JOSEPH CARRABIS

THE AUGMENTED MAN

NORTHERN LIGHTS PUBLISHING

NASHUA, NH

Paperback ISBN 979-8-9878048-0-3
ebook ISBN 979-8-9878048-1-0

Library of Congress Control Number

Editing by Jennifer Day, Susan Carrabis
Front cover image by John Bernard Scullin http://skolenimation.com/
Book design by Jennifer Day

Trailer's standard and return is from Jethro Tull's *Broadsword and the Beast*
The Laqueur quote is from *A World of Secrets/The Uses and Limits of Intelligence*, Basic Books, 1985

Printed and bound in the United States of America
First printing March 2023

Published by Northern Lights Publishing
www.northernlightspublishing.com

Praise for The Augmented Man

"Avatar, Rambo and Robocop films - mixed in with Frankenstein… 5 Massive Stars from me. This is a blistering tour de force that delves into the sociology and psyche of both the Frankenstein monster creator and the monster himself. Joseph Carrabis has created a military and scientific warrior that could mind read and wipe out Rambo, Robocop and 'The Bionic Man' at once, in an instant."

"Joseph Carrabis' *The Augmented Man* at first glance might appear to be just another military SF novel, but it's so much more that that. The story Carrabis tells with consummate skill is a reinvention of "Frankenstein", the classic tale by Mary Shelley."

"Not just a suspense thriller set in the future, this is an astonishing novel of great psychological depth and power that transcends its genre and its themes of love, redemption and what it means to be human will resonate with you long after you finish the book."

"Author Carrabis gives us characters that are believable yet jump off the page as well- which means I'll be seeking out more of his work."

"A master class in how to create a super soldier from a physiological frame work damaged in the right ways to start with. The wiliness of the elite to use the monsters the failures in the system create, then dispose of them afterwards…"

"I was hooked by this line - 'The function of intelligence isn't to discover secrets, it's to instill fear…'"

"Brilliant character driven storytelling, packed with suspense - and the potential for revelation."

"There is a lot of uncomfortable truth in here, which is why it works so well. It's a cracking read, that will also make you think, like all good science fiction…"

"Carrabis writes a masterful tale of how greed and power can corrupt the better judgement of a man."

"…a blistering tour de force that delves into the sociology and psyche of both the Frankenstein monster creator and the monster himself."

"…thrusts the reader into an unknown but realistic world of the future where governments create devastating war weapons of their choosing."

"The Augmented Man takes us into a dark hole of traumatic memories, a God-complex gone awry, military hubris, and science fiction horror that is both riveting and repellant at the same time."

"This is a terrifying account of the depravity of man taken to the extremes of imagination. The idea of a super soldier is appealing until you realize the dreadful consequences of building that soldier on the foundation of fear and despair."

"Is this the future of our military? Another fine book written by the author Joseph Carrabis that I could not put down."

"A fast paced read that kept me turning the pages."

For Susan
(because everything should be)

And AJ
(who said "I can see everything!")

My thanks to
Jennifer "The Editress" Day
John Scullin, USN, Retired
Joseph Della Rosa, Lieutenant, Chief of Incident Management,
USCG
Todd Sullivan, Esquire
and Greg Hickey, Illinois State Police Forensic Scientist and
Author

Thanks also to
Rox Burkey, co-author of the Enigma Series High Tech Thrillers
Dr. John R. Beyer, Ed.D./Ph.D., ex-SWAT, Author of Police
Thrillers through Black Opal Books
Diane Deschenes
Richard Dufrense, LICSW
Bob Hodges, NPD, Jack Killoren, BATP, Michael Levesque,
Armorer, NPD
Dr. Roger Millen
Dr. Victor Santiago-Noa
Gualter Silva
Don Perry

THE AUGMENTED MAN

The ideal experimental animal is man. Whenever it is possible, man should be selected as the test animal. The clinical researcher must bear in mind the fact that, if he wishes to understand human ills, he must study man. No researches are more interesting, more satisfying and more lucrative than those performed on man. Hence, it is up to us to forge ahead in our research on the most developed of animals: man.
    - Mèdecine et Hygiéne, #637, April 1964

In all events, a healthy man does not have the right to be a volunteer for an operation which will certainly lead to a mutilation of the human body, or a serious and lasting deterioration of health. The patient cannot abandon to the doctor all rights to his body, over which he himself has only the right of usufruct.
    - Eugenio Maria Giuseppe Giovanni Pacelli, Pope Pius XII

This experimentation can only be applied to informed volunteers who are completely free to accept or to refuse it, and can only be performed by a highly qualified person capable of reducing the risks incurred to a minimum.
    - Acadèmie de Mèdecine

It is known that free consent is relatively rare. An atmosphere of suggestion, of persuasion, can easily be created, which will succeed in influencing the personality. Naturally, more effective means of pressure can be applied to subjects who are prisoners...This mentality appears to us to be rooted in a regression and a return to the mentality of human sacrifice characteristic of ancient paganism, of those human sacrifices made for a new idol...
    - Psychopathologie expèrimentale, Professor Henri Paruk, P.U.F.

Senator Martha Astin (R.MA): "It sounds like you're making nightmare monsters."

Captain James Donaldson, ONI COS: "Yes, Senator. I am."

Senator Martha Astin (R.MA): "And where do you get these monsters, Captain?"

Captain James Donaldson, ONI COS: "Well, ma'am, you start with those who are afraid of monsters."

- transcript, Gang of Eight Advisory Committee, 310815-1437FF, ONI 17901

IN

Trailer closed his eyes and sat at the end of the bar where the cigarette-burned, cheap black Formica countertop met the wall. He eased himself onto the last stool, tucking into the corner in the dim light, a spider hiding out of sight at the edge of its web. His fingers hovered over the cigarette burns closest to him as if divining their cause, sensing them like small, unhealed wounds, seeing the people involved, learning if each burn was an accident or intentional.

The door opened and he smelled the cool April evening on his skin. It was followed by the alcoholic breath and sweat of two men and a woman they supported between them.

Trailer brought his attention back into the bar, collating the activity immediately around him.

The barkeeper, a heavy smelling man gnawing a toothpick, his face somewhere between needing a shave and growing a beard, walked over to Trailer. "Yeah?"

"A beer. Whatever you got."

The man grunted and walked to the other end of the bar. When he left, Trailer opened his eyes. A river of tattoos flowed up the man's left arm. An old style claw prosthetic served as his right, its hinges and catches polished like silver and glinting in the mirrored bar light. He wore black jeans and a tie-dyed t-shirt over powerful shoulders and an ample gut. Trailer closed his eyes again as the man returned. It seemed to Trailer that the man swam upstream in a river of his own sweat.

He placed a bottle of Coors in front of Trailer. "Six."

"Huh?"

"Six. Six dollars."

"Can I run up a tab? I'll probably stay a while."

The man shook his head. "Uh-uh."

Trailer handed him the money and nodded at the prosthetic. "Amazonas?"

The man eyed him and shook his head cautiously. "Loreto."

"I was there, too."

The man eyed him a moment longer then nodded as he walked away. "Uh-huh."

A five-man band walked onto a stage surrounded by a plexiglass cage reinforced with steel fencing, closed the cage door, set up and tested their instruments.

A woman screamed from a room hidden by a beaded curtain.

Trailer stood up. The barman caught Trailer's shirt in his claw. "You gonna drink your beer or what?"

Trailer stood a head and a half taller than the barman. He said nothing, closing his eyes when the woman screamed again.

"Eddie, Bill?" the barman called out. "We got ourselves a pretty boy here."

Two scar-faced men got up from a table near the door and walked towards Trailer. He shook his head slowly, searching with his ears as a blind man might search out a strange sound. He moved his head from side to side and made a sound, quiet and deep in his chest, a great cat purring. His head snapped back and shook. He whispered, "No...no," as if tasting something tart, bitter, something he wanted to spit out.

Eddie and Bill smiled as they moved closer. Thin and wiry, Eddie had a chain around his waist held on by a drop hook. Rolled back sleeves revealed lean, muscular arms, but with shoulders too high and too stiff for the arms they supported. He wore tight-fitting pants and taped his boots, the laces stopping half way up. The right boot's tape stopped half way down on one side.

Trailer's eyes snapped open wide and he catalogued, his irises retreating as if aflame. "Parkerized Military Machetes, fifty-centimeter, sheath cross harness. Walther P38 9mm Short nine round capacity, right ankle lift grip, Rockwell C57-59 EK Combat Knife left ankle rip release."

Bill's face and scalp looked as if he'd been lyed. Short and squat, the lines on his clothes were clean, hiding no weapons but revealing the scarred musculature common to bikers who played too hard too long.

The woman screamed again. Trailer counted Eddie and Bill's footsteps by sound, measuring the two men by heartbeat. He felt Eddie's muscles twitch as Eddie thought about dropping his chain belt.

Before Eddie's thought became action, Trailer's spine released and he grew.

The barman's claw didn't open in time. He screamed as his prosthetic ripped out of its socket.

Trailer's eyes closed and his face relaxed, becoming calm, pacific, the face of a child fallen asleep. He brought his head down hard onto Eddie's skull and smiled at the sharp-sounding crack.

Major Donaldson and Lieutenant Rivers stood in the cold, early April rain facing a fuel bunker door mounted against the brownish-red brick wall of a small strip mall. They kept their backs to the parking lot, its asphalt cracked and missing in places. Most of the mall's store windows had 'For Lease' signs in them.

The door didn't belong.

Such heavy iron doors belonged on runways and LZs, combat area landing zones placed to provide air support, not on the brownish-red brick walls of domestic mini-malls. On the LZs, the heavy iron doors sealed explosive turboprop and jet engine fuels into the earth, opening like a glass raised in toast to quench a thirst before a mission. Occasionally a Pancho shell would catch an LZ. The fuel bunker doors would glow then melt then slag over the infernos beneath them, first making the LZ sag then run like black sulfur-scented pudding until what remained cooled into a brittle, frozen dessert.

The door broke the regularity of the tiny mall's empty storefronts. Two steel runners, angled slightly up and against the wall, allowed the door to roll shut like a warehouse fire door. A sign - big blue letters on top, small red letters underneath - hung on the wall about zero-point-seventy-five meters above the door's runners:

Henry's Bar & Grill
Live Entertainment
Friday&Saturday Nite

Donaldson nodded. Rivers keyed the lock and slid the bolt back.

Globs of rain arced down from the sky and exploded on Donaldson's shoulder boards. Drops like tiny and persistent mortar fire tapped against the flat metal of his major's shield and hat then dripped from the Corfam brim down his dress blues. He'd turned up his topcoat collar. A few drops of cold found their way in and raced down the back of his neck, only to be stopped by the starched and tightly drawn collar of his regs. Streams flowed from the bottom of his topcoat and soaked his pant legs. The steady rainfall rat-a-tat-a-tatted on his shoes.

Rivers inhaled, grabbed the handles, and, with no hydraulics to aid the movement, slid the door up the runners with a smooth precision and a clarity of movement that pleased Donaldson. Rivers' military dress and topcoat couldn't hide his powerful shoulders and arms. Remarkably well proportioned, with close-cut blond hair, bright blue eyes, strong jawline, and the broad calloused palms of a long-time weightlifter - his size deceived people until they stood next to him, until they had something normal - a doorframe, furniture - to compare him to.

Aryan, Donaldson thought. Rivers is what Hitler wanted his master race to be.

Rivers exhaled as he held the door at the top of the rails. A hook hung on a steel eyelet screwed into the brick wall at the end of the door's transit. Rivers used the hook to hold the door open then stood aside.

Donaldson studied the revealed wall before entering. The remnants of a standard windowless commercial door and doorjamb remained, the doorjamb bowed and cracked. The door no longer fit snugly. One of the hinges hung halfway out of the wall, its bolts stripped as if some monstrous force had pulled the door from its housing. To the left of the doorjamb was a hole the size of a man. An explosive hole. Something, maybe someone, left as if in a hurry, and probably with no choice in the matter.

Inside, Donaldson saw a mix of bikers' bar and slaughterhouse. Harley-Davison, Indian, Norton, and similar decals stenciled mirrors, now shattered, lining the wall behind the bar.

Broken bar taps lay near his feet: Bud, Rolling Rock, and Coors among them. Some local brands. No designer labels. No craft brews, no light beers, no imports.

Shattered bottles of Stolichnaya, Hiram's, Jack Daniel's and assorted bourbons and ryes stood like sentinels behind the bar, against the broken mirrors. No liqueurs, no wines, nothing that could be considered a before or after dinner drink. A screened and fenced stage, both screen and fence remarkably intact, sat opposite the bar against the wall with the explosive hole. Broken glass and crushed beer cans mated on the floor. The smell of blood permeated the bar. Under that, the smell of stale beer, urine, and sex.

At the far end of the bar, in a small room partially obscured behind a beaded curtain, a pool table waited. There were no pool cues, no chalk, no rack, and no balls. Just the table with notches on the side and ashtrays where the pockets would be.

The wall behind it hosted a bizarre rainbow. It started with Polaroids on the left, some black and white and some color. Climb the rainbow's arc and down the other side and you journeyed through the history of modern imaging systems: dot-matrix printouts to grainy color images to glossies to various cell phone screens ending with the latest mobcomms and glasses.

Donaldson parted the beads to inspect the images. Regardless of technology, each image showed a different woman, each sporting leather, each mostly naked and most of them average looking, plain. Each image was autographed and dated - the mobiles, mobcomms, and glasses digitally. Donaldson guessed the date signified when the women'd been inducted as mommas.

He had not witnessed what happened in the bar less than twenty hours ago but it reminded him of a slaughterhouse he'd worked in as a teenager.

In the slaughterhouse, steers didn't know they were on the killing floor until the Judas screamed as its left hind leg was caught in the rail chain and it felt itself upended. Its eyes would go wide as it bellowed in fear. Before the beast could gather itself for a second alarm, the butcher would slit its throat. Donaldson remembered the look of the steer's eyes as they glazed over but never closed, the tongue as it fell forward and wagged from the slack jaws, the blood gurgling from the clean, deep cut in the animal's throat, pulsing from the arteries and draining down over the open eyes, the free legs still twitching - you could tell the apprentice slaughtermen because they'd always catch a hoof in the head or throat or side.

Most of all, Donaldson remembered the slippery, blood-slick footing of the butchers as the cattle were herded, upended, and slaughtered, all in the sick precision of the assembly line.

Rivers surveyed the bar. "Posttraumatic stress disorder, Major?"

Donaldson grunted agreement but wasn't sure. With the amount of stress inoculation Trailer and his team had undergone, PTSD was unlikely. He planned this. Trailer knew what he was doing and did it for a reason.

He inventoried the damage, his eyes stopping, focusing, his mind analyzing, then his eyes sweeping to some other island of destruction until they rested on two knee prints clearly discernible in a pool of fetid, drying, brownish blood, some roaches at its edge like horses at the edge of a stream.

They left the old man like that. The old man Trailer brought to me. "Sir?"

"Yes? What is it?"

"I'm sorry, sir. I thought you said something."

"Oh? No, just thinking about an old man I interrogated once. Pancho sympathizer, I think. I remember he had one hand. Iraqi mercenaries, you know? Trailer caught him stealing rations. He had one hand. That's how I knew he'd been stealing from the Iraqis. Christ. Then the old man tried to steal from us."

Donaldson walked over and ground the roaches under the toe of his shoe.

"Sir?"

"What?"

"The old man, sir?"

"That's all. There's no more. That's all I remember." Donaldson shook his head and continued his inspection. Through the warehouse mounted door, the clouds far on the western horizon broke and revealed the setting sun. Bright orange light ripped through the bar all the way to the mirrored wall. Rivers stood in the doorway, a huge silhouette forcing Donaldson to turn on the bar lights as he worked.

"Major, Mr. Ingman is here."

"Fuck."

Ingman appeared as another set of legs behind Rivers' silhouette and barked, "Make a hole, Lieutenant."

Donaldson remembered Ingman as a tall, thin man. Ingman entered the bar and Donaldson added graying hair, owl rim glasses, and a sparse mustache covering what looked like a cleft palette scar, a conservative gray overcoat, and a purple collar pin to that memory's inventory.

Once inside, Ingman focused his attention on Donaldson. "Incredible, don't you think? One man could do all this and leave no witnesses? I think so. Incredible. He must have really submerged for us not to be able to track him for ten years. I told you we should have rechipped him." He swept his gaze over the room and wrung his hands, his voice now conciliatory and condescending. "Well, looks like the last of the Augmented Men rides again, Jim." He patted

Donaldson's back as if disciplining a recalcitrant horse to accept the reins. "Just think what might have happened if he was upset." He pulled a handkerchief from a breast pocket, placed it over his nose as he went back to the door. "Christ, I told them to turn off the heat in here. You there, Lieutenant. You look like a big boy. You think you could do this?"

Rivers eyed Donaldson. Donaldson shook his head, no.

Ingman's voice turned conspiratorial. "What are we going to do, Jim? We can't afford to keep the man alive any longer. You can only put so much grease on the pig, you know."

"Where is he?"

"In lockup and ready for transfer. Hell of a way for him to surface, Donaldson. Hell of a way."

Donaldson joined Ingman by the door. "I'd like your opinion, Lieutenant."

Rivers walked gingerly around pools of dried blood. Someone had come in and cleaned up the gut pile, but the outline remained on the floor. Like all good hunters, Trailer and the other Augmented Men were taught to clean and gut their kills.

While Rivers worked, Donaldson leaned towards Ingman. "Beat up anymore Cochican barmaids? Or is the pip for some real action?"

Ingman's hand instinctively went up to his lip. His eyes jumped to Rivers and back.

Rivers stood by the lone upright bar stool. It alone remained standing, a sentinel at the end of the bar and against the wall, furthest from the door. A wedge of destruction emanated from it, with the bar on one side and the wall on the other, as if somebody had used a sharp knife to cut a pie then became impatient removing the first slice.

Donaldson asked, "Your thoughts, Lieutenant?"

Rivers studied the bar a minute longer before answering. "He came in and sat there." He pointed to the standing bar stool. One of the puddles had some shoe prints in it and Rivers nodded at them next. "He wore civilian issue leather sole shoes and not Runners - "

Ingman interrupted. "How do you know what kind of shoes he

wore?"

Rivers looked at Donaldson and Donaldson nodded. "The foot placement is for spine stretching and all the other prints were made with various civilian boot treads. Runners have a special sole design, modified on the combat model, to sustain an Augment's leg strength, bone structure, and the increased mass of the calcaneus. The only other possibility is that he was barefoot and I see no footprints.

"The blood pool makes me think he did the first one here. Perhaps some civilians attempted to aid the target. Trailer doesn't want to hurt people." Rivers considered. "He probably stretched his spine to frighten them off."

Donaldson shook his head. "Look again."

Rivers' eyes jockeyed from blood pool to blood pool to overturned chairs to broken bottles, spending an extra moment on each before racing to the next. "What am I missing?"

"You're looking but not seeing. He came out of hiding after how many years in the deep woods? And this is his first noticeable act? He wanted to be found and he wanted to be found in such a way we could only respond one way.

"No, this was completely intentional. Never underestimate him, Lieutenant. Start again."

Rivers went to the stool at the end of the bar, the only one left standing, and sat facing the direction blood splayed on the floor and walls. He closed his eyes. The pupils moved like steady pendulums under his eyelids then stopped. He inhaled slowly, deeply, and exhaled the same way. He nodded and opened his eyes as if waking but not wanting to let go of the dream. His head turned like a camera slowly panning the room.

His nostrils flared. His eyes opened wide as he restarted his narration. "It went like this..."

Rivers voice was lost as Donaldson remembered the Augmented Men.

Trailer, Wartella, and Donaldson huddled behind a wall. Two stone columns, each two-plus meters tall, framed the wall on either side. The wall barely provided cover for the three of them. Every time one of them moved, rapid machine fire chipped at the top of the wall, between the columns and down their sides, splintering rocks and forcing the three of them to cluster.

Wartella sniffed over Donaldson's head, picking up the tinny smell in his sweat, the rime of fear. "Don't fret, Major," he said. "Do what you taught us," knowing Donaldson couldn't, chuckling at his own joke.

Trailer and Wartella folded into small packages, each of them not more than eighty-five centimeters on a side, Trailer slightly smaller because Wartella was the taller of the two. Donaldson had taught them the technique, to fold into a box with the longest dimension the length of the femur, the body's longest single bone - some of the

Augmenteds' physical abilities were just exaggerated contortionist and escape artist tricks. "Make yourself so small you can infiltrate by hiding in a satchel pack, so small they have to be on top of you to hit you."

Donaldson had taught them the technique but couldn't perform it. "We've got to isolate that gunner. The kind of accuracy this man's got, he must be laser-sighting."

Wartella and Trailer looked at him, looked at each other, stood up behind the columns and began stretching. Donaldson knew they could do it. Develop some little-used muscles in the back and along the ribs and anyone could release their spinal column and grow several centimeters, a common escape artist technique. Augmentation pushed it between fifty and eighty centimeters.

Except human skin couldn't stretch that much that quickly. Donaldson stared at tall, deformed bodies with skin stretched thin over their skulls, the hair pulled low and looking like a bizarre, furry tam shading the eyes. He could see and count the heartbeats as blood pulsed up one side of the neck and down the other, as it flowed to the eyes and nose. The tongue and larynx became inoperative because they couldn't stretch that much that quickly either, but that didn't prevent Wartella and Trailer from talking to him. Donaldson concentrated on the cheeks, mouths, necks, and chests, unable to stare into the eyes of men who had become flesh draped trees but fascinated by the muscles so clearly moving under the skin. Wartella and Trailer laughed through long throats, a sound like reedy bass organ pipes, and snapped up over the columns.

Highly irregular. Directly against cover and concealment principles.

And totally effective against a superstitious enemy who saw demons in trees.

Donaldson walked out the door as Rivers concluded his analysis. "Secure it, Lieutenant." Then to Ingman, "You said you had him in lockup? Did he voluntarily turn himself in? Did someone tranq him? Is anybody in the cell with him?"

"You should have read the report before you came."

The two men stared at each other in silence. Ingman broke it. "He waited outside for the police and went quietly when they came. He gave them our clinician's number and then went mute no matter what they tried. We knew enough to silence it and get you here. He's not tranqed. We transferred him to our Manchester facility within three hours and he's under close watch. No one's with him. You think I'm going to risk one of my people because he can't control his hormones?"

The Manchester Veteran's Affairs Medical Center Hospital -

VAMC for short - was an early 1950's pork-barrel project that lost favor shortly after the Korean War. The DOD revived the facility when Viet Nam caused legions of vets to hide in the northern New England mountains. Beginning in 1976, it became a primary care facility for the PTSD sufferers who seemed to come out of the earth in the years following the southeast Asian conference. After that, it became and stayed one of the best houses for people who couldn't let go of war. The Soviets had even asked to tour it in the years following Afghanistan and Kurdistan, as did the Commonwealth of Independent States when the food and water riots hit and led to the Republic Conflicts.

The hospital rested on the top of a hill on the fringe of a suburban area with easy access to Interstate-93. The campus had tranquil, rolling landscapes with beautiful views of the Monadnock Mountains to the west, the White Mountains to the north, and the Manchester cityscape below. VAMC's insides echoed the campus' peacefulness, foregoing sterility for comfort. Each room held two patients with roommate selection based on similarity of need or experience. The hospital also had different units for different problems. Substance abuse was the primary concern with those who returned and continued returning from the South American coca fields. Some hardliners even said, "Goin' South," when they jagged, often with so much punch they wouldn't come back for days. The Coca Wars - Operation White Harvest according to an Act of Congress - officially concluded fifteen years ago. VAMC served as a haven for those still in conflict.

A guard and Trailer's attending led Donaldson to Isolation, deep in the bowels of the hospital and through a labyrinth of reinforced doors, Rivers always a few steps behind as if leaving breadcrumbs to find their way back. They went so far down into the belly of the building that Donaldson could hear the mechanicals operating above them. At the last door, he was asked to sign over responsibility for the calm, pacific-looking man visible through an eight-centimeter-thick screen-meshed window, ten centimeters on a side. Above and to the right of the window, a red warning light flashed over the legend

Hyperbaric Isolation
Decompression when light is flashing

"Why here?" Donaldson asked.

"We heard that part of the augmentation was to the hemoglobin, to increase his strength via oxygen transport. We figured at six atmospheres we could pump in pure oxygen and force his heme to shut down. He can live, but he can't get excited. We thought of AJAX - isn't that what you guys used? Some kind of Lorazepam-XANAX derivative? - but he seemed totally relaxed. Sign this, please."

Donaldson peered through the glass. Six atmospheres and pure oxygen and Trailer, sitting on a cot, showed no discomfort. His skin had a slight blue tinge. Donaldson guessed Trailer's blood was black from oxygenating by this time. He probably couldn't punch his way through the hyperbaric chamber, but god help the first man near him if Trailer wanted to jam once the seal released.

Trailer looked up, smiled, and nodded at Donaldson. Trailer's expression made him uncomfortable. Donaldson studied the Augmented Man's face and went cold.

Trailer functioned as a Hunter/Seeker. He returned from missions only upon completion or if he determined he needed assistance to achieve completion. One time, Donaldson remembered, Trailer returned after six days, his face a mask with eyes of stone.

His eyes, Donaldson warned himself. Don't stare in his eyes.

Donaldson asked, "Good run, Trailer?"

Trailer looked up from the ground, crooked his head slightly to the left as he interpreted Donaldson's words, coming back from readiness as the AJAX coursed through him. He smiled and rumbled, "Happiness is a huge gut pile."

Donaldson shook his head and experienced a chill as Trailer and St.Onge laughed. Donaldson smiled with them and checked his watch.

Ten minutes.

He'd lost ten minutes. He looked at Trailer and Trailer smiled back, his body still swaying slightly, a cobra hypnotizing his prey before striking - a bastardization of Erickson's work in clinical and subjective hypnotic states and useful for compromised kills.

Donaldson shook off the chill of Trailer's eyes as he stared through the eight-centimeter-thick screened glass. *The face smiles but the eyes don't.* The incongruity disturbed him. Donaldson anchored his consciousness to the sounds of the mechanicals overhead, pushed his awareness into the vaguely mossy aromas in the dank, dark hallway, so like a cavern into the earth, cataloguing things around him he hadn't noticed before. Like a diver going free, he took a breath and once again stared into Trailer's eyes. With all his precautions, he still got lost in their maelstroms.

Donaldson blinked and turned away. *He isn't showing recognition, he's showing acknowledgment.*

He checked his watch and glanced at the others. No time had passed.

Or ten years had passed.

He wasn't sure which.

Donaldson shivered as he keyed his mobile for secured, voice-only transmission. "Did you hear me, Major?" the voice asked. "Brazil's found somebody's got to be one of your men."

Behind that voice he heard Ingman. "You tell that prick son-of-a-bitch we're not hazarding any of our equipment on this. He'll have to go get him himself."

Donaldson had lied to himself so many times since the end of the war he began to believe his own falsehoods; there were no Augmented Men left, none survived. The war had been over for years and only a handful of people even knew the Augmented Men ever existed.

Located by a Brazilian CRIP detail one presidential term after the official close of Operation White Harvest, Trailer was about to come home. The Brazilians, assigned the role of Combined Reconnaissance and Intelligence Platoons by UN decree immediately following the war, flew into villages to recruit Kit Carsons, ex-enemy soldiers to serve as scouts. One of the recruits, Vargo Colderra, knew of *um Ianque muito grande* - a very big Yankee. No news there; every war had its MIAs.

Expecting a standard rescue operation, the Brazilians landed a C21-B QuadLift rigged for medical evacuation. Nothing prepared them for what they found.

Trailer had survived ten years in the Orinoco at a 're-education' camp that was as much an insult to mankind as was the directive that made the Augmented Men. His captors had wondered at him, been awed by him, and, to appease their curiosity regarding this big man, had experimented on him, vivisecting body parts to determine rates of recovery, to learn when recovery would be complete but malformed and require permanent removal.

Trailer emerged from the jungle massively scarred. He'd been strapped on his knees, his arms pulled back, barred, and his wrists strapped to his ankles. Even Trailer couldn't remember how long. His arms, armpits, chest, and back festered where his torturers had shoved hot pikes into his armpits. Scars ran up and down both sides of his spine where some kind of animal or animals had been allowed to feast. He had neither fingertips nor fingernails because they had burnt the tops of all the nails on both hands. Blisters formed underneath the nails causing incredible pressure on the tips of the fingers and the inability to move the fingers or hold things, period. Trailer needed to hold things to escape so he bit through his own fingertips to let the fluid out.

The voice said, "I'll have the full report couriered to you in flight."

Donaldson hung up, ordered a car, and in less than an hour was flying to DreamSpace, deep in the Hopi Indian Reservation on Black Mesa in the northeast corner of Arizona. As the last stateside location Trailer had seen, Donaldson figured it would serve as his gateway back. Ingman highlighted important items on the already concise report so Donaldson wouldn't waste any time.

On the vids, Donaldson watched Trailer sitting in a corner, still covered with the filth of his escape, his eyes wide and on his bene-factors, licking his wounds like a dog beaten near death.

Trailer lay on a bed in the hospital compound under guard when Donaldson arrived at DreamSpace. He rose when Donaldson walked in the room and four guards trained their rifles on him. Donaldson motioned them to stand down. Trailer walked up to him, said, "Sig-Rec. Con. MisConCom. RetRem," and held out his arms, palms up, as if carrying an offering to some malicious god.

The meaning was simple and clear. "SigRec. Con" translated to "Signal Recognition. Confirmed." He recognized Donaldson as his superior and confirmed such. Next, he gave his report, "MisCon-Com" meaning "Mission Confirmed and Completed."

The last part, "RetRem," was a direct request to Donaldson as Trailer's mission superior and something only Donaldson could pro-vide. RetRem, for the Augmented Men, meant "Retrieve&Removal from operation" - confirmation that the objective had been reached, the mission successful, a request to stand down from readiness.

Donaldson thought, "Yes, God, stand down. Rest," which Trailer took for his needed confirmation. In return, he held out his arms for his blessed AJAX to bring him out of readiness.

Trailer left the hospital after he'd been there a month, on a deep, high mesa night with a cloudless, moonless sky and mountains on all horizons. They woke Donaldson as lights came on all over the com-pound and DreamSpace's perimeter defenses went active.

"How long has he been gone?"

"We have redundant visual confirmation from fifteen minutes ago."

"What about backups? Do we have anything on Vcam? Anything on BigEars?"

The security chief shook his head. "Trailer asked his guards if they wanted to play some cards. They played one hand - that's recorded - then the guards left, went into SECQ, knocked out the personnel and shut everything down."

Donaldson nodded. He went to the door and walked outside. The installation's BigEars wouldn't pick Trailer up, nor would any IR or US tattlers from overflights. His captors dug his chip out of his ribs and Donaldson's team hadn't replaced it.

Donaldson considered; some would call it an escape but Donaldson wrote it up as a simple dismissal. Trailer didn't officially exist; the misinformation could be easily buried.

The security chief came up to him. "What are your orders, Major?"

Donaldson remembered a pet he'd once had, a dog. When the dog was old and arthritic, Donaldson's father told him that the next day they'd have to take the dog to the vet, have him put down. Donaldson hid so his father wouldn't see him cry, wouldn't yell at him for being a sissy. His father didn't find him, but the dog did. It licked his face and he cried more until he sobbed himself to sleep with the dog beside him. When he woke, the dog was gone.

He ran to find his father, thinking his father had taken the dog to the vet without letting him know. Instead, before he found his father, he found his dog, dead, curled up underneath a table in a quiet part of the house, as if it knew it was causing trouble and decided to get out of the way.

"No orders, Sergeant. Shut it down. Maybe he's just looking for a quiet place to die. Leave him to his peace."

**2 APRIL 2053 1946 HOURS
VAMC MANCHESTER, NEW HAMPSHIRE
SURFACE PLUS 23 HOURS, 46 MINUTES (APPROXIMATE)**

Donaldson had been the last friendly to see Trailer before he went into the Orinoco and one of the last to see him after he got back.

Trailer was thinner now, probably starving himself to keep his energy down, but with a fuller, heavier face. Donaldson guessed Trailer had been eating standard foods for some time. Trailer had brown eyes, but Donaldson knew that from memory. His hairline was receding, which was strange because Trailer wasn't that old, not old enough to be in the normal class of Operation Black Harvest vets.

Trailer stood and walked to the door, his movements deceptively smooth, making Rivers' clarity of motion seem like a mudslide in a fishbowl. Donaldson noticed the fitted pants and shirt, clothes designed for his body, clothes designed not to reveal his physiology. The tailoring was good, but not professional quality. Donaldson made a mental note to add "Acquired rudimentary tailoring skills" to Trailer's 201 file. He also noticed the way Trailer buttoned his shirt: Four buttonholes, the bottom two buttoned, the chest unbuttoned, collar button missing. He checked Trailer's shoes. Freed loafers. No laces. Different clothes, but the same configuration of clothing.

He's still displaying rank and status.

Trailer stood at the door and turned the lock from inside. The steel bars holding it tweaked and started to bend. The guard backed away, pressing against the opposite wall and readying his rifle, a Freon cooled Colt 223 Automag.

Donaldson grabbed the barrel in his hand and pulled the rifle down. "Don't do that. You'll only make him angry."

The guard stared at the bars bending and the look of pleasure on the face inside the small window. He put his weapon down.

"Lieutenant, would you open the door for Mr. Trailer, please?"

Rivers went to the door and began freeing the bolts. Trailer backed away, rapped on the glass and pointed to the light. The physician gasped, "Holy Mother of God we almost killed him," and turned some dials.

"How much do you know about Augmented Men?" Donaldson asked.

The physician focused on the dials and meters to the hyperbaric chamber. "Nothing, really. Just hearsay. My clearance doesn't get me into those records, and we've never had any like him through here."

Donaldson looked at Trailer and Trailer nodded, still smiling. "How fast can you bring the chamber to full normal?"

"I can blow the tanks in seconds but that'd kill your man."

"Do it."

The physician pulled his hands from the dials. "I can't do that."

"You saw him bending those bars to get out? He doesn't want to wait. I think you should do it now. The other option is to let him break the seal while it's still pressurized. That'd kill us."

The physician stared from Donaldson to the behemoth in the chamber. "If that's all that'll happen, why didn't he let us just do it? He's already capped twenty-three people in Chelmsford. What's so special about us?"

Donaldson opened his mouth as if to answer and closed it. Frowning, he stared back into the chamber.

Nothing special about us, Mr. Trailer, correct? Except you want something from us.

Trailer closed his eyes.

From me, Mr. Trailer? Not from us, from me?

Trailer's eyes opened.

"Blow the tanks."

Trailer's attending spun some dials and pushed some buttons on the control panel. The hyperbaric chamber, the hall they stood in, and part of the foundation shrugged as the chamber evacuated to full normal pressure and atmosphere.

"Proceed, Lieutenant."

Rivers finished opening the door.

Trailer stepped out slowly and deliberately, as if each step required an intensity of thought all its own. His clothes had dried blood on them, mostly blotches on the shoes, pants, waist, and sleeves. One thin line of blood, as if done with an artist's pen, arced over his breast pocket.

Donaldson's memories came unbidden, rushing him, attacking from all sides, riffling images at him like a deck of holocaust cards until the riffling stopped and one image remained: the knees in the blood.

The old man kneeled on the floor looking up at Donaldson, St.Onge, Wartella, and Trailer, stiff with fear, like a steer that had just heard the Judas, afraid to move or draw attention to itself, not understanding why there was the pain of the shockrod.

He was thin, his skin a walnut brown and tight over a face sprinkled with stubble, his hair salt and pepper gray and his left hand cut off.

St.Onge and Wartella took the old man's rifle and put it in a corner, letting him see it and leaving a space for him to try for it. Donaldson thought the old Pancho would have been a handsome man, a family man, maybe a store owner or merchant in one of the larger villages. Now they brought him in as a spy, caught stealing ration tins from the wrong hut in the wrong war.

This man's not a spy, he's a thief, a man forced to steal in a terrible situation. That's why he's missing a hand. Iraqi mercenaries think of their camps as holy and don't care who ventures in, they treat all trespassers the same.

The man never spoke, but Donaldson expected silence. As he signaled to let the old man go, the Pancho moved towards his rifle, a steer trying to escape the inevitability of the killing floor. St.Onge and Wartella descended before the man could scream a second time, his eyes glazing over as he gazed at Donaldson and Trailer.

The body, supported by St.Onge and Wartella's undulations, kneeled in its own blood. A pencil-thin stream of blood rifled from the man's neck and left a line on Trailer's shirt, across his breast pocket and mission tag. Trailer wiped the blood from the words, "Save, not all, but serve," and walked out.

Out of the chamber, Trailer walked up to Donaldson, tilted his head back and bellowed, a sound of screech owl and howler monkey and things Donaldson wouldn't guess at, a series of blind vocables, the Augmenteds' cry after a successful mission, Tarzan announcing his kill. It started as infrasound, one Augment calling another on frequencies that non-augments could feel but not hear, peaked at a pitch that could make a man's nose and ears bleed and ended back where it began, a rumble only Augments could hear.

Trailer bore no marks or wounds. The blood on his clothes came from those in the bar. "I have to go outside."

"Show him the way, Lieutenant."

Rivers saluted Donaldson, turned to Trailer, saluted him, and spoke clearly and distinctly, giving Trailer time to measure him and his words. "Sir, I am going to take off my topcoat, then my blue. There is a Beretta 92F in a drop holster under my right arm. Ten clips are in a drop case attached to my belt and located above my left rear pocket. I'm also wearing a belt wire and I have a BaliSong up my right sleeve." Rivers placed his topcoat and dress blues on the floor, open and separate from each other. He then held his hands over his head and slowly rotated right so Trailer could see all sides of him.

Donaldson watched the two men before him. Rivers was shorter and smaller than Trailer, about three-quarters Trailer's size. When Rivers had completed his rotation, he stared at Trailer and smiled. Trailer stared at him a moment then nodded, never taking his eyes off Rivers'. Likewise, Rivers never took his eyes off Trailer's, even as he put his blue and topcoat back on.

"Please follow me, sir." Rivers broke eye contact as he turned and walked down the hall. Trailer followed, each step slow and methodical, like a long freight train slowly gaining speed.

Donaldson started to say something to the security guard when Trailer's quiet voice interrupted them. "Thank you."

Donaldson, the attending physician, and the security guard focused on Trailer's retreating form. He followed Rivers, walking directly away from them. He'd rotated his head one-hundred-eighty degrees to look at them as he walked away. The smile on his face appeared synthetic, like those found on plastic dolls.

"You're welcome, Mr. Trailer."

The security guard put his forehead against the wall and vomited down the cool, damp surface.

Donaldson's limo moved silently along the New Hampshire seacoast on Interstate 95. It was a little after midnight, a little more than one day since Trailer surfaced.

Traffic was light. Rivers sat in front with Merchant, the driver, leaving Donaldson and Trailer alone in the passenger compartment. Donaldson requested this vehicle: a stretch Lincoln Town Car shell on a military transport frame designed for diplomatic use in unfriendly, unsecured, and otherwise hostile environments. The vehicle could go through unreinforced cinder block walls, cross over nitrous fueled fires, pull close to three-G acceleration, maintain cruising speeds past the century mark, sustain repeated AT-7 shoulder mounted rounds without debilitation, and had a modified suspension so as to appear similar weight-wise to any other limo to scanning eye satellites. If it had to, it could take a direct RPG or LAWS hit and maintain compartment integrity. Not that it mattered. After either an RPG or LAWS hit, the driver would be dead. At that point, the AutoNoms would take over, evaluate the situation either independently - if C3I was knocked out - or by coordinating with MasterMind back at TopHat.

Donaldson couldn't imagine that happening, but he couldn't imagine Trailer coming out of the Orinoco, either.

Donaldson had specified no music, no calls, no TXT, no communiques, no intelligence, and the smoothest possible ride. Rivers handled the communications, including the full military escorts - all trained for both immediate action drills and RAM, Random Antiterrorist Measures, although Donaldson doubted such would be necessary - that surrounded the vehicle and allowed it to maintain a steady 70mph for much of the journey.

The limo's orientation took a slight head-up trajectory as they started over the Piscataqua River Bridge.

The smoked windows made it impossible for Donaldson, who sat across from Trailer, to see out of the vehicle or anyone else to see in. Trailer sat back in the seat, his head turned towards the window. His eyes darted and moved in a regular rhythm. Donaldson assumed he read signs they passed and monitored traffic that flowed around them. Trailer glanced up at something. His eyes closed. He opened and locked them on Donaldson as the limo's orientation momentarily leveled then angled down.

"We're in Maine, now."

It was the first time Trailer spoke since leaving the hospital.

"Thank you."

Trailer watched him for a moment. His eyes relaxed, and he returned to looking out the window. "The driver has to go to the bathroom."

Donaldson, unsure of what Trailer would consider a neutral response, simply nodded. "Thank you."

Riding up Interstate 95, Donaldson had the impression this was the first time Trailer had spoken two consecutive sentences to anyone in years and he didn't want to blow it.

"The driver's name is 'Merchant'. What's he plan on doing about it?"

"Rivers told him to piss himself, but keep the car going forward or I'd go off like a tactical." Trailer locked eyes with Donaldson then suddenly smiled. The smile looked like it belonged on a thirteen-year-old who'd cracked his dad's porno encryptions and was sharing the downloads with a trusted friend.

Donaldson smiled back. Trailer nodded and went back to staring out the window.

Senator Carl Wrobleski's drawl could crack china. "Tell us about your Augmented Men, Captain Donaldson."

Wrobleski stared at Donaldson. The message on the Senator's face was clear: Come on, son, give me your best shot. You've been doing an end run on me, boy. Now I'm going to roast your balls on a spit.

"What would the committee like to know, sir?"

Wrobleski called the meeting - unnecessary for all but political reasons - to assert his power, to demonstrate his control. True, Donaldson hadn't kept Wrobleski in complete confidence, but neither had he briefed anyone else concerning the progress of his project.

But now it was time to rotate the Chair of the all-powerful Gang of Eight Advisory Committee, eight individuals with so much collective control that only a handful of people would openly acknowledge their existence. No one knew the complete committee roster but members had to be unanimously approved by the President, the

Directors of the ONI, NSA and CIA, the National Security Adviser, the Secretaries of State and Defense, the Attorney-General, the White House Counsel, the President's Chief of Staff, the Chairman of the Joint Chiefs and the Leaders of both parties in both the Senate and House of Representatives.

If there was a tougher club to get into, nobody knew of it.

A one-meter tall by four-meter wide black baekelite plaque dominated the wall behind the committee members. Engraved in two lines of white letters was John Le Carre's "We do disagreeable things so that ordinary people here and elsewhere can sleep safely in their beds at night." Every time Donaldson saw that plaque he wondered how long Gangs of Eight had existed. Baekelite, discovered in 1907, was one of the first synthetic wonder plastics. Created in Yonkers, it became the go-to compound from the 1910s through the Second World War, finally losing favor in the 1960s. It was designated historic in 1993 and became a collectable "retro" in the early 2000s. That plaque's engraving put it around 1963 and it looked like it had been there ever since.

The Gang of Eight Advisory Committee were Orwell's rough men in tailored three-piece suits and ten thousand-dollar skirt-blouse-jacket combinations, and all with handmade footwear.

The people in this room routinely perused society's underwear, routinely saw when society bled or if there were nocturnal emissions, routinely saw those things society knew but never mentioned, and devised solutions allowing society to believe such accidents didn't exist. No other group in any branch of government had the access or authority, no other group in any branch of government generated the same level of joy when they smiled or fear when they didn't.

Nobody else could question the eight people seated here because nobody knew they existed. They evaluated JUONs - Join Urgent Operational Needs - and assigned JASONs - "independent" elite scientists performing uber-secret research at the government's request. Not even the GAO, the much-honored General Accounting Office, watchdog of the public trust, could question or trace the funds these eight appropriated and channeled. Wrobleski held a true seat of power and had no intention of letting go.

But Wrobleski had been in charge several turns around the sun, and this year there were grumblings. He planned on keeping the chair and, if needs be, Donaldson would serve as this year's convenient footstool to that seat of power. Donaldson had guaranteed the viability of the Augmentation Project eighteen months ago and Wrobleski believed him. Wrobleski had believed him and had cajoled, caressed, finagled and finessed others into believing him.

Wrobleski couldn't lose regardless of the results. If Donaldson produced, Wrobleski won. If Donaldson failed to produce, Wrobleski would crucify him and, thus demonstrating his protection of public funds before more were squandered, win.

The five men and three women of the Gang of Eight Advisory Committee put their heads together and whispered to each other. Donaldson viewed it as his own Sanhedrin. Sometimes he could make out distinct words in their mumblings, often as they glanced at him while whispering amongst themselves.

A woman with a Massachusetts accent and a too-thin body, a dark pinstripe suit and dark brown hair like a luxurious lion's mane that contrasted with her wrinkled face, asked, "What are they, Captain Donaldson? We spent close to six hundred million per and had to secure a three-fifty klick square of Dreamspace with orders to shoot down our own overflights, if necessary. I've got a lot of people down Arizona way ready to walk all over me on this one, so right now I want to know, what are they?"

Donaldson didn't recognize her but her nameplate read *Senator Astin, PhD*. "Senator Astin? Would you be Dr. Martha Astin?"

"That I am. You going to tell me your parents didn't treat you right because of something I wrote in a book?"

"No, ma'am. I read your commentaries on Alice Miller. Childhood psychologies. Impressive work."

"Thank you. Now answer my question."

Donaldson smiled. *This is going to get interesting faster than I* expected. "Are the ladies and gentlemen familiar with Merrill's Marauders? The story of the Augmented Men begins with Merrill's Marauders and goes straight through Britain's SAS and Poland's GROMs to SOCOM, the United States Special Operations Command. If it wouldn't be too much trouble, I'd like to provide some background information that might be helpful in understanding what the Augmented Men are all about."

The Sanhedrin gathered itself and, after a moment's conference, nodded acceptance. Wrobleski sat back and smiled.

"I'd like to preface this explanation with a single thought," Donaldson told the committee. "The function of intelligence isn't to discover secrets, it's to instill fear.

"An operative brings back information that C3I uses and disseminates to various groups: S2, N2, A2, S5, whatever. But such information is only useful on linear battlefields and battlefields have been non-linear since the second Gulf War. What we've learned is that the best use of any mission-specific intelligence is to instill fear by demonstrating a foreknowledge of the enemy's intended action."

Trailer's quiet made Donaldson nervous. He didn't doubt that Trailer could hear the conversation between Rivers and Merchant, that Trailer could hear everything coming through the commlink, would know everything Rivers read or typed through the secured channel. The augmentation selection process specified a high MO - Medial Olivocochlear - Reflex and TCAPS - Tactical Communication and Protective System - like auditory response. They could isolate sounds near surgically by ignoring all other sounds, much like an orchestra conductor can isolate a single violinist souring a note in the midst of a symphony, all of which meant they were sensitive enough to pick up the subvocalizations most people made when they thought, hence they seemed telepathic to the uninitiated. Trailer could probably hear the conversations in cars they passed and those that passed them, and the conversations in their escort vehicles.

Nor did Donaldson doubt that Trailer could see through the

opaque windows. The windows opaqued normal visible, high infrared and low UV. His light spectrum extended on both ends, Trailer could see perfectly in what others would consider a totally black room and couldn't be blinded by anything less than a 200w pulse. He could distort the shape of his eyes and lenses via ocular muscle control, an extension of the orthoptics created to help the visually impaired overcome their handicap. It allowed Trailer to define targets over klicks, or work detailing within millimeters unaided. His skin could feel the minuscule temperature increase should an enemy laser-sight him, and he could release a hormone that shunted dendrite activity, essentially giving him unlimited tolerance to pain, even sending him into shock-state if necessary, keeping him emotionally distant from a given situation's possible harm.

Trailer gave no indications, behavioral or otherwise, of his thoughts.

Christ. We made him perfect.

His eyes danced over Trailer's fingers. Totally healed. As, no doubt, was the rest of his body.

Trailer waved his fingers, now normally shaped and tapered, and nodded.

Listening to my thoughts, Mr. Trailer?

Trailer didn't respond.

Donaldson continued addressing the Sanhedrin. "Foreknowledge is useful but susceptible to disinformation, counter-intelligence, operation and equipment failure, compromise - I'm sure I need go no further.

"Now let's take the concept of fear further, away from theater and mission specificity and into panthetical scenarios. Now what do you have?

"At the very edge, way out there, you have things we've always had in awareness but never really known about. Things everyone has experienced but not thought to name. Today we have the sophistication to give these things names. We call them 'Demoralizing Agents'.

"Let me emphasize that the principle demoralizing agent in theater-specific intelligence operations is not foreknowledge of intended action. Foreknowledge is mission-specific."

Donaldson paused, wondering how long they would wait. He

counted two breaths before one of the Sanhedrin shifted in their seat.

"Demoralization comes through another fear. A fear that no matter what is done, no matter what precautions are taken, those precautions won't be enough; they will be too late, they will be wrong, they will be found out. We've discovered the most incapacitating level of fear is predominantly non-existent in conventional warfare and only slightly more tangible in guerrilla situations.

"We've found that a total demoralization comes with a never-ceasing personal fear that, at any moment and without any reason, the individual will be attacked as an individual, mercilessly and totally, by someone or something that has no concept of any morality intrinsic to demonstrating personal violation, someone or something that doesn't even recognize the individual as having personhood. In short, the individual's self-concept becomes that of a victim, with no hope of escape or reprieve.

"Augmentation creates individuals capable of instilling that fear."

Senator Astin held up her hand. "It sounds like you're making nightmare monsters."

"Yes, Senator. I am."

Senator Astin stared Donaldson straight in the eye, her face showing concern but her voice still strong, "And where do you get these monsters, Captain?"

"Well, ma'am, you start with those who are afraid of monsters."

Donaldson held a TEMPEST class mobile in his hand and thumbed in a code. Two graphs filled the empty space in the middle of the room. "Part of Augmentation involves massive injections of Recombinant Human Growth Hormone and NGF, Nerve Growth Factor. Another part involves the use of osteogenin, a naturally occurring protein in bone that is key in the development of the fetal skeleton. We use enough to ensure the large subepidermal muscles have an extra plating of flexible armor.

Wrobleski snickered, "Thank god for CRISPR." Nobody laughed.

"We used two groups, one treated, the other not, although all other parameters were identical. As you can see by these graphs, the treated group gained height and weight significantly faster, outpacing the untreated group by an average of more than twenty-five centimeters and forty-five kilograms per year."

His thumb swiped his mobile. The graphs disappeared.

"But while untreated candidates added both muscle mass and body fat as they grew, the treated group gained much larger amounts of muscle and lost as much as seventy-six percent of their body fat, mostly from the limbs and face, creating obvious alterations in the candidates' physiques."

He tapped. Another image filled the center of the room.

"The outward changes are not subtle."

Astin spoke quietly, gravely, "Go to the next image, please."

"Of course, Senator." Donaldson put up a plain, white image. "Over time, the Human Growth Hormone is sustained by the Augmented's pituitary and the re-establishment of their own Nerve Growth Factor. Neither serves to increase size or weight any longer - there is a limit to an Augmented's growth as there is with any organic biological.

"And despite appearances, the Augmenteds are fully organic and totally biological. No phase of Augmentation changes that. It does change how the body works, however." He emphasized statements with jabs of his mobile.

"An example of this is growth, which is actually repair and re-generation. Should any Augmented suffer insult - physical trauma or damage - the Augmented's own immune system can guide repair and regeneration. Given enough time and limited damage, they could regenerate just about anything."

Wrobleski's drawl cut through the room. "I appreciate the Captain's studies, but we're here to decide results. You do have results for us, don't you, Captain?"

"Yes, Senator. I do." Donaldson signaled for the lights. "Ladies and gentleman, I'd like to present the best of SEAL Team 6 and the 75th Rangers." He opened the door and nine large, powerful men walked in. "These are the creme-de-la-creme, the best of the best. In all the world, everyone knows there are none better."

Wrobleski rocked forward in his chair and put his hands on the table in front of him. His fingers intertwined and his thumbs tapped as if sending out some kind of signal: long-short-long-long-short, long-short-long-long-short. "Captain, I appreciate the trouble you've gone through to bring these good men here, but we could have gone to Bragg or Coronado and seen the whole damn lot of them."

"That's true, Senator. What you couldn't have seen is this." Donaldson opened the door again and signaled someone in the hall. A minute later nine giants entered the room, none of them under six-six, each of them eclipsing the door. "Ladies and gentlemen, allow me to present the Augmented Men."

The SEALs and Rangers backed away as the Augmented Men entered the room.

One of the Augmented Men, St.Onge, growled at them, "You ain't chief rat no more."

One of the SEALs looked up at St.Onge. "But you, man, you're FUBAR. You aren't even human anymore."

St.Onge chuckled with the other Augments and ignored the SEAL.

The SEAL said, "Hey, man," and reached for St.Onge's arm.

St.Onge closed his eyes and shook his head. Still smiling, he nodded at his eight comrades, said "Right," and before Donaldson could voice a command broke the SEAL's neck - clearly, cleanly, and with one hand.

Donaldson barked, "Down!"

The Augmented Men froze in their position. Not so the SEALs and Rangers. With their comrade silent on the ground, they attacked, with all the efficiency and efficacy at their command, with all the destructive knowledge in their repertoire.

And with all the effectiveness of a team of chihuahuas facing a pack of wolves.

Two gunshots pinged off the ceiling. Everybody's eyes turned to the sound, every ones' except the Augmented Men who stood cold and silent and as unaffected as statues since Donaldson's command.

Wrobleski returned his weapon to its shoulder holster.

The Augmented Men left the Gang of Eight Advisory Committee room. The SEALs and Rangers gathered their dead comrade and left. The eight committee members and Donaldson remained in the room. It took awhile for the talking to quiet down.

"In answer to one of the questions I heard while the teams were leaving, the Augmented Men work entirely on subjective experience. They are socially retarded and locked into a childhood egocentric state. Because of their psychological profiles, their particular egocentric state is one of extreme survival. To them, everything is an attack. Even when that's not true - when there are no attackers - it is true to them because they believe it to be true, believing it as a four-year-old on Christmas Eve desperately believes in a jolly old man in a funny red suit. Technically, what they're experiencing is an hallucination, a trick of the imagination, but anything perfectly imagined is real."

Donaldson closed his eyes and took a slow, deep breath, feeling the car's movement over the smooth road. *Stay in the moment. I am here because I learned enough to do this to him. I am here because I've learned enough to bring him back.*

He opened his eyes to see Trailer staring at him.

To bring him back, I hope.

Donaldson's studies in Psychosynthesis, Neurolinguistic Programming, Neural-, Psycho- and Socio-linguistics, Receptive Listening, Human Dynamics and Psychosocial Modeling, disciplines unknown through most of the twentieth century and that only started to gather steam in the early years of the twenty-first, gave him the psychological tools necessary to create the Augmented mindset.

He had learned enough to do damage. It was easier. He wanted to ask Trailer, "Why did you let me do this to you?", to absolve himself of the crimes he'd committed, but that would be blaming the victim and Donaldson was long past that.

Trailer and the others let Donaldson and his team augment them because Donaldson knew enough to engage each of the nine's Convincer Strategy: the special methods each person uses to understand, accept, and integrate new information. Using Alice Miller's studies as a guide and Erickson's entrancing techniques as a tool, he re-created their family dynamics, thus making them extremely suggestible. Donaldson had to use those techniques again, this time to get Trailer to accept his help.

But now Trailer wasn't a fifteen-year-old frightened kid. He was a thirty-six-year-old behemoth who viewed himself as a concept, something with no objective reality. He had learned and trained to subjugate and void out any BMIRs - behavioral manifestations of internal responses - that Donaldson might use to help him. Trailer gave no emotional affect except what he intended. In that sense he functioned as an emotional process schizophrenic: if he needed to show fear to achieve his goal, he showed fear, if he needed to show joy, he showed joy. Emotional displays were tools and nothing more. As a fifteen-year-old, Trailer was diagnosed as 'functionally depressed'. Now Donaldson wondered if a diagnosis was even possible.

He watched the two-plus meter tall man retreat into a small package on the seat, his head tucked but his eyes still looking out the window, his arms wrapped around himself as if hugging himself, holding himself in, and not chicken-winged at his sides, the only non-standard position in Trailer's small package. Donaldson wanted to comment, saw one of Trailer's eyes wink at him, and kept quiet. Every attempt had been made to ensure a non-threatening environment for the journey and Trailer pulled in on himself as if under heavy fire, as if the entire world had gone kinetic.

What are you afraid of, Mr. Trailer?

As if in answer, the limo started vibrating. Donaldson looked into the forward compartment to see Rivers hands blurring over dials and readouts. Turning back to Donaldson, Rivers shrugged his shoulders, his eyes wide and his head shaking "no."

The vibrations grew explosively until the car started rumbling. Donaldson couldn't isolate the source - the limo had solid-core tires, couldn't get a flat and had met a three-level redundancy before he commissioned it - and he wanted to remain calm for Trailer's sake.

Then Donaldson determined the rumbling's origin.

His eyes white, his face and hands deep blue, his lips tight and quivering, Trailer quaked as a thrumming sound escaped his throat.

He's rotary breathing.

Similar to a cat's purring, rotary breathing, another augmentation, forced oxygen into Trailer's bloodstream, building up reserves so his fast-twitch muscles could go anaerobic.

Donaldson reached for the intercom but too late.

Trailer's left hand smashed through the window. He placed both hands on the door. His shoulders and chest pulsed and the door blew off the car.

Donaldson saw they were on a bridge. A sign flashed past indicating it would soon be closed for repairs.

Trailer's voice rumbled over Donaldson like an earthquake, "Help me."

He leapt.

It took the convoy two hundred meters to stop. The last Donaldson or anyone in the convoy saw of him, Trailer dove under the combers of Casco Bay.

Rivers stood beside Donaldson as Donaldson scanned the bay with binoculars. "Shall I call the Coast Guard?"

"No, he'll just oxygenate and submerge. What were you and Merchant talking about before he burst out?"

"I told him we had another six-plus hours minimum until Dickey, then maybe another hour until Hafey Mountain Preserve."

Donaldson brought the binoculars down. "So he knows where we're going."

Rivers face lost its staid military demeanor.

"Oh, yes, Lieutenant. Trailer heard every word you said. My guess is that's why he left. He wants it secured. For him."

"But, Major, he should know Hafey Mountain is secured. He has no enemies there."

Donaldson snapped back, "Everyone's his enemy, Lieutenant. Every one and every thing. That's how he thinks. I'm his enemy. You're his enemy." He sighed. "Sorry."

Rivers shrugged and smiled.

Trailer swam down to the base of a bridge support pylon and wrapped his legs around it to hold himself still against the currents and tides. He stayed under the bridge, moving in its shadow, hidden from above. He placed his fingers tenderly on either side of the pylon as if caressing a lover's face or a safecracker sensing the tumblers fall, closed his eyes and listened. He waited until, between what he could hear and the vibrations on his fingers, he knew it was safe to move on.

After years of inactivity, his training and augmentations were once again serving him, saving him.

The only difference?

He didn't have to kill.

He almost laughed and caught himself before releasing any air; bubbles on the surface would reveal his presence.

Some bridge ballast, the iron construction rods curved and protruding, had broken free and rested on the bay's floor. Trailer smiled remembering an exercise, The Farmer's Walk, part of every strongman competition as far back as anyone could remember. Trailer had never competed but knew he'd blow through any records, even holding his breath. He floated to the surface, charged his lungs and dove again. He'd stay on the bottom until it was safe.

He picked up the ballast and started walking, periodically flicking out his tongue to test the water's salinity, making sure he headed away from the ocean and north to the rivers emptying into the bay. Sometimes a small mackerel or young cod or haddock would swim up to his face. He'd slowly open his mouth and, when they were close enough, gulp, swallowing some water and the fish whole, then stand for a minute while digesting.

He surfaced far inland, on the dark side of dawn and in the shelter of some elms. He watched the stars for a minute, confirmed direction with the seasonal biasing of the trees, and pulled down some leaves and began chewing. His appendix functioned as any wild omnivore's would, digesting the cellulose to provide fuel, and he could process most woodland toxins with no more than a burp.

He checked the stars one more time then squatted, looking for animal trails that were large enough for him to navigate while remaining under cover. He chose one heading north that had deer sign overlaid with tracking coyote and flicked out his tongue, holding the tip up to gauge the wind, testing the direction so he could stay downwind. Sixtreen klicks on the deer and coyote sign changed. The predator began the chase down. Did the deer know its time was near?

Two more coyote tells joined the first, their scents mingling in Trailer's nose every time he inhaled. Their paths remained separate, distinct; these were good coyote, good trackers, good hunters. They knew this area better than he did. He could learn from them.

He listened forward, careful to stay downwind, wanting to leave them to their kill undisturbed although the scents were old, the spoor ancient in woodcraft terms. He detected their markings, their spoor, marking off their territory, defining their kill. A few moments later he came upon what remained. The coyote had dragged off what they could, probably back to their dens, to their pups. He imagined the alpha male and female joined by the beta male, the uncle of the pack, throwing a deer haunch on a table in the den, proving their right to lead, to provide for the pack.

He slowed and stopped, sniffing the air, listening. Spring. Insects. Voles and chipmunks. Squirrels. Robins and blue jays. Cardinals. High overhead a watching kestrel. Green things erupting from the soil. Leaves turning towards the sun.

The coyotes were gone. He could take his time and, if he didn't rest, reach Hafey before Donaldson.

He sat and dined.

Donaldson locked eyes with Wrobleski for a moment then continued. "I ask the committee to remember what I said previously about fear. The function of the Augmenteds is to demoralize any irregulars or non-negotiables in a given catchment area. Particularly, to create a belief in the enemy that each member of the enemy is individually forfeit at any given time and without any prior warning, that any and all conceivable countermeasures will prove ineffective or be rendered impotent, and that all resistance offered at the time of forfeiture will be futile and inconsequential.

"To achieve those goals, we have created in the Augmented Men the ultimate Snake-eaters.

"So, ladies and gentleman, how do we create the ultimate Snake-eater? We first see what has and hasn't worked in various operations for which there is relevant data.

"For our purposes, that means going back over one-hundred years to World War II's OSS, specifically the group called Merrill's Marauders, which I mentioned earlier. These operatives performed recon and intelligence operations in the Philippines during the Japanese occupation. We took what OSS learned in WWII and created the Rangers and Special Forces under CIA direction in Korea.

"Viet Nam begat another generation with the Green Beret and Rangers under then-President John F. Kennedy's National Security Council directive. Of the seven uniformed branches, the four strategic branches legitimized their own special operations under this same NSC directive. The Green Berets were Army, SEALs were Navy, Flying Tigers were Air Force, and 'Force and Reconnaissance' were Marines later to become Special Operations Capable Marine Expeditionary Unit or SOCMEU, and all of which operated more or less under the CIA.

"The Defense Intelligence Agency created the Rangers, which were a composite of both Army and Air Force tactical service operations. The Army took some of the DIA Rangers and made their own Ranger squads. These special operations contingents remained active, first as white then as black operations, from Viet Nam through Afghanistan, Lebanon, Panama, Iraq, various African theaters and other black operations.

"During the early MIA sweep years in southeast Asia, the ONI took the best of the SEALs and made the Black Berets, also known as SEAL Team 6. USASOC did their part and begat the 75th Rangers - the best of those two groups you saw moments earlier - and both were extended under Operation Phoenix into Afghanistan, the MidEast Water Wars and South-Central Asian StanLand Fuel-Oil Campaigns.

"Although SEAL Team 6 is still legitimized as DEVGRU and the 75th is operational, the Black Berets were only in function briefly. Some of you may remember Project Discovery, the massive security failure that completely compromised Operation Phoenix. In a matter of weeks everyone on the planet knew the Black Berets existed and were told to use and given specific drugs to aid them during operations.

"Neither enhancers nor medicants are process today, but we did learn from it; specifically, aid-dependent learning is not optimized for conflict. However, hypnotic attention and the body's own opiates are optimized when in catchment."

Donaldson paused and met each of the committee members' eyes individually. "Are you beginning to get the picture, ladies and gentleman? We find those who are afraid of monsters, those who haven't lost hypnotic attention and are skilled at producing opiates - endorphins and enkephalins - on demand and give them both training and license to seek out and destroy monsters they were afraid of.

"Except now we specify the monsters," he finished.

The woman from Massachusetts spoke, quietly, "You're talking about abused children, aren't you. Those men you brought in here," she paused and her brow creased tightly, "they were children when you started."

"Mid to late teens, early twenties, ma'am."

"But they were all abused children?"

"Technically and to use your own term, Senator, 'massively traumatized'."

All eyes locked on him. Some faces whitened, the realization forcing bile to rise in their throats.

Astin whispered, "You son-of-a-bitch. I...I have no words..."

Wrobleski said, "Calm down, Martha," his slow southern speech subdued.

Donaldson continued. "We force them into opiate producing states by subjecting them to familial trauma while inducing Naltrexone. The Naltrexone inhibits the production of natural opiates, which forces their bodies to develop multiple strategies for producing those opiates in abundance."

"This is inhuman, Carl. This is...I don't know what." Astin's face flushed and she held her arms tight across her chest, a disapproving schoolmarm waiting an explanation from schoolyard troublemakers.

"Why, Martha. All that Brahmin education you're so proud of

and you can't find a fucking goddamn word for how you feel? I'm surprised at you, Martha. I'm flabbergasted. I'm dumbstruck. I'm - "

"A bigoted, misogynistic prick."

"That's it, Martha. Now you're shitting in high cotton." Wrobleski sat forward and met her eyes, his drawl completely absent. "When you were balling pages to get information on who was voting how, I was sitting in this room making the same decisions about an ugly little war we were about to lose for a second time in some east buttfucked hill country called Afghanistan. You think every war goes like the First Gulf? That was forty-some years ago, Martha my dear. Even before the good Captain here stood to pee, I was signing bills that no one would ever see to do things no one wanted done.

"You want to know something about that little war that was before your time, Martha? The good Captain, here, he didn't tell you what normal, god-fearing American boys learned to do in that ugly little war. And I'll bet your Brahmin fucking father kept you in lace and white satin so you'd never have to know. Well, Martha, honey. Now I'm going to tell you.

"Did you know that towards the end of that war, the Black Berets weren't selected from the special operations teams anymore? We started getting them from Provincial Reconnaissance Units. Do you know where we got the lads in the PRUs? Primarily in jails for murder, rape, theft, assault; and those were the ones we felt safe enough to use! So we got these boys over there and we trained them and gave them a bounty for each weapon, each set of ears, each head, whatever, they could bring in.

"We found something out real fast, over there. You see, there were very few heads brought in, some ears were brought in, and lots of weapons were brought in. Why do you think that was, Martha?" Wrobleski slammed his fist onto the table. "Because you could goddamn tell by somebody's teeth if they were ours or not, but you couldn't always tell by their ears, and you could never fucking tell by their weapons. They started taking out their own teams just to collect the bounty."

He paused, sitting back, his fingers steepled in front of him, tapping, evaluating. Slowly he came forward again, his voice quiet. He spoke to Martha but everyone in the room leaned into his words. "And now I'm going to tell you the sad part, Martha. The boys from the jails didn't go over there knowing to do those things. The boys who were already there taught them.

"Face it, Martha. That Operation White Sphere we had down south slid into White Harvest faster than anybody thought, and that's gone worse than anything else ever did. Everybody on the Hill is calling it 'The Coca Wars' on camera and off, and you want to make nice because something's going to go bump in the night?

"You've always been a Bleeding Jesus, Martha, and if we were outside of this room, let me tell you, darling, I'd vote right beside you on anything you asked. But right now, Martha, right now we need some goddamn monsters, and I'd rather we do it to our boys through this Black Harvest operation than let some little slant bastard or sandnigger or bean-eater do it for us."

No one spoke. No one breathed.

Donaldson measured the room.

Jesus. This guy really knows how to play an audience.

There was no rush. Donaldson dismissed the escorts and Merchant in Portland, checked himself and Rivers into the Portland Harbor Hotel and slept until 0730. He bought a pair of navy blue sweatpants, matching sweatshirt and a pair of no-name sneakers from the lobby shop and ran a ten-mile circuit from the waterfront up Market Street down the length of State Street then to the airport and back.

Rivers briefed him when he returned. "No signs, no mentions, no reports. I even scanned harbor reports. All zero."

Back in their rooms, Donaldson did a quick 3S - Shit, Shower, and Shave - while Rivers shopped online for a nondescript SUV and basic hunting inventory at L.L.Bean.

They finished lunch in the hotel restaurant when a valet walked up to them with a ticket. "Your Sportage arrived, gentlemen. I took the liberty of parking it in our garage for you. And your packages from

L.L.Bean were delivered to your rooms, per your request."

Donaldson sniffed his coffee, put it down, pushed it away. "Small favors."

Rivers closed his eyes and inhaled, first deeply then sharply. "Last night's pizza isn't agreeing with you."

The valet's gaze went from Donaldson to Rivers and frowned. "Beg pardon?"

Donaldson cut Rivers off. "He's talking to me, friend. Thanks for taking care of the car. We'll be checking out in about half an hour. Have the Sportage out front, no need to bring our things down. We'll handle it." He handed the valet a twenty and watched him walk out of earshot. He turned to Rivers, "Civilian standard, correct?"

Rivers nodded. "Straight off the dealer's lot to our doorstep."

Dickey resided deep in the northwest corner of Maine. It showed up on some maps because it was the only town in a seventy-mile radius with a true military designation airstrip, used by hunters going to and from their camps up until four years ago. The Maine Department of Forestry and Game had a post there because of that airstrip. To the immediate north and west lay the Maine-Canadian border, thick, forested woods on the Maine side and homes and farms on the Canadian side, giving the border the appearance of a head with a razor cut hairline. Four years ago Dickey had one street. Not a long street, but a paved one. The only road into Dickey was Maine State Rt 161, which stopped abruptly at the Dickey town line with a sign, "End Rt 161," as if beyond this invisible demarcation lay the end of the world. Someone wrote above the state marker "Abandon hope all ye that enter here." Getting into or out of Dickey meant traveling bumpy, unpaved logging roads. The main street had a bar on either end, a post office/gas station/general store, a remodeled chicken farm that served as a motel, a hunting/fishing supply shop, and a forty-two year old, slightly overweight, squinty-eyed, small faced, half-Indian woman needing orthodontia who served the local gents and lonely big city hunters.

Then the Company built on Hafey Mountain. Now the bars carried good liquor, real motel rooms replaced the chicken coops, the hookers multiplied with none over twenty-five and a party could be had if you asked the right people.

Hafey Mountain itself wasn't impressive, only some five-fifty meters vertical. Hafey Mountain Preserve was equally unimpressive, and all of it intentional. Donaldson had advised on the original design and part of the construction. Lots of money had been spent to make the Preserve as innocuous as possible. The sharpest remotes wouldn't detect anything. An outmoded technique, thermal inertia, might have shown something odd, but the care taken to ensure no solid signatures, negligible recognizability and insignificant interpretation keys quickly became legend back at The Farm. You could find the Preserve by stumbling onto it or by knowing its location and specifically looking for it. Donaldson figured Trailer would go with option two, given his training.

The Preserve masqueraded as a large private hunting camp. The sign on the gate indicated a club name, an owner, a caretaker and a New York City phone number should one be needed and only available 5-5:30pmET, alternate Mondays with no indication of which Monday was an alternate. No one wore uniforms, although everyone there was an SH-11 grade or higher. Shipments of large game, domestic and imported, periodically came through the gates, not much more. Pine needles covered most of the grounds save dirt trails and roads. Pine, oak, elm and other trees claimed any remaining land and much of the sky above. Walk a straight line in any direction and you'd bump into birch, chestnut, and low lying scrub brush. The Preserve's electronic perimeter was disguised as maple sap lines, the collection buckets AIs waiting to be breached.

Most of the buildings looked like slightly oversized log cabins, their arrangement as random as 200 simultaneous runs on the Company's TX-2 could make them. No towers, no dishes, no telemetry sources of any kind could be found on the Preserve or near it if you didn't include the four internet-TV dishes in Dickey. All communications were done via a deeply buried, secured, and hardened laser cable running non-stop from the bowels of Hafey Mountain to Cutler Station's telecommunications web.

Donaldson's Sportage passed through the gates without question early that evening. He parked and entered one of the smaller cabins.

The CO saluted as he entered, handed him a folder, offered his hand and said "Major Distasio."

"When was the last supply shipment in?"

"Four days ago, Sir."

"When's the next? And negate the insignia. For everybody and everyone. First names, no rank. Does everybody here know what's coming our way?"

"Two days. We've all been briefed. A rogue biological, we were told. I have the Preserve alerted to your briefing tomorrow at O-Nine hun-," Distasio corrected himself without a pause, "9:00AM."

Thirty-seven personnel filled the classroom, thirty in chairs, seven standing in back. That left thirteen on the compound listening in on tight channel, directional receivers that looked like earbuds. Any questions they had would be answered when Donaldson met with them after lunch.

Donaldson stared each of the thirty-seven in the eye for a few moments, checking for signs Trailer had hypnotically compromised them. Satisfied, he made a note that the other thirteen were still vulnerable and would check them when they met. He didn't know if Trailer was already on the compound and he'd learned he could never be too cautious where augmentation was concerned.

He nodded at Rivers, standing in the back of the room. Rivers closed the door.

"My name is Jim Donaldson. For purposes that I hope to make clear, there will be no military designations, insignia, ensigns, flags, protocols, ordinances, and so on, of any kind until our task is completed.

"Regarding that task, I know the butt is that my friend and I are here to defunctionalize, deoptimize, dispose, immobilize, liberate, neutralize, sanction, and take executive action upon a rogue biological."

Somebody in the back of the room quietly said, "You forgot 'terminate with extreme prejudice'."

The room went quiet. Donaldson scanned their faces front of the room to back, searching for the one waiting to be disciplined. He smiled, then laughed, and the tension left as if Rivers had opened the door to let it out.

"Despite your training and any orders you may have received regarding the integrity of this compound, there is no action or condition - I repeat, none - upon which our guest is to be engaged by anyone other than myself. If any of you received directives that our guest is to be shopped - "

A second voice whispered, "'Shopped'?"

The original voice whispered back, "Steiner, Jesus Christ, *assassinated*."

Donaldson smiled, keeping it conversational. " - don't. You will not survive. Even if you succeed, you will not survive.

"First, what we're about to encounter isn't simply a 'rogue biological'. Some of you have seen our guest's redacted 201. You'll note there are no significant entries starting the day after the Manacapuru Truce effectively ended the Coca Wars through the following ten years. Then there is a full workup, including psychological, then nothing. Many of you are a little young to know this first hand, but most of you may have studied it either in school or at The Farm. Does anybody here have any familiarity with the Augmentation Project?"

Another voice mumbled from the side of the room, "Oh, shit."

Donaldson didn't miss a beat. "Well, that's one person who has an idea of what we're up against. Probably what you've heard or read is more conjecture than fact. So now you're all about to have your clearance raised ten grades in five minutes. Mr. Rivers, the lights, please."

The room went dark. Donaldson thumbed his mobile and a slowly rotating hologram of a nondescript nude male appeared on his right.

Lifesize and scale, a stationary flat face projection along the right of the image indicated Height 1.7m, Weight 61.23kg and Date 1 March 30. The last part of the legend contained a name, Nicholas Trailer. The image was half a head shorter than Donaldson and looked about fifty kilos lighter, basically a teenager waiting to grow up.

"This is a standard gray man. Nothing special. It was also our guest before augmentation." Donaldson stood at the edge of the hologram, the rotating image not quite touching him and swiped his mobile.

A second hologram appeared and covered half of Donaldson's body. Gasps from those in the front rows broke the classroom's silence as the image rotated before them. Somebody whispered, "Better living through chemistry," but nobody laughed. Donaldson took two steps sideways to get completely out of the projection.

People leaned forward. People in the back stood up to get an unrestricted view. Some murmured "Un-fucking-believable", "Wowza" , "Holy Mother", and the like. Donaldson watched their eyes dance back and forth; check the name in the legend, glance back at the image, reread the legend's particulars, go back to the image, back to the legend and so it went like they were watching a ping-pong match, their eyes darting two and three and more times before returning to their seats, shaking their heads. The two projections were the same person but the brow and cheekbones on the second had morphologized into something vaguely resembling a football helmet, and the subject was massive, even by pro ball standards.

At a first, casual glance, or from a distance, the subject appeared better proportioned and with a pronounced musculature, as if he'd been seriously weightlifting for some time. As the hologram rotated and people came forward, more differences became obvious. Broader hands, for one. And toes both longer and visibly separated from each other, his feet almost long-palmed, short-fingered hands. His eyes opened wider and were further apart. He'd developed a widow's peak. Proportionately smaller genitals than in the first image. His latissimus dorsi and rhomboid muscles spread like a cobra's hood on his back. His biceps looked like cleft footballs forced under his skin. Each head of his triceps showed like a cat's paw unsheathing its claws. His forearms were about as thick as most men's legs and his legs were about as wide as most men's waists. Veins and arteries lined his body like a topographic map of some vast river system rushing to the sea. His muscle definition seemed odd. People came forward to get a closer look.

Donaldson let them explore as much as they wanted and continued his lecture. "And this, you should realize, is after augmentation."

The hologram indicated 1 August 31. Similar scaling as the previous indicated the man had grown thirty-three centimeters taller during the interceding eighteen months. Most impressive was the weight: 297kg.

"The subject before you was one of nine candidated from a pool of some thirty thousand."

Donaldson waited until the classroom quieted down. "Just to let you know, I expect the subject to be on site in the next thirty-six hours. He may, in fact, already be here."

Donaldson waited until those inspecting the hologram returned to their seats. "Our best information at present is that none of you will even know he's here. I don't expect any of you will be engaged at any time, although I can't confirm that. However, I must warn you that he plays strictly Tit-for-Tat.

"And if he wants to play, I tell you in all good confidence, none of you will stand or be acknowledged. If a weapon is involved, it will look like a hunting accident. If not, an animal attack. You'll all be SOL before you let out a breath."

He gave them a minute then continued. "We screened for certain biological signatures: infra-aural hearing, night vision, excessive stamina and endurance, massive tolerance to physical insult. Other things we augmented for our purposes.

"The core temperature, for example, is up from thirty-seven degrees to just over forty-six degrees C. There's neither process disintegration nor cellular protein denaturing from twenty degrees to sixty-two degrees. He can self-induce a complete toxin flush to prevent both ischemia and rhabdomyolysis. Core conversion is, for all purposes, instantaneous. Basically it won't matter what the enemy presents, he'll adapt, overcome and recover within minutes, days at the most. He's invisible to ElInt. Farfoon and Wolff Ears won't pick him up, either. He can shut himself down as if he'd been hit with tetrodotoxin and remain that way until he has to come up."

"Was that to subvert forced interrogation techniques?"

Donaldson wondered how much to tell them, how much they needed to know to close this mission successfully. Bile rose and he forced it back down, his decision made, his years of silence ended. He sought penance and offered his confessional. "Torture was a way of life for these individuals."

He hurried on, wanting his words to outdistance his own memories. "Remember that we recruited them as juveniles, mid-teens to early twenties. Not that it mattered. As I said, torture was a way of life to these kids. They anticipated and expected torture from their quote-unquote caregivers every day of their life. These kids were so twisted being tortured was what they equated to getting attention, being loved. So we never had to worry about teaching them to be vague or evade or escape from being tortured. Besides, they might learn things while being tortured that they could use or report back to us.

"We taught them to relish it."

Silence.

Someone cleared their throat and asked, "Why is the subject tensing like that?"

"Right theory, wrong question." Donaldson paused. "He is relaxed."

He scanned the classroom to make sure he had everyone's attention. "This subject and eight others met the primary selection criteria, which, despite what you see, was not organic and was biological only as a side effect of those primary criteria, all of which were psychological." He paused. "Being caught and captured, what to anyone else would be mind-numbing torture, was simple recon for them."

Chairs squeaked as people shuffled. Throats were cleared.

Donaldson continued, "On a curious side note, Augmentation was only successful with O-Negatives."

Somebody asked, "Universal donors?"

Donaldson nodded. "No idea why. We're not sure if that's due to their ability to force hemopoiesis. They can also force thrombin and fibrin production. They can't bleed out unless there's catastrophic failure. And they're genetically aggressive. Theoretically, they could transfuse each other in the field and maintain augmented stability. But as I say, theoretically. We never tested it.

"This brings us to the secondary selection criteria that were discovered to aid the augmentation process in ways we didn't foresee, but which were much to the project's and individual subjects' benefit.

"The Augmenteds were a Phase Zero answer to developing hardened operatives, an 'economy of force' decision, if you will. Muscle and bone density is increased so that standard combat rounds will bruise but not impair. All the senses are heightened to the limits of organic functional capability and, when in his intended modality state, synesthesia becomes active for increased awareness and communication."

A hand rose and Donaldson acknowledged it. "I don't believe we have an indication of his assigned state," an implied question because no one would ask it directly.

Donaldson answered anyway, "He was a Hunter/Seeker. The - "

"Excuse me, Jim. What is he now?"

"We don't know that."

No sounds. No movement except for a few blinking eyes. Deers caught in headlights.

"So much for rationale, now for individual history. You'll notice that this image is dated 1 August 31. Those of you who know your history may remember that Pancho sued for Mutually Balanced Force Reductions on New Year's Day, 2032. We negotiated a truce and initiated MBFR shortly afterward. At that time the subject before you had 120 confirmed sanctions in 120 days. The 120 days were from 1 October 2031 to 1 January 2032. He became operative 30 September

2031.

"Remember that the subject was one of a team of nine. We decided on a team that size because, as most of you with basic intelligence training know, it is extremely difficult to fix on the position of a small, fast-moving group, which is exactly what this team was. Each member of the team performed equally. In 120 days, these nine men sanctioned one-thousand and eighty primaries, pretty much the majority of Pancho's Decision and Command hierarchy, not including secondaries and collaterals." He studied his audience. "What you see before you is one of nine unofficial but recognized reasons the Coca Wars ended when they did. As a point of psychological reference, the subject was seventeen years old when he experienced immediate, indeterminate aggression. We learned in Viet Nam that no one should go into combat until they were minimum eighteen years of age. Vandenhouck did a study of Viet Nam vets who were adolescents during combat. Because of his work and studies made during Afghan, Iraqi, Panama, the Mideast Water Wars and the Fuel-Oils then again during The Coca Wars, we discovered that the age when most individuals can psychologically handle the stress of combat is thirty-five. At that point, the brain has morphologically and topographically formed sufficiently to handle the responsibilities and decisions involved in such an arena." He nodded at the hologram. "This individual is only seventeen, half the age necessary to endure the stress, psychologically speaking."

A youngish woman raised her hand. "Forgive me, Jim, but you're not giving us much about this fellow's psychology."

"I appreciate that, I truly do. The truth is that knowing his psych makeup won't matter. You'll be dead."

Somebody asked from in back, "Why did the Augmented Men become POWs at the end of the action?"

Donaldson scanned the classroom trying to isolate the voice. His eyes moved to Rivers, but Rivers hadn't found the remark important enough to isolate and couldn't help. Donaldson cut the hologram and signaled Rivers for the lights.

He stared at the audience. "You do not have adequate clearance for me to answer that question."

Donaldson said, "I appreciate Senator Astin's thoughts."

Wrobleski sat back from Martha and brought his hands to his face. Only Donaldson could see him smile.

"The mission this committee gave me was to create hardened operatives, robust specialists, if you will, capable of total submergence regardless of gray status. That's where the concept of the Augmented Men comes from." Donaldson's voice became a quiet chant. "An intensive study of appropriate psychological signatures was made and it was determined we had the necessary pool of candidates available to us. We further selected for biological signatures, specifically signatures we had the technology to modify to fit the organic and biofunctional contingencies.

"I do appreciate your sentiments, Senator, but I assure you and despite what I said earlier, we haven't created monsters." From the corner of his eye, Donaldson saw Wrobleski's smile twitch. "We've done what God would have done if He'd wanted to make a combat regular."

Astin asked, "But what about when they return? How will we reintegrate them?"

"Take a lesson from history, Martha," snorted Wrobleski. "These boys is Jap Zeros, is all."

THROUGH

29 DAYS UNTIL TERMINATION

Trailer sat in a corner of the only place he considered safe in all of Hafey Preserve, a double-walled single room, soundproof and bugproof with hidden external speakers. You'd hear food being prepared, light snoring, an orgy - anything and everything to maintain the desired illusion outside - regardless of any activity inside.

He pulled his legs tight against his chest and his arms around his knees, holding them in. His eyes were half open but defocused, not looking at anything inside the room.

Alone. Waiting.

He'd arrived early the previous morning, moving under the dark, overcast sky like the foraging coyotes and bears he often traveled with. Because he moved with animal rhythms, none of the animals took flight at his approach. That got him to a sturdy, thick-trunked white pine about eighty yards from the compound. He climbed the pine until the trunk and limbs wouldn't support his weight any higher, a hundred feet up. From that perch, he saw, heard, smelt, tasted, and felt the few men walking around the compound. He watched where they walked, then focusing where they didn't walk, saw the heat signatures and heard the minute hums of concealed electronics: security devices, protectives, countermeasures.

He let his eyes and irises open wide, hollowing out his throat and eustachian tubes, then opened his mouth, the Augment's version of echolocation. No other sounds, no other movements, came to him.

He left the pine and moved over the ground until he came to the compound perimeter. There he leapt, clearing the fencing and landing silently, his gastrocnemius, gluteals, sartorii, planar, and great and lesser thigh muscles absorbing his weight and leaving no marks to betray his landing.

Matching the movements of guards who'd just gone around corners, who could no longer be seen by their peers, he moved as if he belonged, as if no differences existed between himself and whomever people saw next, shifting from one man's movement patterns to the next often with a single step, until he heard the thoughts and dreams of Donaldson, Donaldson's mind active even as he slept.

Trailer opened the door. Rivers slept on a cot opposite Donaldson, under a window across from where Trailer'd entered the compound. As Trailer entered, Rivers' breathing changed briefly and he rolled over in his sleep. Trailer froze, holding his position against the door for a full ten minutes, moving only when the guard came by to make his rounds. Rivers didn't move again, although he opened his mouth and took two deep breaths when Trailer fully entered the room, inhaling through his nose and exhaling through his mouth both times.

Trailer listened for Rivers' dreams but there were none. He watched Rivers sleep, concentrating on his features. He recognized Rivers as handsome, even beautiful, and Trailer hated him for that. Under the covers, Rivers had as symmetrical a body as any other man's. Trailer hated him for that, too. It didn't matter that massive engineering on Trailer's body resulted in his morphology and physiognomy, his rage stemmed from the fact that Rivers could lead a normal life. He could be with people. He could enjoy their company. He could love. He could hold someone and not be afraid they'd break.

He could, in Trailer's mind, *be*.

In his sleep, Rivers coughed and smiled. Trailer's hand clenched as he looked down on him.

He shook his head, opened his hand and turned his attention to Donaldson.

Who made him.

To be ugly.

So no one would love him. So everyone would fear him.

He sat between the two bunks, waiting for Donaldson to wake up. He no longer paid attention to Rivers. Rivers was simply 'the other man in the room', not the target, hence irrelevant. He let his senses roam like wild dogs about the camp, listening to conversations, feeling people's touches by listening to their heartbeats and breathing, the intramuscular squishes and clicks as they moved around. Some of the sounds came from people he'd mimicked previously and, knowing them, he let himself see what they were seeing, smell and taste what they were smelling and tasting, sharing their experiences like some ghostly voyeur.

All this you taught me, Donaldson. You taught me to experience them, to be them, but not to be one of them.

28 DAYS UNTIL TERMINATION

Warm, refreshing, morning sun came through the window and caressed Donaldson's face. It mixed nicely with the slight chill and damp of the northern Maine woods. He snuggled under his comforter, enjoying the feel of the distinctly nonregulation feather bed.

Rivers said, "Jim?"

Donaldson grunted.

"Wake up, Jim."

"What in the hell - " Donaldson opened his eyes.

Trailer sat on the floor, cross-legged, arms forward and hands resting on his knees, eyes closed, face neutral as if meditating, between the two beds.

Rivers hadn't moved from his bed but looked like he'd been awake for a while.

Trailer got up from the floor and stretched like a dragon deciding which of the two would be its prey. He nodded at Donaldson, released his spine, turned around and bumped into a coffee table with some folders on it as he walked towards the door. The folders fell and spread open on the floor. Trailer stopped to pick them up, shuffling them together as he did so.

Rivers sat up. "I'll take care of that."

Trailer stood, nodded, and left.

Rivers got up and started gathering the folders after the door closed. "He's getting old. He's getting clumsy."

"Don't underestimate him, Tom. I'd say everything he does has a purpose."

Rivers focused his attention on the papers. "Yeah. Right."

"Tom, trust me on this."

"Okay, okay."

"I'm going to get cleaned up. Finish putting things back in order then go get some breakfast. I'll meet you in the cafeteria in a few minutes."

After the cabin door closed, Donaldson came out of the bathroom and walked over to the edge of his bed. He pulled out the clothes Rivers had purchased for him at L.L.Bean and inspected them carefully. Earlier, when Trailer woke them, he wore the same clothes he'd worn at the hospital in the same way: buttoning his shirt in a recognition signal of rank, preparedness, and readiness. "I don't want that, Nick." Donaldson checked his clothes again for anything that might be misconstrued as either Lettuce - oak leaves, clusters, and so on - or SigRec for rank, preparedness, or readiness.

Back in the bathroom, he stared at his reflection. "Going to bring him back this time, huh?" Donaldson rubbed his stubble and scratched his Adam's apple. He was in good shape for a man staring down half a century and still bore the look of command.

Catching himself in the act of self-appraisal, he laughed. "And you're a fool if you think you're going to bring him back under your terms. Respond to what's happening. Don't anticipate. Don't get sucked in. Take your time. Go slow." He ran his hands down through his belly hair and tapped his fingers against the hardness of his gut. "The Augmented Men are creatures of fear, and fear paints neither a bright future nor a happy present." He took a deep breath and let it out slowly. "Trailer's got to live in your world. You don't have to live in his."

Donaldson joined Rivers in the cafeteria thirty minutes later. Trailer left no signs of his movements nor had anyone seen him. Donaldson and Rivers ate a quiet breakfast of scrambled eggs, crisp hash browns with blackened onions, whole wheat toast, and coffee. "Any idea how long our guest was with us last night, Tom?"

"Sorry to say I didn't hear him come in, although I know he was there for two hours before you woke up. Any idea what he was doing just sitting there?"

"Mapping, I'd say. He hasn't seen me in a while and doesn't know you from Adam. He's so externally driven he probably acquired everybody here, mapping everybody's psychological space, learning everybody's patterns and modes. If I were him, I'd've spent some time trying on those maps so I'd know what to expect and how to react. That's my guess, anyway. I haven't seen him in a while, either. He's a bit of a new beast to me, too. Any thoughts you might have...well, I'd like to know what you think."

Rivers answered between bites. "I try not to. It gets in the way. Clouds things."

Donaldson waited until Rivers had sopped up the last of the ketchup he'd liberally applied to his eggs and hash browns. "Tom, where would you go?"

Rivers pulled a map of the compound out of his hip pocket. He read the legends of each building before selecting one. "That's where I'd go, if I guess him right."

Rivers pointed at The Tank, an exact replica of The Tank at The Farm, the CIA, NSA and ONI training facilities at Fort Peary, Virginia, the double walled, soundproof and bugproof single room with hidden external speakers where Trailer sat alone and waiting.

"It's the closest thing to Isolation on the compound."

27 DAYS, 18 HOURS UNTIL TERMINATION

Trailer sat at the inside north corner of The Tank, slowing his internal rhythms, subsiding his rage, waiting for Donaldson. His eyes, still half open, went back and forth like pendulums under his eyelids. His breaths came deep and once every five minutes.

He heard footsteps, closing outside, and his breaths quickened with the mix of Donaldson's and Rivers' scents.

He took a moment to wonder if he'd have to kill Rivers. Not now. Perhaps later.

Not that he wanted to kill anybody. The people back in that bar had been an opportunistic mistake. He didn't want to kill them, but since he had, he would use it to force Donaldson to do what he needed him to do.

He thought over his plan, considered his moves, evaluated their possible responses. Parts of his consciousness submerged, others rose to the surface. His eyes opened, although his eyes showed like pinpoints in seas of white, and his nostrils flared. For a moment, his entire world became the steady in-out passage of the air on the rims of his nostrils, the constant passage of cool air in, warm breath out, as it traveled through his nasal fossa and tickled his sinuses.

Donaldson and Rivers stood outside The Tank. The door was locked from the inside and all compound personnel were accounted for. Donaldson held the only key in his palm.

He looked at the door. "Nick? May I come in?"

The door opened. Donaldson handed Rivers the key and passed him a note: If I don't come out in twenty-eight days, don't send anybody in. Deploy a small, clean organic and go.

The inside of the Tank was deceptively large considering the size of the building on the outside. Set up like a large studio apartment and painted a pale, supposedly calming, hospital green, a galley kitchen ran along the southeast wall, and two twin beds with white linen and blankets butted the wall opposite the galley. Two writer's desks, a couch and two comfortable-looking recliners, their upholstery matching the white of the beds, and a table with two captain's chairs, each item built directly into the floor thus making the entire arrangement immovable, occupied the center rectangle between the beds and galley wall. A short weave, wall-to-wall rug, a slightly paler green than the walls, covered the floor. The table had checker and cribbage boards carved into it. Everything not upholstered was oak. The Tank had no TV, stereo, pods, players or any other form of electronic entertainment, no exposed lighting and no windows. A full lav with a combo washer-dryer unit sat behind floor-to-ceiling steel reinforced walls at the southeast corner of The Tank, a safe room if necessary.

Donaldson stood in the second, inner doorway, located in the middle of the southwestern wall of the inner room. The first, outer door, located at the south corner, had already sealed. As soon as Donaldson entered the room, the second door would close and the air between the inner and outer walls would be evacuated. Trailer stood as Donaldson entered. The inner door sealed and Trailer stood beside him before Donaldson could move. The Augmented Man stared down at him, his eyes unfocused and his nose twitching as his head and shoulders slowly moved from side to side.

"SigRec Inc. Neg. 'Firm."

Respond to what's happening. Don't anticipate. Go slow.

Donaldson catalogued Trailer's communication: Trailer was in Hunter/Seeker state. He was unable to determine any signal recognition patterns on Donaldson and hence viewed any attempts as incomplete and therefore negative - which also meant he would view Donaldson as an enemy. He was requesting Donaldson's confirmation.

How Donaldson answered Trailer's request for authorization would set the tone for the rest of whatever happened in The Tank and Donaldson didn't want a military tone set.

Answer this right or we all go boom. "It's me. Jim Donaldson. You remember me."

Trailer's eyes cleared as the irises retreated, making his eyes deep, black, and unreal, like some great whale's rising and sounding. He stared down at Donaldson for some thirty seconds.

Donaldson's palms grew cold. Hair rose on the back of his neck.

A few years earlier he'd been diving off Salt Cay and suddenly found himself alone and circled by gray sharks. He tongued his comm.

Dead.

If there'd been a call to surface, he'd never heard it.

The dead comm made little difference. He floated one hundred feet below the hull struggling not to move, hoping the sharks wouldn't have any disturbances to navigate by. One of the sharks rasped his suit, tearing it open and exposing some skin.

The sharks became darts and he was the bullseye.

Then, with no warning and no feeling of bow pressure, Donaldson found himself eye to eye with an humpback whale. No more sharks, just Donaldson and the whale. The behemoth floated, watching him, not moving. Donaldson viewed his reflection in the whale's eye and sensed that the whale watched him dispassionately, ready to crush him and ready to not. Had the whale chased the sharks away so that it could have Donaldson all to itself, but now seeing the size of the morsel, decided he was a waste of its time?

The sharks were aware of Donaldson and that made them the enemy, something he understood. To the whale, he didn't exist. That terrified him all the more. One slight move and the beast, without thinking, could crush him. Donaldson understood his own frailty for the first time, recognized his own solipsism, became aware of his own life as seen through the eyes of another. What was the behemoth thinking? Did it recognize him as a separate and unique, as another life or merely something odd in the water, something trivial, unimportant, something to be ignored?

He submerged into that emotional abyss again. He waited, suspended in an ocean cold with fear. Once again the world rotated into perspective as he stared into Trailer's eyes, wondering what the whale saw.

"They brought me back in a Connex box. I wouldn't have hurt anybody, but they brought me back in a Connex box."

Yes. Uncleaned, your wounds undressed, unfed, with no change of clothes and no aid, in a cage, most of them talking about you as if you either didn't exist or were too dumb to know what they were saying. They lifted the side of the Connex without asking you and blasted you with a 300psi attack firehose, through the bars, taking bets at how long you could stand up.

"They brought me back in a Connex box."

Donaldson nodded. Yes, it's time to pay back the whale.

Donaldson pointed to the lav. "May I?"

Trailer shrugged. Donaldson went in. He lifted the toilet cover. A used prophylactic floated on the water. He urinated and flushed.

"There's wine and cheese in the fridge," Trailer said. "If we had a fireplace and some music, we could become good friends." He smiled.

Donaldson smiled back. "May I ask you a question?"

Trailer nodded.

"Why did you come here?"

Trailer went back to the corner and folded himself into a small package. "So you could kill me."

He didn't move or speak the rest of the day.

27 DAYS UNTIL TERMINATION

Donaldson woke to the sounds of frying and the smell of eggs, hash browns, whole wheat toast, Canadian bacon, and coffee. Trailer stood at the stove. His clothing consisted of three burlap bags - one for each leg and one for a shirt - and two canvas sacks - one for a jacket and the other forming the seat and crotch of the trousers. Donaldson didn't see Trailer's other clothes. The table had place settings for two.

Donaldson got up and Trailer nodded at one of the settings, spooning out generous portions as Donaldson sat. He motioned to the food and Donaldson started eating. A look of surprise came over Donaldson's face. "This is good, Nick. You do wonders with rations."

Trailer walked to the refrigerator and opened the door revealing fresh eggs, a plastic half gallon of milk, a loaf of fresh-baked bread, a few potatoes and onions, some more Canadian bacon in deli paper, a can of coffee, a block of cheddar cheese and a half-empty bottle of Blue Nun.

"I guess somebody's been having a real party in here, huh?"

Trailer went back to the stove. "Do you mind if I eat with you? Some people don't like the way I eat."

"I know how you eat. I was with you during the war."

Trailer stared at him. "Not after New Year's Day, you weren't."

Donaldson finished his breakfast without commenting. Step one in the process of bringing Trailer back: establish rapport. He scanned The Tank. How to do it?

He cleared off the breakfast dishes. "I noticed the game boards on the table. Are there any pieces?"

Trailer opened a drawer and took out a box, which he opened. It held chess and checker pieces, cards and cribbage pegs, each in their own neat little sections.

"Do you play chess?"

Trailer shook his head, no.

"I'm a 2200 level player. Want to learn?"

Trailer stiffened slightly. His pupils dilated.

Damn!

Trailer's breathing became shallow and rapid, his movements lethargic and heavy. He sat at the table with his eyes fixed on the chess board, his speech mechanical and the words staccatoed. "Learn chess. Yes."

Donaldson stopped moving and kept his breaths even. He's gone hypnotic.

He spoke slowly and clearly, "I'm going to remove the pieces from the box and place them on the board." He explained each piece's movements and capturing abilities as he moved each in a slow arc from box to board.

He won the first game in fifteen moves. He lost the second in thirty-three. Throughout the games, Trailer's moves came faster. Somewhere in the fifth game, Trailer started moving the pieces for Donaldson.

Exactly as Donaldson would move them.

Donaldson sat back and watched Trailer play both sides and win games.

I've been acquired. He's learned my patterns, my style. If I were his target, I'd be dead.

Even though Trailer played exactly as Donaldson would play, including variations on proven themes, Donaldson's pieces lost more and more games, each game taking less and less time, each finishing somewhere between twelve and fifteen moves. Donaldson folded his hands under his chin, his eyes unable to follow the blur of Trailer's hands as he moved the pieces automatically, the rules, concepts, and theory of the game more and more instinctive as he played. An hour later Donaldson had lost track of the number of games. Each game went to mate in under five seconds.

Trailer stopped moving the pieces. His head rose slowly, his focus transferring from the board to Donaldson's face. His irises expanded until the pupils were pinpoints. His breathing got deeper and his movements more fluid. "Learned chess."

"Yes, Nick. You're an excellent player."

"Who is the king?"

25 DAYS UNTIL TERMINATION

When Donaldson couldn't give Trailer a condition intensive response to the king question, Trailer returned to his corner, assumed a small package formation and ignored Donaldson without a break. As far as Donaldson knew, Trailer had not moved in two days and the inactivity exhausted him.

This is what we taught him. To instill fear by letting the target know death was near, but not how near, that it was inevitable but not the moment of inevitability.

He chuckled and gave himself a nod. We taught him well.

Trailer could wait him out, no question. And Donaldson had mentally rehearsed every conversation, every engagement scenario he could imagine.

Now he sat on his bunk, watching the small package across the room. Trailer had gone completely internal. He couldn't maintain the small package formation for so long otherwise.

He's waiting for the right moment. Donaldson recounted all operations and procedures active at the preserve. But the right moment for what? The operations and procedures here are pattern perfect. No variations of any kind. He knows what to expect, when to expect it, how it will go, who will do it...

He got up from his bunk and walked over to the small package huddled tightly in a corner of the room. "You said you wanted me to kill you, Nick, but that doesn't make any sense. You could've killed yourself any time you wanted to."

He sat down facing the monster he'd created. Trailer's eyes were unfocused. "So what do you really want?"

Trailer's right arm shot out from its chicken-wing position faster than Donaldson could see. His hand stopped, palm-heel position against Donaldson's sternum as Donaldson inhaled, preparing to speak again.

Donaldson remained calm, collecting his thoughts and focusing them, wanting his words to be clear and exact so that Trailer would hear them as intended.

"You could kill me, Nick, and haven't. You've acquired me, so you must have an inkling that I'm here to help you. I can't un-Augment you, Nick, but I can start you living a life as normal as anybody else's. Let me know if that's acceptable."

Slowly, he took Trailer's massive hand in his and guided it back away from his chest to Trailer's lap, not chicken-winged at his side, all the while watching the behemoth's eyes.

24 DAYS UNTIL TERMINATION

Trailer sat in his corner, neither moving nor noticeably breathing, huddled, protected, submerged in his own thoughts. He closed his eyes and focused all his attention on Donaldson.

Whom he'd acquired.

But the acquired Donaldson didn't match the remembered Donaldson.

The remembered Donaldson would complete the mission assigned him at the Manacapuru Truce and destroy Trailer. He hadn't when they moved Trailer from the Orinoco to Dreamspace. That could be explained. The Dreamspace Donaldson wanted to know how Trailer survived the Orinoco. The Dreamspace Donaldson was just another captor and Trailer had escaped.

This Donaldson, the acquired Donaldson, would not kill Trailer. The acquired Donaldson had not interfered with Trailer since they played chess. He had thought many things but none of them mission specific, at least not what Trailer remembered as Donaldson's mission specific.

This Donaldson's mission conflicted with Trailer's reason for surfacing.

When did the mission change? Who gave the order? Why?

It didn't matter.

The acquired Donaldson would not complete the mission Trailer needed him to complete.

Therefore the acquired Donaldson was no longer useful to him.

He could kill Donaldson. Rivers and the others at the compound would have no choice but to destroy him if he killed Donaldson.

Night.

Donaldson dreamed. Trailer leaned over him in the dark. He undulated slightly, swaying right to left and back again, his broad back and movement giving him the appearance of a cobra about to strike. He'd stood so every night, rising from his corner once Donaldson was somnambrous and couldn't wake. Each night he told himself that he would end Donaldson. He would end Donaldson and those outside The Tank would destroy him.

Each night Trailer prepared and stopped, sometimes hand raised and muscles ready. It would be murder. Intentional. He had not wanted to kill in the bar. They attacked him, his augmentation took over against his will, it was done in the span of one breath. He wanted to be found but not this way, not for this. Once done, however, other training kicked in: use your environment to achieve mission completion. Destroying the bar was as good a way as any.

But here, in the night, in The Tank, it would be murder. And each night he prepared, hand raised and muscles ready, and instead lowered himself out of readiness and hovered over Donaldson, a parent listening to their child sleeping in their crib. Donaldson wasn't somniloquent but his subvocalizations were roadmaps into his dreams.

Donaldson woke in darkness. Dim lights came on as he rose from his bed, indicating The Tank was still in night mode, long before dawn. He made his way to the lav and back. On the way back he glanced at Trailer's corner and stopped.

No Trailer.

Donaldson looked around. He checked the floor cupboards, underneath the bunks, in the shower stall, under the sinks and couldn't find Trailer anywhere. "Okay, Nick. I give up. If you're trying to hide, I can't find you. If you've left, you could've left me a note so I wouldn't make a fool of myself."

The inner door opened and Trailer came in with a plastic grocery bag. He didn't acknowledge Donaldson. He walked over to the refrigerator, quietly opened it and transferred eggs, milk, Canadian bacon, and whole wheat bread. He reached into the bag a last time and pulled out a pint of light cream. "You used to like this in your coffee when you could get it." He placed the cream on the refrigerator shelf next to the milk.

"Thank you. The grocer must be wondering what vandals get in his store at night."

Trailer folded the grocery bag and placed it between the refrigerator and the counter. He walked over to Donaldson's clothes and lifted Donaldson's pants. One pocket opened wide and Trailer dropped some change into it. "You're not as safe as you used to be." He walked over to his corner, folded himself and remained silent.

Donaldson said, "Thank you."

Silence.

"What's it like outside?"

No response.

"I haven't been in Dickey recently. What's it like?"

No acknowledgement.

Donaldson returned to his bunk and slept.

Once again Donaldson dreamed. Trailer rose and stood over him. He listened to Donaldson's dreams, mapping himself into Donaldson, thinking as Donaldson would think, interpreting the input of his senses as Donaldson would interpret them. Trailer synchronized his breaths to Donaldson's to experience Donaldson's dreams more fully, more completely.

Strange things populated Donaldson's dreams. Secret enemies. Half human nemeses chased through dark, South American forests. Vivisected animals, their dissection wounds flowing, dressed in camo gear and walking like men, carrying weapons. In one dream, Donaldson supported a man-sized, mutilated baby rabbit in his arms and screamed for an 18D, anybody with field medical training, tears streaming from his face and wetting the rabbit's fur.

Another dream had elements Trailer remembered pre-deployment, an experience he and Donaldson shared and now shaped by slumber into something different.

Donaldson and Senator Wrobleski argued. Wrobleski said, "Take a lesson from history, Captain. These boys is Jap Zeros, is all." He snorted like it was some kind of joke as he walked away.

Donaldson grabbed his arm. "What do you mean, Jap Zeros? They're men, goddamn it. Men."

Military guards appeared on either side of Donaldson, weapons raised and ready, Donaldson's face in their sights.

Wrobleski turned back slowly, completely in control, as if hearing his name called across the Senate floor. His eyes went from Donaldson's face to Donaldson's hand on his arm.

"Relax, boys. Captain Donaldson just needs to be educated, is all."

Donaldson released Wrobleski's arm and brought his hand down to his side.

"Smart move, son. Now, these fancy soldier boys you made..." Wrobleski paused, evaluating Donaldson before continuing, determining how much truth he could handle. "Understand, they're not men. They don't think they're men and we chose them because they don't think they're men and then we spent a lot of taxpayer dollars to make sure they'd never think they's men ever again.

"What they are, Jimmy-boy, is an experiment." He laughed. "In fact, they's 'Carl Wrobleski's Invisible Group'." He slapped his thigh, his laughter coming out as a hacking smoker's cough. "Yeah, I like that, 'Carl Wrobleski's Invisible Group'.

"Do you know what an Invisible Group is, Jimmy-boy? Well let me tell you, son, in case you don't.

"They's thugs. Originally they's thugs straight from them East German prisons. You're too young to remember, but I do. The SSD got 'em, and the SSD and KGB used 'em. These boys did murder, they kidnapped, they beat the living hell out of whoever their bosses said. Then you know what? They was killed. Each and every one. My pappy got some when The Wall come down and he showed me what they was like before he used them. And when he was done? He got them all in a room with open bottles and lots of food and some fine looking ladies and young looking boys, closed the doors, turned the gas on and made sure nobody got out.

"You understand me, son?

"Them thugs was killed, every single one, and you're going to do the same with these thugs you made. Your boys is Jap Zeros, just another Invisible Group. Do what you've been goddamn told and get the fuck out of here or I'll find someone who can and serve them your ass on a platter to boot.

"Understand, Jimmy-boy? Nod at me so I'll know you understand."

Donaldson stared at the floor, not moving, barely breathing.

Wrobleski grabbed Donaldson's chin and forced his head up. "Look at me, I say, look at me boy, when I'm fucking you. These boys of yours is just a feasibility study. A test. You got no fucking idea what this is about or where this is going."

Fear gripped Donaldson's chest like a cold steel hand, squeezing him, shaking him like a wild dog shakes a kill.

Donaldson's eyes opened. Trailer ignored his gaze. Vacant, open but unaware, Donaldson's mind focused on his dream, not on Trailer arching over him.

Except for the terror, pure childhood terror, in Donaldson's eyes.

What can cause such a reaction in Major Donaldson?

In the dream, someone new, a giant so tall and huge that its head rose above the clouds, its face unseen, unknown, stood with its left fist on its hip, its right hand pointing down at the cowering Donaldson and boomed with a voice like thunder, "Are you going to be a good soldier, Jimmy-boy? Are you going to make me proud?"

Donaldson couldn't speak. Trailer, mapping, pulled back slightly.

Fear's cold steel hand crawled up Donaldson's chest and clamped around his throat.

Donaldson wanted to say no, the word forming in his mouth when the giant backhanded him, the impact so forceful Trailer's head rocked back from Donaldson's dream.

Donaldson pulled Trailer into his dream, taking on Trailer's augmented physiology.

Donaldson-Trailer punched the side of the left knee, popping the joint as the femur slipped off the tibia. Giant hands came down to hold the knee in place. Donaldson-Trailer ran behind the other leg and bit through the posterior cruciate. The body started falling slowly, collapsing on itself like a huge Thanksgiving Day Parade balloon deflating after the crowds had gone.

Donaldson, still asleep, smiled and relaxed, the fear gone.

That dream ended. Brief images of classrooms and farmhouses and tanks like vats from which bison emerged, memories raced through Donaldson's mind looking for places to hide.

Trailer's and Donaldson's breaths desynchronized. Trailer took a step back. He had entered Donaldson's dream, Donaldson's nonconscious adding details both environmental and irrelevant.

You won't even remember it, will you, Major? Jim?

But for Trailer to respond? To sense and feel the impact?

He stared at Donaldson's sleeping form.

To share a dream so vividly he felt the blows Donaldson felt, felt the shame -

Shame?

The hair on Trailer's arms riffled. His skin twitched like a horse shaking off a fly. The ruffling remained.

Goosebumps?

I can still get goosebumps?

Trailer shivered in a room that stayed a comfortable 71°F Summer, Winter, Spring, and Fall. His head cocked slightly and his brow furrowed.

Things didn't match up.

He stood over Donaldson for another hour, listening for Donaldson's dreams. When none came, he returned to his corner and sat.

23 DAYS UNTIL TERMINATION

Ignatius Alphonsus Distasio nodded and smiled as he carried his breakfast tray through the cafeteria. He glanced at each table, its occupants, smiled, nodded, shifted his tray so he could wave at people sitting on the far side of the room from him. He looked at one table and frowned. Two people there stared back, shrugged and shook their heads.

He put his tray down at his table, drained his coffee and went back to the coffee urn, nodding and frowning as he passed tables, waving at people sitting at tables across the room.

Chris Harley, one of the few women assigned to regular duty at Hafey and a red-headed, pale-faced willow among the ruddy hued, alpha male oaks posted there, got up from her table, coffee cup in hand. "Anybody need anything?"

Head shakes all around the table. A couple of "No, thanks." One or two eyes up and smiles.

She may have been the tiniest person at the table but nobody pissed off Momma Harley.

She moseyed to the coffee urn, stopping a few times to chat with people on the way.

Distasio nodded, smiled, and kept his voice conversational as she reached the urn. "Has anybody seen Steiner?

"No. Last eyes-on was 11:30pm last night, on his way to his room. Last signature was 2:30am this morning, leaving the compound."

"Leaving the compound?"

"Before you ask, no idea where he went. He dropped his tags and wasn't chipped."

"How did he get assigned here without being chipped?"

"Paperwork was right. History checked out. Passed all the tests. Good recs. Severe dermal allergic reaction."

Distasio stared into his empty coffee cup and pursed his lips a few times deciding if the coffee warranted another cup.

"Tell you the truth, Boss, nobody's sorry. He was a walking disaster. All he ever talked about was how shitty his life was and how his wife's dying of cancer. He didn't do his work and when he did it always had to be corrected. Christ, his cover was doing materiel inspections but he didn't know a brick from a bullet. They couldn't have posted a more inept SOB here if they wanted to. I was going to ask permission to start Administrative Separation procedures - I didn't want to screw him with Bad Conduct or anything UCMJ - and then this happened."

"He arrives two days prior to our guests, doesn't have a chip, can't do his job, and now he's gone."

"Far horizons search?"

Distasio considered before nodding at Harley. "That would be prudent. Has Donaldson come out of The Tank? Seems like something he should know."

"I'll see to it and no, as far as we know he's still in there with his friend."

"Rivers has been off site for a few days, that I know. Get him on a secure line and patch it through to me."

20 DAYS UNTIL TERMINATION

Donaldson woke unsure of his location and his mind full of dreams. Images of his father, his mother, his training, the Augmented Men, Wrobleski, Rivers…so many dreams on so many subjects he couldn't separate them. Lying still, he looked around.

It was The Tank, full daylight mode.

He pulled his covers off and got up slowly, swinging his legs over the side of the bed. His momentum carried him towards the floor.

His body tensed.

Find your center. Find your center.

His left hand grabbed the edge of the bed, his right went to his still swaying head.

Trailer sat at the table watching him. "You okay?"

"A little groggy. I'll be fine. What time is it?"

"A little after nine o'clock, maybe. Shall I make breakfast?" Trailer began peeling potatoes at the sink.

Donaldson made his way to the bathroom, closed the door and began a complete physical and psychological self-evaluation, a leper checking for wounds, a neurotic checking for twitches.

The pattern's changed. Trailer's not in small package formation.

What's changed, Mr. Trailer?

The smells of breakfast came to him. He relieved himself, washed his face and brushed his teeth.

Opening the lav door, he saw Trailer already sitting at the table, waiting.

Ask him what day it is. Ask him if the Preserve still exists outside these walls. Ask him if he left anybody alive the last time he went out grocery shopping.

A moment later he sat at the table, eating. Trailer sat across from him and started his own, not asking this time, just sitting and eating as if were the most natural thing in the world.

Donaldson counted his chews before he swallowed, anchoring himself to his reality before entering Trailer's. "Too bad you didn't get a paper while you were out. We could've seen what movies were playing in Dickey. Maybe take one in tonight."

Trailer stared at him. "There are no theaters in Dickey. You gave orders for isolation for twenty-eight days. We have twenty left."

We? At least I know the date.

Trailer's chest tensed underneath the burlap sack. His eyes bulged and he hacked as if coughing up phlegm. A bone began to appear between his lips. The muscles in his chest relaxed and his neck tensed. The bone popped from his mouth. Trailer caught it and put it on an unused plate in front of him.

Donaldson kept his eyes on Trailer's and inspected the bone, a small femur, with his peripheral vision. He remembered the Augmented's training. "Fear, gentleman, you will give the enemy fear, and only fear. No bodies, no remains, only a gutpile. You will teach them that they are prey, and that their hunters view them like any other kill."

All Special Operations Forces knew Mao's writings on guerrilla warfare. It was required reading. The Augmented Men took Mao's writings further, into places no one in Mao's time thought to go, preying on the civilians' religious, social, and cultural paranoias. In Viet

Nam, the SEALs painted a target green then dismembered it, finally cutting out the target's liver and taking a bite. Viet Nam had a lot of Buddhists. Such acts - leaving a body no longer intact - prohibited the target from entering heaven. In the Mideast they called it a pigpile: pig intestines, pig blood, pig skin, pig urine, pig feces, pig tongue, pig feet, pig head, ... hell, every mission had at least one man designated "hog handler" who did nothing but carry and deploy offal. Everybody knew pork futures went through the roof during those wars and nobody guessed why. Northern South American paranoias originated in different belief systems, different precepts, different constructs. Donaldson's throat hollowed, his breakfast seeking an escape.

"No," Trailer said. "It's from an old, lame coydog. I showed it mercy." He smiled. "Want to see the rest to be sure?"

Donaldson shook his head. It took another fifteen minutes to finish his breakfast. He cleared the table. All the while, Trailer stood facing one of the walls. His eyes moved back and forth. Occasionally he furrowed his brow as if studying something.

Donaldson watched him as he washed the dishes.

Something whipped back in his mind.

He showed mercy?

The Augments had been taught and trained not to show mercy. They considered it an operational weakness, something that could make the team vulnerable, something not aspect to their conditioning.

But what does it mean? Why did he allow me to wake up that one night and none of the others? And was that pre or post change?

Who's showing mercy to whom? About what?

Or is this Trailer's PsyWar training in play and I'm some piece in the game?

Who, as Trailer asked, is the king?

"Nick, I think you wanted me to wake up that night you were out." He swallowed and a lump of tension crawled down his throat. "I think you want to reach out to somebody. Would you like me to show you how I do it?"

Slowly, Trailer turned to him and walked over to the sink. He stretched and stood eight inches over his normal height. He reached over Donaldson, grabbed a towel from the top of the refrigerator, released himself to his normal height, and started drying the dishes.

The lump in Donaldson's throat made it all the way down.

Okay, time to try a conversation. "What's new, Nick?"

"I'm married now."

A plate slipped from Donaldson's hands into the soapy, grease-slicked water.

"We had to."

Donaldson, the plate back in hand, sagged slightly.

"I was pregnant."

Donaldson's hands took the plate underwater. He left the plate submerged as he rested his arms on the counter. His head dropped forward and he mouthed, "Pregnant?" His head came back up and he stared at Trailer.

Trailer smiled, pointed at Donaldson's face and started laughing.

Donaldson's face relaxed into a sneer. He muttered, "Asshole," and hipchecked Trailer. It was like hip checking an oak and Donaldson grimaced at the impact.

Trailer laughed harder. He grabbed his side and, between fits of laughter, said, "Ow."

Their laughter quieted. Donaldson said, "Tell me about your wife."

Trailer went rigid.

"Only if you feel like it. We can talk about anything you want."

"Her name's Karen. It's common law." Trailer's body relaxed. All external effect gone. "I didn't want to really marry her because I didn't want her to feel she was tied to me if she wanted to leave. I don't treat her good. I don't hurt her. She could do better than this."

Listening, Donaldson wondered if Trailer's Karen had taught him "mercy."

"What do you mean, 'better than this'?"

Trailer grabbed Donaldson's shoulder and spun him so they faced each other. He flexed his arms, shoulders, chest, and back, his muscles spreading and bulging until he was a grotesque parody of a man, the lines where human ended and monstrosity began blurring and fading as he spoke, "This. She could do better than this." Trailer's voice took on the tone, sounds, and patterns of Donaldson's and he quoted from Donaldson's dreams, "...and all of it hyper-extensions of what the body could naturally do, every system amplified and augmented to its operational extreme without impairing or defunctioning the other systems."

He released his muscles and Donaldson, trying to keep the image down in his mind, turned back to the dishes.

"But she stays," Trailer continued. "She says when she can't take it anymore, she'll go, but right now she stays, and that's all I should think about, that right now she stays."

Stay neutral, show interest. We passed rapport and went straight into intimacy. How long has he been waiting for someone to talk to?

"Lately...I don't know. I've been thinking maybe we should get really married. She says she loves me. She says she wants to help." The words stopped, the silence so complete and deadening the plate lapping the water sounded like waves crashing on a beach.

"Do you love her, Nick?"

Trailer's fingers appeared around the edges of the plate he held and it shattered, the sharp pieces bouncing off the skin of his palm. "Love? Love. What is 'I love'? You taught me everything. Do you remember that being one of the lessons?"

Trailer went back to his corner. Donaldson finished the dishes and went over to him. Trailer's eyes were closed.

Yes, what kind of woman could love you? What kind of woman could show you mercy?

He decided not to disturb Trailer and went to one of the chairs.

The behemoth opened one eye and, through a solitary tear, watched the man walk away.

19 DAYS UNTIL TERMINATION

Donaldson finished his eggs as Trailer started washing the pots and pans. Donaldson walked over to him and, when he was about two feet away, Trailer spun on him. One hand clamped on Donaldson's right shoulder, the other's fingers arched into a spearhand. Trailer stopped just as suddenly as he started, returned to the dishes and chuckled to himself.

Released from Trailer's grip, Donaldson sat back at the table. "Everything okay, Nick?"

"Some guy didn't like the way I washed dishes once."

Donaldson remembered the incident from Trailer's 201 file. Trailer's father had been working on one of the family's cars on a Saturday afternoon. He wasn't having much luck and came in for some coffee, his frustration seeking an easy target. Trailer stood at the kitchen sink, about to wash the dishes. According to Trailer, he misjudged the weight of the detergent in the box and dumped the whole thing into the sink. He and his mother laughed. His father got up and boxed Trailer into a corner of the kitchen, punching his face, gut, and repeatedly driving his knees into Trailer's groin.

Trailer was twelve years old at the time.

"Do you want to talk about it?"

"It wasn't my fault."

"No, it wasn't." Are we even talking about the same thing?

Trailer nodded and went back to the dishes.

"When I say that it wasn't your fault, Nick, how does it sound?"

"How does it sound?" He chuckled. "When I was down South, I met a guy who didn't remember me. One time, on the school bus, he walked up to me and slammed his books down on my head. Everybody laughed and he said, 'Hey, Trailer, how does that sound?' I met him again down South, but he didn't remember me. I told him who I was. I reminded him of what he did. Then I hammerfisted the top of his head. I asked while he was falling, 'Hey, Singer, how does that sound?'"

"I remember that," said Donaldson. Trailer compressed Singer's atlas, axis, and cervical vertebra into the space of a single bone, his parietal, occipital, frontal, and sphenoid bones smashed so that it appeared he wore a sailor's cap woven from his own hair.

Trailer stopped washing the pans. "That was my fault."

"Yes, Nick. That was your fault."

"But the other one, dropping the soap into the water, that wasn't my fault."

"No, Nick. There was no reason for what happened then."

Trailer walked over and looked at Donaldson for a few seconds after racking the last dish, sniffed, then went back into his corner. He got up and stretched late in the afternoon, sneezed, then remained silent the rest of the day.

18 DAYS, 19 HOURS UNTIL TERMINATION

Trailer inhaled seven quick, shallow breaths, flaring his nostrils each time, drawing air over his olfactory epithelium, eyes closed, sniffing for danger, for strangeness, for difference, for not-rightness. All that came to him was the cold, clear night air of the thick pine forest outside Dickey, Maine. He stood relaxed but still, giving his skin an extra moment or two to sense otherness, for anything that didn't belong.

Nothing came to him beyond the scent of Steiner's foulness, fifty or so feet above the forest floor. The aromas of Steiner's sweat, fear, rage, shit, and piss mixed with the sharp scent of the massive spruce Trailer tied him to, creating a miasma that clung to him like wasps swarming an invading nest.

Right now, judging by Steiner's sounds and smells, he dreamed.

Trailer didn't dream nor did he sleep as most people slept. Even as a child, he learned that danger came when he slept. An hyperviolent, rage-aholic father and a sexually sadistic mother both crept into his room at night, never together, each waiting until the other slept.

Or had finished with him, exhausted.

He was never sure which.

At most, Trailer dozed, part of himself always alert for the creaking hinge, the turn of the handle, the silent weight falling on the bed. He slept as wild animals sleep, never fully, never soundly, always part of themselves listening for sounds that shouldn't be there. It was another factor in Donaldson's screening, never entering third or fourth stage sleep, never leaving stage one NREM sleep but deep enough so that the brain could repair, could function normally. But that also meant the Augments didn't dream and normal brain function required dream-state rest. The solution was to sleep unihemispherically, one side of the brain at a time, one side at rest and the other fully awake and aware of the environment, switching quickly, cleanly, back and forth and forth and back, some part always alert, always ready, awaiting danger.

But that meant the brain couldn't clear itself out, organize experience into meaning because doing so required whole brain integration. So the Augments microslept, putting themselves into deep sleep for seconds at a time and always after they'd ensured they'd secured their environment. They dreamt but too rapidly to be remembered and only enough to keep psychomotor vigilance at a maximum. Trailer couldn't remember any of his own dreams. Or if he'd ever dreamed, even before augmentation.

But he listened to others' dreams. Often.

He remembered listening to the dreams of those he would kill, wondering. Most of them didn't know he waited over them, listening, learning, mapping himself into them, taking their dreams as his own.

Steiner's dreaming shifted. He sobbed in his sleep.

Trailer put down his groceries at the foot of the spruce, leapt and started pulling himself up arm over arm, branch by branch until he turned and sat on a thick limb, staring at a mummy sleeping bag strapped vertically to the trunk. Steiner's face shown from the hood like a pupa emerging from a cocoon, eyes closed, his breath misting. Trailer leaned into Steiner's exhalations and sniffed cautiously, quick to pull away, a dog leaning forward at the edge of a strange scent.

Two strong scents.

Human and afraid.

No, three.

Human, afraid and stupid.

Pancho always smelled afraid and stupid. Trailer and the others had incorporated it as an activation shorthand; if it smells afraid and stupid, it's the enemy. Kill it. Donaldson sometimes smelled of fear but never smelled stupid. Trailer hesitated to act because of that. The people in the bar smelled neither afraid nor stupid until Eddie and Bill attacked. Then the bar reeked of afraid and stupid in less than a second. He had not wanted to act, only to be found, but augmentation demanded otherwise.

Trailer wondered if the teams that augmented him even knew what subtleties of mind and body human scents, human musks, revealed. Even the most sanitized human reeked of their intestinal, hemetological and neurophysical goings-on, an individualizing sweet rankness that could be tracked for days and miles if necessary, with nothing they could do about it.

Trailer stared up through the trees. These woods had no canopy to speak of, not like in the Amazonas. Dickey had two streetlights and both were shot out, perhaps by some joyriding kids who passed through. Even so, their light wouldn't penetrate this far into the forest and Trailer could count the stars. The dark, moonless night left him a darker silhouette against the pine boughs.

He so preferred the quiet of the night, any night, to the confusion of the day.

Steiner started to stir, to wake. Trailer slid along the branch supporting him, moving silently towards Steiner, stopping just a breath away, sniffing, smelling, slowly countermanding his conditioning, slowly teaching himself to keep this man who smelled of enemy alive.

It was not easy work.

Steiner's eyes blinked open.

"Boo!"

18 DAYS UNTIL TERMINATION

Donaldson awoke to find Trailer sitting at the table, returned after two days absence as if their situation was the most normal in the world. One more day absent and Donaldson would have no choice. He'd have to hunt Trailer down and kill him, which seemed to be what Trailer wanted.

That confused Donaldson. They'd made such headway that last day. Not much conversation-wise but Trailer started opening up, engaging him instead of waiting to be engaged.

Or that could be a standard Augment combat tactic: engage the enemy before the enemy can determine your strengths and weaknesses and engage you.

Trailer hadn't prepared breakfast. He sat, twitching as if fidgeting with something, not oxygenating prior to switching activation states. His sniffled and coughed, almost experimentally, as if not sure how it was done.

More telling, he looked down, directly in front of him. The Augmenteds were taught to look up or level, never down. Look up to incorporate or evaluate visual information, level for auditory information.

But never down. Look down to experience feelings, to understand kinesthetic and emotional information, to incorporate experience as analog, as having shades of gray and not binary, as useful or not.

Trailer was allowing himself to feel.

He's got a cold. Jesus Christ, he's got a cold.

Part of Trailer's psychological signature was being affected. Trailer might get sick, but nobody, including Trailer, would ever know it. Putnam's research into psychophysiological relationships at NIMH showed that psychological states and life traumas can adversely affect the immune system. The adverse effect can be either way, over- or under-compensating. Trailer's PNI - his psychoneuroimmunological makeup - overcompensated, yet another reason Trailer and the eight others made it into the program while some thirty thousand others didn't. Illnesses that left normal people bedridden for weeks would burn through their systems in about a day, twenty-four-hour bugs wouldn't last more than ten to fifteen minutes, and that was before Augmentation.

Trailer never allowed himself the luxury of getting sick growing up because he never got any information that being sick was a part of life. His childhood survival mechanisms kept his healing processes on overdrive. Augmentation completed that overdrive process. As a result, the overcompensation allowed Trailer to survive most CBW attacks. But every plus has its minus. His ability to heal rapidly as a child further convinced him his parents were right; he was a monster.

And now he's got a goddamn cold. "Is everything okay, Nick?"

Nick regarded Donaldson, seeing him as if through a microscope, his focus moving slowly from furrowed brow to eye to eye to cheek to nostril to nostril to cheek to lips to teeth to jawline, like a good PHOTINT operative, his magnifying glass going millimeter by millimeter over some KeyHole image. He felt himself accelerating into Hunter/Seeker state then, as his body prepared to shift, coming back down, slowing, returning to his normal state, like some huge backwoods logger stuck in city traffic, its massive diesel revving, powerful cylinders pounding but unable to get out of first gear because of the lights, bicyclists, and everything else confounding the streets.

He grimaced with pains, pains not experienced before followed by pains he remembered from long, long ago, childhood's pains. The pains merged, swirled, gathered momentum then slammed into him again. He looked into his hand as if expecting to find a phone there then shocked to find none. More memories slipped and slewed, unlashed from their moorings, skidding across the deck of his mind, his consciousness, as Trailer felt himself tossed on his private sea.

He gazed into Donaldson's eyes and saw the whale breach, flume, prepare to dive again, to return to its safety and avoid the storming world into which he surfaced, the storming world in which it needed to breathe.

He dropped completely into Hunter/Seeker state. "Are you here to kill me?"

Donaldson carefully lowered himself into the opposite chair, never taking his eyes off Trailer and making each of his movements as neutral as possible. "No, Nick. Even if that's what you want, it's not what I came here to do."

The only way to be with Karen was to learn how to breathe.

He surfaced, the whale breaching, exhaling his combat persona and inhaling everything that made up his life.

More memories broke their moorings. The whale shrunk as nets surrounded it, pulled it with the weights of experience's pains.

The whale fought to stay on the surface, to stay huge and strong enough to float despite the weights mooring it.

The whale sneezed and the nets broke away. Memories floated around it in the water, unplaced and seeking quiet, seeking rest from the sea.

The man with the whale in his eye said, "Is everything okay, Nick?"

The whale grabbed the nearest memory, evaluating it, confused and wondering where it belonged.

"When was I in the war?"

Psychogenic amnesia? "Let's think, Nick. When do you think you were in the war?"

"I...did I graduate high school?"

His voice is higher, more in his throat and less in his chest. My god what I wouldn't give for pen and paper. "Do you remember graduating high school, Nick?"

"I'm married now?"

"You mentioned a common law marriage earlier, Nick." Never question the subject's reality. Allow them to question their own reality, never do it for them. "Do you think that might not be the case?"

Standard therapeutic procedure: Accept someone's reality to encourage them to stop protecting and start exploring their illusion. That's when they can affect a change in themselves. All the therapist can do is provide a rudder, knowledge of when to raise and lower the sails.

Trailer's speech slowed, as if each word had to be found and evaluated before being expressed. "I made a call last night."

Check all communications in the area. "Go on."

"I talked to Karen. She said she loves me. She... my mother loves me, too. She... my mother... my mother fucked me. Did you know that?"

"I believe we talked about that, Nick, a long time ago. Do you want to talk about that now?" Karen, his wife, confused with his mother? Two female caregivers in psycho-emotive and -cognitive conflict?

"She... Karen. She's not Karen. I never really married her, you know. I was afraid she wasn't real." He started shaking his head violently, then pausing, shaking, then pausing.

God, where is he? Who is he with? He's derealizing, but derealizing what?

Donaldson reached out towards Trailer. "You have to know what is real, Nick. Nothing can change until it becomes real."

"I...change. I...change. I...what happened to me out there?"

"I don't know, Nick. I - " he almost said, 'I wasn't there.' " - think you do, though. Can you share it with me?"

You're changing now, Nick, and I don't have a clue what to do. Do you?

Trailer focused on Donaldson. All of the manifestations of Trailer's cold disappeared. His eyes glazed over and his nose started twitching. "SigRec Inc. Neg. 'Firm.'"

He's gone back to what he knows is safe.

Donaldson corrected himself. A safe hell is where he's gone.

"It's me, Nick. Jim Donaldson. I'm located just outside the town of Dickey, in northern Maine. Where are you, Nick?"

Trailer's eyes cleared, fixed on him, then glazed again. "SigRec... Sig..." his eyes fixed on Donaldson again.

"What is it, Nick?"

Trailer said nothing, staring at him.

Donaldson heard a soft purring sound.

Christ, he's oxygenating, rotary breathing. If I don't do something, he'll switch activation states. "Nick, breathe deeply, slowly. Do you need to know I'm here? Here."

Standard therapeutic technique. Donaldson started extending index and middle finger so Trailer could hold them, could cradle objective reality in his hand.

Donaldson caught himself. Extended index and middle finger could be miscued as a lethal strike, a gun, triggers, any number of weapons. Instead he offered his open right hand. "Take my hand and hold it so that you'll know I'm here with you."

The man with the whale in his eye became Donaldson then went back to being the man with the whale in his eye. Trailer couldn't keep them separate. They merged, breached, and submerged, overlapping one moment then merging into a single body. Trailer breathed deeply, trying to get a scent for one or the other and couldn't. No matter how hard he tried, only one scent remained.

The Donaldson-whale-man held his hand out.

Without taking his eyes from Donaldson's, Trailer's right hand moved slowly towards Donaldson's, took it and brought it up to his nose. He inhaled deeply and closed his eyes, a vintner savoring an exquisite bouquet.

"Friend?"

"Friend."

"You...you won't hurt me?"

"No, Nick. I won't hurt you."

Trailer remembered himself smaller. Much smaller. Being offered a hand. He reached and, when he almost touched the hand, it pulled away, replaced by his mother's laughter.

"Pick me up, mommy." Little hands held themselves up, praying supplicant to the parent-god.

"No, I told you, I have to go out."

"Take me with you, mommy." Little hands formed little fists, slowly coming down.

"No. Shut up. Don't do anything stupid and I'll come back."

"I don't want to be alone." Little eyes looked around a room filled with shadows.

"Grow up. There's some coke and cookies in the pantry. Make yourself some dinner."

"I don't want to be alone." Whispered to a door, already closed, as little arm held little arm tight, squatting, huddled in a corner, alone against the dark.

And again his mother laughed.

In memory, Trailer shrieked his childhood fear and rage, a trust denied.

In reality, he dropped into Hunter/Seeker state. Totally. Blindingly. Frighteningly. His fear and rage masked his face into the plastic grin Donaldson had seen at the hospital. "Damn right you won't." His hand became a vice, its jaws squeezing the mid-digital joints in Donaldson's fingers.

"Nick, you're hurting me. Nick, please. My fingers. You're crushing my fingers."

Donaldson smelled of fear.

Fear, but not stupid.

Trailer needed stupid. His face flowed from plastic and back as he spoke. "So? You left us to die in the Orinoco. Five fingers? Nine men? Sounds like a hell of an exchange to me. Don't you think so?" He changed his grip, now holding Donaldson's mid-digital knuckles between his own index finger and thumb, as if squeezing a tick. "Why is this so important to you, Major? What am I to you that you put yourself in here with me?"

Donaldson's face reddened, his breath erupted from his lungs to make way for pain. He couldn't get air into his lungs and what breath he had went in and out in gasps. His knuckles started separating under Nick's pressure and he wasn't sure how long he'd remain conscious. "You let go of me before I pass out and we'll talk about it."

Not stupid. Donaldson was never stupid. Donaldson was not an enemy. Not the enemy.

Trailer let go and laughed. Donaldson cupped his right hand in his left, pulled it into this lap and sighed. Air raced back into his lungs and blood left his face even though the pain remained. Trailer got a spoon and tore off a piece of burlap, the plastic face gone once again. "Give me your hand."

"You won't hurt me?"

"I don't make promises unless I know I can keep them. Your hand." Trailer used the spoon and burlap to splint Donaldson's fingers.

Donaldson took his hand back and cradled it in his lap.

"Why don't you cry?" asked Trailer. "You want to."

Oh, yes, I've been acquired.

He sat, one hand gently supporting the other, counting his heartbeats through the pulses of pain in his hand, keeping his eyes on the whale, watching Trailer monitor his life signs, listen to his subvocalizations... You're even aware of my being aware of you. You probably even know about the whale.

He took a deep breath and released it slowly. Be real. Be present. "Yeah, I'd like to cry. I'm in tremendous pain, for one. I'm also sick and tired of this. And scared. Let's not forget scared. Damn scared."

"You're scared? Why?"

"Because I've willingly placed myself in a situation where there's extreme potential for massive physical insult, with someone who has a history of cue-reactive aggression and chronic stress response. I have no leads on what all the cues are, and you've demonstrated violence on me physically. You damn near popped my fingers off the bones. I'm only human, Nick. Don't expect miracles from me. Of course I'm scared, damn it."

"'Massive physical insult'," Trailer quoted. "You mean you're afraid I might kill you? You chose to walk in here, I didn't drag you. What situation did you place yourself in, Jimmy Boy?"

Donaldson blanked, the pain in his hand forgotten and the breath gone from his lungs. His body went cold. Trailer spoke my childhood name?

"I'm scared, too."

Donaldson cradled his hand in his lap. "Of what?"

Without moving a muscle, Trailer pulled himself into a small package. Donaldson watched in awe of something he'd never seen, had never even known possible. Trailer withdrew, folding himself emotionally, spiritually, and psychologically while he remained relaxed in the chair, completely inverting everything Donaldson had taught him. Trailer wasn't withdrawing from any external stimulus. He was withdrawing from himself, from his external manifestation, and doing so by withdrawing into himself, not for protection but for comfort.

But Trailer had no comfortable ground to retreat to. Most people under stress attempt to hide in a safe, childhood past, in one form or another. They become a child running to the comfort of home when bullies are teasing them.

But Trailer had no safe past. His earliest childhood memories presaged a tormented life. Somewhere between one to one-and-a-half years old, two of Trailer's cousins, Rosemary and Paul, each some six years Trailer's senior, forced a third cousin, David, some six months Trailer's senior, to beat Trailer up while they watched, laughing. Trailer discovered years later that Rosemary and Paul would beat up David if he didn't beat up Trailer.

What kind of sick bastards were these people? What kind of kin recognition rules applied to such a family? And what fucking cowards these kids must have been. Must be. Donaldson never met any of Trailer's family, nuclear or extended, and he was glad for it. He'd encountered battle traumatized children who showed more humanity to their younger siblings than Trailer's family showed him.

What kind of parents created children like that?

Parents like Trailer's parents.

Trailer remembered running home covered in blood only to have his mother yell at him for ruining his clothes. From there his parents moved and no matter where they ended up, it didn't matter, the pattern had set. Trailer learned to be a victim and that kind of training that young goes deep; Trailer was never allowed a safe personal mythology and such mythologies are necessary for integrating into society and functioning normally.

Donaldson watched Trailer creating a new mythology, a safe mythology, one in which he had a protector, even as they spoke.

But he'd never had a protector in all his born days. That's what made him perfect for augmentation. Donaldson remembered Trailer's stories of hiding in the basement storage areas of the apartment house where he lived, covering himself with books and clothes he'd find in musty old boxes, hoping no one would ever find him.

But someone always did.

So who's finding him now?

Who's protecting him?

And from what?

From himself.

Christ, predator and prey all in one small package. He's dissociating from his own attempts to protect himself.

Without changing position or body posture, Trailer became small and fragile, the behemoth returning to the egg. He answered, his voice was timid and childlike, "I'm afraid that Karen won't love me, that she won't care."

"I care, Nick. I'm still in here with you, and I'm here waiting for you when you come back from wherever you go. I think that's an indication that I care about you."

The voice, still childlike, cried back, "But you told them to make a bomb go off if you couldn't make me better."

There it is, thought Donaldson, there's the crux: personal safety at the price of interpersonal acceptance and stated by the childhood ego state we locked him into.

"No, Nick. The bomb will go off if we - you and I together - can't make you better."

Trailer's face raised up. "Karen..." He stared into Donaldson's eyes. His own went blank as he whispered, "To love Karen..."

"You must first love yourself. You can't give away what you don't have."

Donaldson sat back as Trailer's eyes closed.

Trailer was going on a voyage he'd never been prepared for, going to places that never existed in his world.

Nick continued processing the new information for a full twenty minutes, a direct violation of his training. Or he felt safe enough to explore this new psychological landscape without backup. Or he believed Donaldson would back him up if things went south and he couldn't find his way back, that Donaldson would risk his own life to save Trailer.

Donaldson sat with him, matching as best he could the Augmented Man's breathing and body posture, trying hard to mirror and echo him, to let him know there was somebody there and that it was okay. Nick's eyes refocused and Donaldson met his gaze. They stared at each other and neither spoke for several moments.

Finally Nick spoke, a single word: "Okay."

At no time did Trailer incorporate the information hypnotically, or at least not in the Augmented hypnotic state.

"Where do we go from here?" Donaldson asked.

"You ever done any hunting? Game. Bear, deer, moose?"

Donaldson shook his head, "No."

"Then that's where we start."

Inside, Donaldson smiled. Whatever happened in those twenty minutes, it caused Trailer to take the lead in his own healing.

They spent the rest of the morning and much of the afternoon talking about fishing and hunting. Trailer, Donaldson learned, first found work as a trail guide and tracker, hunting cursorially, flushing game towards his clients. It made sense. Such work allowed Trailer to continue his way of life without effecting rapid change, if any at all. It also made sense historically. Many Ranger and Ranger-like vets returned to find similar work in the wild.

Trailer didn't stay in such work long, however, and offered no comment on what other work he might have done. He steered the conversation over safe grounds and Donaldson followed, reminding Donaldson of a run, at least the ones he took part in. Around 9:00pm they finished the wine and started playing gin. After the fifth hand Donaldson said, "You know I want to help you, Nick?"

As far as Donaldson could tell, Nick didn't acknowledge the remark. He tried a different angle. "It's not fair, Nick. You can remember the cards by riffling them when you deal."

Trailer stopped shuffling and handed the cards over. They played for another hour and Trailer won repeatedly. "You can see my cards by the reflections in my eyes," Donaldson joked.

Trailer put his cards down, slowly. His face took on the same synthetic, plastic grin he had at the hospital and his hand kept pressing into the table until Donaldson could hear the legs and tabletop splintering.

"You want to help me. How can you help me? Do you think you're like me? Everything... anything... I do reminds me of what I am. Does that happen to you?" He stood up, walked over to the door and put his hand on it.

Donaldson tensed. Would Trailer give the hall between the inner and outer walls time to pressurize?

Trailer took his hand from the door and turned to face the room. "What do you do when you first go into a room, Major? You look for a place to sit down? A light switch? Maybe you look for a friendly face, one you know? Maybe one you'd like to know?

"I walk into a room. I don't look for a chair or a light. I don't look to see if there's anybody in the room I know. I look to see how many ways there are to kill, how many ways there are to escape.

"Do you know what it's like having that as your first thought in every situation you're in your whole goddamn fucking life?"

Donaldson shook his head.

"It's not a matter of my wanting to be like *everybody* else, I want to be like *anybody* else. But I can't. This," Trailer slammed his hand onto his chest, "won't let me."

"And this," he slammed his chest again, "is your fault. You did this to me."

"Nick, do you - "

"No." Trailer went into his corner and folded upon himself. Donaldson went over to him and squatted on the floor next to him. Once again he gazed into the eye of some great whale, now trapped behind some immense aquarium glass. The eye didn't blink, nor did Trailer move. Like a whale, Trailer's eye watched, impassive but attentive. Perhaps, like a whale newly risen from the great depths, Trailer looked at him and wondered at what small form of life Donaldson was. Donaldson started to reach out to Trailer's shoulder, to offer comfort, and stopped. Behind the glass, from deep in the ocean, calling to its mates and knowing none survived to answer, the whale cried.

Distasio was impressed by Rivers' grip. "Thanks for hurrying back, Mr. Rivers." A good, solid handshake. Steady eye contact. He smiled his approval.

"Tom, please. Call me 'Tom'."

"Appreciate it. Chris gave you what little we have on Steiner. Do you want to get Donaldson out of The Tank?"

Rivers scratched a few days growth of beard and caught Distasio's grin. "Yeah, going native. Don't get much opportunity on my other jobs. Decided to see what it looked like. What'd'you think?"

Distasio laughed. "You need to stand closer to the razor."

Rivers chuckled. "No need to raise Jim just yet. At least I don't think so." He looked at Distasio for confirmation. Distasio shrugged and Rivers continued. "Nobody's been in his room since he walked off couple of nights back?"

"Closed up tight as a drum."

"Good. Can I get the keys? I'd like to look around."

"I could - "

Rivers held up a hand. "No thanks. Just me. Just for a little while. I want to get a feel for the man, you know?"

"All that 'profiler' stuff?"

"That's what they pay me for."

"Chris will have the keys and anything else we've found out since then. Let me know if you need anything else."

Rivers shook hands again and walked off to find Chris Harley. Distasio checked his watch. He tapped the face a few times and an image of Steiner's room appeared. Distasio pressed a stud on the watch's side and a small, red legend appeared and blinked three times at the bottom of the watch face: REC REC REC. A red ring circling the image of Steiner's room replaced the legend after the third blink.

He lifted a coffee in his free hand and watched. A few minutes later Rivers entered Steiner's room. He took in the room quickly, his eyes pausing on items of interest - papers on the desk, a Boston Bruins hockey bobble, an unwashed glass and an half-empty Scotch bottle beside it - then moved a chair to the center of the room and sat down. He didn't look around, didn't focus on anything, as if resting, like someone catching their breath before starting their next big task. Collecting himself, preparing himself.

A moment later Rivers shifted the chair so that he sat beside Steiner's unmade bed. He leaned over, put his face in the sheets and inhaled deeply two or three times. He stood and walked into the lav, lifted the toilet seat and cover, dropped to his knees as if about to vomit and instead licked the rim, his tongue making slow circles as he licked his way around the bowl.

Distasio's eyes widened. He simultaneously pulled back and stretched his arm out from himself, his eyes locked on the watch's image, a scene too horrible to be ignored, too disgusting to be kept close.

He shook his wrist back and forth a few times, checked to make sure an analog clock face had replaced the feed, sipped his now cold coffee and grimaced.

"Somebody make a fresh pot of coffee." Chairs rolled away from desks in the outer office. He added quietly, "And somebody remind me never to shake Rivers' hand again."

Donaldson awoke disoriented. He rolled over and felt slow breaths on his face. "Everything okay, Nick?"

"I'm hungry."

"Would you like me to fix you something?" He started to get up. The lights, not sensitive enough to detect Trailer's slow motions, started to come on when Donaldson moved.

Suddenly Trailer stood up. The rapid movement made the lights come on full. "No, thanks. I got my own." He held a live brown rabbit in his left hand.

Donaldson chilled. His stomach tightened

He had to get away from the rabbit.

His head snapped slightly. An involuntary reaction. To something internal. Something painful. A non-conscious flight response aborted by his conscious self. A BMIR. Except something twisted free inside, ran away, sought safety, sought protection.

It watched him and Trailer, hiding, peering around a corner, holding it tight, waiting for the fear to subside, for the anger and rage to go away.

It lasted a second. The entire episode. Barely a second.

That's an augmentation technique. Separate the ego, objectify the self, a "protection from threat" strategy. We based it on a childhood survival mechanism, something we screened for in the selection process. We didn't have to train it into them, they already had it. We augmented it, sure, we made it better.

But Donaldson experienced it, not Trailer. Just now, seeing the bunny, he'd experienced self-objectification.

And I don't have any augmentation training. I designed it, I didn't go through it.

Donaldson stared at the rabbit. It weighed about three pounds. Trailer shoved the terrified creature's head into his mouth. The rabbit's claws were useless against Trailer's skin. Trailer bit and the rabbit's body went limp. Trailer's jaw worked twice. The rabbit's skull snapped and cracked, then slowly descended Trailer's throat. Trailer lifted the limp body up and gulped in the blood as it poured from the severed neck.

He took the lifeless form into both hands and shoved one thumb up each side of the rib cage, flicked his wrists and tore open the carcass like it was some overcooked hen. "I caught it munching by the garbage bins. The stomach is full. Want some?"

Donaldson saw the Augmenteds do these things in the field, but not where food was so plentiful. Trailer held out his offering. The smell of the tripe tingled Donaldson's nose. He swallowed hard to keep his last meal down. "No, thanks. But I'll take some coffee."

He walked past Trailer and went towards the lav. "I'm awake now, so I might as well take a shower. Have the coffee ready in ten minutes and we can both enjoy a cup." He started the water running cold, painfully cold, direct from the post-glacial spring feeding the camp from deep under Hafey Mountain, wanting the cold to shock him. His body revolted. He vomited, repeatedly, until his belly offered nothing but air.

Trailer waited patiently, listening.

Donaldson turned the hot water on, letting his body absorb the warmth, waiting for his heart to stop pounding.

A knock on the door.

"Yes?"

"Major?"

He turned the faucets off so he could hear. "What is it, Nick?"

"I'm sorry."

Donaldson waited, unsure if Trailer would offer more. Silence. He turned the water back on then turned the water off again. "Nick?"

"Yes, Major?"

"I'd rather you call me 'Jim.'"

He waited a few minutes and turned the water back on.

Trailer handed him a cup of coffee when he opened the lav door.

"Can I ask you a question, Nick?"

Trailer shrugged.

"When I first came in here, you said you came to Dickey so I could kill you."

Trailer stared into his coffee and nodded.

"Why do you want me to kill you?"

Trailer sipped his coffee twice before answering. "I wanted to die."

Past tense? Change state? Why? "You will, eventually. You'll live maybe ten or twenty years past normal. You know that."

Trailer laughed. "You say it like it's a blessing, ten or twenty years past normal like this. I want to die now."

Back to present tense. What's causing these change states? "But why, Nick? Why now? Why did you surface? You could have gone to Hanscom or Kittery or Loring or Devens and told them to contact me. We would have brought you in. Why go the other route?"

"You kept us secret. We were illegal weapons. I wanted to do something so that everybody would know. Or ask. Now you've got to kill me before people find out what you did to us." He nodded to the south. "To them."

"But why the bar? Why those people? Why Chelmsford, Mass?"

"Because that's the way it went. I got no reason. I didn't mean for it to happen. But you did. I can't be around people because all I see are enemies, attacks, and you made me this way. You think there's some kind of formula for everything? Because that's where I was when it happened. If there is a formula, you created it, I didn't." Trailer spoke plainly, no emotion, no inflection. Tit-for-Tat, simple as that. Maximum efficiency. Maximum expediency.

He did what we taught him to do. It wasn't planned. An accident? "They moved first?"

"Yes. They did what they were taught, I did what I was taught. I survived, they didn't." No emotion.

And then a stumble. "I...I couldn't lose if I wanted to."

Let's try another tact. "You said you were married."

"Some people call it that."

"Is there a problem in your marriage?"

Again Donaldson saw the brief momentary tension travel through Trailer.

"A problem?" Trailer contemplated the phrase as he poured himself another cup and returned to his seat. "You ever loved a woman?"

Donaldson nodded.

"Say this woman really likes you. Say this woman thinks you're the white on rice. Say this woman would sniff your shit for a mile just to find the ass it came out of. Now, say this woman takes a strong interest in you. She's really into you, you know? I mean, she's around you and she wants you. Understand?"

"I don't see - "

Trailer held up his hand. "She wants you. She wants to feel you inside her. Do you know what happens?"

"You tell me, Nick."

"She gets hot."

"Yes?"

"No, see, you don't get it. I mean she gets hot. Her body gets hotter. She starts to smell different because her cooz is juicing up."

"Nick, I don't - "

"Do you know that a woman, when she wants to fuck, her eyes

open up? I mean her pupils go wide? Her breath smells different, too, because she's using more oxygen than normal because her blood's got different hormones in it than usual? Her skin feels different, more electric-like, and you can feel and hear the nerves twitching real easy because she's getting little bits of adrenaline because she's excited she's going to get laid? You know any of that, Jim? Huh, Jimmy Boy?"

Something twisted again. Another BMIR. Donaldson ignored it, focusing on Trailer. "I don't think I ever noticed it before, but - "

"Right, Jimmy, old buddy old pal," Trailer continued, slightly louder. "You never noticed it before. But who gives two shits about you, Jim? I'm the one with the problem, right? So, say your woman is getting ready to get laid. And say you got a nose that can detect the scent of humans three or four miles away. Say you got eyes that can see the changes in heat flow in the human body. Say you got ears that can tell how somebody's breathing and how their heart's pounding and almost what they're thinking?"

Trailer's voice continued its slow rise in volume as he spoke. "And what if everything you are tells you that everything happening to your woman means she's preparing to target, huh?" He came out of the chair, lifted Donaldson over the table and threw him against the far wall. Before Donaldson could rise, Trailer picked him up and held him up against the ceiling.

"Huh? What about that, Jim?" he shrieked, his voice shaking The Tank's inner walls. "What if everything that happens when you're in love is the same as what happened when Pancho is going to target and everything you are decides to target first? Tell me, you fucking god damn motherfucking son-of-a-bitch, what do you do?"

Donaldson flopped like a rag doll in Trailer's grasp. He heard the words, heard his joints snapping and popping, his body in too much pain to form an answer.

Trailer lowered him and sat him in his chair, his voice calm again. "I love my wife, but if she's going to love me, I have to kill her. That's the reason I want to die."

Donaldson's head cleared. He recalled everything in Trailer's 201, then posted that against the 201 on Augmented psychology.

That's the lesson his parents taught him, Donaldson reasoned. They said they loved him then they assaulted him. Is that what all this is about? He finally has a reason to rebel against his parents' scripts?

"Are you afraid you'll kill her?" He watched Trailer's body language but it was pointless. If he said something to set Trailer off, he wouldn't know until after the fact. When he woke up. If he did.

"She loves me."

"I don't think I understand, Nick."

"You selected us because we were never loved."

"That's not - "

Trailer stood up, stretching his spine and spreading his back until he arched over Donaldson like a cobra. "I want to play cards now."

Donaldson stared at Trailer's face, the skin stretched tight over it. Time to find out how much he's changed, he thought. Time to model new behaviors, new information. Time to find out if he can make decisions about his own training. "I have to say something first."

Trailer didn't respond.

"I can't stay in here with you if you're going to continue to hurt me. I'll stay in here and talk with you, if you want. But I won't stay in here and let you hurt me."

Trailer's voice was a deep reed shaking in the wind. "What choice do you have?"

"You can kill me. You can keep me prisoner in here and kill me, if you want. But I won't let myself stay in here if that's what you plan to do. So, if you plan on keeping me in here against my will and hurting me, get used to the idea that that's your decision. You're going to have to do that to me. I'm not volunteering."

15 DAYS UNTIL TERMINATION

Trailer played cards with a pair of Donaldson's socks tied over his eyes. He still won.

Donaldson gave up around midnight. "Nick, I'm too beat to go on. Besides, I'm not much of a challenge for you, even with your eyes covered."

"You should think of music when you play. That's what you taught us to do." Trailer pulled the socks off his head.

"I guess I *am* too tired. I don't know what you're talking about, Nick."

Trailer stood up. He bunched his trapezius and latissimus dorsi muscles until his shoulders snapped like small arms fire, then relaxed. "You taught us to think of music when Pancho asked us questions. That way their acousto-optical equipment couldn't pick up our sub-vocal answers."

Donaldson bit his tongue, hard, to wake himself up. Trailer referenced his time in the Orinoco without phasing into Hunter/Seeker state and Donaldson wanted to be fully conscious in case Trailer wanted to talk more. They played one more game. It took longer than the others and Trailer lost.

"One more game?" asked Donaldson.

Trailer gently put his hand on Donaldson's chest. "You're too tired, aren't you, Jim."

Donaldson looked into Trailer's smiling face and the world went dark.

Rivers woke him up with a gentle shaking. Donaldson sat up quickly. "Where is he?"

"We don't know. When watch changed this morning, the doors were open."

"Nothing? Nobody saw or heard anything? Nothing on ElInt?"

"Sorry, Jim. I was at Loring the past two days clearing the organic you requested. Our best guess is he knows our electronic frontier and moves through when it's cycling."

"He'll come back. We were close, damn it! Close! I think he was going to open up, to let me in. He even lost a game of cards last night. How can he lose a game of cards?"

Rivers shook his head. "Jim, I think you're shitting yourself. He's not opening up. He's not letting you in. I told you before, he's sloppy. Don't you get he's not as tight as he used to be?"

"No. That's not it. He was relaxing. He felt safe. Maybe for the first time in his life. Shit. Do you think I've come this far to only get this far?"

"Jim, listen to me. *You* are losing it. Why is this one man so important to you? So he's different. He's a menace. He didn't work out. The experiment didn't fail, the data's just not what you expected." Rivers smiled at him. "You don't even have to start over."

Donaldson remembered his own trial, the endless paperwork to bury him and have him re-emerge elsewhere, known but blameless. "Because," his gaze went from the floor up Rivers' body to that smiling face, "we crucify the heretic then accepted the heresies. Switch sides for a minute. Would you want to be destroyed or saved?"

"I'd make sure they couldn't find me until I was ready to be found. Isn't that what you taught him?"

"Isn't that what he did?"

"Huh?"

"I need to do some research. Get Trailer's 201 and leave it in the comm room. Tell them that I'm going to need a direct link to The Farm's inventories. And rig The Tank's walls to take EEGSLs."

"Preparation Set EEGs? I don't think that'll do you much good, Jim. We'll know he's about to act, but we won't have time to get you out before he does."

"I appreciate the thought, but that's not what I'm after. Get it in place before 10PM. I'm coming back in tonight."

Donaldson, back in his quarters, held the manifest to Trailer's 201 in his hands. "Okay, Nick, let's find you a way back."

The 201 contained a great deal of information but all of it ten or more years old. He laid Trailer's life out in neatly separated piles, some on his bed, some on his desk, some on the floor. One folder, Trailer's early life, was missing a childhood picture. Donaldson looked around, couldn't find it and shook his head, too focused on his immediate purpose to devote any more cycles to the stray image.

The last folder, Donaldson's most recent notes prior to entering The Tank, held a used napkin in amongst the handwritten pages. He tilted the folder and crumbs rolled out. Donaldson crumpled the napkin in disgust, threw it on the desk and made a mental note to rip Distasio a new asshole.

Ten hours and as many cups of k-coffee later, Donaldson tossed his latest readings on the desk. "Deletions, distortions, and generalities. Trailer's life cauterized in magnetic and optical memories." He yawned, sat back and rubbed his eyes, wanting another cup of coffee and correcting himself. "I wonder if anybody up here has any real coffee?" He raised his empty cup and stared inside, an augurist seeking his future in the residue. He never accepted the synthetic taste of k-coffee. "It may be convenient but it sucks." He knew coffee brokers and food scientists who agreed, and now the false taste, the facade of the real while being not real, fueled his frustration.

He rocked back in his chair, closed his eyes and steepled his fingers over them. "Slow and steady, James, what do we know?"

One hand left the steeple and fell onto Trailer's 201. "One, all of this is who you were, Mr. Trailer." The hand returned to the steeple. "Two, you surfaced." He raised his legs and rested them on the desktop. "Three, so we could kill you." He sighed. "Four, you say you're married now.

"And five, we don't know you. I don't know you. Not anymore."

The whale breached the surface covering Donaldson with its spray.

He pulled his feet down and rocked forward, slamming his hands on the table. "You motherfucking son-of-a-bitch. Jesus Christ, I've been out of the game too goddamn long."

Donaldson clapped his hands and laughed. "Not who you were, not even who you are. It's who you are becoming.

"Oh, fuck me sideways, Mr. Trailer. You said you surfaced so we could kill you. Not who you are now. Who you were then. You're changing and we didn't have a thing to do with it. But the self you're becoming can't integrate with the self you were, that's the you you want us to kill because you don't know how to. Not without killing the emerging Trailer in the process.

"Ah, James, you dumb fuck." He smiled at his own blindness, not being able to see the real behind the facade. "You did run home for safety, Nick. I was too goddamn stupid to realize who home is."

He opened the 201 again, seeing it for the first time. "We took what society gave us and said, 'Here's the map' and forgot that maps are written by tourists. Locals know their way around. Maps get in the way, confuse them.

"I can't be a tourist here. It's time to explore the territory."

Exploration started with the file, compiled at the start of augmentation. All information available came from Trailer, whom Donaldson recognized as an unreliable witness to his own life. Donaldson needed to determine if Trailer viewed himself as moving from something or towards something; was he running away or running to; escaping or questing? Answering that would solve the first dilemma and give Donaldson the clue to the next piece of the puzzle; if escaping, what is he fleeing? If questing, what does he seek?

And let's remember, it's possible to run away from while running towards.

Someone knocked.

"Come in, but watch your step."

Distasio entered with a steaming pot of coffee and fresh mug. "Camp's bug-ears picked up your coffee comments. I share your lack of affinity." He made as if to pour but stopped before any coffee left the pot. "This is my private horde. Seventy-five percent Jamaican Blue Mountain, twenty-five percent Kirapura Kona. Good enough?"

Donaldson stared at the pot as if it held the Grail. "You're kidding. How'd you get it?"

"I know a guy who knows a guy. What else do you need?"

"Who's been reading Trailer's 201?"

"You and Rivers."

"There's crumbs all over it. Somebody even left a dirty napkin in it." He pointed to the desk.

Distasio uncrumpled the napkin and read the legend. "It's not one of ours. This place is on the other side of Jackman, west side of the state near the Canadian border. Good food, good prices."

He turned the napkin over and paused, reading. "Not bad. Not great and not bad. But I'd recognize my staff's handwriting. Ten'll get you twenty nobody here wrote this. Nobody here's been near those files." He handed the napkin to Donaldson.

> *When I grow old,*
> *I will grow old with you.*
> *No others.*
> *All my memories will be of you*
> *All my thoughts will be of you*
> *All my life will have been with you.*

When I grow tired at the end of my days
Let me lie down beside you just one more time.
Your gentle arms surround me
like the fragrance of Heaven's Door.

"Damn."

"Penmanship's shaky, but the soul of a poet never-the-less."

The key in a discarded napkin. Something overlooked and ignored. Like Trailer, prior to being selected for augmentation. The words slapped Donaldson's face.

"He knocked over the files. And everything he does has a purpose."

"I'll leave the pot. Call when you need a reload."

Trailer expended a great deal of psycho-cognitive and -emotive energy generating a personal mythology he could live with when he wrote those words. He generated images, creating intense and highly atmospheric derealizations in an attempt to make things work. The line "When I grow tired at the end of my days/let me lie down beside you just one more time" demonstrated a recognition of physical reality. And all of it about a future, something to look forward to, a quiet reward for a life well-lived.

The mythology he created as a child and that augmentation reinforced was no longer working for him. Something in Trailer's environment challenged his childhood-augmentation mythology.

And on such a massive scale that Trailer's only solution was suicide-by-...?

Suicide-by-Donaldson. His maker, his creator.

His god. People create mythologies about their gods, those they recognize and those they don't. Gods don't create mythologies for people.

Except I did. I created the Augmented Mindset. No wonder he hasn't killed me yet. I'm the basis for his reality.

No wonder he's come to me to kill him. At least he's not chasing me across the Arctic.

He sat, grateful for the taste of real coffee, one less gnat needing swatting. "What exists in your environment that's never existed before, Mr. Trailer? What presents so strong an influence your survival mythologies shattered? Who are you futuring about? What is actively displacing your conditioning? Who and what are you using as the kernel for your new self? Karen?"

Donaldson needed to know if she was real or something Nick imagined. He wanted safety but couldn't find it with anyone he knew so he created Karen, sectioning off part of his psyche to achieve what his training could not?

But that's DID, Dissociative Identity Disorder, what use to be called Multiple Personality Disorder and before that a Syndrome. None of The Augments ever demonstrated DID tendencies. If Trailer was manifesting personalities and this Karen personality had directed him to the bar in Chelmsford?

Donaldson pinged Distasio.

"Need another pot so soon?"

"I need all comm logs for a sixty-mile radius, ten-day history."

"You'll definitely need another pot."

The comm log showed a jacked cell called a bona fide Stacyville number from somewhere outside the Dickey general store at 2:33AM the night Trailer said he talked with Karen.

Was Trailer's Karen at the other end of that jacked cell call? More importantly, Trailer wanted Donaldson to know about this call; he could have lifted someone's mobile, used it and returned it before they even discovered it missing.

Donaldson checked the routing and traced the call to a town about ninety miles north of Bangor: the Stacyville number had a Stacyville address. "People still have housephones up here?" He closed the log and returned to The Tank.

Trailer remained absent. Donaldson made himself a tuna sandwich and drank milk straight from the carton then stretched out in one of the overstuffed chairs and fell asleep. He woke up in the middle of the night, his neck and shoulders sore from staring into monitors all day and decided on a bath, as hot as he could stand it, to seep into his body and relax his muscles.

Naked in the bathroom, he waited for the tub to fill.

A movement caught his eye and he turned, wanting to see Nick back in The Tank.

A rabbit, human-sized, stood outside the door. Blood flowed from deep cuts on its body, its ears hacked almost completely off, dangling as it lifted a paw to move them out of its eyes, only to reveal the side of its skull cracked and one eye missing.

Donaldson fell back against the sink. One hand covered his eyes, the other held onto the sink rim as Donaldson slid to the floor. "No."

His voice changed from a plea to an order. "No!" He opened his eyes, stood up. The rabbit was gone. He turned to face the mirror.

A bison stood behind his reflection.

Donaldson spun. No bison. No rabbit. No Trailer.

He woke up in the chair and leapt out of it, staying low, spinning in a crouch to take in the entirety of The Tank.

It was empty, devoid of threat.

He stood up, adrenaline making him twitch.

It was a dream, Jim. Deep breaths. Steady.

He walked into the bathroom, awake this time, gripped the sides of the sink and watched tremors shake and weaken his reflection's body. "Steady, soldier." He controlled his breathing, forcing color back into his cheeks.

"Transposition, Jimmy Boy? The client's helping the therapist?"

He ran hot water and lowered himself into the tub, soaking, not bathing, watching his fingertips shrivel and pucker, letting his mind roam, hoping his subconscious would come up with ideas. "If what you're doing isn't working, Jimmy Boy, try anything else." He reviewed items in Trailer's 201 and things Trailer shared in The Tank.

The water had cooled. His mind roamed, placed random unrelated events together until he remembered his father yelling at him.

Always yelling.

Always dressed in uniform.

So proud to be a soldier he wore it like a badge of honor.

Donaldson had seen an old movie, *The Great Santini*, and wondered if people had followed his father around taking notes.

Another memory joined the first, a memory he didn't know he had. Something he'd buried long ago, long forgotten.

It flooded his consciousness.

Little Jimmy Boy had an accident. Little Jimmy Boy shook and shrieked with fear, holding up blood-soaked hands as his father yelled at him. "You're not a good soldier. You think soldiers are afraid of a little blood? You're not my son. My son's better than this."

Little Jimmy reached up for his father, blood now covering his shirt and his tear-streaked face, screaming at his hands, wanting to know everything was alright, wanting to know father would take of this and Little Jimmy Boy would be fine.

But no comfort came.

For as long as he could remember, his father yelled.

'You took us because we were never loved.' That's what Trailer said. Basic. What is basic?

He sat up in the tub, his revelation splashing water onto the floor.

"He needs what any kid needs from an adult: reality checks. He wants rapport and communication - shared and validated reality."

He got out of the tub and toweled off. "Fuck explore. It's time to learn the territory. The only way out is through."

14 DAYS, 5 HOURS UNTIL TERMINATION

Trailer knotted the top of the plastic grocery bag and placed it at the base of the spruce. Some of the woodland critters had been nibbling on the bread and cheese when he tended to Steiner. He noticed that they preferred wheat bread and cheddar cheese and, when he could find them, he'd leave trails for them to follow. Animals he trusted. He'd learned long ago that animals never lied, never cheated, never stole, never betrayed.

Wild animals came to him unbidden. At one point, to make Karen smile, to make her aware he wasn't the monster he seemed, he sat at the edge of her property, where field met forest, surrounded by skunk, raccoon, eastern woodlands coyote and other wildlife, tossing them cookies and dogfood from bags in his lap. Predator and prey side by side and no hostilities among any of them. Far off came a gunshot and they huddled closer rather than scatter, somehow aware there was safety in this monster's shadow, safer with him than without.

But he doubted Donaldson, now firmly established in The World, would take to eating foodstuffs sampled by wild animals. The Augmenteds had been taught to eat anything, modified to digest things that would kill normals. But Donaldson wasn't Augmented. He was... well, if not exactly normal, close to.

But normalcy defined Steiner. Disgusting normalcy. Average beyond average and sickeningly so. The once youthful muscles going slack, the trim waistline becoming an ever increasing gut, the once clear lungs now reservoirs of nicotine and city smogs, ill-fitting teeth purchased through Amazon Dental rather than a licensed dentist, the clear eyes now needing lenses and sometime soon, surgery.

Steiner's mediocrity sickened him.

He would give anything - *anything!* - to be as mediocre as Steiner.

But such would never be.

Trailer could accept many things, tolerate many more, and craving Steiner's mediocrity pounded against his heart like a hurricane eroding a beach.

Trailer found Steiner around the Preserve's perimeter one night. Trailer had been calling back and forth with a great horned owl, letting the woods know of his coming and going and that no creatures need fear.

Then a sickening bolus of sound interrupted his conversation with the owl. Smaller animals fell silent, larger animals rustled away.

Steiner made tracking too easy. A dog three weeks dead could have followed Steiner's trail. Trailer found him smoking, a gun in one hand and a knife in the other, a poorly trussed pack on his back, talking as he made his way amongst the trees, sometimes mumbling, sometimes shouting, creating a river of silence in his wake, the woods gone quiet to let this intruder pass.

Steiner complained to no one in particular about the shitty job he had and the shitty life he had and the shitty things he had to do and his shitty kids who called him an asshole and his shitty parents who died without leaving him anything and his shitty wife who made all the family decisions and then told everybody "We decided as a family..." who made him clip his balls so they'd have no more kids and then was always too tired or too busy to fuck him.

The sick but normal bastard laughed. "Maybe that's why you got cancer, ever think of that? You're rotting from the inside out now. But you know what's best for the family, don't you. Did we decide as a family that you should get cancer?"

He burned through his cigarette in one draw and dropped it, unthinking, the end still glowing, onto the forest floor. "How is cancer best for the family?"

Steiner continued bemoaning his life as he walked. Trailer remained hidden, observing, alternately repulsed and awed by the man's normalcy.

Then Steiner said, "And fuck you, too, Wrobleski."

Trailer came up behind him silently. Steiner exhaled. Before he drew his next breath Trailer carried him fifty feet off the ground and tied him to a tree in his own mummy bag.

Steiner took one look down, slumped into the bag and cried until he slept.

Now Trailer climbed as he always had, hand over hand, massive arms, back, and shoulders making his way effortless. He crept up to Steiner, suspended in a spider's web of knots and lines amongst the sturdier branches, tied and trussed like a Thanksgiving turkey ready for carving, making sure Steiner didn't know he was there.

"Hello again. Remember me?"

Steiner flailed in the suspended mummy bag, once again soiling himself, the scents of shit and piss overwhelming the scents of fear and stupid.

Trailer hadn't touched him since finding him wandering outside the preserve's perimeter. Standard psywar practice. Wait the enemy out. Be present, be around but act as if they don't exist. Dehumanize them by a complete lack of interaction.

Then find out what you want and kill them.

Steiner laughed, the sound so out of place that it almost threw Trailer off guard. He registered it but didn't respond.

Steiner's laughter grew until he cackled, high pitched and penetrating.

Trailer realized his cackling might give their position away. He placed his hands on either side of Steiner's neck and pressed gently, inducing a cerebromedullospinal disconnect - Locked-in Syndrome - another fear-instilling technique the Augmented Men had been taught. The subject could feel pain, especially proprioceptive tortures, but only answer questions through eye movement and blinks. No ropes, no drugs, no restrictions of any kind and the individual was powerless while being tortured or, more often, while watching their loved ones tortured.

And once all necessary information was gathered, left to die.

Steiner's face went taught even as his laughter continued. A few seconds later his laughter ceased. He became silent, his face relaxed but his eyes focused on Trailer.

"Blink once for yes, twice for no, okay?"

One blink.

"You know what I am?"

One blink.

"I am not going to kill you. Do you believe that?"

One.

Hesitant.

Blink.

"You sure about that?"

One solid blink.

"Good. Now, who sent you?"

Steiner's eyes widened. Trailer's nostrils twitched. He raised his head over Steiner's face and took three quick sniffs: fear, more intense, far stronger than the normal smell of fear all people wore simply from living in an automated, unforgiving society.

A flight-fear, a fear of discovery, a fear of total and complete retribution.

Trailer smelled it often when ranging down South. The stomach goes acid and churns more bile, the blood goes adrenaline, thins and moves faster, the heart beats faster, breathing goes shallow, the sweat goes basic and flows more freely, the breath goes saccharine, muscles tense and skin tightens. Put them all together and you get the stink of fear, a metallic ozone combination that most people detected vomeronasally and responded to non-consciously.

The Augments recognized it as just another human tell to be used as necessary and when required.

"You're afraid."

One quick blink. Then another. Tears. Another blink. Eyes shut.

"I'm sorry, I didn't quite catch that. Could you repeat it for me?"

A tear. Then two.

Trailer bit through the rope holding Steiner to the tree trunk.

Steiner began to fall. Trailer said, "Race ya," and started descending the tree, hand over hand, facing down, moving slightly faster than gravity pulled Steiner to the ground and catching him just before he hit.

"That's pretty good. You almost beat me. Best two out of three?"

Trailer lifted Steiner to carry him back up the tree and stopped. Even though locked-in, even though Steiner could only breathe, blink his eyes, shit and piss, Trailer could feel his sobs, subvocal though they were.

He put Steiner on the ground, leaned him up against the tree and looked at him. He massaged Steiner's neck and cervical vertebrae, then cut Steiner loose and unzipped the mummy bag, pulling him free. He kneeled so they looked each other eye-to-eye.

"Okay, who are you? Who sent you?"

"Henry Steiner. Wrobleski sent me."

"Wrobleski sent you? To kill me?"

Steiner nodded, wary.

That didn't make sense. Wrobleski would know as much about augmentation as Donaldson if not more. He wouldn't care how science did it but he'd know every detail of what the Augments could do.

"Wrobleski sent you to kill me with a revolver and a knife?"

Steiner shook his head, no.

Trailer rocked backward. This man was either an idiot or a fool, possibly both. "You decided to come after me with only a revolver and a knife?"

Steiner nodded.

"Didn't Wrobleski explain me to you? You know what I am. Did you think you could do me with a revolver and a knife?"

Steiner shook his head, no, never taking his eyes off Trailer.

Understanding brought a new confusion. "You knew you'd fail. You wanted to fail. You wanted me to kill you?"

Steiner nodded.

"Say it."

"Yes."

"Why in fuck's name would you want that?"

Again the scent of fear, stronger this time, as Steiner internally catalogued all he thought wrong with his life, saying nothing to Trailer, keeping it all inside.

Trailer listened to it all, all the memories of failures, none of the successes, all the sorrows, none of the joys. "You're more afraid of going back to the world than you are of me so you're giving up? Just like that? Rather than talking things over with your wife, maybe working things out, at least taking a stab at making things better, rather than commit yourself to enjoying whatever time you have left with her, rather than straightening out your family, you decided giving up is your best option? I've heard of being along for the ride but you don't even want to know who's driving the car. You'd rather die in the crash than grab the wheel and steer yourself to safety."

Trailer pulled back as if avoiding contact with a dangerous organism. "Jesus Christ, Steiner. You fucking scare *me*."

Steiner stared without speaking but his thoughts acknowledged it all.

"Suicide by Augment instead of suicide by cop?"

Again silent acknowledgement.

Trailer stood and stepped back. "Stand up."

"Huh?"

"Stand up. Take off your clothes. You're soaked in shit."

Trailer removed his own makeshift rags and held them out. "About two-hundred yards in that direction there's a rise. " He pointed east. "On the other side is a small stream. Clean yourself off then put these on. Sun'll be up in a few hours. Stay there until sunrise, then look for a brightness on the horizon. That'll be the St. John River reflecting up. Walk towards that brightness. You'll be in Dickey. Tell them you got lost in the woods and found your way out. There's some money in that left pocket. Use it. Buy some clothes and call your wife.

"Live your life, man. Live your life."

"I..."

"Go!"

Steiner ran, Trailer's rags held against his chest, not looking back.

Trailer stood naked beside the tree, shaking his head. Wrobleski would not have sent such a fool to kill him. Except as a decoy. That meant Donaldson might still be on his original mission.

Or a calling card. Wrobleski wants me to know he's still in the game, which means I'm being played.

He reached for his groceries and stopped.

The knot was opened, some bread taken out, a slice bitten through and replaced.

And he hadn't heard a thing.

14 DAYS UNTIL TERMINATION

Donaldson woke to find Trailer back in The Tank and breakfast ready. Trailer had exchanged his burlap bags for a horse blanket he wore like a poncho.

Donaldson studied Trailer for a moment then sat at the table and started eating. "What do you need from me, Nick?"

"From you? Nothing."

"Incorrect. You came back."

"Nowhere else to go."

"You could go home to your wife."

"Can't go there."

"Is there something there you're afraid of?"

"I told you; if I love her, I have to kill her. I'm afraid of her."

She's the key. He's afraid of his feelings, not her, but he can't separate the two. "Care to tell me about her?" Fuck!

Trailer went hypnotic. "Report: five-five, one-thir..."

Silence.

The jungle predator purred.

Donaldson began tightening, tucking, preparing for Trailer to switch activation states, the taste of bile rising as his stomach clenched. I'll never know it until after it happens. Better prepare for the worst.

The purring changed. Slowly, mixed with grunts of augmented effort, as if benchpressing a car by its axles, activation states shifting from preparation sets to something else.

"...one-thir..."

A pause. Veins throbbed on Trailer's neck, arms, and face. A groan. A grunt.

A purr. "...thirty, one..."

A heavy sigh followed by another, a sound of tractor-trailer brakes slowly cycling.

Trailer's nostrils flared. His eyes closed. He exhaled as if releasing steam, as if clearing his insides out.

He shook, a dog throwing off water after walking in a good spring rain. He inhaled deeply, his nostrils flaring. He swallowed, his jaws working, his lips pursing, tasting, words fighting their way out.

What in fuck's name's going on?

Trailer grabbed the edge of the sink. He snapped himself upright. The Tank shook.

He turned, slowly, as if noticing Donaldson for the first time, curious what this small thing was, the behemoth staring at the morsel before him, deciding if it was worthy.

Here it comes.

Donaldson looked to the lav, The Tank's steel-walled safe room.

No time.

Trailer started speaking, his words deep and throaty, coming up with his purrs, talking while rotary breathing, each word coming separately, each word coming as if from a massive bellows deep in Trailer's chest, "...thirty."

Pause.

"Cute, though."

Pause.

"Real... pretty... Doesn't wear...makeup...I...like that...about her."

The words starting coming more rapidly, coming in larger bites, the individual thoughts taking less time to string together.

"No disguises...And she always smells good...like oatmeal cookies, you know?...Frosted...with raisins?...She knows I like them...so she makes them for me...when I'm around."

Trailer closed his eyes. He shook again, his chest and shoulders bunching as if choking up another coydog bone. His voice made a slow, arduous climb from deep in his chest to right in his throat.

"She knows when I'm around...that's another thing."

He's relaxing?

"I think her animals tell her. I don't know..."

And then something much softer, more peaceful, more restful, replaced the predatory purring; the predator became a kitten.

Donaldson stared at him. He's changed his own state. He used the tools we gave him to change his own state.

Trailer's head snapped up. His eyes opened and focused on Donaldson, but his face and posture were relaxed. He pointed at Donaldson's empty plate. "You done?"

Mid-afternoon, Trailer said, "I'm tired." He lay down on his bunk and slept in minutes. Trailer'd been increasingly groggy since he'd started changing his own neuropathy earlier that morning.

Donaldson considered. His brain's restructuring itself? Destroying old connections and creating new ones?

Yes, and consuming all of his body's resources in the process.

My god, this is so important to him he's willing to destroy himself to achieve it? He must know what he's doing, what's happening even if he doesn't know 'forced neuroplasticity' by name. He's able to feel his brain changing.

Does he know it's under his control? He's the one doing it to himself? If he doesn't, that's one thing. But if he does?

Donaldson stood over the breaching whale.

Those old connections and structures never completely go away, Nick. Short of neural trauma, those old memories are still in there somewhere. They can be repurposed but they never go away. The next few days determine if you to live or die, my friend.

But right now Donaldson watched Trailer sleep. For the first time since the initial stages of augmentation, Trailer rested in something other than a small package formation. And he twitched in his sleep. Any nonconscious, unintentional movement could compromise their positions so the Augmenteds never moved when in rest states.

Trailer required little training there; he came to augmentation with a trauma-induced paralysis. If he fought his parents, he was beaten to the point that he couldn't move. He learned in early childhood to not move at all when he slept and not sleep when he knew threats were around.

Donaldson continued to be amazed at Trailer's neuropathic healing ability. He's taken everything we did to him to cause rapid physical healing and regeneration and made neuroplasticity tools of them. He's rearranging synapses, generating new connections, restructuring beliefs about himself, about me, about the war and god knows what else.

He's healing himself of all the trauma he'd endured in his life.

The papers that could come out of this.

Donaldson also understood that the psycho-emotive scars Trailer harbored, the non-conscious hardening both Trailer and Donaldson's team had done to him, wouldn't yield its hold on Trailer's psyche in one day, let alone several. There was lots of work ahead and it'd only begun.

Donaldson's eyes opened to the dim light of The Tank in night mode. Trailer sat on his bunk, staring at him.

"Sorry, Nick. Did I doze off for a while?"

"Why did you let Wartella and St.Onge kill Mancuso?"

"Who was Mancuso?"

"The old Pancho I brought in because he stole some rations. You were the only one of us who needed rations and there was more than enough for you. Don't you remember?"

Donaldson shook his head then caught himself. Don't say 'no', damn it. You were there. Or does 'shared reality' have a different meaning to you?

"Come on, Major. You've got to remember. Mancuso was the old Pancho who'd had a hand cut off because the Iraqis didn't like anyone stealing their mustafa, remember? I do." Trailer's eyes began to glaze. "It was the first day we got in country. We hadn't even gone on a run yet. I found him cradling ration cans in his arm and brought him in. I thought you were going to ask him questions. Maybe even feed him.

"Things got sour and I never knew why. The first thing you said was to put cuffs on him. I laughed because I thought it was a joke. But you didn't know. I remember 'cause you turned around to see what I was laughing at. Then you saw. You told me to guard him. How come you didn't do anything?"

Got to stop him.

Trailer's eyes defocused.

Fuck!

Trailer looked directly into his memories, his language shifting tenses as the past took precedence over the present.

"There's this guy with one hand, so most of us think we can't put handcuffs on him, right? Not St.Onge, no, not him. St.Onge says, 'Sure we can put cuffs on the old man.' But he's got a weapon, so he's forfeit, right? But he doesn't have a hand on his right arm, so we can't cuff him. We cuffed his legs, but he kept on looking at his weapon in the corner even though my weapon's right on him, aimed right between his eyes. And I know he's going to try it, and I don't want to kill this dumb fuck, and he's staring at me and looking at his weapon in the corner."

"Nick."

"St.Onge sees me and says, 'Hey, Nick's too sweet for this. We got to help him.' I think, 'Good, they're going to get somebody else to do this.' And St.Onge gets one of the steel rods we tie fence to, the kind that's flat and has holes in it, and shoves the spade end right into the fire we got burning. He splits open one of the flares, the kind we use to show the QuadraLift pilots where to land, and throws some of the flash into the fire."

"Nick?"

"It goes wild and St.Onge puts a hand over his eyes. I'm not looking at the Pancho, but he's not looking at his weapon either. He's squirming and Wartella is holding him down, laughing because this old man is like a bug in his big black hands. And I don't know what's coming, but St.Onge says, 'Sure, we can put cuffs on him.' And he takes the rod from the fire and says to Wartella, 'Flatten his arm.'"

"Please."

"Wartella holds this old man's arm flat against the ground, the arm without a hand, and St.Onge drives the hot end of the rod right between the bones in the forearm. The old man is screaming because his flesh is cooking where the rod goes through. He passed out and Wartella lifted the rod up. The old man's arm came up with it, the arm without a hand, and St.Onge takes a pair of cuffs."

"Stop."

"He snaps one end on through a hole in the rod underneath the old man's arm, the other through a hole above the old man's arm, then he says - "

"Nick."

" - 'Give me your cuffs, Nick.' I don't know what's happening. I hand St.Onge my cuffs. He cuffed one end around the chain around the old man's arm, then the other cuff to his left wrist. 'That's how it's done.' It didn't matter, because the old man was forfeit, anyway. I think he was dead by that time. He started to fall towards his weapon.

"By the time Wartella and St.Onge got through, there was nothing left."

"Stop!"

Trailer's eyes cleared. He focused on Donaldson, eyes closed, face flushed as if the flash hot fire blazed before him, standing, shaking.

Trailer spoke plainly, clearly, without emotion, relaying a simple fact, "And you let it happen, Major."

Donaldson put his hands on the tabletop to steady himself. Either the room was tilting or he was and he couldn't decide which.

Anchor yourself, Jim, anchor yourself.

His eyes snapped open and he stared at Trailer. Did I say that out loud?

Anchor! Anchor!

Trailer met his gaze, his face neutral, not even acknowledging if he'd heard Donaldson's subvocalized thought.

Anchor to your pulse. Donaldson lifted his hands to steady his head and felt something in them. He opened his eyes. A small dun-colored rabbit.

He shook his head at the image, pulling back but unable to escape. A dead rabbit. His hands covered in blood.

"Yes, I remember. You're right, Nick. I let it happen."

"You know what, Major? It didn't matter, them or us. Do you know what they did to us when you left us there?"

Slowly, painfully, Donaldson sorted through his own memories. The rabbit became a bison calf, lying in his palms. It looked up at Donaldson. "Nothing can change until it becomes real, Jimmy Boy."

"They wanted to know why we were different. How, you know? So they started with Wartella. They got him tranqed - you gave them the tranq, right? - and put him on a table saw they used to quarter beef. You ever seen one of those, Major?"

Donaldson felt himself nodding. The bison calf spoke again. "He needs shared and validated reality from you. Go ahead. Give it to him. Give it to him then ask yourself what you need from him."

"I guess they took him because he was so proud of that big black beautiful body. When they were done with him, they came to me. Did you know that? They came to me and said, 'Take this and eat. He told us about you.'

"I never knew what they meant. Still don't. Do you, Major?"

Donaldson clenched his fists. "No, Nick, I don't." He opened his hands and stared at them as if divining his fate. There was no rabbit. No blood. Nothing but empty palms and the future they held.

"Yeah? Well maybe between the two of us we can figure it out. What'd'you think. I mean, if I could live through it, you can listen to it. Maybe you need to hear it, huh, Major? Maybe you're just as fucked up as I am. Maybe you need to hear this just as much as I need to tell it."

Donaldson, his hands empty and clean, shook himself straight. What do I need from him? "Okay, Nick. I'm listening."

"They took Lukach next. They tranqed him enough so that he was aware but unresponsive? Remember that? 'Aware but unresponsive'? They couldn't lock him in so they used tranq. They staked him out and said to me, 'He told us about you. Now you tell us.'

"But remember what you taught us? What *you* taught us, Major? You taught us to do what we did as kids. Remember that? When we were kids, and our folks and every other motherfucker beat on us, we use to go into a shock state, a 'splitting off of the self' you called it. What else did you call it? 'Dissociation'? You taught us to do that if we were ever compromised.

"I did that. I did that and they shot off Lukach's right hand and said, 'You tell us.' I dropped myself completely, just like you taught us. Then they shot off his right forearm and said, 'You tell us.' But I did what you told us. I didn't talk. Then they shot off his arm, his right foot, his knee, and each time, 'You tell us.'

"They took Baron next. They tied him up and St.Onge says, 'Okay, all right. We're spies. Is that what you want?' I don't think that's what they wanted because they looked at Baron and said, 'Oops! A spy? We kill spies.' and they blew off his head. Clean off. Never saw anything separate so cleanly.

"You ever see anything get its head taken off, Major?

"They sat him up next to me. I remember that. And they said, 'You tell us.' I think I stopped hearing about then, too, because the last thing I remember is the rest of the team screaming at me, 'Tell them, Trailer, tell them what the fuck they want to know!' But I didn't know what they wanted to know. Funny, but I remembered that feeling from before, even as I went out. The last thing I remember before I dropped total, the last thing, is them pissing on me, then pissing into Baron's neck, then jerking off on the body.

"What happened after that, Major?"

Donaldson felt himself spinning, twisting, coming apart as he descended some maelstrom. His hands were white, bloodless, without feeling, his eyes unseeing, numb, blind, the pounding in his head forcing his breath to come in hot gasps, his voice, his body, light, hollow, wheezy, seeking air to speak and finding none. "I don't know, Nick. I wasn't there."

Nicholas Trailer stared at James Donaldson. "You look like you're in a lot of pain, Major. Let me tell you something, something I found out during my 're-education' in the Orinoco.

"Sometimes pain's the only thing lets you know you're alive."

Trailer watched Donaldson, studying, analyzing, moving through him, his augmented senses informing, understanding, feeling something...unknown...strange...foreign.

Donaldson felt himself lifted. The bed came under him, the comforter came over him. Yes, he thought. Kill me. Take your time. Time to die.

"That's right, Jim. You weren't there." Trailer stood and turned away.

Got to keep him talking. Say anything. "It must have been tough, being a POW, Nick."

"Being a POW was no problem. That was just like living at home. That's why being asked a question and not knowing how or what to answer felt familiar back then. I never knew when I'd get hit, never knew what to do not to get hit, never knew what to say or how to say it, never knew when I'd get fed or what I'd be eating. Hell no, being a POW was easy."

Donaldson drifted.

"Loving my wife is hard."

Silence.

Donaldson checked his watch: 2:00AM, deep night, Trailer's absence felt more than seen. Another day had passed. "Hope you're picking up groceries and'll be back soon, Nick. We have eleven days left."

The inner door opened. "You talking to me?"

"No, talking to myself."

"Bad habit. Can get you killed."

"Thanks. I'll try to remember. You came back again."

Trailer laughed, deep in his chest and letting it roll out of him, enjoying the joke. "You're getting safe again, Jim. You're noticing more."

Trailer's laughter focused Donaldson's attention. It took him a moment to recognize what changed.

His posture. He's relaxed. He feels safe here. I'm no longer a threat. "You don't have to tell me if you don't want to, Nick, but why did you come back?"

"I've been thinking a lot lately. Even before I did that bar in Chelmsford. Past couple of days, things started to click. I spent a lot of time blaming you. Then I thought about my parents and blamed them. Then I blamed kids I knew in school, teachers... I'd even get down to people who just smiled at me funny when I was a kid. I been fucked over by a lot of people, but I don't think a lot of them meant it. Most people, they're doing what they think is right. They're making the best choices they can when they got to make them. It's kind of like me, knowing what was my fault and what wasn't. Started thinking about the people who were nice to me, too. Nice for no reason. Couple of teachers. Some people I'd met, before and after."

He's searching for role models, trying to define himself without seeking definition in others. "And?"

"And the good people did what they thought was right. The bad people did, too, probably. And I call them 'bad' because of what they did to me. So what am I going to do? Blame everybody for doing what they thought was right? Everybody's responsible for what they do, but nobody's to blame for it."

The first thing Donaldson noted was the other bed had been slept in. As usual, Trailer had breakfast almost ready. "Sometime you're going to have to let me make you break... Sorry. I wasn't thinking."

"That is a pretty big slip," Trailer paused. "Jim."

"Have you ever talked about what happened before?"

"With who, Major? You? You weren't there. Nobody was there, remember? Nobody's supposed to know. Anybody still alive who was there? No. Not even me. I'm not even alive, according to you folks. You changed my name, my age, my history. When I was a kid, I spent most of my life establishing a lie I could believe in. You took that away with the pass of a pen. Don't be stupid, Major. I'm the last of my tribe. There's nobody to tell my stories to."

"You can tell me."

Trailer smirked. "Sure."

"You know, Nick. There's someplace I'd like to take you when this is all over."

"Yeah? We'll go on a date. We'll have a picnic."

Donaldson took his seat at the table. A newspaper, *The Bangor Herald*, neatly folded to the theater listings, lay next to his plate. Four sheets of paper with small, precise writing half hid under the newspaper. "What's this?"

"When they came to YDC looking for desirables, they read that story and decided I might be a candidate. I wrote it because the doc said to write a story of my life. I wrote it out again last night while you slept. Borrowed some of your paper. Hope you don't mind."

Donaldson remembered the story well. He'd read it several times while studying Trailer's 201. He read it again as he ate his breakfast. Nothing had changed.

I learned about the price of truth before I was ten years old.

My dad was in the bathroom, getting ready for bed, I think. He started yelling. He yelled a lot. If he wasn't yelling, he was hitting us, making fun of us or telling us we were stupid.

Anyway, he yelled for my sister and me to come. My sister is older than me by five years. She got there first. He stood by the sink, pointing at a glob of toothpaste half way up from the drain.

He stood over us and pointed at the glob of toothpaste and his voice was real tight. Whenever his voice was tight like that you knew somebody was going to get a beating and by this point I knew it was going to be me.

"Who left that there?" he says and his face is red and he's shaking he wants to hit somebody so much.

My sister said she didn't do it. "Who did?" I don't know, she said.

He turns to me. "Did you do that?"

No, dad. I didn't.

"Well, you're the only two in the house. I didn't do it and I know your mother didn't do it, so who didn't do it if neither of you did it?"

To fully get this you have to flashback to when I was about 1-2 years old. My room was on the top floor of our house, down a hall from my parents' room. Halfway between was a staircase downstairs and downstairs was my sisters' room. I have two sisters, both older than me.

So one night I woke up and wanted to go see my sisters. I don't know why. Who knows what a kid does at 1-2 years old? So I got up, turned on the hall light and got to the top of the stairs.

Well, my father came rushing out of his room, my mother close behind, and he lifted me up by my right arm. He began wanging on my ass. Not tapping, not even lightly slapping. This was a full grown man holding me up by my arm and slamming me so hard I was rocking back and forth like a pendulum in a bad clock.

I started screaming, my mother started screaming, I could hear my sisters screaming, and my father is yelling at me "Where are you going? You get back in your bed! Where are you going? You get back in your bed!" with each tick of the clock.

I started to pee. Maybe that's why I got up, maybe I needed to pee and wanted my sisters to get the potty seat for me, I don't know.

I started to pee and I'm making a puddle on the floor and my father's really bellowing now and he shouts at the top of his lungs "Did you do that?"

I'm crying, I'm screaming, and there's more tears coming out of my eyes than there's piss on the floor and I'm swinging by my arm and I've bitten my lip swinging back and forth and I can't stop pissing and I'm screaming back at him, "No No No No NO." Looking back it was stupid, of course. I was pissing right there on the floor in front of him, so now he calls me a liar and if you thought he was having at me before, you didn't know my dad. He used to beat me with a rubber hose he got when he installed a washer for my mother. That's another one for you, a full grown man, strong to begin with, swinging a yard long rubber hose like it's a Louisville Slugger at his baby kid because something didn't go right in his goddamn day.

So I'd learned early on that no matter what happened, it would end up with me getting hit.

And here's that old fuck, standing in front of the sink saying "You're the only two in the house. Your mother and me didn't do it so one of you did."

Tell you the truth, I wanted to laugh. Right before he goes completely ballistic, he starts talking logical, like using big words gives him some kind of distance, you know? I remember one time he beat me so hard I shit myself. My god the stench was eye-crossing.

He sees the shit running out my pants leg, he sees my pants turning colors all through the seat and crotch, and he stops hitting me and says conversationally, like he's giving etiquette instructions or something, "Don't you move your bowels when I'm talking to you."

I don't know why, I guess I was in so much pain I didn't know what the fuck I was doing, I looked at him and said, "'move my bowels'? *Move my bowels?* Jesus fuck, I'm shitting myself you goddamn moron. Can't you even tell when somebody's shitting themselves? Are you that goddamn fucking stupid?"

They had to rush me to the hospital after that.

But this time, standing in front of the sink, our father getting louder and louder yelling at us, seeing my sister's face get redder and redder, I basically decided fuck it. It didn't matter.

Remember I had two sisters? For as long as I remember my oldest sister had this scar on her wrist, not like an attempted suicide scar, that I could understand, but this was like a regular hospital scar and you could see where the stitches were and stuff. My parents and aunts and uncles always said my sister got bit by a goose and I always thought that was odd because we never lived anywhere near any geese. I found out years later my father had broken her arm. He'd thrown her down the stairs for some reason and they'd taken her to the emergency room to fix her up. This was before I was born.

But back to the bathroom. I decided it didn't matter. I looked at my dad and I said, "I did it."

My sister let out her breath.

"Why did you lie to me?"

Because it doesn't matter. It doesn't matter if I tell you the truth or if I lie. If you want to hit someone you're going to hit someone, so it doesn't matter and I might as well tell you the truth.

My mother was always telling people I was a deep thinker. I read a lot when I was a kid. Still do. So I'm not sure if I said it just like that, but that's pretty much what I said.

Well, my father stared at me. I could tell he wanted to hit me but I'd told the truth and told him the other truth, that he was a bully and a bastard and it didn't matter what the truth was, all that mattered was if he needed to hit somebody and that somebody was going to be me. I knew he wouldn't hit my sister. She was getting older and for some reason he had real taboos about hitting a woman. I think because his father, my grandfather, use to beat the crap out of my grandmother when he was a kid. Hell, that's probably where he learned it.

Anyway, he told me to go to my room but from then on he plotted. I think I scared him with what I said. I would catch him watching me, looking for excuses. One time I accidentally emptied a box of dish-washing soap into the sink. My mother asked me to do the dishes, I said sure but I didn't realize how loose the cover was on the box and I spilt most of it in the sink.

My dad was out in the garage working on something and not getting it fixed, so he was already frustrated all to hell and when I emptied the box, I don't know, it was some kind of challenge to his manhood or something. I think I was ten or twelve when this happened and he backed me into a corner of the kitchen and was punching me in the stomach, in the face, he was boxing me, again a full grown, strong man punching the shit out of a kid, not holding back, punching me as if I was coming after him. I don't know. After a few minutes he quit. I guess he was tired at that point. My eyes are black, my lips are swollen, my stomach's aching because he's hammered me to the point that I can't breathe.

He storms out of the kitchen, back to the garage and my mother's patching me up. She didn't try to stop him, oh no, but once he's done she comes in to patch me up. She was always like that. Thank god it had already been established at school that I was a clumsy kid and always falling down stairs, over things, tripping over my own feet.

I wonder why it took so long for people to become aware of child abuse sometimes.

But I'd already learned the price of truth was power, and you always get power when you tell the truth. I'm not talking about always telling the truth when you're with friends or that kind of thing, I'm talking about telling the truth when it makes a difference.

That day in the bathroom I got power over my dad and he never forgave me for it.

Trailer's words came back up Donaldson's throat like a piece of bad meat: You selected us because we were never loved.

Never loved. A bison asked him, "Were you ever loved, Jimmy Boy?" His vision blurred. He started thinking of music, one of Bach's Brandenburgs. Images of rabbits and bison swirled in front of him. He looked up, his mind grasping at topics to engage Trailer while struggling to control his own mind. "Talk to me, Nick."

"About?"

"Anything. What got you into the Youth Detention Center?"

"Spaghetti."

A rabbit asked, "Spaghetti?" Donaldson heard the words come out of his own mouth.

"Yeah, spaghetti. You know all this."

Donaldson didn't respond.

Trailer looked at him and shrugged. "I forget how old I was, I think I was fifteen. My mom invited some people over. Was my dad there that night? Yeah, I think so, but it didn't matter. I remember that no matter who my mother was with, I was always supposed to call him 'pop'."

As he talked, Trailer's voice took on the tones and inflections of an adolescent. "I remember I once had five pops in five nights. There was one night I was supposed to be asleep, but I wasn't. I got up and peeked through the doorjamb into the living room. I had three pops at the same time that night. I think one of them spent the night. Probably the one who brought the Fentanyl. I don't know, though.

"Mom and dad had some people over, Pip and Josie. There was a big bowl of spaghetti on the table. I'd had a bowl and was just sitting there, thinking about, I don't know, I guess maybe about this girl in school. I was just thinking, staring off into space, you know? Not really staring at anything at all.."

Trailer paused. "Major, are you all right?"

Donaldson nodded, not fully aware. His hands felt sticky, blood covered. Somebody kept shouting, "Kill it, dammit. Kill it."

He forced his mind to focus on the man in front of him. Memories of The Augments' last run clouded his vision like cataracts covering his eyes. He saw Trailer wearing a BDU, one of the few times the Augments wore battle dress in all their time in-country.

Of nine Augments, only Trailer survived and only because he was the youngest one selected for the program. His body hadn't stopped growing when he entered the program. The Augmentation process worked with his body's own building process, not starting over or reawakening it as it did with the others. Of all the others, only Trailer fulfilled his last mission: sanction and confirm, and only because nobody knew how much his young body had taken to Augmentation.

"Major?"

Donaldson nodded again, unseeing.

Trailer stared at him a moment then continued. "But I guess my eyes were staring into the bowl of spaghetti. So dad says, 'What the fuck you looking at, kid? You want some more, take it. Don't stare at the bowl like that.' Pip says, 'Ya, I was going to have some more but I saw him looking and felt like I'd be taking it out of his mouth so I decided I'd better not.'

"I looked up and said, 'What?' and dad hits me for making everybody feel bad about dinner.

"I shook my head. I didn't care anymore. They're all laughing at me. Pip and dad point at me and Pip stuffs his face full of spaghetti right from the bowl. My mother hit me again and everybody laughs harder and I just stop caring. I just fucking stop.

"I say 'Why me?'. I said it real quiet. I wasn't asking anybody a real question, I was just, I mean, why me? Why is this happening to me? What did I do to deserve this?

"Right about then I realize that hey, I'm just a kid. I didn't do anything. I didn't do anything, I didn't say anything and I sure as shit didn't deserve this.

"I didn't deserve this, I didn't deserve these assholes in my life, I deserved better and I realized ain't nobody going to make it better for me, I got to make it better for myself, and they're all around the table, and I smiled. They're laughing at me, my mother's smacking me, my old man's hitting me, I bet Pip and Josie would've gotten up and taken a few swings, too, I mean, who's going to help the village idiot when the village wants to play?

"That's when things changed.

"I got up and opened the cupboards beside the stove.

"My dad goes, 'What the fuck are you doing, kid?'

"I'm moving things around, couldn't find what I want, opened up the next cupboard down. 'I'm looking for something.'

"My mom says, 'What're you looking for? You don't know where anything is. Tell me what you're looking for.'

"Not there, either. I go to the next cupboard. 'No, I can find it.'

"'You dumb fuck, tell your mother what you're looking for.'

That's when I find it. A big cast-iron frying pan. I knew we had one. We had three, really. One really big mother and then a smaller one and then a little tiny one you could cook maybe one egg in.

"I stood up, the biggest cast-iron frying pan in my hand. God that mother was heavy. Took both hands to lift it.

"'What are you going to do with that?' my old man says.

"I swung it at his head.

"Big fucking splat. I swing it with both hands and the damn thing is so heavy it kept me spinning after it cracked his skull and knocked him out of his chair.

"My mother screams. I hold up my finger, you know, like 'Wait a minute, please.'

"I kneel beside my dad and I lift that frying pan as far over my head as I could with both hands and I bring it down on his face with all the strength I can. I mean, I'm grunting, it's like doing crunches with a weight across your chest I'm swinging so hard. Four times, five times, six times.

"And nobody moves.

"I mean, fuck, I would've gone lightning getting out of there but nobody moves.

"Then Pip says real soft, 'Jesus, fuck, kid.'

"I went back to the cupboard and pull out the tiny frying pan. I still got the heavy one in my hand but it's slipping because of all the blood and brainsplatter on it and I can't hold it anymore, I can't get a good grip, you know what I mean?

"Pip goes to get up but he's having trouble because he's sitting between the wall and the table. He yells at his wife, "Get me outta here, Josie, get me out,' only it comes out more like he's pleading than angry or anything else.

"And then I got it, I figure it out. Pip's afraid of me. Maybe because he doesn't want to go on me one-on-one, I don't know, maybe he thinks I'd never turn, maybe he thinks I'm the little rat-fuck he always thought I was, I don't know, but I say, 'Oh, that won't be necessary,' and I swing that tiny frying pan at him. It's still heavy and he blocks it but he's working to get out from behind the table so he doesn't block it square and I could hear his arm break right before he screams.

"I swung that tiny frying pan edge-on into his open mouth and it breaks his jaw, he's swallowing teeth he's not spitting out, his mouth is split open like The Joker's smile and I'm fucking laughing my head off.

"'Have some more pasta, Pip.' And I pick up a handful of spaghetti and shove it down his throat. He's gagging, he's choking, I'm laughing, I don't ever remember feeling this good, I mean liberated. Christ is this what freedom feels like I don't know but I'm not going to let it go.

"I wipe my hands on my pants and pick up the big frying pan again. 'Chew your food good before you swallow,' I say and I sail that mother flat against his face with all I've got and his head goes back into the wall and halfway through it. He just stands there, his head back like he's looking at the stars and it's the only thing keeping him from falling to the floor, his head smashed into the wall and I gently place that big pan on the table and I'm thinking I should thank it, give it a place of honor, you know, on the mantle or something, show everybody how it freed me from slavery, that kind of thing.

"Now Josie opens up. She's making to run, fuck her husband, Pip, she's leaving him there and getting out, and now I'm dancing with the tiny cast-iron frying pan, I'm fucking ready for Dancing with the Stars, and I smash her head on one side, swing around and get her from the other side, and she's hobbling, no idea how she's still standing up, so I go at her again and spin around and go at her again and spin around and go at her again and I'm going back and forth so fast her body doesn't have time to fall and BaBing BaBang BaBoom her head's about as wide as her neck. Her eyes are coming out of her skull, her teeth are falling out of her mouth, her tongue is hanging out like a dog's on a hot summer's day, she's got blood coming out of her nose and ears and mouth and I am fucking loving it.

"Anyway, she goes down. Now it's just mom and me.

"Good old mom and me."

Donaldson brought his mind back to Trailer, to Trailer's language. He's mixing tenses again. My god, how long has he been phasing like that? He acknowledges himself then takes it away. His parents taught him that.

Yours did, too.

The thought came as a whisper, intruding into his analysis of Trailer. He forced it down and focused on Trailer's switching verb tense and what it meant.

No sense of time, no sense of place. Does he even know where he is now?

Do I know where I am now? "Excuse me. Back in a minute." A few controlled steps got him to the bathroom. He splashed cold water on his face as his eyes met his reflection in the mirror.

Have I been phasing in and out of the past and not aware of it?

He shuddered as memories overran him like worms on the dead. The war ended too soon.

Donaldson challenged his superiors when he found out Wrobleski ordered the Director of National Intelligence - authorization for The Augments came under a special Office of National Intelligence charter, ONI GCATTCS 17901 CENTAURS - to compromise the team by giving next run locations. That and enough Remoxipride, an early 1990s attempt at a non-extrapyramidal replacement for the schizophrenia drug haloperidol, to make the Augmenteds manageable.

Remoxipride itself behaved as anticipated on the general population. It had the added benefit of affecting the Augments like Delilah cutting Samson's hair; small amounts caused weakness and fatigue. A little more caused confusion, headache, and fever. Still more and you got internal bleeding and hypersensitivity to light. Enough of the stuff caused severe convulsions and, eventually, death. It affected Trailer quite differently; it made him want to sleep.

"You did what?" Donaldson demanded of Wrobleski.

"Captain, do I have to give everyone here a goddamned history lesson? These boys are Jap Zeros, son. We never meant them to come back."

"What the fuck're you talking about, Senator?"

"Jap Zeros, *Captain*." Wrobleski emphasized Donaldson's rank, his drawl disappearing as he spoke. "Nobody could figure how the Japs got their Zeros to fly so fast or maneuver like that. Then we found out how they did it. It's easy to design a ship to do what those Zeros did if you never expect to get any back.

"That's all these boys are," he finished, his drawl back in place. "These fancy soldier boys you made is Jap Zeros. Hell, I personally don't want them back. That's why they read like any other Special Forces team on paper, Jim. We can lose them that way."

"But why Evangelista? He'd be tried for war crimes fifty years ago and probably again today."

"MBFR negotiations, Captain. He and his friends are a little curious how your boys came about."

"What the hell did we make them for if we were just going to give them away?" he screamed.

Wrobleski smiled. "Because we could, Jimmy-Boy. Because we could. Sometimes, it's nice to know what can be done."

A bison asked, "What did you do when you found out what Wrobleski did, Jim?"

A rabbit stood beside the bison, both covered in blood. The rabbit had no ears. "Did you do the right thing? Did you kill them, Jimmy?"

We didn't have enough time to get Congressional approval.

Congress, even the Armed Services Committee, thought of file ONI 19701 as another DARPA pork-barrel project. The file didn't go into detail. It merely stated that "males from selected unstable environments were optioned for technically modified combat readiness development and training." So, with eighty percent of the service cycling stateside either dealing or using, with thirty-two percent of the body bags coming in without bodies but with pure grade, and with the majority of civilians protesting because either the price of their fix went up or the prediction of an Amazonas Syriana coming true, and especially with no northern South American country able to pay its World Bank, IMF and ITC loans and debt without trafficking grade, when Pancho sued for MBFR Congress was perfectly ready to commit.

When Pancho discretely told the negotiators he wanted the "ghosts who walk the jungles," the ONI saw a perfect solution. They didn't need to explain an internationally illegal activity to anyone and Pancho guaranteed the US rights to cultivation of the fields.

Donaldson held the rabbit, his hands covered in blood. The bison lay at his feet, much of its head blown away. Across from him sat Trailer as he had come out of the Orinoco; naked and soaking wet, his left knee cap cut out and beginning to regrow, ribs broken and ruptured through his skin, the soles of his feet beaten flat, and one eye partially out of his head, withdrawn into a small package and huddled in the far corner of a Connex box.

"I'm so sorry, Nick."

Trailer smiled, his features a little wider than normal. He inhaled deeply, lost in the memory and unable to return. "My mom's backing away, shaking her head, her hands are in front of her, her eyes are wide and she's crying and then she backs up into the counter and there's nowhere for her to go.

"Come on, ma. All the times you took me to bed and you think I'm going to hurt you? All the times you gave me that great mother love?"

"And her head slows and she looks at me. And she's got that look she gets when she's going to two-time the old man, you know? That *How can I do this and get away with it?* look? She's figuring how to get out of this. She's thinking maybe the kid's got some fur on his balls after all and she can make a break for it.

"'You won't hurt me?'

"You don't want me, mom? You always wanted me when there was nobody else around. How come you don't want me, mom?"

"And she smiles. She thinks she's out of it. She thinks she's going to survive.

"'You know there's nothing better than a mother's love, right, Nick?'

"She called me Nick. Every other time it was shit head, moron, you little SOB, you fucking bastard, even when she was fucking me or making me lick her, I was never Nick and now I'm Nick to her.

"'You want some mother love?' She lifts her dress. She spreads her legs and shows me what she's got. What the fuck was she planning? She's sitting down to lunch with guests and she doesn't have any underwear on?

"So I swung that little cast-iron frying pan for all it was worth, from behind my back and up between her legs and you should have heard the crack when it broke open her twat. I mean, I didn't know women had any bones up there.

"She screamed.

"'Shut up.' And again, Bing BuddaBang BuddaBoom. I split her from the bottom up.

"God, I never felt so good, so safe. Nobody's going to bother me ever again. I got a paper plate out of the cupboard and sat down. I hadn't had a chance to finish my lunch."

"When the police came, I was finishing. It was my first lunch where I didn't get sick when I ate, always wondering if I was eating right - my dad would grab the back of our heads and smash our faces into the table if we didn't eat right. Funny thing was we never knew what was right - or if I'd get enough to eat. I think the neighbors called the police.

"They must have heard something."

The man in the Connex box stood up and hobbled over to him. "SigRec."

Donaldson answered with Trailer's standard. "I see a dark sail on the horizon set under a dark cloud that hides the sun."

"You sent us in to die."

Donaldson remembered his response, his rationalization: I'm a soldier. I follow orders.

Trailer stopped talking. Donaldson looked up.

Across the table sat a monster with a plastic smile, the kernel for the Augmentation project. Trailer bludgeoned four people and completely separated himself from it, first driving the act into his own private DreamSpace then creating a surrogate self who could protect him. A primitive defense, splitting himself into two people, one good and the other evil. Trailer the good bore no responsibility for what

Trailer the evil did. He might as well have been stepping on an ant. A pure sociopathic schizophrenic act, devoid of any human feeling except one: Survival. Trailer produced an extremely healthy response to a recognized threat; he protected himself.

Now the sociopath sat across the table from him, its eyes wide open, its irises pulled back, letting all the light in the room into Trailer's mind. In the center of those eyes, Donaldson saw himself and the drop of sweat coming down his brow. Trailer gripped Donaldson's neck and lifted Donaldson until they stared each other eye-to-eye.

Trailer pulled his other hand back into a fist. "I remember one time, when I was about eight or nine, my mother took off with some friends. The baby-sitter split when her boyfriend wanted to get laid. I called Ma and told her I was all alone. She said that I was a big boy and to call her if anything went wrong. Well, the doorbell rings. Usually it's this cop my mom knows, big mother, who comes over after a drug bust. He brings over whatever he can score during the bust, brings over a couple of other cops and they go into the bedroom with mom and party. But mom's not home tonight so I don't know what I'm gonna do."

Trailer shook Donaldson like a small bell, dinging him every time Trailer wanted to emphasize some point. Donaldson's body flapped limply, a rain-soaked flag wrapped around its pole by the wind, his struggles futile against the Augmented Man's strength. Trailer's shaking him back and forth moved him closer and closer to Trailer's fist. Trailer's voice never rose or fell but remained steady, as if in a bar talking to a friend.

"Well, it's this guy I've never seen before. No idea who he is. They were supposed to get together that night, but good old mom, any chance to shoot, snort or fuck and she was there.

"This guy's standing in the doorway looking at me, looking into our house, I have no idea what's going to happen or how I'm going to get it this time.

"He asks me, 'Are you home alone?'

"'Yes, sir.'

"He smiles and kneels in front of me. 'Your mom's not home? Is she coming back soon?'

"'I don't know, sir.'

"'Maybe you could call her, find out when she's coming back. Could you do that for me?'

"Well, guess what? Nobody answers the phone. I call and I call and nobody answers the phone. This guy watches me and about the third time he says, 'Maybe I can help,' and he takes the phone from me. I'm scared cause I don't know what's going to happen and my hands are sweating and I'm shaking and this guy smiles at me, holds out his hand for the phone and says, 'Maybe I can help,' so I don't know what the fuck to do and I give him the phone.

"'I notice you were punching in the number. Do you know about speed dial?' and he puts her number on '5'. 'Here,' he says. 'All you have to do is press and hold 5 in the middle of the keypad to call her,' and he's got his eyes on me, real concerned like, and he's smiling but he's not really smiling, it's that *Jesus fuck what did I get myself into?* smile, and then he says, 'In case of emergency,' and I don't know what to do. Is this guy being nice to me? When's this guy going to bail? Everybody else does. I mean, what the fuck is that?

"This guy waits with me for about an hour and a half and then says try again. And I do, and you know what? This time mom answers the phone.

"'Where've you been, ma? I called before and you never answered the phone.'

"'You must have dialed the wrong number, Nicky.' So right there I know she's wasted because I'm never called Nicky unless she's drunk or pissed and wants something from me.

"'No, ma, I dialed it ten or twelve times.'

"'No, Nicky, it never rang here. You're wrong.'

"And this guy stares at the ground and pats my shoulder and we both knew. We both know because I'd either get voicemail or the phone would go live for a second and we could hear party noises on it.

"So we both knew there was never fucking going to be anybody there for me. Nobody was ever going to answer the phone."

Trailer's eyes fixed on Donaldson's. "You should learn to concentrate better."

Donaldson closed his eyes as the fist swung towards his face. It occurred to him that this situation felt comfortable. He was about to die and had no responsibility in the act. He couldn't stop it, couldn't thwart it. It felt like childhood with his father, like acting on those last orders sending the Augmenteds to their deaths - of being powerless, emasculated, violated.

A rush of wind pressed against Donaldson's face as Trailer's fist approached, blowing away that comfortable feeling, the rushing wind ripping away the lies he'd repeatedly told himself.

The floor came up under his feet. Trailer's hand release him.

Donaldson opened his eyes as Trailer screamed. He covered his ears but not in time. The Tank shook.

Trailer fell into one of the chairs by the table. Donaldson, momentarily deafened, couldn't hear but felt The Tank shaking with Trailer's wails and sobs.

Trailer looked up and Donaldson read his lips. "Why did this have to happen to me? Why did I continue? Why did I survive? Why did I go on? Why couldn't I die like the rest of them? Why me?"

Trailer's fist whipped past Donaldson's face and smashed into his own. "Why me?" Again the leviathan's fist slammed into its own face. "Why me?" he shrieked, again swinging his fist in.

What you going to do, Jim?

He reached out and took Trailer's fists in his hands, holding them down, hoping Trailer wouldn't lift him and use him as a cudgel to inflict any more self-damage.

Trailer shuddered a few times, the spasms passing through him and jarring Donaldson's teeth. He quieted and stared into Donaldson's eyes. Between sobs he said, "You took quite a chance. I could've killed you."

"You had lots of chances before this. Besides, you didn't resist when I held your hands. It isn't me you want to kill."

"But you were handy. You would have done nicely."

"Yes, Nick. That's the whole thing. I was handy. I'm not the one you wanted to kill, but I was handy."

"So who'm I trying to kill?"

"The last killing you did was in the bar. You didn't want to, but you used it to get our attention, correct?"

"You didn't respond to my TXTs and emails."

"You sent us TXT and emails?"

Trailer laughed so hard Donaldson covered his ears a second time. Once Trailer's laughter subsided, Donaldson continued, "You said you wanted us to kill you. Is that still true?"

"Sometimes I cry when I think about Karen."

Again, she is the crux. "Karen makes you cry?"

"No, not her. Just sometimes when I think about her."

"I don't understand."

"She married me." He tapped his chest."This. That's enough to make anybody cry."

"Nick, you understand we can't un-augment you. I can't give you back the body you came to us with. But you're not some kind of monster. You're a product of everything that happened to you as a kid - "

"And what you did to me during training."

Donaldson hesitated. "Yes, and what we did to you during training."

"I didn't want to be this way."

"You did sign consent - "

Trailer cut him off. "I was fifteen years old. You chose me because I was so psychologically damaged I didn't know down from up."

"Yes, yes. You're right. I'm not going to defend what we did. If it was defendable, we wouldn't have spent so much time covering it up."

Trailer's face again went plastic. He started moving towards Donaldson, slowly. "Damn right you covered it up."

"Nick, listen carefully; we can't un-augment you. We can...I can help you learn to live with your augmentation."

"You made me so that doing damage was a reward, remember?"

Trailer quoted from one of the many ONI briefs on Augmentation, "Minor CRISPR modification to the incentive salience pathway, specifically within the nucleus accumbens shell, ventral pallidum, and parabrachial nucleus of the pons, the insular cortex, and orbitofrontal cortex will cause a endocannabinoid release closely but not exactly mimicking sexual release when the augment initiates violent behavior.

"Talk about sex and violence. And I'm suppose to love someone? You fucking designed me to kill what I love."

"Tell me about Karen."

"What?"

"You're right, we designed you for violence. But you haven't told me you killed Karen. And you've hinted that one of the reasons she loves you is because wild animals trust you."

"So?"

"So some part of you has already learned to not kill what it cares about. And that's the point. We can give you new training, different training. Hell, what you did the other day right before you took that nap…"

Trailer started pacing. "No woman could want me this way."

"You're making a decision that's not yours to make. Karen's already made that decision unless you've been lying to me all along and she doesn't exist."

"Of course she exists."

"Then the only decision you have to make is if you want to live with her decision. We're not done, not by a long shot, but the first part is you deciding what you want and going for it."

Trailer stopped pacing and stared at him. His voice rumbled from his chest. "Don't you think I want to be well?"

A pause.

"Do you think I want to be like this?"

Another pause. He shook his head. "We…"

A final pause. He shook his head. His traps, mastoids, pecs, and delts tensed, the osteogenized skin surfaces softly crackled like wax paper unwrapping a sandwich.

He took a breath in while he moved his head in an arc, as if trying to see something on a far horizon. "I..."

Quiet. Let him do the work. Just be here when he's done.

"I...choose..."

A soft voice, a song, not a rumble, and quiet, private, something not to be shared, something only to be heard by those willing to hear, whispered through the woods and drifted across the fields.

Medea, the horse, raised her head, her eyes and ears focused on the edge of the field. The llamas looked up and focused their ears. The ewe baaahed, gathered up her two lambs and trotted off in that direction.

"Sheila!" Karen called out. "Get those lambs back here." She hurried into the barn and came out with a double-barrel shotgun. "Goddamn sheep." She loaded two shells and snapped the barrel up.

The shotgun moved faster than she intended, something lifting it up and away quicker than her hands could adjust.

"Please tell me you aren't afraid of me."

"Nick." Karen's voice changed from frustration to joy in one word. She grabbed his horse blanket poncho and pulled herself up to kiss him. He bent over, not touching her, just making himself an easier target for her.

One on each cheek and then on the lips.

He purred.

Then she slapped him.

"Hey."

"You scared me. I thought you might be a bear coming for the lambs."

"Doesn't mean you have to hit me. Besides, bears would make more noise. And no bears will bother you."

She ignored him, pulling him towards the house. "I made you cookies."

"The horse?"

She shook her head.

"The llamas?"

Another shake framed with a smile.

"The sheep? The chickens."

"Guess again."

"Who?"

"The raccoons. They came last night, stood up and stared at the barn. They know the kitchen door's too small for you to fit through. I came out and they stayed so I asked them, 'Is Nick coming?' They came up to me looking for cookies and looking at the barn, so I knew you'd be here sometime today."

"Little snitches."

"A friend of yours came by yesterday. At least he knows you, who you are."

Nick stood up, his movement lifting Karen off her feet and into him. "Who?"

"Tom Rivers. Nice guy. Good looker, too. Blonde, blue-eyed, nice smile."

Nick's chin quivered.

"Don't you know by now that nobody's handsomer to me than you."

"I..."

"For the past seven years, He-Man, I've waited only for you, I've wanted only you. There's been no one for twenty years before that and they'll be no one for the rest of my life and whatever comes next."

He lifted her gently, cradling her in his arm as a father might cradle a child. "Will you...will you love me the rest of my life?"

"The rest of your life, the rest of my life and whatever comes after."

He kissed her gently, butterfly wings brushing her lips.

"That tickles."

"What did he want?"

"Just said to say hi, that he'd been hoping to meet you on the trails sometime, that he'd be looking for you."

He put her down. "I can't stay."

Her shoulders fell, the joy left her voice, she turned away. "Take some cookies with you then. And I made you some clothes. Take that rag off. Medea wouldn't even wear that." She smiled at the horse. "Sorry, girl. No offense."

"I may be gone for a while."

"More than your usual 'a while'?"

He nodded.

"I'd like you to stay the night. Some time."

"So would I," he whispered into the wind, then to her, "Do you remember one time you made a video of me with the llamas? You wanted to share it with your family and I asked you not to. Do you still have it?"

She reached into her blouse and pulled out a tiny gold heart memory chip locket on a thin gold anchor chain. "I keep it with me always. I watch it some nights when you're not here."

"I will be here. Soon. Forever. I promise."

She shook her head. "Promises make a thin soup, Nick."

"Have I ever lied to you?"

She shook her head again.

"I'm promising you. I will be here, soon and forever." He lifted her hands in his and kissed them. "I promise."

"I believe you, Nick. I do."

"I need your locket."

She pulled her hands back. "What for?"

"I just do. Trust me?" He got on his knees, their faces almost equal height. "Please?"

"Take it. Just bring it back to me. You bring it back to me."

"I promise." He debated asking her to leave, to pack up what she needed, send the animals to some other farmers for a while, get in her truck and go.

He lifted her up as he stood. It wouldn't matter. Rivers knew who she was, what she looked like. The Farm probably had aerials of her circulating through its memory tanks back in Virginia.

He cradled her in his arms and kissed her.

She shivered slightly. He kissed her so rarely. And his touch, so gentle, excited her so.

He breathed deep, inhaling every scent of her. "I love you."

She pushed away slightly, still in his arms, waiting until his eyes met hers. "You've never said that before."

"Now I know what it means. All that it means."

His massive hands moved like feathers. She breathed deep, filling herself with his scent. Her heartbeat quickened as the taste of his lips met hers. She closed her eyes.

And then he vanished, not even footprints showing where he'd been.

She clenched her fists and screamed, then shook, frustration commanding her body.

7 DAYS UNTIL TERMINATION

Donaldson woke to The Tank in daylight mode. He lay quietly, eyes closed, evaluating and debating.

Definitely a pattern. Donaldson didn't know if Nick recognized the pattern but a pattern existed nevertheless; there's a breakthrough of some kind, some revelation of Nick to his psyche, and then he's gone for a day or two.

The other day was, perhaps, *the* breakthrough: the first phase of the intimacy model skewed for Augmented psychology. Seven days remained, something both knew. If the intimacy model held, sometime and hopefully soon, Trailer would do something to determine if Donaldson was still emotionally available to him. After that, Trailer would share "real information," the core thoughts and beliefs that made up his existence. Donaldson had done his part. He had listened and been rewarded with a piece of Trailer's belief system: "Karen married me. This." Trailer's somatic remained psychologically distinct from his physical self.

The next part of the intimacy model moved from emotional

availability to intentional availability; a demonstration by Donaldson that Trailer had personhood, had meaning in Donaldson's life, that Donaldson placed a real value on Trailer's existence, that Trailer's existence enriched him and losing Trailer somehow diminished him.

People who are naturally intimate demonstrate intentional availability automatically via active and attentive listening; the amount they focus on a person demonstrates that person's value both in the moment and in their life. To demonstrate real value, Donaldson needed to demonstrate active and attentive listening, an indication of Trailer's importance in Donaldson's life.

But Trailer's augmentation might misconstrue active and attentive listening as presaging an attack; untrained combatants focus on their adversary to the exclusion of all else. Warriors focus on their environment until the moment of attack. Augments use their environment as an element of their attack, there's no difference between target and non-target to them.

The question, Nick, is what will your point of view be during this next phase; your own history will be in direct - fuck that, probably violent - conflict with the new information I'll be modeling. You'll work to prove to yourself your old worldview is correct. You'll do everything you can to force me to give up on you.

Well, I hope not *everything* you can do.

But you will work to make me leave, stop listening, stop caring and give up on you.

You'll need that to prove to yourself that you were always correct about others hence yourself, that you're not worth anybody's time.

That first part is going to be easy. It's the last part we've got to dance real slow; I'll have to empathize, to associate with your pain.

A good therapist doesn't let their own bullshit get in the way of the client's work. Or they recognize their own bullshit's going to get in the way and recuse themselves before engaging with the client.

Well. Ain't this going to be fun, then.

Donaldson rolled over to see Nick's broad back poking out of the sheets on the other bed. Where he'd been, when he left or when he returned, remained mysteries.

"Nick? You hungry?"

Nick got up to make breakfast. Donaldson noted the home-tailored shirt and pants.

If you're not making your own clothes, Mr. Trailer, who is?

"Why did you choose us?" A simple question but the tone was aggressive, anticipatory.

The next phase is coming sooner than I thought. "What do you mean?"

"I talked with the others. We all had shit lives. That was the only thing we all had in common: Wartella, Caron, Cummings, MacNeil, St.Onge, Vergato, Lukach, Baron, and me. Why us?"

Donaldson hesitated. He'd already formed the answer and knew Trailer had heard his subvocalization. "We only selected individuals with catastrophic trauma in their childhoods. We needed individuals with strong survival instincts and drive already built in. Children with your background, they either 'failed to thrive' - that's what it's called - or developed acute survival skills. The Augmenteds were the ones who'd developed all the necessary tools for psychological survival. You came to us from a psywar worse than anything anyone'd experienced in any real arena."

"I remember you telling us 'Nothing that's going to happen to you is going to be as bad as what has happened to you'."

"Yes, I remember that. It was true as far as we knew. The crux of the Augmentation Project hinged on that. We selected people already suffering from PTSD. All of you had already developed powerful mental defenses. All of you came to us emotionally hardened. All we had to do was give the bodies a chance to catch up to what the mind and spirit had already done."

"But you said you were going to help us."

"Yes, Nick, we said that."

"No, not *we*. You said that. You, Jim Donaldson. You said you were going to make it okay for us. Did you really think you were helping us?"

The bison asked, "Were you being a good little soldier, Jimmy Boy?"

"I was following orders, Nick."

"Yeah? Whose orders are you following now?"

"Nobody's. I was called and asked if I wanted to be here, given the option. If I said no, they would have liberated you while you were in the hyperbaric chamber, at the hospital in Manchester."

"So why're you here?"

The bunny had no ears.

"I... don't know. Because it's important to me."

Someone screamed, "Are you a good little soldier? Are you going to make me proud?"

Donaldson focused on Trailer. Trailer no longer maintained Tank discipline. They'd finished breakfast an hour ago and Trailer still hadn't cleaned the dishes, another aspect of Nick's signature being affected. The Augmented Men left no trails, no traces. Even something as subtle as not doing the dishes demonstrated a submerged desire to negate his training, to come to surface, *to be found.*

"If I leave again, will you come for me?" Nick's voice faltered, its resonance gone. Each word seemed to migrate up from his chest.

"You usually come back."

"I know, but if I don't. Will you come?"

"I'm afraid I'd have to, not that I'd want to."

"I'm not worth it?"

"Oh, it's not you, Nick. You're worth it. I'm afraid I'd have to come after you - "

"To kill me, right? If you don't prove me negotiable in seven more days, you have to kill me."

"I don't want you dead, Nick. Besides, you could have killed yourself without all this in the past month. You're too much of a survivor. You've spent most of your life trying to kill what's inside of you. But that's who your parents are, not who you are. You're caught in the ultimate paradox. Trained to kill and trained to survive. You can't complete the primary sanction but your target is always right there, staring at you. Now you're going after some kind of secondary function. Nobody can give it to you. You've got to find it yourself. Last month the pressure got so bad you sanctioned whatever was handy."

"Like the other night, you were handy."

"Something like that, yes."

"Then how am I handy to you? If I'm suffering from something like PTSD, what're you suffering from?"

"What?"

"Come on, Major. I'm ugly but I'm not stupid. You want to help me? You should know the best way for you to help me is to let me know you're just like me."

"I am just like you."

The smile left Trailer's face as it slid back to plasticity. He walked to his corner and started folding, caught himself and stood up, leaning against the wall. His face remained plastic, the whale watched Donaldson from behind a great glass. A voice came quietly, sneaking over the table like the roll of distant thunder across a plain. "Whose orders you following now, Major? Jim?"

"Nick, I - "

"You made me kill children," he interrupted. "That last run you sent us on. You knew it was a schoolhouse, not a command post, right? They were kids. You set us up, didn't you? There was no reason we had to kill those kids."

Yes, I set you up. I agreed to it, anyway.

"We didn't have to. It was our last run. You knew Pancho was going to capture us. What was the point of killing children if we were going to be captured anyway?"

Because I...

"I'm sorry, Jim, I didn't quite catch that. Could you repeat yourself?"

Because I...

Donaldson's breakfast came up, fast. Trailer met it with one of the plastic grocery bags he'd left between the cabinet and the refrigerator.

"That's a violent bioneurophysiologic response there, Jim. The brain produces a thought so terrifying, so abhorrent, the body evacuates itself in preparation for a flight response. Usually a memory causes such responses, something the body couldn't escape at the time it engrammed so the body violently attempts an escape at the time of remembrance."

Trailer tilted his head to the side. His tone changed, became privately conversational. "How'm I doing so far, Jim?"

He straightened his head up, his tone back to his previous. "We need to go further, Jim. We need to finish that thought."

Because I also learned to abuse the innocents.

He violated himself again.

"Go on, Jim. Finish the thought. Bring it all out."

"Protocol forced me to go in with a Recon team and give the appearance of finding you. The Augmenteds. We knew Pancho had immobilized you the day before. Nothing...wasn't ready...wasn't prepared."

"Go on. You can do it, Jim. Get it out."

"Your last run...deployed as a group...you rarely deployed as a group. You traveled as a group but handled objectives individually or two-man teams comprised of Hunter/Seeker and Liberator."

Trailer handed Donaldson a dish towel. Donaldson wiped vomit from his lips and chin.

"This time you went all together. Each of you knew your job. You..."

"Yes, Jim?"

"Your job was to plant a thermally sealed dry ice charge with a photosensitive fuse and a core-suspended threshold detonator."

"That almost sounds nice, like your describing some kind of fancy Christmas ornament I was supposed to hang on somebody's tree."

"That was your part in the mission."

"And pencils misspell words, cars drive drunk, and spoons make people fat. Like I said, I'm ugly, not stupid. Don't mistake me for an idiot. Our job was...?"

"To blow up children. To kill innocents."

Within a few minutes of children taking their seats in the class-room, after their teacher had opened the doors, blinds, and windows to let air in, there would be enough light in the room for the photosensitive fuse to rupture the thermal seal. The dry ice began evaporating, which drew room air around the detonator, blowing the dry ice apart and sending pieces out radially up to one thousand meters per second, a sound similar to someone popping their finger out of their mouth the only warning. Within minutes the dry ice went straight into gas. You'd need good eyes to find pieces of the seal and a gas spectrometer to detect a slight staleness of the air.

The bodies, shattered and torn apart, revealed the ingenuity of the bomb. The smaller dry ice pieces got razor-sharp edges as they melted against warm flesh.

Outside they found a bison with a broken leg, the leg clearly sliced by one of the dry ice projectiles, licking its wound and bellowing. Licking to perhaps keep off the ants swarming it and bellowing to perhaps lament its frustration in its hopeless task.

One of the recon team took out his pistol and blew the beast's throat out, yelling, "Shut up, God damn it."

Like Trailer, the bison didn't die.

"I'm sorry, Nick."

"There's nothing to be sorry about. We knew what you were planning. We didn't know they were kids, though, until we got there and there was no scent of grownups. But we hadn't any dust on us to stop us from what we were ordered to do. You did that. You made sure we would complete our mission. Soon as it went down, up comes Pancho halfway between us and ground and he's dusting us. They took me back. They made me look. Nice mission to send me on, Jim. Thanks. I appreciate it, truly I do."

I'm sure you do.

The legacy of the abused child, Nick spent most of his life trying to finish the job his parents had started, his mind adapting and swarming like ants over that bison's leg to survive his childhood, then his body made practically indestructible to do it. Donaldson sent him on a mission Trailer could never allow himself to complete. Killing a child meant Trailer became his parents, whom he had already killed. But becoming his already dead parents meant he had to die and above all else, he survived. Everything. His entire structure, brain to bone, designed to survive.

"The reason that last mission was to kill children," Donaldson explained, "was in case anything went wrong. Pancho could accuse you of war crimes. There would be no one to defend you."

"There never was."

Back in the forest, back in the jungle, in the Orinoco where the schoolhouse had been, Donaldson walked over to the man who shot the bison and knocked him to the ground. The man rolled with the punch and turned his weapon on Donaldson.

Donaldson screamed at him, "Is that who we are? Is that what we're all about?" He drew his own revolver and fired into the bison's skull. The bullet ricocheted off the horn and buried itself in the beast's right eye.

It didn't move, except for some slight twitching of its broken leg. A bubbling sound escaped its throat as it breathed.

Donaldson fired another shot into its skull. The beast stopped twitching, but it still breathed. He grabbed the pointman's duckbill, pressed it between the bison's eyes, and fired all four barrels into the creature's brain. What remained looked like a bowl of brain stew.

The men around him laughed at his failed attempts at mercy. One of the men picked up the good remaining horn. "This has gotta be worth something, man, it's just gotta." He placed it in his pack.

In his mind's eye, the bison, as he'd last seen it, gazed up at him with its single remaining eye. "Is it okay, Jim? Can I die now?"

"I didn't want to do it. They made me do it. I didn't want to hurt you. I - " I'm no different from Trailer's cousin, David, fearing retibution from Rosemary and Paul. Is this how oppression starts? We so fear for ourselves we'll willingly sacrifice another? His eyes misted and his voice cracked. "God damn but I didn't want them to kill you."

"What's-a-matter? Want to kill us yourself? Afraid to kill me yourself?"

"Kill it, son." Donaldson looked up, his head shaking, snapping as he focused from point to point to isolate the voice's origin, finally staring into his hands.

"I said kill it!"

He held a dead rabbit in his hands, its blood still flowing from multiple wounds.

The voice screamed, "Are you going to be a good little soldier? What do you do when you're given an order, son?"

Donaldson fell to his knees before the whale, Nick's face shifting back and forth too rapidly for Donaldson to determine his state, only the whale's large eyes, maintaining their focus on his, remained unchanging.

"I was following orders." Donaldson shook, wanting to die, not knowing how to do it, his own rage coming out. "No one would help me. I wanted to die and no one would help me."

"I can kill you, if you want. I've thought about fragging you since New Year's Day."

Donaldson looked at the behemoth before him. He nodded, violently, unable to speak, now drooling, bubbling spit foaming out of his mouth.

"Tell me about the rabbits, George."

Donaldson's eyes fixed on Trailer. His mouth opened and he shook slightly. A snort followed by two tiny laughs. He wiped his mouth with his sleeve then reached over and gently slapped Trailer's face and laughed harder. "'Tell me about the rabbits, George'?" He sat with his back to the wall as the laughter caught every few words. "I didn't know you were that literate, Nick."

"Karen reads to me. We read books together. *Of Mice and Men*, one of my favorites. So tell me about the rabbit, Jim."

Donaldson rolled onto his side, laughing, laughing until his laughter turned to tears. "When I was a kid, six years old, I was out in the yard with my dad, mowing. I was steering the mower and he was walking behind me talking with a friend. I looked down and the grass was all red. I stopped and saw a little bunny at my feet. A baby bunny. I reached down to pick it up. It had no ears, just two red stumps where the mower had ripped them off. I turned to my dad. My hands were covered in blood. 'Look what I did to the bunny, Dad. Help me. We've got to help it.' My dad said, 'Kill it, son,' then started talking with his friend again. I said, 'No, Dad. We have to try to save it. We hurt it. Now we have to help it.' I remember my dad. He's upset, maybe embarrassed. 'Kill it, son. Just kill it.' I started crying, feeling the pain of the bunny and wanting to die for it, to make good for my mistake. 'No, I can't, Dad. I want to help it.' My dad yelled at me then, 'Do you want to be a good little soldier, Jimmy Boy? Are you going to be a good little soldier and make your father proud? Or do you disobey an order when I give it to you? Is that the kind of soldier you are?' I was crying hard then, 'I can't, dad.' So my father took the rabbit in my hands and made me toss it in front of the mower again, then he held my hands on the mower handle, and he made me push it back and forth over the rabbit. When the rabbit was dead, he wiped his hands on my shirt, adjusted his uniform, and went in the house with his friend.

The bunny, its bleeding head in his hands, stared up at him. "Is it okay for me, too, Major Donaldson? Can I die now, too? I'd really like to die."

"I can still remember hearing that rabbit's screams over the sound of the mower."

"You're just like me, aren't you."

"Yes, I guess I am."

"I kind of think everybody is. The lucky ones know it."

Donaldson wiped his nose on his sleeve and wiped the tears from his eyes. The bison and bunny, both on the ground before him, put paw in hoof, waved, and said goodbye.

"Tell me about us, Jim. You didn't want to help us - " Donaldson looked up and Nick smiled, " - at least not then. What were you trying to do with us? Were we some kind of experiment or did you have something in mind?"

"Oh, we had something in mind. Laqueur wrote 'The only promising way to improve intelligence performance is to select recruits who have at least some of the faculties needed, and then give them a good training' in the mid-1980s. He was right as far as he went with it.

"There were lots of key characteristics in the recruitment protocol. Fear and distrust were near top of the list and always come together, never singly. Or rarely. Anyway, we wanted to foster that fear and distrust.

"Some people who survive your background develop various schizotypal states as part of their survival mechanism. We wanted to trigger you people into a perpetual schizo-affective state, to instill a controllable social psychopathism in all of you. That's why we fed you Naltrexone during training. It made you desperate for the traumatic bonding that went on in your homes. Most of you had already learned to ignore massive physical insult. All we needed to do was finish the job.

"We gave you permission to live out your wildest childhood revenge fantasies. Do you remember we had you read about Amin, Gaddafi, Pol Pot? Hell, we had records about sadistic motherfuckers as far back as Caligula, King Herod, and the Ceasars. We showed you videos of Hitler, Baby Doc, Shwe, ... it's amazing what these men knew.

"And we showed them to you like they were home movies. Hell, to you Augments, they were."

Trailer's eyes closed. "Yes, they were."

"We said, 'Here's your blueprint. Here's your template. See if you can do better,' because we knew you couldn't experience guilt about your missions because you were already driven by the primary belief that you were guilty, period. You didn't think humans were going on your missions, you thought monsters were, and monsters never have remorse or seek forgiveness for what they do, so we were covered, we were good. We selected you because you thought you were morally wrong before we ever got to you."

Donaldson wiped his mouth, finished explaining. He got up and took the towel into the lav. "But any functional society's role is to protect, not to exploit." He ran water. There were splashing sounds.

Trailer called after him, "That part about schizotypal states. That's like hearing voices? Stuff like that?"

Donaldson, wiping his face with a clean towel, stood in the lav door. "Why do you ask that?"

"There was a time I thought I could read minds." Trailer waited for the reaction, waiting for the parental dismissal. "I guess that was just some of the schizophrenia, huh? Just paying so much attention to everybody else I thought I could read their minds?"

"I don't know, Nick. It's not uncommon, though. People subjected to what you went through as a kid. It's called *Forced Adaptation*, an aspect of *Theory of Mind*. Some people call it mind reading. Theory of Mind is how we anticipate someone else's behavior, how we understand their reality. We need it to socially survive. Forced Adaptation is one step further, when one person has to adapt to the another person's reality. You got good at it, way better than most, so you could survive. Maybe that's why you thought you could read minds. I'm sorry you had to go through it."

"You know I can tell when you're lying?"

"Am I lying?"

"I had nothing else to do, so I remembered my life. I don't even know everything they were doing to my body, but I remembered everything anybody ever did to me growing up. Hell of a refuge, don't you think? But you know what? It was safe. It was safe because it got me away from where I was. And so I was a kid all over again, hating where I was but finding safety in the pain I'd always known. Is that what you meant to teach us?"

"No, Nick. Again, I'm sorry. I wish it'd never happened. Unfortunately it did. There's nothing I can do about it. There's nothing you can do about it. It's going to be with you until you let go of it."

"'A' can torture 'B' for a month. Maybe a year, depending on how strong 'A' and 'B' are. But 'B' can torture 'B' forever. Funny thing is, usually 'B' will take on the job if 'A' stops."

"Yes, Nick. That's right." Donaldson tossed the towel into the combo washer-drying and stared at the buttons, searching for one labeled "Bison/Bunny Blood." "That's right."

Nick waited for Donaldson to come out of the lav. "You remember that guy I told you about, the one who stayed with me when I couldn't reach my mother? I remember him. He never left. When my mother got home, he yelled at her for leaving me alone like that and coming home fried on Fentanyl, coke, whatever it was she was high on. I yelled at him to leave her alone. I took it out on him and all he did was let me know somebody was there for me."

"Do you want to talk about that?"

"Yeah, I do. I want to talk about a lot of things. Not right now, though. But that guy." Nick's words slowed. His eyes defocused and his head tilted slightly, like a dog trying to understand its master's command. "I remember him."

Bingo! That's his kernel, that's his role model, that's who he's basing his new mythology on.

And it's somebody I'll never know.

Nick continued, his attention again on Donaldson followed by defocusing and repositing. "He's like Karen."

He's doing a trans-derivational search. He's selecting memories to base a new mythology on.

Donaldson's eyes roved The Tank's one room, searching for things to support Trailer's transition. His current external information is insufficient for him to function. He's searching his own internal libraries, his memories and experiences, for the missing information.

Nick's next words came without a repositing to his immediate reality. "Like you."

Here it comes. This is it.

Nick was redesigning how he experiences reality, coming up with new methods for understanding his environment, directing all his augmented faculties internally, computations clicking faster than a normal man could think or follow as he sought new ways to match information to existing values and beliefs.

He's using his programming to change his programming. And all I can do is sit back and watch.

Nick's external behaviors testified to his internal work of redefining his life - the defocused eyes, the slowed speech, the head slowly tilting right then left then right again, the dog trying to understand, different cerebral hemispheres going on- and off-line to understand and incorporate the new information.

"Every time I come back here, you're waiting. Every time I go home, she's there, waiting." The eyes focused, the head became straight upon the shoulders, and the words paced as for normal conversation as Nick finished, "She loves me, you know. I have proof. You wanted to know if she's real. She made this a while ago and let me have it to show you."

He handed Karen's locket to Jim.

"Thanks. I don't have a reader in here, Nick. Mind if I go get one?"

"Before you go, tell me something; can two sick people get well together?"

Donaldson considered. "I don't think so, no."

"That's what I thought, too. Do you know that when I came back I was so righteous nobody would shake my hand." He held his hand out to Donaldson.

Donaldson took it. Trailer's hand enveloped his like a hurricane enveloping a child's toy boat. He waited for crushing pain.

But Trailer shook his hand gently and stared into his eyes. "You know, I've never hurt Karen. I've been afraid to touch her. Time to go change that, don't you think?"

4 DAYS UNTIL TERMINATION

Donaldson regained consciousness slowly, alone, The Tank's inner and outer doors open with daylight streaming down the hallway between the inner and outer walls. The world rotated and he fell back onto his bed. He could breathe without difficulty and move without pain, albeit lethargically.

And three times pays for all. The next time, Nick, the next time I can't let you live. Half crawling and half staggering to the outer door, he saw nothing but bodies in the compound. He called out and got no response. The nearest body was breathing, and that gave him hope. His vision blurred and he started falling again.

A strong arm grabbed him around the waist and held him up. Instinct overrode logic and he snapped his elbow back to where a face might be. Something caught and gently lowered his arm.

"It's me, Jim. Rivers."

Donaldson let Rivers lift him up and didn't remember anything else for the rest of the day.

He woke up in his cabin sometime during the night. Rivers sat in a chair across from him, waiting. Donaldson asked, "What happened?"

"Nobody knows. I was in the hole getting the EEGSL transmitted when it went down." He tossed a packet onto the coffee table. "None of the surface personnel saw him or know what happened to them. ElInt shows negative. Security is neither breached nor compromised. And by the way, he showed no preparation sets. He's not going off, he's continuous."

"Yeah, but continuous what?"

"Nobody knows."

Donaldson ran his eyes over the room and then back to Rivers. Rivers nodded.

"Can you track him?"

"I think so. I have the element of surprise. I should leave as soon as possible, though."

"We still don't know - "

Rivers cut him off. "Let me try." He smiled and, as his smile grew, nictating membranes moved out of the corners of his eyes, stopping when they popped out contacts covering feline pupils. His nose twitched and a prosthetic fell off his upper lip, revealing split and flowing membranous nostrils, a horseshoe bat's nose on a human face. He snapped his head and prosthetics fell off his ears. The prosthetics flattened his real ears back against his head. Now free, his ears moved independently, prehensilely. They were larger than normal ears, ribbed for acoustic channeling and veined to act as heat sinks, adding to a normal body's heat dissipating neuro-venous and -arterial contacts during long distance pursuits and cursorial tracking.

Donaldson, staring at Rivers, corrected the assessment he made thirty days earlier at the Chelmsford bar: Not Aryan. An ambush predator, a ground hunter.

Donaldson, when told that Trailer had surfaced at the Chelmsford bar, summoned a Hawker Hunter X, a VTOL in civilian trim minus the optically guided antitank guns, 20mm cannons, and TOW missiles, to a local airpad near his rural Vermont home. Once airborne he had nothing to do for a while, so he slept.

And dreamed.

Of young men, the youngest fifteen, submerged in vats, old wines being given new skins while they slept, for many days, weeks, years in subjective time, as electrodes and enzymes tickled and teased their flesh, their bones, their minds. Fluids moving through sluices in the vats making their bodies as pliable as newborns, as eager to grow, to change, to adapt.

He dreamt of surgeries, of fetal cell clonings fostered inside these young men, of organogenetic implantations to modify vital functions using differentiated cells under forced oncogenesis; creating targeted, beneficial cancers to add mass to bone and muscle. He dreamt of stimulating muscles to grow muscles and bone to grow bone, electro-osteal, -dermal, -cortial, and -immunal manipulations to their bodies, growth growing growth, and of feeding his young men fevers and fears, hormones and hyruonics, and how it changed these boys into monstrosities in the shape of men.

He dreamt of the supraliminal conditioning that he, personally, had done to them.

To each and every one of them.

To make their minds match their bodies.

Those young boys.

His cattle.

And when he woke up, he was drenched in sweat.

The VTOL landed in the heart of the Georgian Appalachia. As they approached, Donaldson saw what appeared to be a manufacturing plant the size of a four-square football field. ArborVitaes, easily visible from the air or as one approached from the highway, neatly spelled out "Welcome to Berman Pharmaceuticals." He consulted on the design and served as DO for its use, but he'd only been here once before, years before he required its services.

The standard array of corporate communications equipment - from fractal-core antennae to telecomm whips - festooned the roof of the building. In the midst of these stood another antenna, almost innocuous amongst the others. It looked like a weird old-style TV antennae except for the top that flared slightly into two bulbous nodes, one facing up and the other facing out. That and that alone, if you knew what was what, meant that this facility handled more than corporate communication. It surprised Donaldson that a more secured or hardened means of contacting Washington hadn't been instituted, but it didn't matter if only negotiable data were exchanged.

Behind the facility a rather obvious looking electric fence held back mountains, separating them from a landing pad. He noticed small boxes the size of Christmas tree ornaments placed on each fencepost, each fencepost carrying four such boxes evenly spaced on their surface. Wires ran from a few of the fenceposts, finishing the image of standard electric fencing, but Donaldson noticed the grass around each fencepost grew contragrade to the grass surrounding it, and all the contragrades grew inside the fence, designed to keep those within the fence inside the fence. He remembered it this way. He'd planned and designed it this way. He found no changes or tamperings.

Nothing came in and nothing went out.

He hoped.

He walked through Berman Pharmaceuticals' corridors without a word. Occasionally he smiled. As the facility's ArborVitaes indicated, the plant was designed for pharmaceuticals and, as far as anyone could make out, that's what it did.

As he neared the geographic center of the plant, he started to pass through a series of offices. He'd already passed through some standard operations offices when he entered the plant. This second set of offices had no windows and only one door entering from the outer plant. Donaldson walked through to a still smaller set of offices.

Here differences became obvious. Active equipment replaced the passive pharmaceutical testing and development equipment, more and more people hurried about in full-length, white labcoats, so like the robes of some religious order, moving like acolytes unsure of the altar, more and more life-support, cloning, histology, hemetology, oncology, dermatology, osteobiology…but no test animals. Simply signs of augmentation technology and labs.

He continued towards the geographic center of the plant. People greeted him with "Sir," capital implied.

Finally he came to a corridor with a single door. The door had both secure-entry locks and pressure bolts. A set of eyecups, like binoculars set into the wall beside the door, with a speaker above and an horizontal electronic card reader beneath, stared at him. Someone had drawn a nose between the eyecups and card reader, barely discernible, barely recognizable and still there. Not a normal nose, it hinted at what waited inside.

Donaldson pulled what looked like a store discount card out of his pocket. He passed the card through the reader and looked into the eyecups as the backglow of low power lasers washed his face.

A rich, male voice, a melodious tenor, came over a speaker above the door. "Yes."

"It's Donaldson."

The locks sighed as pneumatic cylinders released. The door's pressure bolts started to unwind. Once unwound, electric motors swung the door slowly open.

As his eyes grew accustomed to the low lighting, his skin tingled with the laboratory cold and his nose scrunched at the familiar smell of maggots.

No, he corrected himself. Necrosis.

Maggots would eat away necrotic tissue and leave healthy tissue alone, hence found favor in certain surgical theaters. Underneath that came another familiar scent, slightly stronger than the odor from a moist cut after removing a band-aid. He looked around and saw a bleeder of Factor VIII Recombinant blood substitute.

Some things never change, he thought. It had been twenty years since he'd smelled that mix of hospital antiseptic, agars, high-yield cell cultures, and nutrient soups. The fumes came together with the sour smell of destructive recomposition. He breathed in short gasps, as if oxygenating before an ocean dive, giving his lungs a chance to adapt.

The melodious tenor spoke from the room's center. "Takes a

moment, doesn't it?"

Monitoring equipment covered the walls from floor to ceiling and Donaldson glanced at them as he continued into the room. Various black cables and tubes ran from the walls through concentric rings suspended from the ceiling to equipment, some permanently mounted into the floor, some on casters.

The cables and tubes never intertwined or overlapped, each cable and tube kept separate from its neighbors and so many of them they blocked out all overhead lighting. Illumination came from the multiple readouts, dials, and gauges located on the walls and machinery, leaving everything in the dim shadows of blue, green, red, and gray afterglow. Some of the cables and tubes were as thick as Donaldson's thighs, and he had the impression a monstrous and meticulous spider had been busy building a web from which to descend. Sounds of electric and pneumatic switches opening and closing filled the room, steady as a machine and as subtle and rasping as an old man's last breaths.

Donaldson followed all the equipment and suspended hardware to its focus: a clear-walled, cylindrical tank, two meters across by three meters tall in the center of the room. All the cables and tubes either descended or ended there. The image of a spider remained, patiently waiting in the center of its web, waiting for prey. An old style TV set with a cable feed running off the back rested on a platform above the tank and facing it.

"Programming?" asked Donaldson.

"Movies," came the voice, now coming from the tank in front of him. "I like to watch old movies."

Something sloshed inside the tank and a mannish form lifted itself out. Donaldson couldn't be sure due to the lighting but the face seemed malformed, or not finished forming, basically something incomplete about it.

The fluid in the tank still sloshed. Donaldson felt more than saw the spider start to descend.

The man held out his hand. "Hi, Dad."

"It is customary to offer a salute before the salutation, Lieutenant."

"Sorry, Sir." Rivers saluted and held it until Donaldson's release.

Donaldson offered his hand and Rivers took it. Rivers' hand was as cold and wet as the body from a damaged grave.

"Go back to your movies, Lieutenant. We'll be traveling north in a few hours."

Rivers moved like a snake, folding himself up and over the rim of his tank. As the fluid sloshed and lapped, the cables and wires and lines reattached themselves to his body.

Donaldson left the room. The door swung back into place and motors screwed the pressure bolts into their channels.

Rivers reminded Donaldson of an alien who'd learned to mimic human facial expressions but didn't have the equipment to pull it off. "Go ahead. Requisition what you need. Anything you can't find here, leave a list and I'll have it waiting for you at Loring in five hours. He's got a wife, Karen, in Stacyville. He might head there. I don't know."

Rivers left.

Donaldson came out of the shower a little while later, his neck and back sore, but he couldn't feel any swelling and had no bruises. Rivers left his list on the dresser and Donaldson started packing. The 201 files were still on the coffee table in the middle of the cabin. Donaldson picked them up and counted through them. "Baron, Caron, Cummings, Lukach, MacNeil, St.Onge, Trailer, Vergato, Wartella; Phase Zero." He stopped.

He held the files up and read the names as he went through them again. "Baron, Caron, Cummings, Lukach, MacNeil, St.Onge, Trailer, Vergato, Wartella." He opened the cabin door and called over a guard dressed as a trail guide. "Corporal, has anybody been in this cabin since I arrived?"

"No, sir. Lieutenant Rivers stood station while you were in The Tank. I took duty when he left."

"How long ago did Rivers leave?"

"About twenty minutes, sir."

"Get him on the comm."

"He left on foot, Major. He didn't take any supplies or comms with him."

Donaldson nodded and closed the door. The 201s still in his hand, he opened and scanned them individually. "Baron, Caron, Cummings, Lukach, MacNeil, St.Onge, Trailer, Vergato, Wartella." He threw the 201s on the bed. "Lieutenant, there is no element of surprise anymore. Trailer knows a Phase One exists."

Half an hour later a Cobra Helistar sliced the early morning sky as it took Donaldson from Hafey to Loring. Three hours later a red-on-white Suburu Grande Sport sat outside the Officers' Club. Staff Sergeant Levesque, a sunburnt, carrot-topped man with a marathon runner's leanness and farmer's strength, assigned as Donaldson's aide, leaned against the Grande waiting for orders. At 1700 hours he got them: Be on comm until you receive direct authorization otherwise, my corneal only.

OUT

1

The picnic area filled with vacationers stopping to tap their thermoses when Trailer emerged from leafing oaks and elms. Leaves, still small and richly verdant, pushed past bud. He washed his clothes using stones and sand as he came down the Allagash Waterway, being careful with them, feeling Karen's sure hands in them, and now they carried the scents of forest and river. The morning was late spring warm with wisps of ground fog crawling along where the sun - hinting of a hot summer - drew moisture from topsoil blackened with the detritus of last summer's life, dead and rotted into the ground, the mists carrying a rich earth smell.

He walked across the road towards some empty tables, the mist swirling around his feet as he walked, at times masking them, at times rising up his calves like playful pups demanding attention. He chose a stone bench and table as being most able to support his weight. He didn't need rest, he needed time to think.

A family got out of a van and took a table some twenty feet from him, paying no attention as they walked past, and he watched them set up their breakfast. Three women and two men, all middle-aged, one woman in her twenties, no children, and one incredibly old man. All except the young woman wore brightly colored clothing of reds and blues and yellows, all of it too light for this time of year. The young woman wore fashionable, seasonal clothes that accented her figure. Their scent and bone structure indicated a shared parentage except for one of the men. Their coloring, features, speech, and the scents of the foods they placed on the table told Nick they came from Ecuador or northern Peru, possibly Waica, Cubeo, or Jìvaro.

Nick started tensing.

"No," he whispered. "That war's long gone." He closed his eyes and breathed deeply, remembering where he was.

The old man came over slowly, using a walker, his black, polished oxfords coming down slowly but purposefully with each step. Nick could see he was arthritic, but the old man's body and footwear revealed more; he'd been interrogated, strapped into either a tiger cage or a crow perch, and his left shoe had the distinctive shaping and pattern necessary to accommodate a foot with a sole beaten flat by a metal rod. The rest of the family already sat at the table, already starting to eat, and the old man not even halfway across the parking lot.

He smiled at Nick and looked away. Before he looked away, Nick noticed a tear in the man's right eye. A moment later he wiped a tear from his own eye.

Nick stared at the family for a moment and nodded, understanding.

He was probably a storekeeper. He probably got caught stealing bread to keep you fuckers alive.

The old man wore black suit trousers with black suspenders and a worn black belt, the buckle polished smooth from many years of use and the leather frayed and falling forward like some old and crippled stallion's penis preparing to piss. His pants practically fell off him, the suspenders alone providing security. On top, he wore a white cotton shirt and a shiny black tie, properly knotted. He had a white Panama hat with a wide black band that highlighted his cherry wood skin. His suit coat was draped carefully over the rails of his walker as if the rails were the arms of his best friend, and had rolled up his sleeves in the warm sun. The flesh hung like sacks of old wine. Nick wondered how long it took the old man to knot the tie, knowing he wouldn't have accepted any help. As he got closer, Nick also detected the scent of esophageal cancer.

You don't have much time left, do you, Grandfather. This is probably your last family outing.

Instead of sitting with his family, the old man sat at Nick's table. He smiled, took out a frayed white handkerchief, wiped the sweat from his face, and started talking about gardening.

Nick tried to understand, but the cancer in the old man's throat and his broken English made comprehension difficult.

One of the women noticed the old man at Nick's table and approached rapidly. "Hey, pa, leave him alone - "

Nick waved her off. "No, he's all right. I can't understand him too well, but I don't mind the company. I'm just waiting for a friend to show up." Nick turned to the old man. "*¿Qual é seu nome?*" *What's your name?*

"*Nicolas Jolero. Prazer em comhecelo.*" *Nicolas Jolero. Glad to meet you.* The old man held out his hand and Nick shook it gently.

"*Meu nome e 'Nick', tambem. Nicolas Trailer. É um prazer.*" *My name's Nick, too. Nicolas Trailer. The pleasure's mine.*

The old man laughed and coughed, catching some phlegm in the same handkerchief he'd used to wipe the sweat from his face. He called to one of the women and pointed to a paper bag unopened on the table.

"Pa, he's not interested in your greenhouse."

"No, really, I am."

She brought the bag over and gasped when she caught a full glimpse of Nick's face. "Excuse me. Something caught in my throat."

Nick nodded. The old man shooed her away and tapped Nick's hand as he opened the bag slowly, more out of reverence than age. He smiled coyly at Nick and pulled out one tomato, then another. Next came a zucchini, followed by peppers. With each item, the old man gave Nick broken English instructions on the care and feeding of each, each vegetable from the old man's private garden, a garden he alone tended, and no one else in the family cared or even paid attention.

The old man continued issuing instructions on how to garden.

Does he know I'm the only one paying attention?

The old man nodded at Nick and flashed a two-tooth smile. He grunted something and pointed to the richest looking pepper he'd pulled out of the bag. Nick returned the nod, not knowing what he was getting himself into.

The old man's eyes went wide and he clutched his chest, coughing. The phlegm collected at the corners of his mouth as his arms shook and veins bulged on his face and neck. Nick reached out to help him but the old man waved him off. The coughing stopped and the old man shrugged, wiping his mouth. His eyes no longer going in and out of focus, the old man made a wild grasp, not a calculated reach, and his hand fell as if by chance on the pepper he'd drawn to Nick's attention. He cast an eye to the other table and snorted, his focus regained as he looked back at Nick.

Nick's perceptions changed. He accelerated into Hunter/Seeker state, but it came with confusion. There was no desire to harm or hurt, no intention to kill or destroy.

What's happening? The old man? I'm afraid of the old man?

No, I fear for the old man.

He sat back slightly, watching the old man, savoring the new thought, a desire to protect another from harm.

I fear for the old man.

The world became just the two of them, the old man and Nick sole witnesses to the old gentleman's work.

Everything he was, everything he'd learned, he now used to pay attention, to engage, to interact, to demonstrate honor and trust.

Nick put out his hand for the pepper. The old man said, "*Espere um pouco!*" Wait!

A sun-dried hand went into a pocket and pulled out an old knife, so old and so used that the ivory matched the color of the old man's hands.

Nick's pupils went wide as the old man's wrist snapped and the knife opened. Nick could feel his blood surging, blackening, as he gauged the response limits and receptivity speeds of the old man's movements.

He heard his own voice whisper, "No." For the briefest moment, he was back in the Chelmsford bar.

The blade swept through the pepper, cleaving it in two with no effort, the morning sun glinting off the blade. Nick's eyes dampened the spectrum slightly. The rose-greenish sweet smelling juice of the pepper oozed down the blade, onto the dark ivory handle, onto the old man's cherry wood hand, all in slow motion as Nick's senses continued increasing his perception index. The old man's tongue slid from between his lips as his knife hand went up and he licked the juice from the blade. Nick felt his jaws opening, his ears pulling back. His hand started to move and, as it did, the old man put half the pepper in it.

"*Vamos comer!*" said the old man. Eat.

Nick looked at the pepper in his hand, then back at the old man. "What?"

The old man smiled at Nick's confusion."*Vamos comer!*"

Nick lifted the pepper to his lips.

Sweet. Natural and real, not hollowy, and without a pesticide aftertaste, so sweet that Nick tasted the juices of some late April sun. He looked at the old man and noticed that the old man watched him intently.

"*Voçe é Jivaro*" Nick said, not asking a question. You're Jivaro.

"*Sim. Sou porque?*" Yes. Why?

"*Precisote dizer uma coisa.*" I need to tell you something.

The old man seemed to think for a moment, staring into Nick's eyes until Nick felt the ocean swell around him. "*Sí,*" the old man said finally, "*sim penso quesim.*" Yes, I think you do.

"Hey, pa, come on and eat," one of the men called.

The old Jìvaro stood slowly, grasped the arms of the walker and turned it, rocking it, infinitesimally to bring it around towards his family. "*Mas primeizo vamos comer.*" But first we can eat.

From Nick's table to the old man's family's was some twenty feet. Glasses of lemonade and cups of coffee waited on the table's edge. The old man's walker came down, he pulled, one leg lifted, the other dragged. He sighed and began again. Nick walked beside him, taking small steps.

Very small steps.

At times Nick didn't move at all, instead watching the old man's progress.

The lemonade was gone when they got to the table. One of the Jìvaro's sons, the one who did most of the talking, patted Nick's back. "You've got a lot of patience."

Either the old man didn't hear or paid no attention to his son's statement. Nick watched the old man listening to conversations at tables they passed. "You understand what they say, don't you, Grandfather?" Nick spoke Jivaroan, speaking the exact tongue of the old man's tribe.

The old man smiled and winked, then sat down, easing himself into a folding chair with a satin pillow on the seat. He reached out for a similar chair and patted the back, indicating Nick should sit down beside him. "Nick."

Some other people at the picnic area, a man in his mid-thirties and his son, started playing catch. Nick sighed, remembering the day his father came home with a bat, ball and glove and took him out to play catch. After a half hour of failed attempts, Nick's father patted him on the head and uncharacteristically said, "Maybe later, huh?" Nick threw the ball well but little else. They went once and never again. Nick found the gear some months later in the closet with his father's high school trophies.

The old man grunted something and nodded towards the father and son playing catch, reached over and wiped Nick's cheek. Nick was surprised by the wetness there.

One of the old man's daughters offered Nick some lemonade. The old man took Nick's glass before she could begin pouring and turned it upside down. A china cup and saucer lay on the table in front of the old man. He tapped the cup into the saucer, pointed a finger at Nick and grunted something.

"But, pa - "

The old man looked up from under his hat. She shook her head and walked towards the van.

The old man and Nick started talking about the father and son playing catch again. They talked the way they talked about gardening, now speaking pure Jivaroan. The old man's cancer still made understanding difficult, but Nick didn't mind. Nick found himself listening and nodding, hoping his nods were at least synchronized to what old man was saying.

Nick relaxed listening to the old man's guttural tones, getting thirsty and thinking about the taste of the lemonade, wondering why the old man wouldn't allow him any.

His daughter returned from the van carrying a tray with two china cups and saucers, a small silver coffee pot, a china creamer filled with light cream and two pony glasses filled with a black, oil-thick liquid with a pungent, slightly bitter smell of weak sage and burning coriander. Nick looked at her. She rolled her eyes in sympathy, cast them at her father, shrugged and rolled them again. The old man pushed the empty cup and saucer away from him and tapped the table. She put the tray down and left. "Call me when he's done." She and the rest of her family started clearing their things.

The old man placed a saucer and cup in front of Nick, his hands and voice as animated as when he gave Nick the pepper. He lifted the creamer and said something. Nick nodded as the old man poured some cream followed by steaming hot coffee.

The smell caught Nick for a moment. He expected the store bought, k-coffee so prevalent since the US government sold the rights to cultivation of the South American fields. Instead the thick, rich scent of La Minita and Maragogipes beans, coffee smells from a forest an equator and some away from the northern Maine woods, enveloped him. The bitter scent intruded on his nose, making him sneeze, then the fact that he could sneeze made him laugh.

Everyone else had gone back to the van by the time the old man had finished the ritual, leaving the two of them alone again.

The old man pushed the tray away and lifted his pony glass to Nick. Nick returned the gesture. He grunted something and Nick said, "Salute," because he didn't know what else to do. The old man laughed and they drank.

Natém.

Nick recognized it instantly by the salty, burnt soy taste, a drink of Jìvaro shaman. It slid down his throat and Nick started flexing his esophageal muscles, forcing the liquid down so he wouldn't vomit. The old man pointed to Nick's cup of coffee and Nick gulped it down. Nick coughed and the old man laughed, slapped Nick's back and laughed again.

They sat there sipping their coffee, talking about peppers and fathers and sons. The old man talked. Nick listened.

Eventually the old man said, "You were in the war? You killed some of my people?"

Nick's eyes watered. "I killed all of your people."

The old man placed a hand on Nick's back and rubbed back and forth, letting Nick cry. "No, you didn't kill all of my people. Many of my people died, but many people had a hand in killing them. Some of the killers, my people themselves."

Nick sobbed. "I'm sorry."

"You should be. That's good. You should be sorry, and you should cry. But that's enough. You cry until you don't have to cry anymore. You be sorry until you've been sorry enough. That's all. You don't need to be anything else. When you're done with those, you're through." The old man prepared another cup of coffee for Nick. "Drink."

Nick drank and coughed again. This time the old man didn't laugh. "You want me to punish you for what you did twenty, thirty years ago?

For what a child did? I might punish the child then, but I'm not going to punish the man now. What can I do you haven't already done to yourself? There's only one thing. One thing I can give you but it will mean nothing until you can give it to yourself. I give you now what I would have given the child then. I give you your worst nightmare.

"I give you forgiveness."

Nick stared into the space between them for several minutes before his gaze returned to the old man's face.

"Now, Nick, can you forgive yourself? I never knew the boy so I can't forgive him. Only you can forgive him. Forgive him, tell him there's no reason he has to be punished. Or will there always be some reason for you to hate him?"

"How do I forgive myself?"

"By realizing you have the right to be forgiven. By realizing, inside of you, there is forgiveness. You see, I can't give it to you, it has to be there. You have to look for it until you find it. You're not an old woman. I think you'll find it. All you really need to do is want to find it and you will.

"But first you must truly want to find it. It must mean your life if you don't find it. It all depends on what you want to see, what you want to find. If you don't want to find forgiveness, there is no hope. If you want to find it, it will be there."

"I don't understand, grandfather."

"Here is a story. A story to help. Old men, we have lots of stories. This is about the shaman boy and the old women..."

Ten minutes later the van horn blared. "I have to go. My children, they want to see everything now." He laughed. "They haven't learned. In time, everything is exactly what they will see."

"Were you in the war, Grandfather?"

"Yes."

"And?"

"And now I am not."

The old man tapped Nick's chin up until they stared eye-to-eye. "*Now I am not.*"

The horn blared again.

"Except when my children want me to hurry."

Nick cleared the table and walked, slowly, patiently, with the old man to the van. Before his children closed the door, the old man pulled another soiled, stained handkerchief from his pocket, gave it to Nick, and winked. Nick tapped the side of the van and the family drove off. Nick went back to the table where he and the old man sat. He pulled out the old man's handkerchief and brought it to his nose. As the handkerchief opened, an uncut pepper fell out.

2

Donaldson found Levesque waiting outside the Officers' Club with the Grande in the late afternoon sun. Levesque tucked his services beret tight under his left arm and went to attention at Donaldson's approach. Donaldson had never seen hair so bright orangy-red in his life. For the moment, he dismissed it.

He returned the latter's salute. "Do you know why I selected you, Levesque?"

"No, Sir."

Donaldson opened a folder and thumbed some pages. "This is your life, Levesque. You want to tell me what's in here?"

"I don't understand the Major's question, Sir."

"Let's start with Special Forces Jungle Operations and Unconventional Jungle Operations Courses, both of which you've taught. You're SERE certified, so you know Survival, Evasion, Resistance, and Escape on all continents. You're top of your class Pathfinder, Scuba, Amphibious Reconn. You've got top honors from the Mountain Warfare Training Center, you've got Insertion/Extraction and

Infiltration/Exfiltration, land navigation and aerial interpretation." Donaldson lifted another page. "Damn, I didn't even see this one. You're all communications certified, you're offensive and defensive on nuclear, biological, and chemical, conventional and field expedient demolitions certified, Night Observation and Starlight employment, Personnel Radar PPS-15 and RABFAC PPN-18 Employment, and fully field medical.

"You just rotated here from clean-up in Iraq and the Amazonas. JFK Center also says you're SOF trained." Donaldson watched Levesque for reactions. "You disagree with any of that?"

"No, Sir."

"All this and you save your money, don't drink, don't gamble, don't whore. Either you're planning on going merc when you get short or you got some kind of religion. Which is it, sergeant?"

"Neither, Sir. Just like to study, Sir."

"You got no dick, is that it? Figure all of this is going to buy you a real big one?"

"No, Sir."

"Maybe you want to prove to mommy and daddy that you're a good little soldier?" Donaldson winced at his own words but continued looking for cue reactivity in Levesque. "Figure this is going to prove you're a man?"

"No, Sir."

"Maybe you're doing all this so pappa'll love you when you get home?"

"No, Sir."

"Good, then relax, Sergeant." Donaldson opened the Grande's gate, pulled back a quilt and some space blankets, and pointed at foam-walled boxes. "Tell me what you see, Sergeant."

Levesque opened and moved the boxes quietly and quickly. "454 Casull Tenby, five 300 grain rounds per cylinder, ten cylinders. Five-hundred boxed 300s. Greenfield 45-70 SuperMax, five 405 grain per cylinder, also with ten cylinders. Five-hundred boxed 405s, uranium cased. Five-hundred boxes each 300 and 405, Devastators."

"Any comment, sergeant?"

"Nice weapons, sir."

"Ever fire either of these?"

"The Casull, sir. I've never seen a 45-70 this close before."

Donaldson lifted the weapon, checked the cylinder then slapped it back and spun it, waiting for the chambers to stop clicking under the firing pin. He pointed to a pile of bricks thirty meters away. "Be my guest."

Levesque took the weapon and fired. He received the recoil laterally, his arm jumping up a foot from level. The brick pile exploded.

"Comments?"

"Comfortable grip." Levesque handed the weapon back, keeping his eyes on it while Donaldson cleared the expended shell, took a round from his pocket and dropped it in.

Donaldson smiled. He put the 45-70 back.

He heard the Officers' Club door open and a long, light stride came towards him. "Show him what's on the bottom, Donaldson."

Donaldson spun. "Stay out of this, Ingman." He noticed the latter's mustache was a shade darker than before and fuller. "Really trying to hide that scar, huh? Those Cochican barmaids are tough."

Ingman's hand instinctively groomed his mustache into place before dropping slowly to his side. His face tightened and he smiled at Donaldson. "Can't stay out of this anymore, James. They asked me to clear your reque order. Wanted to know why you requed those cannons during peacetime." Ingman looked at Levesque. "Did he show you what else he's got, Sergeant? Or did you think the base marksman was going to sally some desk jockey major on R&R? Didn't you wonder what he was hunting if he's got handguns that'll stop elephants?"

Levesque, still at attention from Ingman's approach, didn't answer.

"Show him the rest, Donaldson."

Donaldson turned back to Levesque. "I was just about to show you these, sergeant. There are no secrets here. After you're fully briefed, you can back out if you want. No questions and no comments. Is that understood? And at ease."

"Yes, Sir." Levesque returned to parade rest.

"No, no. At ease."

Levesque studied Donaldson, reading him and the situation before transferring his services beret from under his arm to his shoulder epaulet. He eyed both men as well as he could then relaxed some more.

"Good." Donaldson moved the boxed handguns and their ammunition aside. The Grande had a false bottom and he removed it. "You're doing good, Levesque. Let's try again." He pointed at six long boxes in the Grande's hidden compartment.

Levesque's eyes snapped over the box's contents once, twice, then stood there as he spoke. "Benelli M1 Ultra 90 12 gauge eight shot Semi Auto, thirty magazines 12 gauge, thirty magazines flechette, 480 rounds total. Ruger AC-556-A Full Auto, 5.56 NATO full metal jackets, hollow point." He lifted two separate boxes and studied them. "Explosive tip and armor piercing 5.56 NATOs, all steel rounds." He placed the boxes back and continued. "M16 Master full auto, Synthetic 99 magazines." He shifted the Synthetic 99s to read their legends. "Mixed uranium cased CrowdPleasers and CBW 5.56 charges. HK-91 308 NATO Casing Heavy Assault Rifle, 300 magazines, boxed. M203 lightweight 40mm grenade launcher for under the Master, 400 meter service range. Mk-79 Hurricane single barrel magazine loaded pump-action grenade launcher. Thirty grenades per magazine. Twenty magazines." He checked the legends on the magazines. "Mixed stun, coned, and sonic doublebugs. AT-8a shoulder mounted antipersonnel missile launcher set for thermal and cardiac response. M40 A-1-A bolt action, single shot rifle, Terminator sights. LAWS III handheld rocket launcher, sixteen rockets in cigar grips. Vulcan 770 40mm high explosive, rotary chamber Gattler minigun with full charge and pack. Liquid gloves for improved grip on all the weapons."

"What do you know about these weapons, sergeant?" asked Donaldson.

"The LAWS are a light antitank weapon. It's a handheld anti-armored weapon rocket launcher. That, along with the explosive tip 223s, were used to stop the Tienden one-man tanks Pancho bought over the weapons market. The M40-A is considered to be the most accurate rifle in the world, good to over a klick and a half, depending on the shooter. With the Terminator sights, more so. The Vulcan is heavy equipment. I'm told it can knock through trees like solder through spring snow."

"I find it hard to believe that someone with your background has so little to say about what's in these boxes, Levesque."

"And, by all means," Ingman added, "speak freely."

Levesque focused on Donaldson. "How freely, sir?"

"By all means."

"Well, I know I'm fucked if I use them. Most of these are outlawed. CrowdPleasers were developed during the South African anti-apartheid redo movement. They're designed to take out groups of people with a single shot. The Vulcan was disused due to its size, I thought. I've never seen one except on paper. It's based on the StreetSweeper and the 12 gauge Striker, another South African weapon design also used during the Apartheid riots and now used by British Combat Forces. It'd take two strong men to carry, unless you're wearing a 'brace. The CBWs are binaries, all with lethal mix chemistries, with contact and penetration fuses. The 8a is for jungle combat. I hear it was also used to bring down large game in the Amazonas and Loreto when troops got hungry. The doublebugs give your target brain jam. You, too, if you're not careful. The HK-91 is credited with keeping the Eastern Block Ground Forces on their side of The New Wall when Krobochev decided Putin wasn't militant enough. The Benelli is standard riot armament for most US SWAT teams. The flechettes are high velocity, high power, flying razor blades. You need something out of armored division to stop those."

"Anything else you'd like to say, Levesque?"

"I believe the gentleman is correct, sir. You are not some desk jockey major on R&R. I am not to sally you around and make sure you bring back a nice wallmount. The '8 wouldn't leave enough of anything up here except for soup or stew. The powder burns alone wouldn't make it worth the meal."

"That's all?"

"I'd like to know what I'm expected to do and what I can expect for return hostilities. You don't go out like that unless you expect somebody's really going to get pissed at you being there."

"Good, Levesque. I don't want either an iceman or a showboat on this run. The '40 and '91 are for you. I understand that you're maximum-range certified on the M40 and have extensive training on the HK-91."

"Yes, Sir."

"Well, we're going to sit you in a tree with enough deer piss on you to make any buck that finds you damn angry. As for when you're going to use all that SOF training Congress spent so much money on, ever hear of a rogue biological?"

Levesque shook his head, no. Ingman stepped closer.

"Well, that's what's out there. My guess is it's not friendly. There are some files on the driver's seat. Read them. Before you do that, though, I want all the weapons equipped with holographics, Night-Eyes, and lasers."

Levesque saluted and started away.

"Sergeant?" Donaldson pointed to Levesque's hair. "That's quite a crown you're wearing. That's never been a problem before?"

"I go bald and wear monkey-black when I'm on station, sir."

"One last thing, Sergeant?"

"Yes, Sir?"

"Why in hell did you study all those things?"

"I'm hoping for a job in intelligence when I get out, sir. Perhaps a position as diplomatic courier or aide-de-camp."

"Congratulations, Sergeant. You just left both of those grades way behind."

Levesque smiled, saluted, and left.

Ingman inspected Donaldson's weaponry. "No hives?"

"Swarmbots would be as useless here as they were in the Amazonas. Foliage's too dense. Lower the recognition and they'll start taking out bears and gnarled trees. Besides, the normal load would be worthless. We'd have to increase the load to the point they'd be unstable in flight. Let's go with eyes-on-target and sensory backup for now."

A piercing ringing, not enough to deafen, definitely enough to demand attention, came from Ingman's shirt pocket and rattled each man's teeth.

"This'll be for you." He pulled out a small, cherry red mobile. "Before you ask, it comes sonicked." He turned the phone over to reveal some earbuds before handing the device to Donaldson.

A holo appeared in front of him as soon as it touched his hands.

"And you can QC the video. It's got about ninety-seven uses. Ninety-nine if you want to use it as a phone."

Distasio, sitting in his office at Hafey, stared at Donaldson from the holo and asked, "Is this secure?"

Ingman nodded. "I'll go over it with you before you leave."

Donaldson said, "Evidently it is. What's up?"

"Do you remember Corporal Steiner from your visit?"

"Should I?"

"He was the one, during your briefing, didn't know what 'shopped' meant."

"Go on."

"He went missing while you were in The Tank. Did Rivers tell you?"

"What was he supposed to tell me?"

"He went missing maybe half your time here. Never returned. We did a far horizons and came up empty. Today we learned why. About an hour ago, in fact. Picked up a sheriff's emergency request. Poor son-of-a-bitch wasn't keeping his food down any too well when he called it in."

"What's this got to do with me?"

"I'm transmitting video from the scene. Ready?"

Before Donaldson acknowledged, the holo blurred from Distasio's office to a forest scene. Strung between two leafing poplars was a square-looking bundle leaking something.

Donaldson heard Distasio say "Can you hear me, Captain?"

Chris Harley's matter-of-fact, no holds barred voice answered. "Here, Sir."

"I've got Donaldson on relay. Narrate the scene for him, please."

The holo jiggled and bounced a bit as Chris Harley's shouldercam took over, moving them closer to the bundle and showing it at an up-angle. "I'm one-point-six meters and armored. The package is at a little over two. Depends on the winds and water saturation in the soil. We suspect it was hung higher and I'll get to that in a minute.

"What you see dripping and pooled underneath," the camera dipped to reveal some clawed, damp earth then returned front and forward again, "is blood. The amount and placement indicate slow exsanguination. We estimate he's been like this for a day."

Harley walked the camera around so Donaldson could see all sides, the bottom of the bundle saturated, torn in some parts and scratched through revealing white fibers in others. Something hung out the bottom, between tears. As the camera circumnavigated the package, two drops of blood fell from the clump.

Donaldson said, "What is that?"

Harley's matter of fact voice answered, "Near as we can tell, sir, a piece of ass."

Distasio snapped, "Captain."

Donaldson cut him off, "Continue."

"The package is fifty-three centimeters on a side - "

Donaldson interrupted. "A box? A fifty-three-centimeter box?"

"Yes, sir. Roped and tied. Use to be a mummy style sleeping bag." She spoke to some others off camera. "You two. Make a stairway."

Two large males in BDUs entered the line of sight. One got on all fours, the other bent over beside him. The camera climbed as Harley walked up them then peered down into the top of the package.

A human face. A man's face, the neck snapped back so the face stared up into the sky. The eyes were missing and the face was pocked as if riddled with acne scars. The clothing seemed strange.

"You can't tell from the face but this use to be Steiner. We matched the blood. We don't know what to make of this. From what we see, he's wrapped in or wearing burlap bags. Based on the tears and teeth marks in his rump, we think a bear took a liking to him round about midnight. The sheriff got a call from some hikers on an access road this morning. Seems lots of carrion eaters were gathering - that accounts for the face and eyes - and that tipped him off that something was dead or dying."

Distasio blurred back into the holo. "Thanks, Captain. Donaldson, you want to claim this? We can release it to state or go on our own. Doesn't matter who takes it, they'll start with samples of the bag and burlap."

No, Nick. Not this way, no. "Can we hide this?"

Ingman said, "How long?"

"I don't know."

Donaldson returned to the Officers' Club and stared for a moment at his reflection in the wall mirrors.

Ingman dropped a folder on the table in front of Donaldson. "He escaped, didn't he?"

"Yep."

"Looks like you did a good job with him. Now he's only taking out single families at a time."

"What's this?"

Ingman nodded at the folder. "Clean and neat, Donaldson, just like he'd sanctioned them. Everybody thinks some coyotes or bears got noseworm. I think different. Am I right?"

Donaldson measured the destruction in each photograph, then read the opening paragraphs of their accompanying reports. Each one assumed animal attacks. "Something doesn't feel right. I don't know what it is, but something isn't right."

Ingman pulled a map out of the pack. "Then what do you make of this?"

The map indicated where in northern Maine the attacks took place. They followed the Allagash Wilderness Waterway from Dickey over The Traveler. Donaldson completed the line on Ingman's map down the Wassataquoik Stream to Stacyville. "He's going to kill his wife."

An SP ushered Levesque to Donaldson. "Everything's ready, Sir."

"Get that Grande parked outside into a Sky Stallion. Get two sets of Wolff Ears and Farfoons. We'll need helmeted Zeiss NightEyes. ACA Motion Detectors with one-kilometer sweeps. Fluxgates and Finders for both of us. Extra power packs for all of the above. Four bags of full body armor and cage braces - just like you wanted - designed to hold all ordnance and munitions. Make sure the M16 and the Vulcan are on swing struts. Organic armor on everything. The braces have to allow full lateral mobility and balance. Full camouflage gear and thermal reconns. Vanadium and titanium smithed K-bars on both boots, belt, and both shoulders."

"Sir?"

"Yes."

"We're going on a bughunt, Sir?"

"You might want to load up on razors and monkey-black, son."

Levesque's eyes snapped straight forward. "Yes, Sir."

"One more thing, Levesque. We need to be in Stacyville ASAP. What you can't find here, make sure it's there waiting for us." Levesque saluted and left. "Looks like I'm hunting some bear."

Ingman sat down. "Are you sure that two men will be enough? Or are you trying to avoid detection?"

Donaldson rested his head in his palms, his elbows on the table, gauging his level of exhaustion. *Am I ready for this?* "Yeah, I think just the two of us."

"What? No, I mean you and your two men; the sergeant and the aide you had in Chelmsford, Rivers. He met me when I deplaned and checked the reque order, escorted me halfway here then left."

"Rivers is on base?"

Levesque came in, an SP running in tow. "Sir, the vehicle's gone."

Donaldson ran to the door. Ingman and Levesque followed. He turned to Ingman. "What was his status? Was he damaged in any way?"

"No, he seemed fine. A little flush-faced, maybe. And he was in civilian trim. Hunting garb." Ingman's lower lip curled up and pulled down on his mustache. "No, wait a minute. He was mumbling to himself and stopped to salute me. I didn't think of it then, but he was half humming half singing something, real quiet. Sounded like nursery rhymes, something like that. Barely stopped when he saluted, almost like saluting was an inconvenience. Why? Wasn't he with you at Hafey?"

"Yes, but I sent him on ahead when Trailer escaped. Tom thought he could bring Trailer down unaided. I guess he's finding out Trailer's not so old and feeble as he thought. Still, he should have notified me before he took the Grande."

"Maybe he's got a real good fix and didn't want to waste any time?"

Donaldson pulled out the red mobile. "Can this do tracers?"

"Just ask it."

"Tracer, DDS&T PO Rivers 13-29-32."

A holo popped up in front of the phone. "Expand, two-cubed eye frame."

The holo grew until a two-meter cube appeared, the top eye level to Donaldson. A topo map of northern Maine appeared in the background, the foreground the exact route shown on Ingman's map. The location-time stamps matched the estimated times-of-death on Ingman's map to within a half hour.

Donaldson's eyes danced over the hologram. "Yeah, maybe. Trailer is leaving a good map of where he's headed."

Levesque said, "Sir, the tracer reports the lieutenant as local and static. If he just left with the Grande then the tracer's incorrect."

Donaldson studied the tracer map. "He must have thought Trailer figured out how to monitor the primary tracer channels to stay ahead of him and pulled out his chip. It's got to be around here somewhere. Check where the Grande was parked."

Five minutes inspection revealed a tiny silver slab, about the size of a dime, blood still drying on it and a greenhead horsefly merrily sipping away.

"Levesque, reque me another Grande, identical. Get my last reque order from Ingman." He looked at Ingman. "You still got it, right?"

Ingman nodded.

"Good, get me everything on that reque order plus what I just asked for. Let me know when everything's ready and we'll rendezvous. Until then, get me whatever's in the motorpool that's simple, and now."

"Yes, sir." Levesque double-timed it to the requisitions office.

Donaldson watched him go and slumped against the doorjamb. "I wish we never made them. Any of them."

"Jim?"

Donaldson's brow furrowed. "It's 'Jim' now? I don't know whether to be angered or relieved. Why the familiarity, Ingman?"

"I'll deny I ever said this, but we were all to blame."

Donaldson smiled. It led to a chuckle. He composed himself, looked at Ingman, and laughed.

"What is it, Donaldson?"

In between fits of laughter, Donaldson repeated Nick's revelation. "Everybody's responsible, but nobody's to blame."

3

Karen Trailer sat at her wooden kitchen table under a bare ceiling light. She stared into the dark morning beyond her window, listened to the soft sounds of her animals waking as she sipped some hot tea from a chipped mug. She'd shown Nickie - she called him "Nickie" because it made him laugh. "Do I look like a 'Nickie' to you?" he'd ask. She'd put her arms as far around him as she could and answered "You look like my 'Nickie' to me." - how to throw clay and this was his best attempt to date.

He could do better, far better, but refused to because he thought if she thought he needed her she would keep him around.

Foolish man.

People saw Nick as a monster. He'd gone into Stacyville with her once and she swore she'd never put him through that again. The stares she could deal with but Nickie... Somehow Nickie knew what they thought. He could quote what they said in their own voice using their own words and all he had to do was look at them once. He could even mimic how they walked. If you didn't look closely.

Her pocketbook contained a datebook she got from the bank, the kind nobody used anymore because it required penmanship and writing skills, something else Nickie asked her to teach him. She opened it and counted the red marks. Red marks on every page. Red marks in every month. Red marks wiping out whole weeks and sometimes two months at a pass. She took out a red pen and began counting from the last time she'd seen her husband. In precise but tear-stained letters, the word "alone" appeared in several of the marked out passages.

And it was getting worse. Nickie's last visit confirmed it. Even without him telling her. He wouldn't say where he was going. She would have said he'd gone on a drunk but she'd never seen him drink anything but water.

But she heard that sound in his voice once or twice before, the sound of loneliness and wanting to be alone, but wanting her with him in his loneliness. When he'd sounded that way before he'd always go away, coming back weeks later, usually with game he'd hunted, food for the freezer.

"See? I can take care of you," he'd say. But never like some great white hunter throwing his kill on the table, more like a great cat bringing home fresh meat for its kittens.

He would even purr when she hugged him.

"I know you can take care of me, Nickie. We can take care of each other." Then she'd sit with him in the quiet, in the dark, knowing he cared and knowing he feared but not knowing how to help him let the fear out or her caring in.

So she'd sit with him, patiently, trusting. It'll happen when it happens.

She pulled other, similar datebooks out of her purse, feeling Nick's presence in them. She had no pictures since giving Nickie her locket. Only the datebooks she kept and a bowl of rose petals, petals from roses he gave her with irregular regularity, in her bedroom. "Our bedroom."

She closed the safety pins that held her pocketbook together. The earliest datebook started shortly after she met Nick. She counted unmarked days. In seven years together they'd only spent six months of actual time together. The rest of the time he was gone, leaving her alone. As she counted unmarked days, she also noted where she'd written in milestones in their courtship. Where others might mark trips to the beach, picnics, or a marriage proposal, her datebooks marked that a year passed from the time he met her until he would touch her. She remembered his gentleness and passion.

He was the first to touch her in years. She didn't trust the hands of others. A year passed before he let her touch him. Even then, he held her hands, gently holding her hands as she explored, his body still as if frozen, distant, fearful, in the dark, asking her not to question the mysteries her hands revealed, and they passed another six months.

Finally, one night when he came home, he woke her with a gentle kiss on the lips. She held her hands out to him. Usually he lifted her to him. This night he said, "Cover your eyes, babe."

"What's wrong?"

"Please, just cover your eyes."

He turned on the light. "You can look now."

His body reminded her of a Touch-and-Talk topographic map she'd seen during a visit to UMO as a child. You could run your hands over mountain ranges and feel their steepness and deep valleys, experience the cold of glaciers or the depth of the oceans on your fingers, the dampness of swamplands and the graininess of deserts.

Nick's body had mountain ranges where bones had erupted to the surface then miraculously found their way back under the skin, skin stretched and healed over burns like cool lakes in a burning desert. Some wounds he described, some he didn't and never how he got them, only what caused them, his narration cold and rational like the map she'd touched as a child. Some wounds she couldn't even guess at. Sometimes, when she got a cut or scrape or bruise doing her chores, he would pick plants and flowers he planted in their garden, mix them into a poultice and balm her wounds, explaining the properties of each, what to mix with what and to what purpose.

At times his comings and going reminded her of a quiet, gentle pet, an old, faithful dog that finds the quietest place in the house to rest, perhaps to die, as if to make sure that its remains will be out of the way, never underfoot. Wherever he went, whatever secrets he kept from her, she accepted because she accepted him.

As her mother said, "You learn to live with some things."

Her teakettle started its soft shrill whistle and gained volume rapidly. It drew her attention away from the dark beyond the door for a moment.

The doorbell rang and she jumped, then put her datebooks and pen back into her purse. It wasn't Nickie. Nickie never rang the doorbell and she never heard him come in. A rose would drop in her lap and then he'd be there, filling the room as he filled her heart. But the doorbell's ring signaled fear, someone not Nickie, perhaps a message of her fears realized.

The doorbell rang again and she started to cry. She swallowed her tears and got up to look out the window. The outside light hadn't come on at his approach so she flicked the switch.

A Suburu Grande Sport, a blue-lit interior indicating driverless "Ready" mode, waited outside. No one she knew drove a Grande Sport and a man, about six inches shorter than Nick and smaller all around, in jeans, workboots, a flannel shirt, and hunting cap, stood outside facing the road.

She called out, "Yes?"

"Mrs. Trailer?"

"Who's asking?"

"Is Nick home?"

"You didn't answer my question."

"Tell him Donaldson's here."

"Major Donaldson?"

"Yes, Major Donaldson."

"What's Nick's favorite song?"

The door burst off its hinges before Karen could move, knocking the wind out of her and landing on top of her as she sprawled on the kitchen floor.

"Fucking bitch!" The man lifted the door off her and picked her up by her hair.

He pulled his hat off, revealing close-cropped blond hair. His face was red, not red from the cold or wind, but an unnatural red as if the blood flowed just beneath the surface. His lips pulled back into two thin white lines that highlighted pulsing red gums and white teeth. His tongue snapped up and licked an inflamed and running nose. Most of all, Karen noticed his steel blue eyes with pinpoint pupils, almost no pupils showing at all. "I can smell him. He's around here, somewhere. Where is he, Karen?"

Rivers, but not as she remembered him. He smiled revealing manicured teeth.

She did what Nick had taught her, smashing her forehead into Rivers's nose, reaching into his groin and pulling up anything her hands found.

Rivers smiled, turned his face away and spit something out. When he turned his face back Karen saw a mouth of teeth filed into points and the skin of his nose turned up like a leaf-nosed bat, making his face look like a raw, open wound.

She looked aside and saw an upper and lower bridge work on the carpet, beside it a flesh colored lump.

"No, Karen. He's not there." Rivers drew his head back and opened his mouth, pulling his lips back from his teeth like a shark about to feed.

The ceiling above them opened. They looked up. Nick smiled back as he crushed a five-pound bag of black pepper. Rivers dropped her and started sneezing, whirling to the right to get away from the pepper dust. A slight breeze brought a fine mist, a powder Nick made from one of his plants, down from the ceiling onto Rivers' face. He fell to the ground.

A rose came over Karen's shoulder, her coat surrounded her, Nick lifted her over Rivers and outside. He stopped outside the door and wedged an envelope under a shingle. They got in the Grande and left.

4

Donaldson's hands tightened on the wheel as he drove up to Karen's home. The front door, knocked out of its frame, reminded him of the Chelmsford bar. State police swarmed like flies over the dead. His throat hollowed and the bitter taste filled his mouth.

A Stacyville patrolwoman saw his Kia's Mobile Air Command plates and waved him over to the side where a Stacyville PD captain asked for his credentials.

A tall, athletically built mid-40's black man, a Maine State OSI Captain's shield clipped to his belt, walked over, his hand out. "Let me see those."

The Stacyville captain handed them over.

OSI said, "Wait here," and took Donaldson's ID to an aging black on black Chevy Impala. It gave Donaldson a moment to settle, to observe. The OSI Captain wore clothes so well-tailored Donaldson assumed he'd severely pissed somebody off to warrant a northern Maine station. His Impala had an exhaust pipe and a tag on its state-issue plate that identified it as having no autonoms, wouldn't respond to autonoms, could not send or receive and that a human controlled it.

An animal control officer tended some animals in the paddock. The officer unfurled a thick black hose, entered the paddock and filled a trough. He also filled two green buckets. He placed one in front of the llamas and the other by the sheep. The horse neighed then drank. The sheep bleated, the llamas made their honking bark. They looked well-tended, cared for.

"They okay?"

The officer nodded. "Untouched and in good shape. You know these folks? Anybody coming back or do we farm them out to neighbors?"

Donaldson shook his head and shrugged.

He gazed over the gardens and fields, taking deep breaths of the corn and hay growing in the sun.

The normalcy of it lulled him. So long as he didn't look at the door, didn't get out of his car to look in the house, he could convince himself he'd parked at a subsistence farm's vegetable stand: one or two people getting by year by year. Idyllic. Quiet. Peaceful. Local grown. No pesticides.

The OSI sat in his Impala, talking to a holo floating above his dash.

Donaldson asked the Stacyville captain, "Who's he?"

"Maine State Office of Special Investigations Specialist Detective Captain Jonathan Douglas Eckhardt."

Donaldson glanced up. The captain nodded. "That's the way he says it, too."

"Looks too pretty to be up here."

"And don't he know it."

Eckhardt came back with Donaldson's credentials and surgical gloves. "Put these on."

Donaldson did so. Eckhardt handed him an envelope with 'Major Donaldson' written on the front in Trailer's handwriting. "You read that and tell me if it means anything to you."

Donaldson read the note: "Here there be Dragons."

Dragons? The Shaolinists said dragons are spirit. Nick's telling me he's going back to being a ghost? He's going into Hunter/Seeker state?

And the handwriting is precise and clear.

He wrote this before he got here? Before anything went down?

He knew something was coming down.

Donaldson stared at the message, taking a moment to realize its full meaning. Nick's controlling his state? He's deciding how he responds to his environment?

He smiled and let out a single, low chuckle. Ah, Nick, you're my hero.

Donaldson placed the note back in the envelope and walked to the door. Inside, police turned the house into a forensic pathology classroom. "What happened?"

"At 0530 hours this morning, two officers responded to a neighbor's complaint. They didn't report in reasonable time so we sent a second squad to investigate. Both officers were dead. One had a front to back hole in him the size of a baseball, the other looked like some animal turned him into lunch. We got descriptions from some of the neighbors, although they don't agree. We got definitely one and possibly two UNSUBs active. So far, if Augusta knows anything it ain't much. But you being here tells me you know something I should. So what do you know that I should?"

Donaldson took the descriptions from Eckhardt. "UNSUBs? Unknown Subjects? Nobody IDed them?"

"You see anybody left to ID them?"

Donaldson read over the descriptions. Although not the best, he recognized one as Trailer and the other as Rivers. "Did the neighbors have any idea which of these two killed your officers?"

Eckhardt's eyes popped. "Those descriptions are accurate?"

"How should I know? How reliable are your witnesses?"

"Let me see your credentials again." Eckhardt read them, walked to the front of Donaldson's sedan, read the license plates and reread the credentials. "You know your bona fides don't match?"

"I borrowed a friend's car."

"What are you doing here?"

"Saw all the activity, thought I'd see if I could help."

"My god, your mouth works better than a New York City whore's. Where'd you learn to come up with answers like that?" He glanced at the Staceyville captain then back at Donaldson. "Cuff him to his steering wheel. And blacken his windows so he can't see out. Then roll up his windows and leave him in the sun. We should be done in five, six hours. We'll come back for him then."

"That would be a negative career move, Detective."

"I look like I've made a lot of top-drawer choices regarding my career?"

"Okay, let's start over. Yes, those descriptions are accurate. Yes, there are two of them. And before you ask, yes, they are mine."

"Geez, I feel so secure knowing you guys are on the job. Look around here. The nearest house is two hundred yards away. These people were just waking up and staring into a rising sun. I told my men to test for hallucinogens. Now you're telling me we've got two men about seven feet tall built like bulls pissed off at somebody?"

"One's seven feet, the other's something over six." Donaldson checked his watch. "They've got three hours on me."

Eckhardt blocked Donaldson's path. "Don't ignore me, flyboy. Whoever did this, in case you didn't hear me, just did two state troopers. We in law enforcement tend to come down a little hard on that. We don't like to admit it, but it's the truth. You see, we tend to want to stop a cop-killer real fast because, if some asshole don't mind doing a cop, he sure in shit ain't going to mind offing some poor bastard civilian."

Donaldson went to his sedan and pulled the red mobile from its harness on the dash. He put the mobile back after a few minutes of talking into it and walked back to Eckhardt. "Wait a minute."

Eckhardt's mobile starting ringing. He glared at Donaldson before answering. Donaldson watched the man yell, slam his fist into the roof of his car, curse most everyone in sight, look back at him, then take a bullhorn from his trunk. "Everybody out. This is Eckhardt.

We're closing this one down."

Donaldson walked over to him. "I'd appreciate some guards being posted here."

Eckhardt nodded vigorously. "Oh, you'll get a lot of volunteers for that."

"Don't worry. This won't happen again. I just want to make sure no civilians try to loot this house."

Donaldson sat in his sedan while the police closed up the house. "Where would they go?" He called up a holo surveyor's map of Maine on his mobile. "Nick would prefer deep woods, Rivers is augmented for urban combat."

Eckhardt walked over to Donaldson's car and leaned over. "We just got a call. Karen Trailer is at Old Town Bank in East Millinocket, about half an hour south of here, withdrawing everything in her account."

"Tell the bank to delay her. I'll be there in fifteen."

5

Donaldson cut his sirens and lights entering the town. At the bank, he walked up to a woman matching Trailer's description of Karen. She stood at the teller windows clutching her purse to her chest, her eyes darting around but mostly watching traffic passing the bank's big front windows.

"Karen?"

She spun at him and held her purse like a shield, protecting herself as she scrutinized Donaldson's face. "Do I know you?"

He expected something, someone, different, but studying her he appreciated Nick's choice. Not plain yet not striking, either. In her early forties and not over forty-five. Farm muscular, not gym muscular. Blond hair, green eyes. Ruddy complexion. A good mix of crows' feet and laugh lines and still someone who's seen too many winters and not enough springs, someone whose life had been gauged by extremes. Someone who will survive because she knows how to survive, not someone who withers away waiting for help. The kind of thing that comes from long years of sacrifice.

He stared into her eyes and saw an exhaustion matching his own, a surety that the prize was worth the effort but damn that effort was a stretch.

He gave Nick's mission standard. "I see a dark sail on the horizon set under a dark cloud that hides the sun." He didn't know how much Nick told her, or if Nick told her anything.

He waited for Nick's confirm.

She searched his face, seeking hope, for answers. "Bring me my Broadsword and clear understanding." She had a solid, strong voice, neither wispy or wind driven, nor husky or sensual. All her words came from inside her, her heart. She filtered nothing before it came out.

There is nothing hidden about this woman. How did she end up with Trailer? He smiled at the cashier. "Sorry, we made a mistake. This won't be necessary."

Outside, he stopped her. "Karen, stay close. Somebody's moved my car."

"No. Nick said you'd come here to find me if you knew. He switched cars with you."

Yes, I've been acquired.

They walked to the original Grande. Donaldson put his arm through hers. She didn't pull back. Instead, it seemed she placed more of her weight on him with every step. He opened the passenger door for her and, once both were seated, her gaze roved up and down the street searching for something. Her expression collapsed from longing to sorrow and she started to cry. Donaldson, remembering protecting Trailer against his storm not too many days earlier, now put his arms around Karen as the anger and fear came out of her. Holding her, he wondered if this was the ultimate product of augmentation: trauma and release.

Finally she calmed enough to tell him what happened; after Nick calmed her down, they drove to Millinocket. He told her to get all their money out of the bank and be ready to travel.

"When Nick talked with you did he look right at you or did he seem preoccupied? Distant, maybe. Maybe confused? Maybe even tired?"

"No, but he had something on his mind. A woman can tell. A wife knows."

The red mobile rang. He listened, acknowledged, and replaced it. "We're monitoring police frequencies. Rivers has been spotted up by Patten. You know where that is?"

6

Governor Mark Hatch achieved several terms in office by listening to everything his handlers said. Increasing popularity and national recognition, not all of it good, was making him bolder. "I don't care what the President says, dammit. I want my boys in there."

Ed Sylvio, in his late forties but still looking thirty-five due to an early athletic career, weight training, and several tens of miles of running every week, watched his boss carefully.

Play it slow, Sylvio. The man's unstable right now and that's dangerous.

Lately Sylvio found more and more evidence that Hatch's instructions and information came from outside of his usual circle and concluded whoever the hell else is feeding him is making him dangerous.

Sylvio had been with Hatch from his beginnings as an early 2030's arch-conservative in Portland fighting the influx of designer drugs into the schools. Sylvio, like several of Hatch's other aides, didn't believe in Hatch's policies as much as he believed Hatch would provide a steady coattail into state and eventually federal government. Several others of the governor's top aides had deserted in recent years as Hatch's uncompromising and outspoken conservatism increasingly rankled federal policymakers, but Hatch always came out clean. When Sylvio questioned him about his other sources of information, Hatch grinned what Sylvio called a shit-eating grin. "Be careful, Ed, there might be another rooster in the hen house." Sylvio's time was getting short but he felt a debt to Hatch for the ride thus far, a debt that would be repaid when Hatch's current term ran out.

One more year, Sylvio. One more year and you can move to Georgetown on some nice, fat appointeeship.

"Governor, I don't think this is a good idea. Lots of eyes are going to be on you during the next year. This might not be the time, not with so many defections in your close counsel."

"That's exactly why I think I should act now, Ed. Show the people that I'm not shaken by the cowards." Hatch walked back and forth behind an expansive oak desk, gesturing only when he reached a corner of the desk before turning back. Maine's state shield - a northern white pine with the word "Dirigo" - covered the wall behind him.

Hatch reminded Sylvio of a target in an arcade shooting gallery. "Governor, every federal and military official we've spoken with says to keep all state personnel out of this. They don't want the state police, the wardens, the foresters, and especially not the National Guard, involved. I think that's sound advice, considering what little they've told us."

"And that's another thing, Ed. They haven't told us much, have they?" Hatch stopped parading in front of the state shield and brought his fist down toward the desktop. He stopped it an inch above the desktop, then resumed the motion after checking neither his hand nor anything on his desktop would be damaged. The subdued office lighting and drawn curtains reminded Sylvio of every political thriller he'd ever seen. The smell and blue haze of cigar smoke were missing but little else.

"You know what that state motto means, Ed? It means *I Direct*. Well, it's time. Federal has nothing to do with state services, and the

National Guard are under the command of the state office. Besides," he grinned that shit-eating grin again, "I think this will be over before anything happens. You tell my boys and the press crews to get ready. Mark Hatch's going to show the people of Maine they voted a real man into office."

The governor's secretary opened his office door and the sharp, incandescent lighting framed Hatch against the state shield. He looked up, not startled, but smiling, as if caught in a photographer's flash.

7

Karen and Jim drove in a silence interrupted only by her directions to Patten and once when he stopped to examine the weapons, field inspecting each in turn, neither hurrying nor wasting time.

Karen didn't have to say anything when they got to Patten. Police and emergency vehicles blocked the roads. State troopers held their firearms at the ready.

Jim's car's plates got him through the roadblocks. He stopped about a hundred yards beyond the last EMT station.

"That's it? Patten is an ice cream stand and a motel at a cross-roads?" He turned around and headed back. What looked like a no-tell motel sported a sign in front that read, 'Motel-like rooms' and on the next line *Phones Welcome*. "I'll have to remember to bring my phone."

The focus of activity was a red-on-white Ford Explorer parked in front of an ice cream stand. The Explorer appeared untouched and showroom new. The ice cream stand stood about fifteen feet kitty-corner to a house that owed a lot to bigbox advertising. Stacked wood, power tools, and the chalk outlines of bodies lay on the ground in between. Jim and Karen drove slowly, weaving their way through several police barricades until they got back to the Explorer.

Eckhardt, already on site, mocked surprise when they pulled up and stopped. "Oh, Major Donaldson! Major Donaldson, sir! We're so glad you're here! Look at what's happened! Oh, please, Major Donaldson, help us, please." Then with no mockery, "How did I know you'd show up? Come here. I've got some pictures I want to show you."

"Stay in the car, Karen."

Eckhardt opened a briefcase resting on the hood of his Impala and flipped up a screen that started a slideshow at ten seconds per. The images showed the ice cream stand surrounded by what appeared to be amazingly lifelike but oddly positioned manikins. The slideshow progressed through a series of images of the same subjects, each image rotated to show different angles around the subjects.

Something caught Donaldson's eye. He paused the slideshow, magnified the image and started it over.

"These are CSI photos?"

"Yeah, takes you a second, doesn't it? First team on the scene couldn't understand why somebody parked all these dime store dummies out in the middle of nowhere. Then they noticed the flies on everything."

"Okay, I get the picture."

"Ho, ho, Donaldson. Very funny. No, don't go yet. There's some more I want to show you." He called up another folder. Another slideshow started. "You see, we got here about, oh, twelve to fifteen hours after it happened. That's our guess, but we're not sure if it was pre or post the Stacyville rampage. Maybe you can help us with that?

"Anyway, it went down at night. Lots of animals foraging for food, you know? Friendly little critters like fox, coydog, raccoon, crows, stray cats and dogs; you hear what I'm saying to you? They probably know the routine and show up about an hour after closing to scavenge the puddles of ice cream, knocked over soft drinks, dropped hot dogs and hamburgers.

"That's what they'd normally find, anyway. This time they came here and found, guess what, a party! Christ, they must've loved it." Eckhardt's thumb flew backward like a manic hitchhiker's. "We found bear shit back there. They must have smelled the blood and joined in the fun. I mean, damn, there was more than enough for everybody.

"Ah, but wait, there's more." He stopped the slideshow and pointed at the image. "Notice how most of them are standing up, but kind of funny? Whatever you let loose up here, it took some lumber and nails from where they were remodeling the house and..." He paused, looking around at the investigation team taking more photos, cataloguing more body parts, analyzing more blood spray patterns.

"Donaldson, I was in DC and New York during the homeless purges, I was shot down in Loreto, Pastaza, and Pando in the Coca Wars, and in the DEA during the Triangle cleanup - my cherry's long busted and I've never seen anything like this." He called up yet another folder. "A few of the civilians got knocked down by the animals. We'll figure out who they were from dental records."

Donaldson held up his hand.

"No, we're not done yet. There's one more thing you're going to see." He tapped another red folder. The screen flashed a key requirement. He inserted a chip from his keychain. A video started. "One good thing about modern society is that crime goes everywhere. These folks been complaining about vandals so they went and installed this fancy video surveillance system."

"I don't need to - "

"Oh yes you do, flyboy. I've seen this damn file twice and I still don't know what I'm looking at. You're going to watch it with me and let me know if I suddenly slipped into some Saturday night Twilight Zone bingefest."

Donaldson eyed him for a moment. "My name is James Donaldson," he said evenly. "You can call me Donaldson, James, and if I get to like you, Jim. If I don't like you - and you're getting real short - it's Major Donaldson, Sir.'

"Right now I've got my own shit to deal with here. It seems to have mixed with yours. Truly sorry about that.

"However and I could be mistaken on this point, you seem to have an attitude that is prohibitive to teamwork. You know, the kind of thing your kindergarten teacher checks off when she sends home your report card to your parents: Does not play well with others. So let me make a suggestion." His voice hardened. "Fuck off. Either fuck off and get your people out of my way - because, as you know, what's out there could hurt them - or trash the attitude so we can get some work done."

"You going to look at this file," Eckhardt hesitated, his jaw and lips moving as if discovering he was sucking on a lint-covered sourball, "Donaldson?"

"Yeah, okay. Go ahead."

Watching the video, Donaldson saw the Ford Explorer come down the road and park between old Chevys, Fords, and various pickups. Rivers got out and the locals checked him out, their expressions classifying him as someone passing through, another vacationer lost on a backroad. Rivers fit in, he was designed to fit in. Only slightly larger than the average man, with his prosthetics in place his face didn't bear the obvious marks of augmentation Trailer's did.

He fit in. To a point. The locals' looks said, "Hi, Tourist, leave your money and go, don't stay, you don't belong."

Donaldson cringed. First trigger. Lack of social acceptance.

The video showed Rivers cataloguing the family staring at him from the nearest pickup as he walked to the ice cream stand's Order window. Anybody else would have ignored the locals' social rebuff as some kind of Down East or Yankeeism. A kind of "Lived here all your life?" "Not yet" exchange.

"What'll you have?" asked a middle-aged woman behind the Order window.

"How much further is it to the next town? Oh, and a Coke, please."

"Which way you going?"

"My guess is north."

The woman pulled a Coke bottle from a sixpack in a refrigerator and opened the window screen. She smiled. "You don't know which way you're going?"

A loud, nasally, tenor voice hollered from the parking lot, slurring the words, "You stupid son-of-a-bitch bastard don't you know anything?"

Donaldson backed up the video.

Eckhardt said, "What? We haven't got to the good stuff yet."

Donaldson watched Rivers pull himself in and tuck his head slightly when the man hollered. "Just wanted to check something."

Second trigger: You couldn't find a better match for Rivers' father's voice if you hunted for it.

Rivers turned to the sound of a car door slamming behind him.

A man in his late forties, early fifties, with an empty holster on his belt, staggered beside his pickup. He had the look of someone who weightlifted then stopped but didn't stop drinking. About the same size as Rivers, the drunk carried more of his weight in a gut that rolled over his belt. Spider veins spread from his nose across his face, stopped only by puffy cheeks and eyes reddened from long drunks.

Rivers turned back to the window but stopped when the man grabbed a skinny, brown-haired boy in his early teens sitting in the bed of the pickup. The boy stood up, staring around him. His eyes fixed on Rivers. Without warning the man buried his fist in the boy's gut, doubling him over.

Rivers stared at the people in the parking lot, finally returning to the drunk and the boy. The boy's eyes swelled with tears as he coughed and gasped for air. A woman came out from her side of the truck. "No, Benny, don't hit him again."

"Shut up and get back in the truck." Benny pulled his fist back again. Nobody in the parking lot made a move to help.

Suddenly Rivers stood beside Benny. "Don't do that."

Benny looked Rivers up and down, then puffed his chest out and hooked his thumbs at his belt, his gut billowing around his arms. "What-do-I-have-to-do-be-a-god-damn-saint-to-my-own-kid?" It came out as one word, almost indecipherable as Benny slurred the sentence.

"Don't hit the boy again."

People started getting out of their trucks. The lady in the ice cream stand called out, "The next town north's Hersey. Here's your Coke. No charge."

Rivers evaluated the people in the parking lot. "You're going to let him hurt the boy, aren't you?"

Nobody answered. Benny laughed. "Hey, don't he look real good in them new clothes and fancy car. He don't have no guns, though. Hey, don't you know you need guns to hunt? I don't see a gun rack. You got any guns?"

Rivers twitched. Donaldson played back the clip twice to make sure. Watching again, he saw Rivers with his arms at his sides, straight-backed but relaxed, releasing his vertebral column without gaining height. "You haven't had a serviceable weapon in your holster in six - " he sniffed twice, his nose wrinkling " - No, more like seven years."

Benny's eyes focused for a moment. "Wha...What?"

Rivers watched as people gathered around him. "And not a one of you with a phone out, nobody doing a thing because you all know each other, you all cover for each other, nobody sees or hears a thing." Rivers shook his head. "This is institutional violence. Any of you get that? Or are you all so backwoods fucking stupid you've never heard the term before?"

Donaldson shook his head, almost in rhythm with Rivers. Third trigger. It's all over now.

One of the other men, his hands in front, open, hopeful, pleading, said, "Hey, hey, Benny. He didn't mean nothing. You didn't mean any trouble, right, friend?"

Rivers continued shaking his head then laughed. "Hell, yes. Trouble is exactly what I mean." He spit and snapped his head.

Donaldson stopped the video.

"No, no," said Eckhardt. "This is where it gets real interesting. For one thing, that blonde guy stops being human. I'm convinced they wired this wrong and started picking up a Saturday matinee."

"I don't need to see anymore."

"No, I think you do. There's one more thing you're going to see." He fast-forwarded the clip then let it play.

The boy remained in the back of the truck, now standing too stiff and too quiet, his eyes open too wide and his breathing too shallow, surrounded in an ethereal landscape of standing corpses, some still twitching at random nerve firings.

Rivers walked into view, his face and clothing covered in blood, his prosthetics held in one hand while he brushed off some dirt and gravel with the other.

He lisped at the boy, "It's okay. No one's going to hurt you now."

The boy didn't respond.

"Hey, kid. It's okay now. I took care of that asshole for you."

Still no acknowledgement.

"I'm talking to you, kid. I saved your life. That fat prick's not going to trouble you anymore. Can you understand that? Say thank you or something."

"Thank you."

"That's better."

The boy got out of the truck and walked to two bodies, their arms intertwined. Donaldson recognized one as the boy's father and guessed the other was what remained of his mother. The boy stood beside them and started tapping his father's arm. "Hey, dad? Dad? Can I talk to you, dad? Dad? Are you okay, dad?" He started tapping his mother's arm. "Ma, something's wrong with pop. You want me to undress him and get him into bed? Ma? Talk to me, ma. What's wrong?"

The boy reached for his father again and Rivers grabbed his arm. "Kid, they're gone, wasted. They can't hurt you anymore."

The boy shrugged off Rivers' hand and started tapping his father's corpse again. "Dad. Wake up, dad. Come on, dad, wake up. You want me to get the truck ready? Come on, dad, we got work to do."

Rivers jerked the boy away from the bodies. "Damn it, kid. I'm telling you they're gone. I saved your life."

The boy moved towards his parents.

Rivers twitched. "Don't you get it, kid? They don't love you? Fuck, if they were still alive he'd be beating the shit out of you and she'd be standing there screaming at him to stop but not doing a thing to save your sorry ass."

The boy shrieked and pounded on the bodies. "Dad. Come on, dad."

"Grow up, you little bastard. Grow up and get real. They're dead. Gone. I killed them. Thank me for saving your life."

"Let me go. I want my dad. Dad? Make him stop, dad. Mom, tell dad to make this guy stop."

"No-o," Rivers growled. His arms came up and down, almost too quickly for the camera to catch. "I saved your life. They didn't do anything for you." His arms swung again. "No."

The boy disappeared.

Rivers shook as spasms snapped through his body. "I took care of it," he whispered, then screamed, "I took care of it."

He pulled his head back and filled himself with air, releasing it as a bellows reddening a flame. Then calmly, "I can take care of it."

He screamed again, "I can take care of it."

Then, like the boy, Rivers disappeared.

Donaldson asked, "What happened to the boy?"

Eckhardt pulled a third red folder. It automatically validated his key chip. "Wait for it. He was found walking around I-95 by a trucker."

The screen went black and lit up again, this time on the skinny, brown-haired boy, wrapped in a trauma suit from the neck down.

"What's wrong with the suit? The right side didn't inflate properly?" Donaldson pointed. "He looks lopsided."

Eckhardt shut the viewer off. "Part of his problem is that he's got lots of Percocet in him. Other than that, Blondie smashed through the shoulder, arm, and upper ribs. Tore the arm clear off.

"So, you want to know why I have an attitude? It's because something's walking around I know nothing about and that scares me. I don't like being scared. Came way the hell up here so I wouldn't be scared. Now, just like momma said, whatever you're afraid of, it's going to find you.

"My attitude back in Stacyville pissed you off? Gosh, Major Donaldson, I'm real sorry about that. By the way, does this UNSUB have a name? No, screw that, what the hell did you let loose in my woods? It does some cops, okay. It does a whole town and then special this kid? This thing is way, way wrong."

"He's starting to cascade."

Eckhardt pulled back. "Cascade? What kind of shit is that? And what the fuck do you mean 'he's starting'? You say it like the next thing I'm going to hear is 'he's going to get worse'."

"His name is Thomas Citroen Rivers, Lieutenant, and yes, he's going to get worse. I can get you all the information you want. None of it will be useful because he no longer exists." Donaldson answered but kept his eyes on a Suburu Grande Sport that approached, the windows tinted so he couldn't see the passengers. "More correctly, you won't have access to any relevant information about him.

"What he's demonstrating is *surplus killing*. Normally, a specific sequence of events leads up to a prey animal's death and shuts off the predator's impulse to kill. Right now and I don't know why, the sequence is jammed. Something's interfering. In the wild, it's usually something quite rare: a nova keeping the night sky daylight bright or mid-winter temperatures equaling summer temperatures for a prolonged period of time or the prey doesn't flee for whatever reason. Whatever causes it, the predator just keeps on killing, way beyond what's necessary for its own survival."

"Christ, Donaldson, do you listen to yourself? You're talking like this is some kind of rabid wolf."

Karen walked up to them, her eyes moving from one abomination to another. "My Nickie couldn't do this."

Eckhardt monitored her approach. "And you are?"

"Karen Trailer, meet Detective Douglas Eckhardt, Maine State Office of Special Investigations."

"You're Karen Trailer? You mean 'Nickie' like 'Nicholas Trailer'?

You think your old man could do *this*? No, let me rephrase that. You think your old man *could* do this?" Eckhardt shook his head. "It sounds stupid no matter how I say it."

Donaldson said, "Rivers isn't Nick Trailer. He's looking for Nick Trailer. Nick Trailer is the other man your witnesses saw."

Karen added, "Rivers' is the one who killed your police. Not Nickie, if that's what you think. My Nickie knocked him out and we left in his Suburu."

Eckhardt rested his elbows on the hood of the car. "I've got two questions to ask you. First, what pissed this Rivers off? Second, what did your husband do to knock him out?"

One of the uniforms handed Eckhardt an order form from the ice cream stand. "You're a real popular kind of guy, Donaldson. Everybody's leaving you notes." He handed Jim the paper. Written with a precision mimicking typesetters, scrunched between 'DRINKS' and 'ONION RINGS' was

From DDS&T PO Lieutenant Rivers To DDS&T Roam COS Major Donaldson Re DDS&T PZ Trailer MESSAGE FOLLOWS There can be only One END MESSAGE

Donaldson leaned back against Eckhardt's car and sighed. "It's from some old movie he saw, kind of. Some kind of battle cry, if I remember correctly."

The Suburu pulled up in front of them. Before it came to a complete stop the passenger door opened and Ingman stepped out. "We should've shopped that freak when we found him in country." He groomed his mustache as he nodded at the note in Donaldson's hands. "What's that? More noseworms?"

Donaldson debated handing Ingman the communique. His eyes roamed from Eckhardt to Ingman and past them into what was left of Patten.

The driver door of Ingman's Suburu opened. Levesque got out, head shaved and camouflage coded. He scanned the area, his eyes resting on the number of ambulances and emergency vehicles and the remaining cleanup.

Ingman looked around him, his jaw and lips twitching as he studied the intensity of the violence, his hand forgetting to groom his mustache. "He's going into optimal state, isn't he?"

"Nobody sees the elephant in the living room, right?" Donaldson said.

"These attacks," Donaldson waved at the destruction around them, "the photographs you brought me at Loring, the remains of Steiner Distasio found; these weren't done by Trailer. I knew something was wrong when I saw them. Trailer would avoid detection, and he knows how to draw attention to himself if he wants to. Besides, if he did kill, it would be because he evaluated something as a threat and there's no gut pile. Even in Chelmsford he left a gut pile."

Karen exclaimed, "What?"

"I'll explain later, I promise. Right now, don't worry, it's history and already taken care of." His gaze returned to Ingman. "If he was killing for pleasure, he'd've surfaced by now."

"So what are you saying, Donaldson? You trying to tell me there really are some bears out here with noseworm?"

Levesque, still at attention, cleared his throat.

Donaldson asked, "Is there something you'd like to say, sergeant?"

"Are we hunting the individual who did this, Sir?"

"We're hunting two individuals. I suspect and can not confirm that one of them, Nicholas Trailer, is friendly. The other one, Thomas Rivers, did this, so to answer your question, yes."

Ingman yelled, "The other one? God damn 'the other one'?"

"That's right, Ingman. There are no noseworms. Rivers did these. My guess is he did all the others, too."

Ingman stared at the destruction surrounding them. "You made another one."

"Are you upset because nobody told you or because somebody actually made another one?"

Ingman laughed slightly, more a sad chuckle than an actual laugh.

"Should I alert anywhere else?"

"To what purpose?"

"Should I tell the forestry and wardens to evacuate the woods? There's nothing anyone can do, is there? Can we send in the toy soldiers? To help evacuate?"

"Again, to what purpose? What if there's an encounter? They'll just be fodder. Nothing conventional could stand against either of them if it came to it. Nothing readily unconventional, for that matter, and massively unconventional I have there." Donaldson pointed at the vehicles.

Eckhardt said, "We have to get civilians out of harm's way. You're saying we can't stop them, can we at least get people away from them? Radio broadcast coupled with emergency 'net and TXT to all mobile signals in the woods?"

Donaldson shrugged. "I don't know. Yeah, go ahead. I'll brief whoever you want via closed-circuit monitor."

Ingman asked, "How do you want this going out?"

"No offense Ingman...Don...but you were pretty good at coming up with plausibles. Care to take a whack at this one and let the rest of us know before it goes out?"

"I'm on it." He lifted his own red mobile to his ear.

Donaldson turned to Karen. "Do you have any idea where Nick might be headed?"

She pointed west. "Nick wanted to get Rivers into the woods, past Katahdin because of vacationers so maybe in the lakes around Kokadjo. He thought he'd have a chance there. He said he was going to keep Rivers away from people as much as he could. If he could make it, he was going for the old POW camp at Spencer and into Bigelow. He thought of Seboomook but said it had too many people and Bigelow would be deserted this time of year. He considered Bog Brook in Gilead but there's people between here and there and he didn't think any Rangers stationed there would survive."

"Eckhardt, I'm going to take my man and go looking. If I can't find anything, I'll be back." He laughed. "Hell, I hope we'll be back if we do find something. Especially if we do find something. Hopefully, I'll be able to brief you in three hours."

Ingman cut in, "We've already got a plausible deniability - a neuro-organic got dropped during transport, the canister ruptured crazing wildlife, some bears got a whiff and this is the result - ready to go. That works for everybody?"

Eckhardt looked at his uniformed and plainclothes personnel. "You're telling me nothing my people could do would work?"

"Exactly that, yes."

"You got three hours. Go."

8

Donaldson drove as Levesque channeled the PPS-15 and RABFAC cones, the earplug and guidewires blending into the camouflage on his scalp. Fifteen minutes up the road Levesque adjusted his equipment. "This Rivers. Is he roughly two-hundred k's?"

"Got him? Trailer'd go about three-hundred."

"Must be Rivers. He's moving fast and flanking about a klick and a quarter up. There's no heavier bipeds in the woods."

"Could mean Trailer's gone silent."

Three-quarters of a klick up they came to a walking trail with a sign indicating a picnic area at the trail head. A gray sharkskin BMW 950i snugged the treeline at the foot of the trail, red lights blinking from the mirrors, dash, and doors, showing the car in armed mode in case anyone tampered with it.

"Rivers driving this?" Levesque asked.

"I wouldn't think so. He wouldn't lock it if he was."

Levesque adjusted his instruments. "Just picked up some civilians on SSR, Sir."

"Get the Wolff Ears out."

They heard, "Throw me the ball, Andy. Come on, son, throw me the ball."

"Sir?"

"Yep, time to boogie." Donaldson opened the back of the Grande, pulled out the M16 and a belt of armor-piercing shells out, and handed them to Levesque. "Yours." He strapped himself into a cage brace and attached the Vulcan with full packs. "If it's big and it moves, kill it." He handed Levesque a set of Wolff Ears and they started up the path.

The Wolff Ears picked up four voices; male, female, a young boy. Donaldson guessed their ages as thirty, thirty, and seven. The fourth voice, Rivers, could only be picked up as infra-sound, singsonging a bizarre children's playground chant, as if choosing sides for some frightening game, "MY mother punched YOUR mother RIGHT IN THE nose. WHAT color WAS THE blood?"

The infra-sound went silent. Then the same voice, higher pitched, almost audible, "Orange, ooh, orange," followed by a sound like a dog snuffling the ground picking up a scent.

The voice a third time, fully audible. "Come in, children, lunch is ready."

Levesque whispered over the Wolff Ears audio. "Prepare for a major shitstorm, Sir?"

"Affirmative." Donaldson nodded and listened as they walked, getting winded by the weight of the armament and the unexpected climb. If Rivers was phasing in and out of his past experiences, they were ones Donaldson knew nothing about.

A different sound over the RABFAC and SSR, strange.

"What is that, Major? It's not bipedal motion."

Donaldson's stomach churned. "It's Rivers. He's skipping up the trail."

Rivers, fully audible. "Pardon me, I know you, don't I?"

Donaldson jogged, his lungs throbbing, unable to pull enough air in.

The male voice. "Oh?"

"Your name's 'Andy', right? You're a doctor."

"Why, yes, I am. How did you know that? Have we met? Do I know you?"

Rivers chuckled. "Yeah, I thought that was you, Andy. But you wouldn't remember me. I was nothing back then. Nothing to you, anyway. I thought we were friends but you, Andy, you made sure I knew just what I was."

A pause and a breath. "To you."

Another pause. A heavier breath. A piston building pressure before detonation. "Remember me now, do you?"

The RABFACs detected shuffling feet - Donaldson guessed the woman and child's - the steps not neat, not clean, but quick, nervous, moving through leaves, moving away from Rivers towards the trail head, towards Donaldson, towards Levesque, towards their car.

Rivers. "No, wait, folks. Don't leave yet."

The man's voice. "Take Andy to the car, Sherrie."

Rivers moved.

The woman shrieked.

"Hey, kiddo. I knew your dad a long time ago."

The woman, her voice high, tight, angered. "Put down my son."

"This son?"

The woman, raging. "I said put him down."

"This your son?"

The man's voice, uneven but still confident. "What do you want?"

Rivers' voice. "And he's the father? Really?" A deep inhale. "Does he know you're sleeping with somebody else?"

Another inhale.

"For that matter, so is he. Don't you people wash when you're done? Or do you like carrying somebody else's stink on you. Maybe so you can waft past each other and stick the proverbial knife in a little more?"

The woman hissed, "Put my child down, now."

A pause. It seemed only Rivers and the child breathed. Rivers said,

"Come here."

The woman's voice. "What?"

"Come here."

"Why should I come over there?"

"Do you want me to put your son down?"

"You'll let go of my son if I come over to you?"

"What are you, negotiating a contract? You some kind of attorney? Get your cuntlips over here." Then to the boy in his arms, "Ever seen your mom's cuntlips? Up close and personal? I'll bet they're real pretty."

Donaldson heard a click. A red uplink warning light blinked on his cage brace.

The woman spoke slowly, clearly, as if standing before a crowd. "As a matter of fact, I am an attorney. I'm in the State AG's office - "

The man cut her off. "You're an assistant to the deputy State AG."

Rivers again. "Isn't this amazing, kid? Pay attention. It's things like this that'll scar you for the rest of your life; Your parents pissing on each other rather than saving your life. Get it? Their egos are more important than you."

The boy. "Mommy?"

"Quiet, Andy." Her voice shifted towards the man, again hissing. "I'm in the State AG's office." Her voice turned towards Rivers, a sound of defiance. "And I'm now documenting this."

A click followed by an uplink warning light.

She's wearing commspecs? She's streaming live video? To where? To whom?

The 'brace didn't have signal blockers.

Fuck!

Rivers laughed. "Are you really that stupid, lady? I mean, you said you're an attorney, are you also going to admit to being a moron?"

"I am documenting this."

"You are a moron. You are situationally stupid. What do you think that uplink's going to do? Do you think help's going to magically appear? Don't you understand that I can kill you all long before help arrives? Or that telling me," Rivers perfectly imitated her voice, "'I'm documenting this'," his voice returned to normal, "is not helping you win your case? You think title and position equates to safety, power, and authority? Here? Fifty miles the other side of east buttfuck?

"You're an attorney? Big fucking deal. I'm the devil incarnate, I'm about to kill your son, slowly rip the flesh from your bones and you know what? There's not a damn thing you or weasel-dick over there can do about it. You think being an attorney, a state AG, gives you safety? You think you got power and authority over me?"

Rivers voice but quieter, confidentially. "What's your name, son?"

The child, timid, unsure. "Andy Junior."

"Andy Junior, do you know your mommy and daddy hate each other? Do you know they'll drop kick you over the side if it gives them the chance to shove the knife a little deeper into each other?"

He pressed the little boy's bladder. "Pee for me, kid." Clothes saturating. A deep breath.

"Do you know that guy over there's not really your father? She's your mother, but I have no idea who your real father is. Not him, though."

His voice louder, towards the woman. "Do you even know who the father is?"

Levesque over the audio. "Sir?"

"Go full hot. He's mapping his family of origin onto these people."

"Mommy?"

Rivers again. "Hey, good idea. Hold your arm out just like that, straight out. Point at your mom for me, okay, Andy Junior?" Then to the mother, "Still documenting this?"

The woman. "Wha...Wait." She shrieked, "Wait."

The child, shrill, screaming. Repeatedly screaming.

Rivers' voice again, calm but the words slurred. "Ah, that's some good eatin'." A pause. "Document that, did you?"

Donaldson's legs moved like lead. The trail became molasses. Rivers was talking between bites.

The man moved.

Bones cracked.

The man screamed.

Rivers. "We went to school together. I use to call you Ange. See you grew a mustache since then. I remember you told me men with mustaches were trying to make their mouths into cuntfaces. I wonder if Ingman knows that?" Rivers' voice, towards the woman. "No, no, Sherrie. You stay right there and keep those commspecs recording, okay?"

Rivers. Moving. Walking. His full weight coming down with each step. Leaving a trail? His voice, low to the ground. Kneeling?

"But that was when I could grow one and you couldn't, so you'd have to say it back then because you always found a way to make others feel small." A laugh. "You were so fucking insecure. You masked it well, I'll give you that, but you were way more insecure than I ever was."

A sigh. "Doesn't matter. I couldn't grow a 'stache now if I wanted to."

A pause. "But... Ange, ever heard the expression 'Wipe that smile off your face or I'll wipe it off for you?' How about I wipe that 'stache off your face for you?"

Ripping flesh. The man, howling, insane.

Rivers, towards the woman. "Does this make me look fat?"

The woman, moaning, on the ground. "Oh, come on, get up. Give us a little kiss." Then, "Oops, sorry. Damn thing won't stay on."

Donaldson slipped, got up, slipped again.

"Did you hear that? Think somebody's watching your video?"

The woman screamed, "Help."

Movement. Quick. Rivers.

The woman again. Half a scream. Cut short. Silence.

Rivers, spoken while standing. "Well, that was stupid. Who's going to document this now?"

A kick. A howl. Ground level. "You know, Andy - Ange, remember when I use to call you 'Ange'? - I always knew you were stupid but I never thought you'd marry stupid."

Donaldson fell under the weight of the Vulcan and signaled Levesque to go on ahead.

Rivers spoke conversationally, casually. "Yeah, we knew each other, but that was a long time ago. I was shorter and fatter back then. We were in the same class, but you always got the good grades. Looks like you did right through college, being a doctor. What kind of doctor are you? What do you call them? Proctologist? Are you an asshole doctor, Ange?

"Do you remember you once bet me a dollar that Sirius was the brightest star in the sky? And I said not absolute brightness? And you said I was stupid because I kept on saying it was Deneb - "

Whack!

Air rushing from collapsing lungs.

"and when I got a book and proved Sirius wasn't - "

Whack!

Blood, pumping out of open wounds, the heart struggling to keep pressure up.

"you refused to pay me what you promised."

Whack! Whack!

"What you promised!"

Whack! Whack! Whack!

"You said I was too stupid to know anything, anyway, and I was so stupid you didn't have to pay."

The *Whack!*s too quick to count, jackhammers breaking bones.

"I had to fucking chase you through the school hallway and what did you do?"

Whack!

"You turned and threw the dollar at my feet. You didn't even hand it to me. You weren't even man enough, gentleman enough, to do that."

The jackhammer kicks falling as Rivers talked. "You. Fucking. Loser. Ange."

The jackhammer stopped.

The child quiet until now, in shock, sobbed.

Rivers kneeling.

"I remember you called me up once to come over, but by the time I got there another one of your friends showed up. You were..." Rivers paused, remembering. "Embarrassed. By me."

"Come to think of it, you only played with me when nobody else was around to play with."

Where is he getting this? There's nothing like this in his 201. Donaldson kept climbing, kept hoping, kept hurling air into his lungs, fighting up the rise even though he knew it was too late. Rivers had gone way over into cascade. Nothing would bring him back.

Another sound. Some kind of sucking? Wet. Floppy.

"You still in there, Ange?"

He's picking through the bones.

"Do you remember seventh grade? We stood outside waiting for the school bell to ring to go in in the morning? You started whispering things, taking all the guys we hung out with and walking with them away from me. You'd look over your shoulder and whispering, real quiet, making sure that the only thing I could hear was my name. That all I could hear was 'mumble mumble mumble mumble Rivers. Mumble mumble mumble Rivers.' Then you'd nod and they'd nod and you'd look at me and shake your heads and start all over again? Mumble mumble mumble Rivers. Mumble mumble mumble Rivers? Huh? Remember that old buddy old pal dear old friend of mine?"

Donaldson stopped. The RABFAC showed only one signature: the Rivers-child composite.

"Huh? Do you?"

Donaldson hoped it was a composite.

Rivers voice. Too calm. "Do you remember when you and Hank Stoadt came over to my house? We were, what, maybe ten? You came over after you and I had a fight. You said you wanted to play. You sat there and waited for me to get dressed. You fucking watched me and smiled. You knew what you were going to do. You must have been laughing all the time. I was so glad to see you. I thought you really wanted to be my friend. We went outside. You tried to get me to look the other way, but I saw something move and guess what. There was Hank. And stupid fuck me, I was so glad Hank was there with you because it meant the two of you really wanted to be my friends. And you said we could play. And Hank said we could play. And you two decided to play hide-and-seek. And I was so happy you guys wanted to play with me I said sure. And you guys said I was It. And I said sure. And then, as I closed my eyes, you two knocked me down and started beating me up, laughing all the time you were hitting me, remember?"

The composite separated. Rivers held the boy at arm's length.

"Well, Ange, I remember."

The boy, held by his feet, swung in an arc onto his father's remains.

"I - "

Bones cracking.

"fucking - "

Fluid sounds, blood spray.

"remember."

A sound from Donaldson's slaughterhouse days, something the slaughtermen called a flat-fuck fall: the disemboweled carcass, nothing more than a bag of blood and bones, flopping to the floor to be discarded.

Donaldson, his lungs collapsing, falling to the ground, crawling.

All movement up the rise stopped.

Rivers, calm. No exertion. Not breathing heavy. "No. You don't remember. You don't remember any of it at all. That's how little any of what you did to me means to you."

Donaldson got up. Levesque would be facing Rivers alone with no element of surprise.

"Yeah, you did some rotten things to me when we were kids, Andy."

Silence.

How much farther? Donaldson's legs offered as much support as blades of grass.

"Hey, you dropped your wallet. No, you just stay there, I'll bring it to you."

The Wolff Ears went quiet save a slight rhythmic rustling. Levesque, ascending the trail.

Wallet pages flipping.

A pause.

"Oh, shit. You're not Andrew LaCoff, you're Andrew Bardene."

More pages flipping. Another pause.

"But you are an asshole doctor. I got that part right."

Hysterical laughter.

"Oops. Sorry. My bad. Hey, two out of three, right? At least Sherrie got most of this on uplink. It's stored somewhere." Now as quiet infrasound, spoken intimately, as if by someone at his bedside, the whisper of a deep-throated lover, "I know you're out there, Major."

Levesque's M16 fired.

"MISSED me MISSED me NOW You got TO Kiss me."

The M16 fired again. A tree splintered.

"I'll give you one more shot, okay? Go for it."

The '16 released another round.

"Boy, you suck. Put it on automatic. Go ahead, I'll wait. Ready? Good. Now - "

The '16 went full auto, stripping trees of their leaves and limbs.

"Clever boy! I was about to say 'keep up'."

The '16's continuous fire shattered boulders and carved the ground around the picnic site as Levesque swung it hoping to finalize Rivers. Tree limbs fell, the '16 cutting through them like a mad chainsaw. Donaldson saw Rivers jumping from treetop to treetop with the '16 spraying wood chips in his wake.

Then only a whirring, the weapon's ammunition spent, and a thud.

"Come here, handsome. Give daddy a great big kiss."

FUCK!

Donaldson's squawkbox activated. Levesque had gone silent to sanction Rivers. Now it showed open and active on Leveeque's channel.

Donaldson wheezed into it, "CarrotTop, mission status."

After a few seconds of dead air, Donaldson checked the contact light. Green. Communications established and active.

Donaldson tapped his squawkbox. "CarrotTop, status."

Nothing. He stopped moving. He swallowed. "GoldenBoy, confirm status."

"Target neutralized."

The squawkbox deactivated.

Donaldson ran, his legs failing at every third step until he crested the path.

Levesque sat directly in the path, a clean hole about the size of a fist went from his chest to back. He had no heart. The M16, snapped in two, rested in his lap, his right hand still holding the trigger guard.

His left hand covered the hole in his chest. He said, "Sorry, Maj..." and his eyes glazed over, dead. What remained of the family were piled on top of the picnic table.

Rivers called to him, his voice clear but too distant to be tracked, "You sent a man? Not even an augmented man? You don't respect me, Major Donaldson. We're going to have to change that."

Donaldson, almost rolling back down the path, set his commgear to wide-channel. He called Emergency Medical first then Loring.

Later, after confirming the ambulances were back on the road and safe, he drove back to Patten. The town already had the elements of a ghost town; lifeless, the buildings empty shells, the only activity five heavily armed state troopers, Eckhardt, Ingman, and Karen.

Ingman spoke first. "I heard your call to Loring. I told Eckhardt here to order a forced evacuation in an eighty-klick radius using this spot as ground zero."

Donaldson nodded. "I've ordered Air Cav to do a dust-and-burn, Karen. Sorry."

9

Nick waited in a tree at the edge of Rivers' response limit. Rivers stood beside a parked Chevy Aero about five hundred meters down the road, his attention on two young female hikers. He had one by the throat and prepared to shove the other's head through the windshield.

Trailer jumped off the branch and faced Rivers, landing beside some tree trunks stacked for skidding, their chain draped over them but not secured.

Rivers looked up.

"I see you like pretty things." Nick's voice echoed down the road like distant thunder.

Rivers smiled and pulled his lips back from his teeth. "You want to stop me?"

"Hell, no. You want to waste your time with small game, go ahead. That's the best you can do, go for it. It's good that you know your limits. You won't get hurt that way."

Rivers dropped the women and started towards Nick.

"The last time you had your chance, I put you to sleep and you never even knew I was there." Nick turned his back.

Rivers picked up speed like he was a deuce and a half under full load.

Nick gauged Rivers' steps and speed. He placed his feet and leapt straight up.

Rivers' steps were closer than they should have been.

They didn't gauge his top speed accurately.

Nick braced himself. Four meters off the ground a freight train slammed into his back.

Rivers reached one hand around Nick's left side grabbing for his ribs, the other hand came around Nick's right.

Nick flexed his shoulders, back, and chest, layering the muscles as he would to protect himself from combat rounds. He rotated his head and saw Rivers' smiling face, his teeth coming down on his spine.

Nick tucked into a ball, using Rivers momentum to start them spinning. He snapped his head back into Rivers', grabbed Rivers' forearms and dug his fingers in between the radius and ulna until Rivers' wrists and elbows popped.

The ground came up fast, Nick on top of Rivers, elbows and knees in the vitals then rolling aside and up on his feet.

Rivers sat up, blood trickling from his lips. "You know what I am?"

"Phase One, Urban Combat Unit."

"Phase One. Better than you. They corrected their mistakes with me."

Nick shook his head. "They compounded their mistakes with you, my friend."

"I had your lunch when you were outside Dickey with that idiot and you never even knew I was there."

Trailer clapped his hands and laughed. "Didn't they teach you any-thing? That little stunt with the bread under the tree? I was waiting for that. You're mapped, junior. You're acquired. You can't surprise me anymore."

Could Rivers spot the lie through Trailer's augmentation? He be-gan to shake.

Nick stared at him. That's not Augmented movement.

Rivers' shaking got worse. His face reddened. A moment later he blanched. His mouth foamed. "I'm the best. *Me.*"

Nick mapped what he saw against Rivers' 201 file. That's rage. Blind rage. No Augmentation can remove that. Did they foster that rage and anger in him the way they did in me?

He backed away.

Rivers singsonged, his voice a jeering child's, "Scaredy-Cat, Scaredy-Cat!"

Nick laughed.

"You're scared!"

"No, amazed." Something new moved through Nick, tickling him. He laughed again, but at what?

He adjusted the awkwardness in his mind until the right word surfaced: Pity.

I pity him.

Rivers, not shaking any longer, ran his tongue over the blood and laughed. "Must have bit my lip." He got to his knees. His hands flailed at the ends of his arms. He flopped an arm on the ground until the hand rested palm up, his arm placed as if to curl weights. "You know what your problem is, Nick?" Rivers stepped on the hand and pulled his arm back. Nick heard the bones snap back into place. "Your problem is that you don't want to kill." Rivers took his foot off his hand and wiggled the fingers. "Me, I kind of like it." He held his hand up. "See? Just like new."

Nick threw some of the powder on Rivers he used back at his house.

Rivers sneezed, violently, once, then smiled. "Sorry, Nick. I've already adapted to it." Rivers flopped his other hand until it rested palm up on the ground.

Before Rivers could snap his wrist back into place, Nick kicked Rivers' head, toe-on, coming off the ground with all his mass in the strike.

Rivers rolled back with the impact, coming up on his feet and shaking his head. He picked up the skidder chain and whipped it at Nick. The chain wrapped around Nick and Rivers pulled him in.

Nick stretched to his limit.

The chain fell away. Nick snapped his forehead into Rivers' skull.

Rivers stepped back, dazed but not stopped.

Nick followed him, jumping off the ground with his left and front snapkicking with his right.

Rivers came off the ground with the power of the kick, landed in a lineman's three-point stance, grunted and started towards Nick again.

Nick took a step back and repeated the maneuver, this time jumping off his right and kicking with his left. The kick lifted Rivers from the ground. Bones cracked in Rivers' crotch.

Rivers smiled and took another step towards him. Nick came off the ground again, his right foot shattering more bones in Rivers' crotch as his left snapped Rivers' head back. Rivers' legs were weakening. He staggered, then laughed and took another step towards Nick.

Nick dropped into Hunter/Seeker state, Rivers too powerful an enemy to engage otherwise. His own rage and frustration overtook him, forced him to become what he wanted to flee in order to survive.

He tackled Rivers and knocked him against a tree.

Rivers started to fall.

Nick spread his legs, stretched, released and smashed his brow into Rivers' face, digging his fingers into Rivers ribs, pulling until Rivers' intestines ruptured into his hands.

Rivers raised his arms.

Nick snapped his torso, driving from the hip, smashing his forearms and elbows, left and right, directly under Rivers' arms, splintering Rivers' upper ribs into his lungs, shattering his clavicles.

Rivers' arms fell limp at his sides. His left eye had swollen shut and he had no prosthetics.

"I remember you as far more handsome when I first met you."

Rivers looked at Nick through his right eye and laughed. "You don't remember shit, old man."

Nick remembered facing his father, feeling that no matter what he did, his father would be there to beat him, laugh at him, mock him.

His point of view shifted. He saw himself through his father's eyes, tiny, frail, frightened and afraid, knowing the hand was raised and soiling himself because he had nowhere to run, nowhere to hide, nowhere to be safe. The point of view shifted further, approaching the little boy like a circling hawk until Nick saw the world through the little boy's eyes, felt the cold wooden floor on bare little boy feet, felt the wetness in his pajamas on thin little boy legs, tasted the blood and felt the heavy hand slap his small little boy mouth.

Nick felt the hawk, its talons digging deep as it rested on his shoulders, lifting him back, up, into the sky, until Nick remembered everything, remembered how it was and realized how it was supposed to be.

"I remember me!" he screamed. "Me, God damn it. I remember me!"

"Big fucking deal, Trailer," Rivers slurred through broken lips. "Who gives a shit?"

"I do," Nick said. "I do." He swung uppercuts from behind his hips, landing them in Rivers' neck and jaw, grunting and pounding, his body a destructive machine, Rivers' head snapping back and forth against the tree like a flesh covered speed bag.

The machine gained speed, momentum. Blood covered splinters flew from the tree as Rivers' head banged against it.

The trunk snapped. Nick brought both fists up in a double backhammer. Rivers' head smashed onto the splintered trunk.

He backed away. Rivers didn't move, his body supported by his impaled skull.

Nick walked down to the road and stopped. He turned back.

Rivers remained supported by the tree, immobile, blood flowing from the back of his head down the tree and forming puddles at his feet.

Nick turned away, took two steps and stopped.

"I can't be anything until I'm willing to be everything."

He faced Rivers again.

"Everything. Everything I've ever been.

"Everything."

His face went plastic, his back arched and released without gaining height, his muscles bunched and bundled under his skin. Walking to the skidding pile, he picked up one of the tree trunks and walked back to Rivers.

His eyes opened wide. His irises retreated. His breathing changed. His skin gathered a blue tint.

He swung the trunk like a double-ot Louisville slugger into Rivers' knees.

"Never make an enemy you can't afford to keep," he rumbled, and swung the trunk into Rivers' chest.

10

Hatch closed his office door and stepped into the hall. "They did what?"

Sylvio looked towards the closed door.

"Well?"

"They called a forced evacuation with a fifty-mile radius centered on Patten. The official word is that some experimental gas got dropped in the area and the Air Force wants to go in and get the tanks. Once that's done, the forest will be open again."

"Stacyville's south of Patten, isn't it?"

"Yes, and the animal attacks come down the Allagash to Stacyville."

A messenger came up to them and handed Sylvio a note. "The Bangor air tower just picked up a scramble from Loring."

"Good, I'll - "

A tall, thin, late-30s, white-haired, blue-eyed, blue-suited bureaucrat staggered out of the State AG's office two doors down, leaned against the wall and slid to the floor, his leather-soled shoes skidding and scuffling as his legs refused to support him.

His hands cupped over his mouth. Vomit shot through his fingers and dripped from his hands, covering the front of his suit and the floor where he sat. He breathed heavy but shallow, panting, his face as white as his hair. His hands fell away from his face as his bowels and bladder released.

Sylvio thought the man was having a heart attack and moved to administer first-aid. Hatch yelled at the man, "What the hell's wrong with you?"

The man looked at Hatch, tears washing his face. "Sherrie. We got a video from Sherrie. They went picnicking west of Patten."

Hatch opened his office door enough to slide through. He pointed at the man on the floor. "Look after him." He squeezed into his office and closed the door before Sylvio got near.

11

We have a Green Go for the first sweep, air-tranq, on station, confirm," Wing Commander Robert Minich tongued the comm switch in
his gargoyle, the bug-eye helmet fitting snugly on his head and linking
him to much of the firing and surveillance systems on his ship, one
of five Apache WarCloud heavy-attack helicopters hovering over the
Maine forest.

A voice crackled back, "Two Seven Oh Niner confirmed. Tree
level, armed. You got everybody on gas-passers, Bobby?"

"Pooh Bear to Piglet, drum confirm, aye?" The Apache WarCloud
two ships starboard flanked belly up. "Drum confirm, aye. Pooh Bear
to Tigger, drum confirm, aye?" The WarCloud between Piglet and
Minich flanked belly up. "Drum confirm, aye." Minich checked his
port. "Pooh Bear to Kanga, drum confirm, aye?" The WarCloud two
ships port flanked belly up. "Drum confirm, aye. Pooh Bear to Roo,
drum confirm, aye?" The remaining WarCloud belly rolled.

Piglet's voice snapped over the comm, "Back to your mother's
pouch." The comm picked up chuckling from the other ships.

"Drum confirm, aye. Pooh Bear to Christopher Robin, all air-tranq, affirmative."

The red ready light came on underneath the green station light. "Christopher Robin to Pooh Bear. Good hunting, Bobby."

Minich tongued closed Support's channel and put the Wing channel on the ship's horn. "Gentleman, low and lazy. I'm on point. All armed, one dangerous. Crop dusting jonnies." The position lights went green across his mission board as the five WarClouds swung down in goose formation, tight wing, to thirty meters over treetop and spread until they hovered one thousand meters from wing tip to wing tip. Minich's ship hovered over Rt.11 until the others showed ready at their positions. They started forward, slow and steady, Remoxipride and AJAX coming down from their fixed-wing dusters in a fine mist.

Two hours later they passed over the Northwest Piscataquis, coming up on Seboomook. Minich called, "All stop, close tanks, tighten." The WarClouds stopped in the air. The gas drums rolled into the ship's bellies as the WarClouds moved back to the tight goose formation. Minich's ship's 30mm chain gun rotated forward. The FFARs, folding fin aerial rockets, swept back allowing the Mistrals to slide front. Minich aimed the Mistrals to cross six hundred meters up the west side of the Northwest Piscataquis on a logging road. "Pooh Bear to Roo. Stretch your legs. Ed, you're 18D. I'm getting a low heat signature at 600 by 12 by standard. Confirm?"

A low, gravely voice came back. "Confirmed affirmative. We got him, Pooh Bear. At the base of the shattered tree."

Minich called back over the Wing Channel, "I'm calling Support. Everybody stand easy until we get word."

Word came less than a minute later. "Ed, your call. I'm not getting any lifesigns, but I'm told that's not golden."

"Can you tell me what I'm looking at, Commander?"

"Sorry, Ed. My eyes only."

"Oh, what the fuck. I've been cramped up too long." Roo slid under Pooh Bear and held station at four meters airborne with its

Hellfire antitank missiles and chain gun pointing up the logging road.

When Minich's mission board showed a ship's integrity violation light for Roo he knew Ed had opened the hatch and prepared to drop out. "One more thing, Ed. Your weapon is to remain shipside when you go medical."

Barney, Roo's pilot, called back. "Hey, Commander, I'm not sure I like this." Roo's integrity violation light went out.

Ed said, "You're saying that like you think I might need it, Commander."

"I don't think you will, Ed, and it's orders. Seems like something we can live with."

A moment's hesitation, then, "Aye, Commander. I can live with this one if you can. Okay, Barn?"

Barney said, "I still don't like it," as he released the hatch servos. Ed dropped out of the WarCloud unarmed and bent over, a field medical kit over his left shoulder. He kept his gargoyle over his head and jogged, still bent over, away from the WarCloud that rose once again.

"Stay low until I'm up, Ed," said Barney. "Don't want to bang your head on the blades."

When the WarCloud rose six meters, Ed stood up. "It was either this or sub duty," he rasped to the hovering pilot.

"You still on, Ed?" asked Minich.

Ed gave a thumbs up and pulled up his sunshield, revealing a boyish face inside the gargoyle. "Can everybody hear me? I'd like to know somebody's listening before I go medical."

Minich switched Ed's helmet mike to the Wing channel. "Hot mike, Ed. You're true on ships. Put on your special forces field medical shield in case he can see you. His name is 'Rivers' and he's to be considered dangerous."

Ed mumbled the shield's legend as he pinned it over his name tag, "'Remember to first do no harm'. I hope he knows that." He looked around and listened for a moment, then approached Rivers' body, kneeling beside it and opening his kit. "Shit this guy smells bad." After a few minutes of running his hands over Rivers' body he took a stethoscope out. The scope had a cable that ran back to the kit. Ed put some monitors on Rivers' neck, chest, inner thigh, and throat. He looked at the kit for a minute. "Commander, patch me to Medevac."

"Come on, Ed," Barney said. "I can see him from here. Why call them? Put it in a body bag and we'll make sure all the pieces are there when we bring it in."

"You don't get it, man. This guy's alive."

"Medevac will be here in twenty minutes," said Minich. "We can expect a red on white Suburu Grande Sport coming up the logging road soon. I'm also told whoever did that might be close by."

Ed stood up and looked around as color left his face. He reached down his side for his missing firearm and barked into the link, "You mean whatever did this might still be around and all I can do is talk nice to it, Commander?"

"Gentleman, I think our brother would appreciate all reasonable support."

The WarClouds split the goose and descended until they hovered level with Roo. As the ships moved, the goose spread into a five-pointed star, all facing out from the center, with their rear, anti-torque rotors slightly more than blade-width apart. Ten meters beneath the rotors' center stood Ed with Rivers a bloody pile at his feet. All the WarClouds rotated their gun turrets, chain guns, FFARs, Mistrals, Hellfires, and grenade launchers forward and aimed deep into the trees.

"Better, Ed?"

Ed went back to studying Rivers' body. "He's damn hot. No wonder you were getting thermal from him."

Minich kept a close eye as Ed worked on Rivers. Ed jumped back and Minich called out, "Talk to me, Corpsman."

"That...that son-of-a-bitch - "

"Fast, command status."

"His abdominal closed. Just as I watched. This fucker should be fried and his guts just shut up like a drum. What the fuck am I babysitting, Commander?"

"Just watch him, doc." A moment later Minich's voice sounded on the horn again. "Damn. How about that. Looks like my puppy ate my homework. I can't read these orders anymore." A Barrett 5760 50 caliber rifle, Semi-auto, came down a cable from Pooh Bear.

Kanga called out, "A 5760! Son-of-a-fucking-bitch, Commander, who the hell d'you think's out here, Jesus Christ himself? What in hell did they tell you we're hunting?"

Ed checked the weapon's supply as he slipped it over his shoulder. The WarClouds didn't break the star until the Medevac arrived. They headed back to Loring without further dusting.

When he could no longer hear them, Trailer pushed the rocks off his chest and broke the surface of the stream. "He's not dead?" He ran his hand through his hair and considered.

"He's not dead" didn't make sense.

Trailer walked back to where he and Rivers fought. "He's not dead."

He knelt beside the splintered tree, still covered with Rivers' flesh and blood, and touched the surface of one of Rivers' blood pools. A skin had already formed, the osteogenin forming hardened tissue to protect itself from further attack.

Trailer stood and looked towards Loring.

"He's not dead."

Trailer shook his head.

"I've been played."

12

Trailer jogged towards Patten, alternately laughing and cursing at himself for falling into such an obvious - in hindsight - trap. "Maybe Rivers is right. Maybe I am getting old."

A klick and a half down the road he spotted Donaldson, Karen, and someone else in the Grande. Someone he didn't recognize.

He moved into the trees before anyone saw him.

They stopped about a hundred meters beyond where he hid. Karen got out. "Nickie? It's okay, Nickie. Major Donaldson said he knows it wasn't you. Mr. Eckhardt's with us, too. He's with the state police. He said he doesn't want to arrest you."

Eckhardt nodded towards Karen. "What makes her think Trailer's here?"

Donaldson shrugged. "Women's intuition?"

"Nickie? Can you hear me?"

Donaldson, staring up the road, turned in Karen's direction. A wall of rich, blue-tinged flesh reared up and gently pushed her away.

"No, Nick - " was all Donaldson got out.

Nick lifted the Grande from the passenger side and rolled it onto its roof.

Donaldson struggled to keep his eyes on Nick and Karen. He had her under one arm, moving into the woods.

"You okay?" Donaldson asked Eckhardt once the Grande stopped rocking.

"Yeah. He rolled the car before I could pull my piece. I'm starting to believe what you've been telling me. He's the reason Pancho wanted quits?"

"He and eight others like him. The rest never made it back."

"What's so special about him?"

"We started working on him when he was fifteen. All the others were older, some entering their twenties when we recruited them."

Eckhardt looked at him but didn't say anything for a few minutes. "You going to call the auto club or are we going to right this ourselves?"

Donaldson reached for his phone and Eckhardt pointed to the red mobile, crushed and poking out from under the car. "Unless you build electronics like you do Trailer, you're going to need a new mobile before you can make any calls."

They got the Grande back on its tires and stopped to catch their breath. "What'd'we do now?" Eckhardt asked.

Donaldson picked up his crushed mobile. He'd followed Minich's mission status on it. When he heard Rivers'd been evacked, he ordered a heavily guarded emergency Med field station set up in the middle of the tarmac with a hundred-meter perimeter and ground support, hoping Rivers would stay lazy for a while. Trailer took Karen, so she was safe for the time being. He hoped they would talk and Karen could convince Nick to surface without harm.

"We get drunk."

13

"They said the woods are okay to open?" asked Hatch.

"No, they said they found the canisters and needed more time to determine if there's any residual biohazard," replied Sylvio.

"Ed, I have it on good authority that no canisters fell in my woods. As a matter of fact, I have it on good authority that this could get me into the White House if I play it right. I want my boys up there, Ed. What they're looking for is still up there and we're going to find it first."

"Governor, I don't doubt that the biohazard story is bullshit, but I'm still not sure about sending in any of our National Guard troops. All we got from Eckhardt was that everything was taken care of and that he'd report later when he returned to base. I - "

A little used door opened into the governor's office. The door led to a smaller office that had been vacant since the first desertions from Hatch's staff. Behind the door stood a man, old beyond counting and barely filling a suit obviously expensive and tailored to do the best it could with what it had. The man's head was a Q-tip topped prune on a toothpick body, but his face seemed familiar. Behind the man, Sylvio saw the smaller office was laid out efficiently and comfortably. The man in the door shuffled towards them. Sylvio moved involuntarily to get a chair to the man before he fell, the old man's movements seeming so slow and pained.

The man spoke, his voice broad and powerful, resonating the body that projected it, and with a distinctly non-Maine drawl. "No, thank you, Mr. Sylvio. That won't be necessary. I'm old, but I'm not an invalid, not by a long shot."

"You have me at a disadvantage, sir."

Hatch laughed. "Ed, meet Senator Carl Wrobleski. The Senator recently came on board to help me plan my presidential strategy. Damn good timing, too. Approached me just a few weeks before things went South - forgive the phrase, Senator."

Wrobleski smiled.

Sylvio held out his hand. Wrobleski took it and Sylvio touched the cold hand of death. He let go of the hand without shaking.

"Thank you, Mr. Sylvio. Put this out under the Governor's seal. We do this right, Mark here will be in the Senate in the next election. Tell the press corps that Mark Hatch is personally going to help his boys secure the forests."

Ed nodded and left. Wrobleski looked familiar because Ed Sylvio was a student of political issues, not necessarily politics. At the top of Wrobleski's career, he became persona non grata. Something to do with the Coca Wars, Ed knew, and something to do with some Black Projects Committee that, according to rumor, Wrobleski chaired.

What am I getting into?

He stopped halfway down the stairs to the media room and asked himself another question; *how much can you swallow, Sylvio?*

14

A clear dusk brought stars and cold to the mountains. Karen and Nick camped near a peak, in an area with a flat spot on a west slope, the last rays of the sun turning their steaming breaths into vaporous gold maelstroms. Tall, sheltering pines and oaks with little undergrowth framed the setting sun, looking like some leviathan submerging into the New Hampshire mountains. Bird calls went from territorial and mating to hunting calls as the sky darkened. Insects stopped buzzing, peepers and crickets started chirping from the trees and under leaves. Far off they heard loons and bullfrogs making their way across ponds, lakes, and rivers.

"I can either keep you warm myself or build you a fire."

"Either's okay, but I'd prefer you keep me warm."

"I... Uh... "

"Like this." She put her arms as far around him as she could and rested her head against his massive chest.

His arms hovered over her, gently.

"Relax your arms, Nickie. Hold me. Rest on me. Lean on me.

Those are ways you show me you want me to help you."

He kept his arms over her without resting them on her.

"Nickie."

He lowered his arms until they appeared as pillars on either side of her, touching her as gently as feathers falling to earth.

"Better. We're going to work on this. Now, what's going on?"

"What do you mean?"

"I mean, 'What's going on?' This is the first time since we met that I've been afraid - "

"Of me?"

"No, silly. Never of you. But I don't know what's going on. Major Donaldson said some things that don't make sense to me."

"About me?"

"Yes, about you. It doesn't change anything, though. Even if what he said is true, it was you then, not you now.

"It's not you now, is it, Nickie?"

"No, not now."

"Good. But I'm still scared. I'm cold, I'm tired. Somebody I thought was a friend is trying to kill us. The Air Force and Maine State Police are either hunting us or helping us, I don't know which. I can't cry anymore because my stomach aches from sobbing and I don't have any tears left. I don't know what's happening and my own husband is afraid to hold me.

"Nick, I love you. You can believe that or not, it's up to you and I love you. I love you if you believe me, I love you if you don't believe me.

"If you love me back, then let me help you. I don't care if you think there's nothing I can do to help you, let me decide if I can help you. Even if I can't help you I can be with you. Sometimes being with someone is help enough.

"Do you understand?"

A tear got caught on his eye ridge. "Yes."

She tore a piece off her dress and wiped his eyes.

"I love you, Karen."

"I love you, too, Nickie."

He brought her close so that their faces touched.

"I'm...I'm afraid, too."

"You're afraid? Of Rivers? Of what they'll do to you?"

He chuckled. "Rivers? No. What they might do to me? Maybe. What might happen to you because you're with me? Yes. They might fire at me and hit you."

"Tell me what's going on, Nickie. Who are 'they'? What might they do? Why? Help me to understand. What did you ever do to them?"

He looked down as if inspecting something on the ground. "'They' are the government. The Black Ops branch that made me, anyway. What did I do to them?" He stared at the emerging stars and snorted. "I survived."

"Can Major Donaldson and Detective Eckhardt help?"

"I don't know. Maybe. Not yet, anyway. I'd like to be with you, alone, for a while. Is that alright?"

"More than alright." She wrapped her arms around him as well as she could. It was like hugging a wall. "I don't know much but I do know that right now we can hold each other. For right now, we can make it better. We can hold each other and be with each other, and that makes things better. At least for a little while.

"So for right now, hold me and let me hold you, okay, Nick? If we're not going to get Major Donaldson and Detective Eckhardt and I'm going to die in the middle of the woods, I'm going to die being held by you."

"You're not going to die."

"I will if you don't hold me."

His arms encircled her slowly, his biceps larger than her head.

"I'm not going to break, Nickie. Hold me."

He held her against him, letting the weight of his arms rest on her and she on him. She sighed and he lifted his arms faster than thought. "Am I hurting you?"

"No, Nickie. It just feels so good to have you hold me. I feel like nothing can happen when you do that. That's one of the first things

I knew about you. You would never hurt me."

"You believe that?"

She nuzzled into his chest, muffling her words. "Yup, uh-huh, most certainly do."

"Did you know I…I hold you when you're asleep."

"You do? How come I don't know that?"

"Because you're asleep."

"Why don't you wake me up? I love you holding me."

"Because," he hesitated. "Karen, I'm afraid. I was afraid. I was always afraid I would hurt you. I have hurt you. You want to tell me being my wife is easy? You never see me, and when you do I hardly talk."

"But you listen to me. That means a lot. Even when I'm not saying anything. It's like everything about you is listening to me, like your whole world comes down to my every breath. I like feeling that special."

Her interpretation of his attention amused him. It amused him and he preferred her interpretation over his.

Karen asked, "Do you remember when we met?"

"Of course I do."

"So do I. I remember that no man gave me more than two looks until you. I remember that I was bringing some food to the Dittman's farm - remember them? Twelve kids on twenty acres of land and less than six thousand dollars a year in hard cash?"

He closed his eyes, his arms relaxing even more as she snuggled against him, feeling her nestling against his thighs. He rumbled, the sound a quiet earthquake escaping him. "Yes."

"I've known poor but nobody that kind of poor. Do you remember I was on the porch with Mrs. Dittman and their younger kids? We were watching Mr. Dittman plow with that old, half-blind gelding of his. Then the horse fell into a furrow and broke its leg. Do you remember what you did? It was the first time I'd ever seen you."

The feeling of her, the smell of her, aware that she continued relaxing against him even as he strengthened, tensed, prepared for terror.

"I helped the man plow his field."

She pushed back and stared up at him. "Is that all you remember, Nickie?"

He opened his eyes and shook his head, no, then started to oxygenate.

"He sent his son to get his rifle, to put the horse down. You came out of the woods before the boy got back. You knelt by the horse, rubbing its neck, quieting it. I remember that so clearly, Nickie, because I'd never heard anything in so much pain and fear before."

Nick mumbled, "I have."

"You have, Nickie? When?"

"Nothing. It doesn't mat - " No! "I'll tell you sometime. Promise."

"Okay." She looked at him, dimly aware of his changes. "Okay. Well, when the horse quieted you twisted your arms and snapped the horse's neck. Dittman and the rest of us couldn't believe it. We'd never seen anything like it. I know none of them had ever seen you before. You removed the horse's harness then lifted it over your shoulders and walked back into the woods."

"I showed it mercy."

"Yes, you did. But none of us knew that's what you planned.

"Jed, Dittman's oldest boy, was ready to let the dogs out after you. But then you came back. You came back and put the plow reins and yoke on yourself and pulled. I'd never seen anything like it. Dittman said he'd never seen any man so strong. Or so quiet. You finished his field with him, then you were gone."

Nick heard his voice getting lower. "I showed it mercy," he repeated.

No! She is my wife.

"It was a fair trade. I took his horse. I plowed his fields."

She buried herself in him again, unaware of what the changes inside him foreshadowed. "The both of you plowed his fields, Nickie. It might not have looked that way to you, but you pulled the plow, he guided the share. I watched you all day, walking steadily out there, saying nothing.

"Marriage is like plowing that field, Nickie. I've always believed that. Two people work together, you'll get a good harvest. I've been waiting for you to let me onto the field."

His toes spread, his time-sense slowed, the world opened up before him until he heard the scents of her body and saw the colors of her voice.

No. Not again.

"You okay, Nickie?"

His voice rumbled, more infrasound than audible. "Go on."

"They didn't see you for a month. I kept coming back but you never did. I left food out where I thought you might find it. And cookies, too. Oatmeal raisin. I don't know how I knew you liked them so much."

He closed his eyes, listening to his lungs quake. "I remember that."

"I hoped it was you finding the food, Nickie. I didn't think anybody else would have put the empty cans back in the bag. Then, I remember, I found a whittled hickory stick with red and blue ribbons next to the bag. I thought that was so cute, kind of like a bouquet, and so like one I'd expect from you." She pulled back slightly. "You know I never thought to ask. That was from you, wasn't it, Nickie?"

He opened his eyes. His brow furrowed. He spoke, slow and strained. "Yes."

Yes. She fed you, treated you well, never harmed you, thought well of you.

Just like your mother! Just like your father! Just like all of them! She'll hurt you! She'll kill you!

She'll kill you!

He dropped into Hunter/Seeker state.

Sweat mottled his brow. He concentrated on Donaldson, on the old Jìvaro, on his mother's boyfriend who stayed when he could've left.

What would it be like if she doesn't intend to kill you?

His eyes opened, the sounds, colors, smells, tastes, and touches of the world went back to their assigned places. "Yes. I gave you the hickory stick. Do you know what it means?"

"I think so. I still have it. Did you know that?"

"It is a wedding stick. When you took it, it meant you married me."

"That's what I thought. Still, it would be nice if you'd ask."

He knelt, crouching so they'd be the same height. He touched his heart then extended his hand to her, reaching and straining towards her without touching her. He saw her confusion but didn't see fear.

Not fear. Not stupid. She's not frightened of me. I am a person, not a monster.

"Will you marry me, Karen?"

Following his lead, she reached out and took his hand in hers, then entwined her fingers in his and brought his hand to her own heart. "Yes." Tears washed her face.

They remained quiet for some time, holding each other. Nick wasn't sure when it happened, he stopped monitoring himself at some point. At some point, he started living right there, in the moment, in their embrace, no longer afraid, only alive.

"Nickie, you're such a teddybear. I don't understand why you worry about hurting me. You couldn't hurt anybody if you tried."

He remembered the bar and things he'd done in his life. "No, Karen, you're wrong. I can hurt people. I can hurt people without even trying."

"Nickie, if you're going to tell me you were in the war, I know. We talked about that."

"No, Karen. I told you I was in the war. I didn't tell you what I did or what happened."

"Is it important? Do I need to know? My dad was in StanLand. He told us some things about what happened over there. He was in some kind of intelligence unit - Rangers? No, Pathfinders - behind enemy lines." She shuddered. "At least the things he told us about...Do you really think I need to know? Isn't it enough to know you were there, but that you're back here safe, now? Do I really need to know what happened over there?"

"I'm back here, safe, now." He repeated it, slowly, letting the words, the idea, settle in. Rivers, he decided, was for tomorrow and not today.

"Do you need to know what happened down there? I don't know. I know I need to talk about it. There's nobody else I can talk to.

"You don't have to listen but I need to talk about it, to share it because sharing it makes it real. You don't even have to believe it. It's probably better if you don't believe it. But I have to share it anyway.

"I need you to know my life. Once you know it, you decide if you want to be part of it. If you don't, I'll understand."

"Does this have to do with you going away for so long?"

"Yes. Sometimes. Sometimes, when I go, I just need to be alone."

"My dad used to do that, too, sometimes. I remember momma always used to cry because she thought he was running away from her, that it was her fault. Is that what all this is about? Is this because of something I've done, Nick? Something I didn't do? Is there somebody else?"

He laughed and pulled her into him, making his body warm to keep her warm. "You think somebody else could want this? You're a prize, Karen, a gift. You want me, not what I can do. Do you have any idea how much that means to me? No, Princess. It's nothing you did or didn't do. It has nothing to do with you. Is there somebody else? Yes. Two that I know for a fact. I'm not sure how many others."

She tensed and sobbed into his shoulder, pressing her head under his jaw and into his neck. "Is that why you never seem to want me?"

He lifted her head and kissed her gently. "No, Karen. Not other women. The two I meant were my mother and my father. There haven't been any others."

He sighed. "I need to tell you about my childhood, what I did in the war, and why I was away for ten years in a three-year war. That's what I have to tell you about. You have to have information before you can have awareness, and I want you to know about me before we go any further because...because if you don't want me after this, I want it to be your decision, not mine."

She let go of him and planted herself on the ground, patting the ground for him to sit beside her. "Okay, I'm listening."

"I have to show you something first." He reached into a shirt pocket and pulled out an old, black and white picture of a young boy, maybe four years old.

She held it up to catch the fading light. "What a beautiful child, Nickie. Who is it?" She held it close and studied it. "What sad eyes, Nickie. He looks like he's already seen the world. Is this somebody from the war?"

"Kind of. It's me." Events of his life attained lives of their own, demons gathered and herded since childhood, their weight about to be exorcized as the lyrical child they had buried broke free, as a rage so thick it had gagged him since childhood started to bleed away.

"When I was three years old, my father left my mother. Not for good, but she didn't know that. She decided I was the reason he left, and that I was going to make it up to her. In every way. ..."

He led her through parental abuse so horrible she wondered how he survived. From teachers who so shattered their own lives they found meaning in shattering his, through Augmentation, through training, through runs, through capture, through torture that Augmentation allowed him to survive when mercy would have granted death, through escape, through being found and flown back, and so it went, through the night and into mid-morning, stories from childhood through stories from five days ago.

When he finished, when she had no more tears for him and only wracking sobs as solace for the life he'd lived, he said "Hold me?", which she did, and for the first time, acting because he wanted to, acting *for* rather than *against*, understanding what his actions meant to another, letting himself be seen, letting himself be held, knowing he was heard, he cried.

Later she asked him if they could go home. "I could make you some more clothes."

"No, Karen. We can't go home. They'll be looking for me soon enough if not already. I want to learn what they say about you. Probably say I either kidnapped you or killed you. We could go over the border and start a life in one of the little towns way up north. If Rivers comes back, he's going to try to kill me. I'm afraid of what he might do to you."

"No one can stop him? You can't shoot him or something?"

"I tried the last time, Princess. The man's strong, but not like me."

"Not like you how?"

Nick laughed. "Different," he paused, looking into the distance, evaluating. "Very different now. Not that I know how that might help.

"But I'm worried about you. He won't be satisfied with me. He'll want you, too."

"And you really think he's going to come back?"

"I don't know. I would. Would have, anyway."

"But he's not here now," she said. "Right now I'm here with you. And I'm tired of not being with you. This is practically a honeymoon. I think it's the longest we've been alone together."

"I have several caches throughout northern New England. We could kind of have a honeymoon now. If you wanted to, I mean."

"Is that what you'd like?"

"We'd have to steal or borrow clothing. For you. Or make it. Maybe a car, depending how long we stayed out. I could carry you."

"I've always thought Bonnie and Clyde were kind of romantic. But we have a home, Nick. We can have a honeymoon. I'd like that, but then we go home. Then, if we want to, we can close up that part of our lives and move on. If we want to."

"How come you stayed with me?"

She thought for a moment. "Because I wanted to. Because I knew my life would be better with you in it. Because you're worth it. To me."

She put a hand on his chest. Nick's senses told him what Karen felt, what she wanted and probably before she herself became aware of it. He felt her, unsure and afraid her needs might drive him away again.

Then he stopped. He refused to let his fears, his past, define his future, and let her desires and his course through him, an AJAX that cleansed rather than crippled, that prepared him for joy and not sadness.

For the first time that he could remember his body responded as he'd like it to, on its own, without him having to monitor every breath and every pulse it made. He lifted her up, in his arms, carrying her deeper into the sheltering woods.

"Well." She held onto him like a vine claiming a tree, letting her body share her feelings for him freely. "How nice."

15

Donaldson sat in the Loring Mess writing up travel orders for Rivers and the support team assigned him. Rivers hadn't gained consciousness during the entire month he lay in the field station. Much of the time, his flesh roiled and bubbled as if infested with maggots and viewed on high-speed film. At one point he began twitching so violently the corpsmen and attending physicians strapped him down. Along with that, he started throwing off enough heat to make the med team uncomfortable in the close quarters of the field station. Rivers' body was healing and mending. He didn't know when Rivers would regain consciousness but knew it would be soon and wanted to have Rivers quartered at The Farm when he did. The ONI had nixed moving him sooner, fearing his body could consume itself regenerating if moved too soon, thus depriving them of a chance to examine their mistakes.

Ingman came in. "We're ready anytime you are. The ground crew finished prepping your Black Hawk. An HH-80iM? Hell of a ship for dustoff, don't you think?"

Ingman referred to the modified Star Wars iM that Donaldson ordered for use as a Medevac to transport Rivers from Loring to The Farm. The iM series were highly sophisticated helicopters flown by Task Force 160, the Night Stalkers, an army aviation unit charged with getting SOF into and out of hostile environments and used for SeaSpray to transport Delta Teams anywhere, worldwide, after the decommissioning of the Hughes 500 series. Donaldson commissioned a modified iM to carry Rivers, the support team, SOF personnel, and some heavily armored Marines in bio-support suits. If Rivers even hinted he was going to wake up, they had orders to fire and simultaneously release GB and VX nerve gasses and Remoxipride in the support chamber.

"You go. I've prepped The Farm so they'll sign over as soon as you land. I'll finish this paperwork I'll send it down ahead of you, then I'm going to meet with that detective to let him know his world is safe. After that, I'll see if I can find Karen and Nick."

"Don't you think they're long gone by now?"

"Don't know until I look."

Ingman shrugged, tugged on his mustache and walked out. Donaldson listened to the turbines revving to flight pitch on the iM and its WarCloud escort. He looked down at the paperwork as the iM got airborne. "This can wait."

He called Eckhardt. "Any chance we can rendezvous in Bangor?"

"Yeah, I've been keeping tabs on petty thefts, lost clothing, missing camping supplies, B&Es at cabins, and any unusual animal reports and sightings. Still no idea where Nick and Karen are. You?"

"Negative."

As Donaldson hung up, the sound of the iM caught his attention. The turbine was screaming but the blades weren't biting a thing, as if somebody held the throttle in a death grip but didn't know the collective existed. He heard the helicopter sweep down and towards the far end of the tarmac.

He stood and looked out a window. "What the..."

Heavy arms fire made him duck.

One burst. Two.

Something exploded.

A WarCloud, its turbines screaming, climbing skyward at the limit of its design.

Ingman came through the doors. "He got airborne."

Donaldson looked down at his unfinished paperwork. The next box read "Fit to Travel." He checked it off.

Donaldson hadn't gotten to his car before the Bangor Air National Guard Base's control tower got a triangulate and confirm request from Minich at Loring. That done, Minich donned his gargoyle and ordered his team, "Wheels in the wells, boys. Wheels in the wells." He ran to Pooh Bear and demanded a GO code.

Ingman's voice came over the comm. "Stand station, Commander. I will be joining you ASAP. Your flight and mission orders will come codex DDS&T Roam COS Major James Donaldson or from my lips visual confirm only. Acknowledge?"

Minich stood silently beside his ship. The ambulance drivers closed their doors, looked at him, and shook their heads. The iM and Medevac field station teams were dead. They started making calls as soon as their ship left the ground. Barely seven meters up the collective went to a dead-man's position. The throttle went wide and the cyclic eased the swashplate slightly forward, making the ship slip forward and down. The pedals went to full right rotor and the ship started spinning. Minich had seen it before, in StanLand, Gulf IV and the Coca Wars, the flight signature of a dead pilot whose body had slumped left in his chair. The iM landed, the doors opened, but nobody got out. Minich called but no one answered. Loring Control couldn't raise them either, although their comm channel showed clear.

Ed and Barney, watching from their own airship and closest to the iM, looked to Minich, who nodded. They left their ship powered up but with all systems disengaged then walked over to investigate, weapons drawn.

Rivers, red-faced and dressed in a pressure suit, rolled out of the hatch.

Barney was thrown up into the iM's still whirling blades.

Somebody in ground support yelled over the comm, "Go kinetic. Go kinetic."

Rivers grabbed Ed and wrapped him around the pressure suit like an extra long scarf. Minich saw Ed scream but couldn't hear him over the sounds of ground support's oppression.

Rivers limped over to Roo.

Ground support continued to lay down heavy fire.

Command came through the comm again, "Corral him. Corral him."

Ground support switched to continuous, their fire forming a box closing Rivers in.

He laughed and ran through it, kissing Ed as he closed Roo's hatch.

Ed, no longer screaming, grabbed his face and fell to the tarmac.

Roo lifted as Minich and others ran to Ed.

He had no face from nose to lower jaw, just a bleeding hole and a look of pure terror in his eyes.

Ingman walked up and Minich saluted, dropping his hand before Ingman returned the salute. "I want a fucking GO or I go without one."

"Commander Minich, stand at station until we find out what's going on, please." They waited, the two men staring at each other.

Ingman's mobile buzzed. He listened then keyed it off. "We have reasonable surety regarding the WarCloud's destination, Commander."

Minich's right arm went up and whirled over his head as if snapping a whip. The remaining WarClouds' FFARs and Mistrals rotated forward. The tarmac was awash with the roar of turbines generating full lift.

Ingman pulled on Minich's arm and shrieked the order into his face, "Stand down."

They stared at each other for another ten seconds. Minich's hand, palm open and facing away from him, went up slowly. He clenched a fist then rotated it counter-clockwise and backwards, finally pulling it down to face level. The turbines released, the Mistrals and FFARs receded into their berths.

When the tarmac grew quiet enough for Ingman to speak normally, he let go of Minich. "I need a pilot for an Kiowa OH-58T, someone who's familiar with TARPS."

"Oh yeah, I feel confident now. You're taking an unarmed two-man scout ship to hunt that thing down?"

"That's what I need, Commander. Do you have anyone available?"

"I started on both."

16

Donaldson met Eckhardt just north of Monson, at a rest area western side of Route 6. The latter activated a topographic holomap of central Maine and floated it above a picnic table. Red arrows indicated westward movement along Golden Road then down Greenville Road to Silas Hill Road.

"Is this their migration during the past month?" Donaldson asked.

Eckhardt nodded. "It's my best guess. There's some Natives in the department who've known about Trailer for a long time. Abnaki, Passamaquodi, Micmacs. An Abnaki passed my desk and saw some notes, started talking to me. Trailer has quite a rep with the tribes. He has a cache near there that he shares with them. Karen mentioned Kokadjo. They seem to be taking a leisurely, scenic way of getting there."

"What else is this showing us?"

"Not much. You know the Governor's mobilized the National Guard for Ratissage, right?"

"I can get that squelched."

"I don't know about that. I got an old buddy who owes me. He keeps me informed. Hatch's ordered at least two HULCs, two Solo-Quads, and a Stryker."

"A Stryker? He planning to go eight-wheeling up the Kennebec?"

"That I don't know. I do know he's got people training on the Solo-Quads, flying point and guard for the Stryker in the northern forests."

"And he's got HULCs? Human Universal Load Carriers? What are the HULCs for?"

"He's got a team turning them into IronMans. Whatever you did to keep this quiet, I don't think it worked. My buddy also told me he knows somebody who's getting him a CIA Wet Team because, whatever goes down, it's going to be bloody."

"The Wet Team'll be a waste of time. And he's a fool if he thinks IronMans and SoloQuads'll help him. He's an even bigger fool if he thinks he'll protect civilians."

"Yeah, but he's our fool and I have a duty to him and the people he represents, so I'm not here and we're not having this conversation."

Donaldson looked around. "I'm sorry, did someone say something?"

"Maybe the last thing I'm not going to tell you is that he's got a hardon for the Presidency, is convinced this is his ticket and somebody with serious knowledge is whispering in his ear."

Eckhardt waited for a response. "You know anything about that?"

"Do you have a name?"

"No, I'm asking you, do you have a name?"

Donaldson shook his head, no. He looked down the road for a bit, every once in a while shaking his head, negating possibilities. "I can't think of anyone. Nobody still alive, anyway."

"Yeah?"

"Yeah. I'm on your side, remember? Even though you're not here and we're not having this conversation."

"Yeah, well... Evidently Hatch's waiting for something to happen so he'll know where to send the Guard. Anything major he likes to know about, in case he gets asked a question. This one came and went faster than a white man in Watts. There's a rumor he's got a zombie-video - it's got to be a joke because the tagline is 'He bit her head off' - of a family getting dusted during a picnic. A handful of people have seen it. Half of those say it's a RedTube fake, some kind of vid-trailer. But the other half aren't sure. After Patten I'm not either."

"You seen it?"

"I don't fly that high. The only other thing I know is that he's got Bangor north and west covered with people looking for any signs of dead animals from that biohazard warning you gave out."

"But Nick and Karen are safe? Trailer can keep himself hidden if he wants to. Should I be worried? Can't we explain the situation to him? The man's rational, isn't he?"

Eckhardt looked at Donaldson. "Hello in there, Jim, what color is the sky in your world? Should you be worried? This is an election year and we've got an incumbent who makes Trump's presidency look like a left-wing liberal's. He wants our fishing trawlers to carry nuclear warheads in case the Canadians fish our waters. He wants UMO to develop speech-sensitive mines for the northern roads so Canadian truckers won't use our state as a shortcut without paying highway taxes. I got a commendation a few years back and, after he shook my hand, he told me it would be okay to dance or sing if I wanted to. Forty years after Obama and it's okay to sing and dance? Is this something that should worry you? Hell no. Why do you ask?"

"Kokadjo, you say?"

"That's my guess. I checked up through there the day of the last report. None of the natural and hiking trails looked used and I couldn't see any new trails. He had to leave the roads to get to some of the places where we had reports and somebody that big would have to leave a trail."

"No, he wouldn't. He was specifically augmented for dense forest warfare. He was actually the first pass at something else."

"What else?"

"Our goal was to create GCATTCS: Ground Cavalry All Terrain Tactical Combat Specialists."

Karen's voice made both men turn. "Before you can make the

ultimate warrior you have to know what you're fighting, Major."

"Where's Nick?"

"I don't know. About two hours ago he said Rivers was coming for him. About a mile up the road he smelled you so we stopped and he carried me here. He doesn't want any of us around when he meets Rivers so he didn't want to bring the car in case you tried to follow him.

"He's going to draw him west, away from people, to Spencer Lake or the Bigelows, if he can. He figures Rivers will land around Seboomook because that's close to where they fought and Rivers will try to pick up his scent. He also said that Rivers' 201 is either wrong or incomplete. Rivers didn't let you know everything he could do."

Donaldson said, "I'm going to need a navigator."

"In for a penny, in for a pound." Eckhardt transferred equipment to Donaldson's Grande.

Karen stood by the open door. "I'm coming, too."

Donaldson shook his head, "No. Sorry. This isn't going to be pretty, Karen. We're going to have to kill Rivers, which he won't appreciate. What I'm hearing from you is that Nick's rational and emotionally okay, which is good, but there's no guarantee he'll stay that way once Rivers engages him. That means I can't assure you of Nick's safety with any confidence, and I can't have you compromising this mission. You'd be safer far away - "

Eckhardt laughed. "Like Antarctica, maybe?"

"Nick explained everything to me. He doesn't want to die, but he knows that might happen. Besides, he taught me how to wrestle. I could even win, once in a while."

Donaldson stared at her. He shrugged. "Yeah, sure, why not? Come on, Karen. This is turning into one hell of a party. Everybody can dance."

17

The Warcloud's speakers blasted the northern Maine forest. "Come out, come out where ever you are." It descended erratically a few hundred meters ahead of Nick on the road and he moved into the trees. He planned to wait until the WarCloud's turbines completely disengaged then rush the ship. As he waited, the turbines continued to whine but the rotor slowed.

"Autogyro. He disengaged the rotors and let the ship land itself." He heard a sound to his right. Instincts took over. He tucked and rolled into the sound. Rivers passed harmlessly over him.

"Come on, Nick. I'm better than you. You know that. I took your best and here I am again. You can't get rid of me like that."

Nick, back on his feet, watched Rivers smiling up from the forest floor, pine needles and leaves in his hair.

"You jump from the WarCloud?"

Rivers' eyes shifted right and left, a child caught with his hands in the cookie jar. He sat and made a show of brushing pine needles, leaves, and dirt from his clothes, not looking at Trailer, only grooming. "No."

Nick shook his head at Rivers. *That was me not long ago.*

But now I must be everything I've ever been to survive.

"I don't have to kill you, Rivers. You're going to take care of that on your own. You won't need my help."

"What?"

Nick started backing away. He'd misgauged Rivers' response limits once before. He wouldn't do it again. "You can only underestimate your opponent once."

"Right," screamed Rivers. "And I won't do it again."

He waited until Rivers stood up then turned his back on him and pivoted his head until he stared into Rivers' eyes. "Catch me if you can."

Like the ghost Pancho thought he was, Nick vanished into the forest.

Rivers moved awkwardly, carelessly. He let out a sound Nick had never heard before. Far worse than his own war cry, it came like a banshee over him, dulling his mind and senses. He pulled himself in and dropped into Hunter/Seeker state. Back on the road, Nick heard the WarCloud's cockpit windshield shatter.

18

Hatch stood behind a makeshift forward observation post. "Would anybody care to tell me what's going on?" The tent was erected smack dab in the middle of a hunting camp landing strip deep in the woods west of Jackman, essentially making the landing strip inoperative to anything but rotary wing and quad traffic.

The hunting camp - known as 'Camp Delta' to its regulars - was a camp in name only. There were four beautiful houses, an advanced communication system with up- and down-links to several satellites. The landing strip was flat grass that could have handled a C130 had it not been for Hatch's tent. It rested on a mountaintop with clear views into valleys in all directions and the mountains beyond, and the only way in was by that airstrip, on foot or via technical ATVs. Sylvio didn't know it existed until Wrobleski whispered in his ear about a friend, a Delta Airlines CEO and hence the name, who owed him a favor, but one aerial pass over it and Sylvio knew it would make a great base of operations.

Until Hatch got there ahead of him and put up his tent.

Hatch wore a three-piece St. James suit and a standard issue helmet with the strap tightened under his chin. The helmet had some webbing and he'd placed grasses, twigs, and pinecones in it with the end result being that he looked like a Greek myth gone corporate. Behind his desk, on the tent wall over Hatch's right shoulder, hung a picture of George C. Scott as General Patton in full battle array. The state flag hung directly behind Hatch and a flat topographic projection of northwestern Maine completed the Greek Chorus over his left shoulder.

Sylvio stood beside Hatch in full BDU, National Guard out of Augusta, his frame filling the battle dress uniform comfortably. A camera crew and two National Guard waited across from them at the tent's opening.

Sylvio said, "We don't know exactly, Governor. An Army helicopter landed close to Seboomook, but there's nothing on any channel our equipment can monitor."

Hatch turned to the camera crew. "Could you folks excuse us for a minute? I promise you nothing will happen while you're away, but there are some security questions I have to get clear before we proceed. Thanks." The guardsmen escorted the news crew out and returned. "You, too. And seal the tent when you go."

Hatch waited until he and Sylvio were alone. "What's going on here, Ed? Senator Wrobleski's going to be here any minute and I have nothing for him. I'm looking like a fool and I don't like it."

Sylvio glanced at Hatch's helmet and said nothing.

"Ed?"

"Yes?"

"What's wrong with you now, Ed? You're the last one here I can trust. Everybody else booked out and now you're failing me? Damn it, Ed, I thought I could trust you. If you're not going to do your job, get the hell out." Hatch sat at his desk, his hands busy finding things to do. He opened a drawer and pulled out some sheets of paper that he began shuffling on his desk. "Well? What's it going to be, Ed?"

"Sorry, Governor. A little tired, is all."

"Yeah, well. Look, Ed, everything seems to be coming this way. I want you to take all the teams and fan out. Find out whatever's going on. Once you've secured the perimeter, confirm secure channel and affirm your cargo - "

"I'm sorry, what?"

"Pay attention, Ed. I said it right, 'Secure the perimeter, confirm a secure channel and affirm your cargo'?"

"Yes, I'm sorry, Governor. That's right."

"Okay, good. When that's done, you call me. I'll have someone alert the news crews and have some of the boys drive me wherever it's going down in the Stryker.

"This'll look great, Ed. If you don't screw it up. Okay, now. Let's go over this once more. It's got to go exactly like this and I don't want any mistakes. You've been with me a long time, Ed, but remember, shit rolls downhill. If I look bad, you're going to look worse. Understand?"

19

Traveling in the silence of his Grande, Donaldson couldn't help but wonder what the people with him made of their situation. Eckhardt had come to a position with the Maine State Police as an escape from cities gone mad. Karen had given herself to a man only a handful of people wouldn't see as a monster of some kind. And as for himself?

I'm up here seeking salvation for my own sins.

Three different people coming together for three different purposes and now together traveling a back road through the Maine woods. He had no idea how safe they were together and equally no idea how safe they'd be apart. Rivers was his problem. He had help out of Loring, and he believed he could count on Eckhardt, too. Trailer was also his problem, but of a different sort, and the only help he had on that end was Trailer himself.

He stared at the rearview mirror for a second. Karen tucked herself into the seat, against the passenger-side door, her head pushed into the corner where the seat and door met, her arms folded tight across her chest, her forehead resting on the window, her eyes closed tight. She must have sensed him looking because she opened her eyes and stared back, then shyly smiled at him before closing her eyes and resting against the window once again.

Karen, too. Let's not forget Karen. Trailer would do anything for her, I'm sure.

Donaldson smiled a moment more then his eyes returned to the road ahead.

Karen cleared her throat and he glanced back in the mirror. She was smiling with her eyes closed, her face relaxed. "Nick plans to cross over 201 north of West Forks. He's heading for Spencer."

20

Ingman and Minich stayed high and used the RTARPS on infrared and visual to pick up any movement in the forest. The RTARPS, a Realtime Tactical Aerial Reconnaissance Photography System, could pick up the heat signature of day-old bat shit in a snowstorm from a ten-klick ceiling. Ingman knew standard V and IR would be useless so scanned for secondary signatures, hoping to detect either Rivers or Trailer before either could see or hear him. "Hold it. The 'TARPS is fucking up. I'm getting multiples. It looks like ants on a Hershey Bar down there."

Minich checked the display. "There's nothing wrong with the equipment."

"Go to three hundred meters. I'll recalibrate."

The Kiowa came down. The signals got stronger, but now the 'TARPS added form and definition to the signatures.

"Oh, shit. I thought we closed off the woods. Looks like we've got some hunting parties looking for moose." Ingman switched the RTARPS to full visual. The screen showed uniformed teams. Ingman adjusted the 'TARPS' eye to see the team patches.

"Holy Jesus Christ I don't believe it! Get us down, as low as possible. I need a visual confirm." The ship stopped at two hundred level. Ingman checked down starboard and slumped back into his seat.

Minich's eyes went from the RTARPS to the forward and port windows. "Meat."

Three National Guard teams waved at their ship. The RTARPS showed ten other teams in a five-klick radius of the ship's azimuth.

"Who the fuck let them out?"

Ingman opened the comm. "This is Recon 5 out of Loring to the Guard units positioned at field square 39-02. What is your authorization?"

A voice came back, "The Presque Isle Cannoneers, Maine's Finest. We also got some Bangor and Augusta people in the other teams."

Ingman widened the RTARPS' camera and rotated the eye so that it shot directly below their ship. Ten men stood like tenpins, all looking up, smiling and waving at the Kiowa.

"We got some beer here. We'll trade you if you can get Verne to his daughter's birthday party and back before The General shows up."

Minich muttered, "You never have an advanced weapons system when you need one."

"Who'm I speaking to, soldier? Who's in command of your troops?"

The RTARPS started pinging rapid movement. Hoops, hollers, sidearm and semi-automatic fire came up from the ground. Ingman ordered, "Report."

"Holy Christ look at Bobby!"

A second voice came over the comm, "It's that bear-neurotoxin thing."

More gunfire. A second scream. Ingman set the 'TARPS to all frequencies scan. "Get your men out of there," he yelled. "Get them out, do you hear me?"

A mix of voices came over the comm.

"What happened to John?"

"Where's Tommy and Jacques?"

They broke ranks, running in random directions, firing at the wind as it twisted leaves and rustled twigs.

"What the hell got John?"

"Oh, my god."

The 'TARPS started pinging then grew silent. Ingman's hand brushed his mustache, not grooming it this time, and it stood out like little boar bristles leaping from his upper lip.

The ship's ANSC frequency hopper picked up and fixed on another voice, steady and controlled. "This is Lieutenant Edward Sylvio, 00Xray-29-372Delta, National Guard Light Arms Brigade Mentor Company 7-76Charlie, Augusta Barracks. Copy?"

Ingman linked the RTARPS to the directional antenna and began scanning. "Switch the horn to 6770N, Minich."

"Secured and confirmed."

The RTARPS pinged and locked. "Affirmative on the copy. We've got you, Lieutenant." They found him under the exposed root cluster of a dead oak. "You trained regular?"

"Affirmative. Three years kinetic in Pancholand, Guard ever since. There's somebody five-hundred meters to your three o'clock who's killing my men. That's a 'TARPS carrier, isn't it? Do you have anything that'll get us back home?"

"Affirmative on the 'TARPS. Sorry, lieutenant. We have our standard 9mms and nothing else. You got any other regulars down there?"

"Negative. Repeat, negative. Can you dust him until I get these men away from here?"

The woods fell silent except for Sylvio's signature. Animals over half a kilogram burrowed, flew or ran out of the killzone.

Minich asked, "How can he move without showing on the 'TARPS? He's got to show on the 'TARPS."

"No, he doesn't. We won't be able to differentiate his signal if he moves with the natural flow of the land."

Sylvio called from the ground, his voice starting to crack. "Come back, Recon 5, come back."

"Stand easy, soldier," Ingman ordered, then to Minich, "There's only one man down there, now. The rest are just bodies."

"So what do you want to do? We can't get down to him with these trees. We can't offer him any air support."

Ingman brushed his mustache again. "Get as dead over him as you can."

Minich maneuvered their ship until the landing supports slapped the tops of the trees. Ingman cramped a drop line to his chair and the doorguard. He took a belaying pin from the ship's flight pack and threaded the lead of the drop line through its eye. He rammed the opposite end into his 9mm.

Minich caught on. "This badboy's only got six hundred-fifty-seven horses, Ingman."

"When I count to three, I fire. Tell him to grab on and, as soon as he's sally, lift. We can drop the 'TARPS." Ingman counted as steady as a watch ticks off seconds, "One-Two-Three."

Ingman opened his door and fired straight down.

Minich yelled over the comm, "Get it, Sylvio. Grab it."

The belaying pin buried itself a meter from Sylvio's left foot. He grabbed it and threading it through his pack straps.

The RTARPS started pinging madly, picking up a flat unrecognizable signature, low to the ground and some two-hundred meters from Sylvio.

Minich called out, "Negative visual."

"I hear him! Get me up! Get me up!"

"Lift him, Minich!"

The RTARPS' detectors became a steady whine instead of distinct pings, the monitor's image taking on more and more of a human form.

Below the strain of the engine, Ingman and Minich heard a wailing banshee call and watched the ship's windows crack.

"Get me outta here!"

Below them they heard the steady three beat "Pa-thwoo Pa-thwoo Pa-thwoo" of Sylvio's M16 as they started to black out, Rivers attempting to pasteurize their brains, using his voice as a sonic doublebug.

Minich put on his mask and switched it to a fifty-fifty mix of atmosphere and pure oxygen.

He rammed the throttle to full open. The Kiowa strained.

He pulled the collective straight up. The main rotor's blades were twisting lifting the ship. He flattened both pedals, locking the rear rotor out of a dead man's spin.

The Pa-thwoo Pa-thwoo Pa-thwoo of Sylvio's weapon went silent.

Sylvio screamed as if caught in an auger.

Minich felt a tug on the cable below the ship. The last thing he remembered was Ingman slumping forward, nose and ears bleeding as he released the drum claw and the 'TARPS fell from the ship.

21

Governor Hatch waited with an RTO in his hunting camp observation post, way up north of where the National Guard units had entered the woods. Wrobleski sat beside him in a beach chair, the only additions to his business suit a Panama hat and sunglasses.

"Good spot, don't you think, Senator? Excellent place to call the shots."

Wrobleski nodded. An hour earlier they picked up the cries and death throes of the Presque Isle Cannoneers. After that the radio went dead.

"Are you sure that thing works, son?" asked Hatch.

The RTO, a boy of nineteen who still used more Clearasil than Wilkinson Swords, lifted his bugeye from its hook for the fifth time that hour. "Yes, sir. I'm sure."

"Well, go outside and see if you can get anything, Sylvio should be calling in by now. He won't let me down. If there's any trouble, Sylvio will cover it. He's a good man, that Sylvio. A good man. He's leading my boys up here to report anything he finds."

Wrobleski handed the RTO his mobile. "And take this with you. Let me know if you get any signal."

The youth saluted them both. "Yes, sir."

Hatch changed into a standard issue BDU and measured himself under George C. Scott's watchful eye. He strapped pearl-handled revolvers on, tapped the gunbelt to test its security, tapped the revolvers to ensure their place at his sides, and saluted the picture.

Wrobleski called, "What's the story out there, son? Got anybody?"

A wall of flesh came through the door. Hatch fell back into his chair as the behemoth approached. He got up in time to place the chair between them.

The man carried the boy in his arms, the boy's radio unit on his back. He laid the boy on the oak desk. "He's not hurt, just asleep. He'll wake up in a few hours. You can't stay here. You've got to call the National Guard out of the forest. They'll get killed if they haven't already."

He unstrapped the radiotelephone and dropped it beside the desk.

Hatch slid his hand down to his right holster.

"You're not even right-handed, Governor. Nor do you have the composure of someone ready to kill."

Wrobleski put his hand on Hatch's arm. "That won't be necessary, Mark." He stood up with some effort. "You're Nicholas Trailer, correct?"

Nick stared at the sack of flesh. "Senator Wrobleski. Quite some time, no? And you've lost the shoulder holster. Clever, I suppose."

Hatch kept the chair between them as a shield. "You're coming in with me."

The senator's eyes diverted slightly. "Shut up, Hatch," he hissed. His eyes came back to Nick, his voice and tone back to congeniality. "I lost all my hopes because of you, Mr. Trailer."

"My mother said that to me once."

They heard a car bouncing along some trail ruts until it gained the landing strip. Donaldson, Eckhardt, and Karen came in. Karen went immediately to Nick. He moved between her and Hatch's sidearms.

Donaldson stopped and stared. "Wrobleski? Is that you?"

Eckhardt said, "Hey, nice poster. George C. Scott. That must have cost a bundle."

"Nice to see you again, James," said Wrobleski.

The silence was broken by a few moments of static from the dropped radio pack.

Donaldson asked, "What's going on?"

Hatch started to speak. Wrobleski dismissed him with a sharp "Shut up, Mark."

Hatch sat down, his hands in his lap and his eyes straight forward.

Wrobleski continued, "I've been helping the good Governor here develop a White House strategy. Never thought I'd catch you two in the bargain. Ha! Astin would have to laugh at this." He turned to Nick. "That bitch didn't have the balls for this once she found out what you people were."

Nick's brow furrowed as he met Wrobleski's gaze. Donaldson watched the whale's face work.

Nick's back. He's here. He's showing what's going on inside.

"Can you plan the reunion later?" Eckhardt asked. "We've still got some maniac out there wiping out villages. How do we stop him?"

"Who the hell are you?" Wrobleski said it as only an old-time Southerner could, his drawl minimizing Eckhardt as few words could.

Eckhardt laughed. *"Was ist das? Ein schwartze? Nicht hier, nicht im meinem Staat!"*

Nick's face cleared as he backed out of the tent. "Sorry, Senator. I've got some things to take care of up here. After that, we'll see."

"No, we'll see now." He pulled the RTO's gun out. "Drop your weapons, all of you. Bagging you two will let me die in peace. Sweet Jesus, there's still time to campaign and bringing you in, dead or alive, could get me to Washington again, vindicated. No, Mr. Trailer, you're coming in with me."

Nobody moved.

"Senator, those bullets won't even bruise me. The most that will happen is that someone else will get hurt. I'm telling you for your own good, get out of the forest."

Wrobleski stared from one face to the next. "Hatch, get over there with them. Toss your sidearms over here first."

"Me?"

"Move!" Wrobleski stared at the six of them on the other side of the desk. "The woman your wife?" Nick said nothing but Karen moved towards him. "I thought so. You," he said to Karen, "over here." He grabbed her arm and held the gun under her chin. "Promise me you'll come in with me, Mr. Trailer, no harm to me, or she dies."

"No deals." Nick kept eye contact with Karen as he spoke.

"You think I won't?" He aimed the gun at the sleeping RTO. "You brought this boy in. You cared about him enough not to hurt him. Now I'm going to blow his head off, just to prove my point." Wrobleski lowered the gun to the sleeping RTO's ear. "Then, if you still think I'm kidding, I'm going to kill this pretty lady here."

Eckhardt shook his head. "You're fucking kidding." He turned to Donaldson. "You took me down cowpaths worse than anything I saw in Pancholand, I'm thinking the next person I'm going to see is Banjo Boy and now this? Tell me he's fucking kidding."

Nick said, "I guess the boy dies," and nodded.

Karen arced both arms up between her and Wrobleski, catching him under both his arms, knocking them up and away from the RTO and everyone else in the tent. She grabbed his jacket, leaned forward and kneeled as she moved.

Wrobleski somersaulted onto the tent's dirt floor, a flat fuck fall, his arms and legs flailing through the air like a spider separated from its web.

Eckhardt clapped his hands. "That was beautiful."

"Thank you." Karen looked at him and Donaldson as if she'd been caught sneaking some cookies to her room.

Nick smiled. "That's my woman."

"And I'll wrestle any man that says otherwise," Karen said.

Eckhardt held up his hands. "I'm good."

Donaldson laughed. "No challenge here."

Eckhardt picked up Wrobleski's revolver then placed Hatch's sidearms in his belt. He tapped Wrobleski with his foot. "Over there with Hatch, where I can keep an eye on both of you."

Wrobleski didn't move. "I think she broke my back."

"Yeah, I know. I think you're breaking my heart." Eckhardt hoisted Wrobleski by the collar. "Over there!"

Wrobleski gathered himself into the shadow of the desk, straightening his clothes and dusting himself off. "I don't know what you think this is going to gain you. There's only seven of us here. One's asleep, one's a biomedical freak with a price on his head, one's a woman who's foolish enough to marry and harbor him, one's black, Donaldson knows what it's like to be indicted and I'm sure doesn't want to go through that again, Hatch still rolls up his sleeves to take a shit and I didn't hear any of this."

Eckhardt shook his head. "Somebody tell me this isn't what's heading up our government."

Nobody spoke, the only sounds the cackle and hiss of the radio.

"Oh, come on. Somebody tell me."

Hatch, staring at his prized picture, whispered, "Jeez, it *is* George C. Scott."

Eckhardt looked at Donaldson. "Let's go with Wrobleski's idea. Let's change it up a little. If I shoot these motherfuckers - excuse me, Karen - you folks won't tell, will you?"

Wrobleski looked at Eckhardt's gun. His fingers twitched.

Before his thoughts became action, Nick picked him up by the back of the neck and shook him, a mother cat chastising her kitten. "Sorry, no. You don't get to use that gun."

"Shoot him, Donaldson. That's an order! He's going to kill me!"

Wrobleski struggled in Nick's grip. He stopped, his breathing strained, his arms limp at his sides. Nick's arm never moved, the old man no burden at all. "You don't frighten me, Mr. Trailer," Wrobleski gasped. "I know who you are. I know what you are. I've read everything Donaldson ever did to you. I can do the same thing, only I can do it better."

Nick's eyebrows raised in disbelief. "Oh?"

Wrobleski started in without pausing, his drawl replaced with neutral voiced cadences and pronunciations. "You can listen to me now, Nicholas."

He started loud and let each sentence grow softer, quieter, adding emphasis to certain words to wrap one message within another within another, a Russian doll within a Russian doll, to draw Trailer in.

Donaldson eyed Trailer. An Ericksonian induction? Where'd Wrobleski learn that?

Nick's eyes started to defocus, to half close as Wrobleski continued working his trance.

Slowly Nick lowered him to the ground.

Wrobleski finished, whispering so softly only the Augmented Man could hear him, "Protect me from them, child, and I will comfort thee."

Nick turned and faced the others in the tent.

"Nick?" Donaldson slowly raised his weapon.

Nick started to rotary breathe.

He frowned at the weapon in Donaldson's hand, purring. "That used to work on me? Christ, it's boring and dull." He lifted Wrobleski again, holding the old man like a sack of soiled children's clothing, holding him far away lest the odor overpower him.

Trailer's face changed. "I am so far away from what you need me to be right now. So far. And you have no hope of catching up, do you." He shook his head, the question answered with no words spoken.

Wrobleski hollered, "You pious bastard. You think I don't know what's been happening to you? You think I haven't been informed?"

"You think it matters?" Nick began exhaling. One minute, two minutes, three minutes and more until even his lungs had been emptied. As he exhaled, his skin grew pale and his face plastic, his eyes glazed and rolled up in his head. He waited like that a moment until his skin returned to color, then drew Wrobleski's face close to his own and began to breathe again, this time taking long, slow breaths, exhaling into Wrobleski's face.

Eckhardt whispered, "What's he doing?"

"He's discharged his normal oxygen and dropped into Hunter/Seeker state so his body can use alternate chemistries. Right now he's CO_2 driven, instead of oxygen driven like we are. His body chemistry right now has more in common with a sixty-year-old four-pack-a-day chain smoker than us. It's a technique used when assaulted by biological and chemical weapons. By breathing into Wrobleski's face like that Nick'll suffocate him. Wrobleski won't get any oxygen for as long as Nick holds him."

"Hey, I think the guy's an ass but I don't think we should kill him."

"Neither do I. And I'm willing to bet Nick doesn't either."

Wrobleski began punching and kicking Nick as he gasped for air, the combination of physical activity and Nick's CO_2 gagging him. "You son-of-a-bitch. Go ahead and kill me. Go ahead!"

"Alright." A smile came across Nick's face as his jaws opened wide. "You say you've kept informed of what I've been doing, Senator. Then you should know what I've been doing is dying. A lot of dying. I've learned how to die anytime I want to."

He placed his mouth over Wrobleski's nose and mouth then massaged the old man's diaphragm, forcing him to breathe Nick's stale air.

Wrobleski held his breath as long as he could, gulped a mouthful of air and held it, all the while striking Nick's face and arms. In less than a minute he had stopped moving. Nick pulled his mouth away from Wrobleski's face and massaged until Wrobleski gained consciousness then pulled him back towards his grinning mouth. "How many times can you die, Senator Wrobleski?"

Wrobleski panicked. He screamed into Nick's mouth, his words echoing in Nick's body, "You think I matter? You think any of this matters?"

Nick pulled his mouth away but still held Wrobleski close, their noses centimeters apart. "You think I care?"

Wrobleski snorted a laugh in the behemoth's face then bellowed, "You goddamn sorry fool. Nobody cares."

Nick opened his mouth wide and pulled Wrobleski towards him.

Wrobleski had both hands pressed against Nick's face, trying to hold him back.

"Nobody cares, dammit! Nobody cared then and nobody cares now. Do you know why we did what we did to you? Because we knew we could and no one would stop us. You were just kids, god-damn it. None of you was much over twenty, twenty-one. None of your families cared. What difference would it make if we fucked up a bunch of street brats, anyway? The entire population was terrified every time they saw two punks taking a walk. You think they'd stop us? They wanted it without saying as much."

Wrobleski grew limp again in Trailer's grip. "Go ahead and kill me, Mr. Trailer. People won't care until the next time something un-comfortable comes along, and when it does they'll all look the other way again and let us make the next unmentionable weapon to take care of it."

Nick let go and Wrobleski sprawled on the dirt.

"'Because we knew we could and no one would be there to stop us'. Because nobody cares. You're just like my old man. You're just like my old lady. You're as much a product of your fears as I am."

"Ha. You think this is about fear, Mr. Trailer? This has nothing to do with fear. You, Donaldson, the others like you - you're all a mea-sure of expediency. Expediency and power, that's what it's all about.

"The whole point of the Coca Wars was to get control of the coca fields, to regulate the trafficking. We were going to put a tax on the drug. We started planning the war back in the 1980s, back when we started looking for any way possible to finance our debt. Then when the time was right, we sat in Congress and orchestrated a war, not because *We, the People* were threatened. We engineered a war because our way of life, our power - not *The People*, us, the people you idiots continued to vote into office, into power - was threatened. There were no more enemies left, so we created one."

Wrobleski clapped his hands and laughed. "And the people be-lieved like they always do, because governments learned Christ's lesson better than any Christian ever could: 'The People' are happiest when they're as stupid as sheep."

They stood silent, listening, the slight breeze outside, loons calling on a nearby lake, chickadees arguing over seeds and the occasional static of the radio the only other sounds in the camp.

"Every politico since they hung gardens in Babylon knew that; you want to stay in power, tell the sheep somebody don't look like them is threatening their way of life. Hell, you don't even have to make them suffer, just make picking up groceries a little more difficult. Make sure there's not as much bread or milk on the shelves or the beach is closed or they got to boil their water before they can drink it or god forbid they got to wait an extra thirty seconds for some moronic download and the goddamn sheep'll back you to the hilt."

Wrobleski held his stomach as he laughed. "So we made you creatures because it was expedient to do so, because we needed you and then we didn't, and when that time came it was expedient to be done with you.

"Now tell me, Mr. Trailer? You think what you do here is going to make government change? Are you a better person for hearing it? You didn't hear anything. I'll swear to it."

Nick smiled and nodded towards the radio unit.

Donaldson lifted it to see the status indicators. "Commercial and emergency broadcast frequencies, all hot!" He showed them to everyone and laughed.

Eckhardt patted Nick on the back. "Oh, that was nice. Very, very nice."

Nick smiled at Wrobleski. "If the people are the sheep you claim, this won't amount to much. But whether they are or not, I'm sure your days are over."

Nick's eyes went from Donaldson to the radio unit and drew a thumb across his throat. Donaldson switched the unit off.

Wrobleski sat in the dirt, his eyes wide on the fading radio status indicators. A line of red rage marched up his face. A cross between a lunatic's laugh and an animal caught in a trap gurgled out his foaming mouth.

Trailer said, "Maybe they'll come up with an expedient solution for you?"

Wrobleski pulled a Kahr Arms P380 from an inside pocket, put the barrel in his mouth and pulled the trigger. George C. Scott's Patton would never look the same again.

Nick held Karen against him, not letting her see what remained.

Donaldson's eyes went from Wrobleski's shattered skull to Nick and back. "Nick, you knew he was going to do that. You must have known he had the Kahr. Why didn't you stop him?"

He held Karen close and answered in order. "I did. I did. To show him mercy." He kissed Karen's head. "You okay, Princess?"

She nodded, her arms around him.

"Jim, there's an old logging camp, Collection Area 9571, on Old Spencer Road, about ten clicks as the crow flies from here." He pointed to it on the map. "I'll get Rivers there, if I can. Then it's up to your people."

"I'll do my best."

"Karen's going to be safe?"

"Like I said, I'll do my best."

"Jim, when it comes my time, remember the bunny."

Donaldson nodded.

Nick kissed Karen again then was gone.

Donaldson called for a team to escort Hatch, Wrobleski's remains, and the still sleeping RTO from the woods.

Eckhardt said, "Saddle up?"

Donaldson wasn't paying attention. He walked up to a crate on a deuce-and-a-half and read the manifest. "Help me open this and get it into the back of the Grande."

"What is it?"

"A combat modified HULC. Hatch's IronMan."

22

A loud screaming woke Minich. His hands went to the collective and cyclic from instinct even before his eyes opened. When they did, they opened wide and passed over the instruments. They hovered two hundred meters above the Kiowa's operational ceiling and swung slowly east. The screaming came from the engine and rotors. Blood soaked the front of his BDU.

Then he remembered. He tapped his arms, legs, chest, and gargoyle. No broken bones. He took a deep breath. No internal damage, although the breath almost made him blackout.

"Ingman, we still got our package? Don't bother with the 'TARPS. I dropped it. At least I think I did. That must be Sylvio. I can feel the sluggishness from here."

Ingman didn't respond.

"Ingman?"

Ingman still didn't respond. Minich looked at him. Ingman faced his window, his gargoyle resting against it, his head slightly bowed. Blood covered his lap and the bottom half of his window. Fresh blood dripped from his gargoyle.

"Ingman?" Minich shook the latter's shoulder. No response. He unstrapped Ingman's mask. A cupful of blood splashed into Ingman's lap. Minich removed Ingman's gargoyle. Blood dribbled from Ingman's ears, nose and mouth. His eyes, also bleeding, had liquified in their sockets.

Munich checked his watch. They'd been out for two minutes.

"Ingman?" He shook the man a second time, harder. "Ingman?"

Minich checked Ingman's pulse. Blood trickled from the bristles of Ingman's mustache.

"Sorry, Ingman." He radioed for a medteam.

Sylvio started on exposure, frostbite, oxygen deprivation, pressure sickness, and fluid loss treatments when Minich landed at the Jackman Maine Regional Health Center, which now served as an emergency field medical station. Sylvio, although conscious and aware, lay immobilized on a cot, his left leg a traumatic amputation from the knee down. He'd cut off an Alice strap and used his M16 to make a tourniquet, then jammed his weapon into his belt to hold it in place in case he passed out: not pretty but effective.

"How you doing, soldier?" asked Minich.

"They say I'll live. I think I have you two to thank for that."

"I'll say you're welcome for both of us. My partner didn't make it. Sorry we couldn't do anything for your men."

A field medic gave Sylvio an injection.

"Been nice talking to you." He saluted then shook Minich's hand. "Thanks again." Sylvio's eyes closed and his breathing eased and became regular.

"Is he going to make it?" asked Minich.

"Yeah. He'll be respiratory symptomatic in winter, probably, and I don't know if he'll need dialysis, but he might. I'm taking him to Northern Medical as soon as I'm sure he's stable. But don't worry. He'll live."

23

Donaldson remained in constant contact with Minich as his Grande bounced down washouts and rock-strewn trails. As it was, he had to show his ID about every fifty meters as trucks full of Army National Guard stopped him at gunpoint in case the blonde man-eater was in the car.

They parked Donaldson's Grande under a cluster of elms where the trail narrowed for portage crossing and got out.

Donaldson said, "I have to take Rivers down." The comm opened and he spoke into it.

"There's a tactical Wing coming to give me air support. They should be here in a half, three quarters of an hour. This is going to get real nasty. Lots nastier than I thought. If I'd known it was going to go down like this, I'd've argued otherwise back when we started."

Eckhardt said, "You mean a couple of months back or this morning?"

"I'm ordering you two to leave. The last 'Track is coming down the trail and you two are on it. Get out of here." He turned to Karen. "You're my responsibility, and I don't want Nick thinking I failed him." Then to Eckhardt, "Can you get her out of here?"

A blond, blue-eyed, red-faced, wide-grinning snake uncoiled from the tree and wrapped itself around Karen.

"Sorry, I need her here."

Karen screamed.

Blonde lightening struck Eckhardt. He crumpled to the ground.

Something snapped into Donaldson's stomach. He flew back against the Grande and remembered nothing.

24

Donaldson opened his eyes to see Nick's face smiling down into his. "He's got Karen, Nick."

"I know."

"Sorry. I didn't know."

"You couldn't know. No one can know everything. Besides, it makes it easier to track him."

"Eckhardt?"

"He has compound fractures on both legs and his right lung is punctured, a sucking chest wound. I made some splints, immobilized him and used some cellophane from a cigarette pack I found on the trail to stop the chest wound. He's going into shock so I put him to sleep. He'll be okay, but he'll need real attention when he wakes up. He'll be in lots of pain."

"The old ways serving new needs?"

"Something like that."

"Did you find a first-aid kit in the Grande?"

"Did what I could with what I had."

"I had some firepower. Is it still there?"

Nick nodded. "But I don't know if it's still operational. Did you not finish filling out Rivers' 201 or did he withhold from you? His 201 says he can regenerate from thirty-five percent failure in about three weeks. I know I achieved near one hundred percent failure and he came back in under thirty days."

"First thing is, he's not mine. I was long gone, a tenured college professor, when they started on him. I'm here because you're here."

"What?"

"I reactivated because you surfaced. My options were to reactivate and either neutralize or rehabituate you or not reactivate and let them neutralize you with no option for rehabituation."

"And I always had trouble getting dates. How does Rivers figure in?"

"He was the pricetag for my involvement. I didn't know he existed until I reactivated."

"Meaning you probably didn't have a complete 201 on him."

"Like you said, no one can know everything. As for Rivers' regeneration ability, it's one of the new things they learned how to do. He can achieve a complete central nervous system shutdown, essentially turning his systems pre-limbic so he can regenerate. They only tested down to thirty-five percent because they thought more would destroy the work."

"Rivers let them demonstrate thirty-five percent failure? He stood there, said 'Do it' and let himself be a WIAMan and nobody thought that was an indication there was more wrong with him than there ever was with any of us? Come on, Jim."

"Nick, he's not my boy. A flesh and blood Warrior Injury Assessment Manikin and nobody ever made the link? I'm sure they made the link. I'm sure they wanted the link. I'm sure they reinforced the link.

"But test the link? Hell no. Run the risk of destroying the work? Fuck that."

"So I was the test? If I destroy him, it's back to the drawing board, if he destroys me, put a check in that box and on to the next, is that it?

"Not part of my plan."

"What else do I not want to know?"

"His hallmark is a massive delayed identity development disorder coupled to process schizophrenia. They aggravated the process schizophrenia rather than indulge any hypnotic attention. It provided a superior learning curve for target acquisition. Basically he's got no identity other than his target's."

"He's constantly becoming what he has to kill?"

"And the only way to alleviate the paradox is to sanction the target. Once the target's gone, he's back to being Tom Rivers."

"Who was such a sweet, lovable guy to begin with."

Donaldson mimicked old commercials, "But wait, there's more. He's got a secondary acquisition mode when he's on mission: ask him a question, you become an intermediary target."

"Ask him where the lav is and he blows your head off?"

"Any direct address, identity question, yes."

"Anyone who questions who he is, what he's doing, where he's going or where he's been?"

"Correct."

"What a brilliant way to maintain mission anonymity; he kills anyone who questions him."

"They made him as indestructible as they could, Nick. That way he never has to change from what they made him. In his own mind he can't die so he's got no reason to change what he does or how he does it, he's got no reason to try something new."

"He can't change internal states?" Nick answered his own question. "Anybody who can regenerate from that level of failure doesn't need to, they just need to wait until they're operational again. That explains a lot."

"Two for two, Nick. Once he's active, he's active. He can't situationally evaluate and modify. He can't innovate."

"He's got no reality to check other than the target's so any question that requires a reality check defaults to an immediate sanction?"

"It won't always be immediate. He may rescind to his childhood ego state, map any external reality to some recognized internal state. He already did that once that I know of, at a picnic area. Mapped a family onto some transcendent childhood origin myth we were completely unaware of and killed them all."

"I read in his 201 that he's especially sensitive to state-inducing phrases and actions. What does that mean? Can it help us?"

"Sticks and stones won't break his bones but calling him names can incapacitate him."

"You're fucking kidding."

"At least minimally confuse him. I have no idea if there is a maximal side. They intended it as a failsafe: a direct parental frame assault will stop him cold. He won't drop like a fly but he'll want to. All his resources go into staying out of fugue state when he's subjected to the abuse his family gave him."

"You're going to slap his face?"

"And laugh as hard as I can when I do, if I can get close enough. If I do, you'll have your chance."

"But first I'll have to get you close enough."

"It'd help."

"I'll try to remember that. Anything else I should know? You got any Phase IIs or IIIs coming down the pike?"

"Not that I know of."

Nick's eyes darted to different parts of the woods.

"Is he up there? Is he getting close?"

"Yep." Nick walked into the trees and disappeared. Donaldson took off his shirt and body armor. A purpling welt covered his right side, from armpit to hips, emanating from where Rivers hit him. He guessed a bruised rib. He went over to the Grande, checked on Eckhardt and field inspected each weapon, then started putting on the other armor, followed by the HULC and weapons. He caught his reflection in one of the Grande's windows. "This is what twenty-first-century knights look like."

The WarClouds approached from the northeast. He launched a flash grenade straight up. Half a minute later the airships' guns stared down at him.

He raised his left hand and signaled; fist up, open fist, index finger circle in the air, closed fist, open fist spread fingers, palm down and lower hand. The WarClouds raised their guns. Pooh Bear lowered a comm on a cable.

"I've got a wounded man here, field dressed for multiple femoral fractures. Can I get a medevac?"

Pooh Bear moved up. Piglet hovered over him. A slingbed descended.

"Donaldson, this is Minich. Rivers got Ingman."

Donaldson said nothing for a moment. "Sorry to hear that. Anything else I should know?"

"TopHat gave us clearance to liberate both Rivers and Trailer. SOF is on its way."

Donaldson maneuvered Eckhardt onto the sling and signaled them to lift off. "Sorry to hear that, too. Does it matter that Trailer is on our side?"

"No can do."

"Rivers has Trailer's wife up there. Or are we in the business of burning civilians again?"

Pooh Bear hovered. Donaldson saw the gargoyles looking down at him.

"You have three hours. After that this real estate goes kinetic."

Donaldson snapped the comm to the HULC and headed into the woods.

Half a klick in he came over a freshly made path. It had to be Rivers because Nick would never leave a mark. Either Rivers was stupid or he wanted to be found. Walking into Nick's environment, Augmented or not, proved Rivers stupid, inexperienced, and probably both. Donaldson assumed Rivers was also cocky enough to want to be found. He switched on the motion detector strapped to the HULC brace across his chest. Something coming fast two hundred meters and flanking him. The 8a showed no heart or thermal. The Benelli swung over his shoulder and he flattened himself to the ground.

Rivers called out, "It's okay, Major. I can take care of him."

Donaldson didn't respond. He stayed flat, a drunk gripping the earth for safety.

"Major? I've got Karen, Major."

Don't move, don't breathe.

Donaldson couldn't move. Rivers' augmentations were for urban combat but he was the equal of any twenty men even in this unfamiliar arena.

The HULC's motion detector beeped.

Rivers singsonged, "I KNOW where YOU AR-e. I KNOW where YOU AR-e."

Donaldson came up. The Benelli receded as the Vulcan swung around him, rocking him with its weight.

The motion detector starting pinging like heavy rain on a car roof. A tree trunk cracked followed by Rivers ear-shattering ululation.

Nick called out, "I've got Karen, Jim."

Donaldson looked at his motion detector. One blip moved rapidly on his left. Out of the corner of his eye he saw a little girl riding piggyback on a Bigfoot. The motion detector blipped something in front of him to his right. He squeezed the trigger on the Vulcan. The 40mm high explosive shells cut through all but the oldest trees like a chain saw through deadwood.

25

Minich watched a blip move through dense tree growth from high over treetop. "Donaldson, do you copy that signature? I'm getting a negative confirmation." Neither he nor his equipment had seen anything like the blip's configuration before. "Donaldson? Can you hear me? Donaldson?"

Eeyore, Roo's replacement ship and manned by a crew new to Minich, opened their comm. "I don't think any buck or bull moose could move that fast through that growth and it doesn't read like a quadruped."

Tigger called over the Wing channel, "We'll know soon enough. It's coming towards the clearing. Let's hope it's the nice one."

Minich switched everyone to hot mikes as Nick moved into the clearing with Karen on his back. Eeyore's chain gun opened fire, shattering boulders, splintering trees and making stones fly.

Nick stood there, in front of Karen, his body spreading until he formed a shield around her.

Minich hit a killswitch on his mission board. Eeyore's weaponry went silent. He opened Pooh Bear's speakers. "Do you have wounded?"

Nick laid Karen on top of the Grande. Blood flowed down her face, neck, arms, back... jagged-edged stone fragments, wood splinters, and shrapnel penetrated most of her body. "You're not going to die, Karen. I'm here. I'm holding you, just like you asked."

The WarClouds hovered at two hundred meters. Nick's hands started moving faster than Minich could follow. He ripped the leather off the seats, took the padding from the rifle boxes and cushioning from the seats and made pressure tourniquets, tying them off with the strings from her jacket. He ripped off pieces of his own clothing and made battle dressings. As Minich watched, Nick tore the hood off the Grande and pulled the fanbelts out of the engine and wrapped Karen in the Grande's rugs, immobilizing her against the hood with the fan belts.

Nick stood back and checked her breathing and pulse, then knelt over her as if in prayer.

"I'm here, Princess. Can you hear me? I'm holding you. Feel my arms around you, Princess? It's okay, I'm here."

He checked her vitals once again then raised his head and yelled into the sky. Minich's Wing felt the sound rock them over the drone of their own ships.

Karen's eyes opened. She attempted to move an arm but Nick's strapping held it down. "Don't move, Princess." He patted her softly, making sure she was immobile.

He turned to face the Wing. His hands blurred overhead then down in front of him and again over his head.

Kanga said over the ships' horn. "Did anybody get any of that?"

"What I got was he's going to stabilize her," Tigger replied. "We're to evac her to support. Anybody else get that?"

Minich confirmed, "Aye."

Once again the ships maneuvered to let Piglet drop a sling.

Back on the ground, Karen whispered. "I want to hold you, Nick. Free my arms so I can hold you."

"I don't think - "

"I'm going to die, He-man."

He heard the balmic swish of fluid filling her lungs.

"No." Nick grabbed the Grande's field medical kit. His eyes opened wide, his irises retreating until only pupils remained, his eyes black as night.

His breathing went rotary. His face went plastic.

"Acquired."

A pause. His eyes locked on her.

"Mapped."

He pulled transfusion lines from the kit and bit through the skin on his forearms so the needles could penetrate. Blood erupted in rhythm to his pulse. His hands hovered over her arms for the briefest second, seeking the heat signature of arteries and veins. The other ends of the transfusion lines found their marks.

"Synchronize."

He bent so that his lips were over hers.

"Heal." The word came out slowly as Nick exhaled almost pure oxygen into her lungs.

He placed a hand over her heart, his other fist clenching and releasing to her heartbeat, his hands working to stabilize her, his heart pumping blackening blood through the transfusion lines into her, one hand massaging her heart to move his blood through her body until each wound leaked black fire.

Piglet whispered over the ships' horn, "What is he doing? The Laying on of Hands?"

Tigger said, "Either that or the Kiss of Death."

Nick pulled back, his mouth and face away from her and inhaled again.

Karen whispered, "Hold me, Nick. I want you to hold me when I die."

Nick's tears made a warm summer rain over her face and neck, washing the blood from them.

"You're not going to die."

He grabbed the straps and snapped them. She held her arms out to him. He snapped the remaining straps, lifting her into his lap as he sat on the ground. "You are everything I have ever loved," he whispered, brushing the blood clotted hair from her eyes.

She smiled up at him. "You are everything I have ever loved."

She coughed. Blood rocketed down her chin. "It hurts, Nickie. How long will it take?"

"I don't know...I - "

She put a finger on his lips. "Hold me while I die, Nickie?"

His augmentations allowed him to feel what she could no longer say. Her thought came into him quickly, quietly, like a butterfly on the wing; I trusted you in life, I trust you in death.

"Yes, my love."

He held her closely, tightly. His hands moved along her back. His fingertips found nerve plexus and pressure points. "For mercy's sake."

He pressed.

Her heart fluttered.

He dropped into Hunter/Seeker state; all augmentations active, sharing her last moments, guiding her, loving her, giving her peace.

Minich watched unsure of what he was seeing. The Bigfoot rocked the little girl in its lap while it cried, its agony shaking the forest from floor to sky. It seemed he rocked her to sleep.

To Minich, it seemed to take a long time.

When he could mourn no more, Nick's stood. His body hardened. He removed their lines, gently tucked Karen's body in the slingbed and signaled for liftoff. When the slingbed was shoulder height he touched her body. "Everything I am, I give to you. Let's hope I kept my wits about me, Princess."

Piglet lifted her and bent its rotors heading back.

Nick raised his left hand to Minich's ship, the speed of his signaling too fast to follow.

Minich watched. When Nick lowered his hand, Minich signaled, "Slow. Repeat."

Nick signaled a second time, his hand still a blur.

Kanga asked, "Did I read him right?"

"He wants us to scatter, with all the ships heading back to Loring. He wants me to double back to Camp Delta and maintain silence." Minich hesitated before he went on. "He'll call us with instructions when he's found Rivers.

"Gentleman, spread the goose."

26

Donaldson waited until the Vulcan's echo died down. Something was wrong. The WarClouds flew away.

"What the fuck is this? I throw a party and nobody comes?"

Everything grew quiet. Donaldson checked his motion detector. Nothing. The Vulcan's belts were spent. He dropped it. The Benelli swung over his shoulder. "Well, that's better. I feel so much lighter now."

Something grabbed him by the back of the HULC and upended him, holding him by the foot. His knee and hip slid out of joint under the weight of the armor, cage, and weaponry.

He pulled the Casull from his right holster and pointed it at Rivers' face.

Rivers pulled him up and bit through the barrel before Donaldson could fire. "Little boys shouldn't play with guns, Major."

Donaldson stared into Rivers unblinking eyes.

"What's next, Major? Aren't I the best?"

Donaldson whipped a K-bar with his left hand. Just as he began to feel the putty-like resistance of augmented skin, his motion detector went off.

Rivers looked at it.

The diversion let Donaldson thrust the knife into Rivers side.

Nick jumped and grabbed Rivers around the legs.

Donaldson fell and twisted so the cage would take the impact. He got up and checked the K-bar. The guard had rich red blood, the tip covered in black.

A mass of arms and legs landed in front of him.

Donaldson once again heard a side of beef being slammed onto a cutting table.

Rivers' limp body flew backwards through the trees, snapping limbs and crashing through smaller trunks. He got up and ran further up a dried creek bed.

Nick pointed at the K-bar. "You want to be careful with that thing?" He went after Rivers. A cut oozed black pitch from his thigh.

The AT-8a snapped free of the HULC. Donaldson mounted it on a tree, set it on automatic, then swung the Benelli and Ruger into opposing left and right positions and followed.

27

Nick walked slowly, blending his movements to the swaying of the trees. It all came back. Watching for mosquito concentrations to see where people hid. Watching how long it took a spider to build a web in a footprint to determine when someone walked through. Reading the wind on the grass and heat flow and dissipation to determine movement patterns.

Nick heard something approaching him. He slowed and froze, hiding in the thick Maine woods by being most obvious of all around him.

Rivers came through the bushes ahead of him, bearwalking, his nose to the ground, sniffing his way along.

Nick waited until Rivers was directly in front of him and kicked right into the top of Rivers head.

Rivers stood up slowly. Blood flowed from a large gash in his scalp. "My turn."

Nick braced for the impact; Rivers' 201 noted the smaller, tighter Phase One design in order to bulldoze through urban environments.

The impact nearly severed his head and sent him rolling ten meters.

He heard something ticking about a hundred meters away and came up running.

Behind him and coming fast, he heard Rivers go pure arboreal, using the trees as he would telephone poles, fire escapes, and rooftops to remain aloft if he were in a city.

The ticking grew faster. Nick leapt up into Rivers path, not grabbing branches or trees, instead tucking and rolling in mid-air as Rivers reached for him, dropping before Rivers caught him.

The ticking stopped. The 8a launched three missiles into Rivers' face.

Nick didn't stop to figure out if the missiles had any effect. Rivers was totally unknown, his 201 completely invalid. He ran at top speed deeper into the forest, towards the old POW camp and Collection area 9571, the discarded logging camp that had grown up and died close by.

He had a plan.

28

The trees went kinetic over Donaldson's head. He looked up in time to see Rivers tuck his head as the AT-8a fired. The missiles exploded in the tree immediately above him and Rivers fell. Donaldson shut down all his equipment and sank to the ground.

Rivers got up slowly, one hand to his head, the other holding a tree for support. His eyes were closed. Blood flowed from his right ear.

The 8a started ticking.

Rivers stilled and the 8a swept past him, fixing and tracking something big moving downwind of Donaldson. Rivers pulled his good ear back, moving it to let the veining channel sounds in.

It was moving fast and straight for Rivers.

"I've got you now, Mr. Trailer."

The AT locked and Rivers hit the dirt in time to see a bull moose get blown away as the AT released its remaining missiles, one missile going straight down the moose's throat and out through its butt without even detonating.

Rivers smiled. "Nice, I'll have to remember that."

The AT-8a grew silent.

Rivers got to his feet, shook his head, and sniffed the air. He started running.

Donaldson watched from ground level. *Christ, he's not even shutting down to repair.*

Donaldson lifted the Benelli, but there were no clean shots. His motion detector showed Rivers moving fast and away from him.

"Minich?" he called on the comm. "You there, Minich?"

No response.

"Is anybody there?"

Nothing.

"I'm getting damn tired of this." He closed the comm.

The motion detector grew silent, its last sweep heading north northwest. He called up a topomap and compass on the HULC's HUD.

"I'm too old for this." In full BDU with armor, mounts, and weaponry, some hundred-fifty kilos over his body weight, he had trouble negotiating the forest terrain. The HULC gave him perfect balance with its powered and self-bleeding structural servos, but its original purpose was moving loads, not moving through dense undergrowth with low lying branches, brush and vines. The IronMan rigging didn't help because it was intended for urban combat, nothing that would get him over the terrain the map indicated.

He inhaled deeply. His side ached. His hand moved to the HULC releases and hesitated. "No, I'll keep my coat on, if that's okay. Never know when we might expect a chill."

He folded all the weaponry in so that he could use his hands to help him move and started in the direction indicated by the last sweep.

29

"That's Donaldson, Commander. You going to answer him?" asked Pooh Bear's pilot.

"No, I want a clear channel for Trailer. I've got to bleed the monster. Power down so we can refuel and bellow if he calls."

The field station had no more casualties and was being torn down. A tanker remained with a line running to the WarCloud. Coca War issue Greenbags covered the ground like little death mounds. Half-tracks came in and out, carrying the green bodybag-wrapped dead away for identification, cocoons that would never grow moths.

Minich left the ship and walked over to a sergeant in charge of the bugout. "Juice her," he said as he pointed to the WarCloud. On his way back, he stopped by the same sergeant, "I brought in two people, special. I'd like to know what happened to them. One was Ed Sylvio. We brought him in under a Kiowa. The other was a civilian caucasian female, Karen Trailer."

The sergeant scanned through some papers. "Sylvio's in Northern Maine Medical and is going to come through okay. The woman, at least you brought her in in one piece. She special to you?"

Minich shook his head. "The wife of a buddy of mine. Friendly fire." He pulled down his gargoyle and walked back to the ship.

30

Nick walked up the old logging road towards the camp upwind, exposed and at a disadvantage. Every hundred meters or so he'd stop and listen. A few minutes later he stood in the center of rusted and rotting logging equipment, as if various forestry machines had found their way here to die in peace, an elephants' graveyard of technology no longer needed.

Nick inventoried his surroundings: the remains of a dragline, a skidder, and the end of a railroad spur used to bring logs down to the main trunk and on to the lumber mills to the south. Black, blue, and red berries grew on bushes all around the camp. One side of the camp had a well surrounded by entanglement wire to keep adventuresome teens, hikers, and critters from falling to their death. Beer cans, various bottles and lots of shitpiles - some human, some not, the human piles demarcated by used toilet paper left by hunters who stopped in the old camps to rest and drink - were scattered around.

"And so we begin."

He went to the bushes and began eating berries by the handfuls.

He went to the well and drank three buckets of water without stopping. He went to the skidder and opened the battery box. It still had all five batteries, three full, one cracked and bone dry and the last with three of five cylinders full. Disconnecting the battery cables, he touched the positive and negative leads from the last battery to his tongue. The snap of electricity made him snap his jaws shut. "You're alive and well. I'll keep you out and hope your brothers are just as happy."

He searched through the debris for bottles with heavy bottoms and no cracks then used a piece of hydraulic tubing to siphon the battery acid into three whisky bottles he found. The skidder's fuel tank was empty, but plenty of high-grade oil remained in its crankcase.

He went to the rail spur and grabbed handfuls of the seven-centimeter flattened granite stones used for ballast on the rail line, took off his shirt and pants and tore the fabric into fifteen-centimeter strips. He gathered up the dragline, some railroad ties, irons, and the entanglement wire.

He pulled one of the rails sideways until he could brace two ties against it. It hummed with the tension and the ties started running cracks, then stopped. Nick placed a finger over his lips. "Shhh."

One end of the dragline he looped around the pulled rail, the other end he whipped over the trees and into the woods.

He came back to his stockpile and gathered some uncrushed beer cans. "They won't be the greatest CBUs, but they'll be the damned dirtiest cluster bombs he's ever seen."

He covered the bottoms of the beer cans with a layer of high-grade oil. He took apart the skidder's seat to get the Styrofoam cushions, tore the tops off several undamaged cans, then began relaxing the muscles along his urinary tract. A moment later he started pissing into the cans.

Some of the stones he snapped into smaller pieces and mashed into dry feces, along with the toilet paper, which he pressed into the cans with the high-grade oil. He soaked the strips of his clothing in his urine and tamped the mixture down, twisting the cans until only a strip of clothing remained exposed. Some he strapped around the bottles filled with battery acid, separated from the bottles themselves by the seven-centimeter granite stones, one on each side of a bottle.

He piled all of his makeshift CBUs by the remaining live battery and connected the battery cables to it, using the skidder's lighting wires to thread through the bombs. At the spur, he pulled loose two rails and grabbed some ties, wrapped the remaining drag line around him, and carried his booty into the woods.

Two hours later Nick came back down the road. It was turning dark. He leaned against a birch and heard, "On the seventh day, he rested."

Nick turned and looked into Rivers' smiling face. He leapt backwards, turned in the air and ran as he hit the ground.

"Oh, come on, Nick. We've been through all this before."

He heard Rivers charging after him, felt the wind blast of Rivers' reaching for him.

Nick tucked, rolled and sprang sideways into the woods.

Rivers' hands closed on empty air. "You son-of-a-fucking-bitch!"

Nick jumped up ahead of Rivers and rammed full speed into a thirty-centimeter thick pine.

"Boy that was - " Rivers didn't complete the sentence. He ducked as one of the rails thrummed over his head, the railroad ties splintered so that their ends resembled a logger's version of punji sticks.

"Good try." He laughed and stood up.

The second rail swung down from behind him and into his spine, sending him skyward and into a waiting web of entanglement wire.

"I thought so," said Nick.

Rivers screamed, "Didn't hurt." His hands and arms flailed the air, pulling the wire from deep cuts all over his body.

Nick didn't stop to find out if Rivers lied or not. He ran towards the logging camp.

He heard Rivers behind him, moving slower. Perhaps dragging a leg, perhaps still bound in the wire. Nick didn't give his trap that much credit.

Rivers let loose a banshee yell. It felt like someone was shoving a K-bar into Nick's skull. Rivers hit every frequency Nick could selectively hear.

Nick flexed some muscles in his neck and opened his mouth and throat wide, protecting his inner ears by balancing the vibrations on both sides of his eardrums, resulting in his hearing going dead. He kept moving.

He stopped at the perimeter.

Rivers popped up in front of him. "Knew you'd block your hearing, Nick. Read you did that against doublebugs in Pancholand. Guess you don't learn. Guess you never heard of trial and error."

Nick started somersaulting backwards.

Rivers followed him. "What a show!" He clapped his hands as he followed Nick into the trees.

Nick did a double somersault and banged into a tree.

Rivers leapt sideways. He shouted, "I'm not falling for that again."

He landed. The dragline caught and snared him straight up.

"Trial and experience," Nick corrected. "Something you don't have. Fifty-fifty chance and you always evade right."

The dragline slid Rivers down towards the skidder.

Nick picked up one of the stones he'd left by the snare and winged it at the bottles lined up on the side of the skidder. They broke, the urine soaked rags closing the circuit on the battery and lighting wires. The CBUs exploded as Rivers smashed into the skidder.

Rivers hung there, motionless, blood running from him.

Nick came up behind him, kneeling at the perimeter of the camp and crawling towards Rivers. He flexed his throat to open his ears.

Rivers didn't make any sounds, but experience told him that didn't mean much. "I fucking hate this part of the movie. You're screaming at the hero to get the hell out of there or pump every last round he has into the creature and get away." He stood up and moaned, "I don't even know if I'm the hero in this one."

He closed to three meters when Rivers snapped up and bit through the dragline, landing on his feet. "Christ, Nick. I thought we could've been friends through this. I thought we could've been pals."

Glass and metal shards protruded from Rivers' face and chest. It looked nasty. The wounds bled profusely but amounted to little more than shaving cuts. None would slow him down. Many of them closed while Nick watched. The acid made his face look like an adolescent's who hadn't heard of Clearasil. The entanglement wire on one leg already had skin folding over it, like a tree growing over and around some obstructive fencing.

"Now I'm really pissed, Nick. Now I simply have to kill you."

Nick jumped and tucked, slamming Rivers into the skidder and driving his knees into Rivers' gut.

Rivers howled as he bounced off the skidder.

Nick spun towards him, arcing his leg up and across Rivers face, wheel-kicking him one, two, three times.

Rivers pivoted on the last kick, adding to the momentum, and smashed his fist into Nick's arm. Both heard the elbow snap.

Rivers smiled. "Oh, and you can't repair the way I can. It'll take you at least a couple of weeks to mend that one."

Nick jumped and delivered two flying front snap kicks into Rivers' groin.

The kicks lifted Rivers off the ground. He sighed heavily, rubbed his groin, then smiled again. He undid his pants and kicked them off his ankles.

One hand ran through the hair in his groin. Nick looked. Rivers had no genitals, only pubic hair.

Rivers said, "My friends call me Ken."

"No wonder you're angry." Nick ran back into the trees.

"Give it up, Trailer. I have twice your strength, five times your speed. I'm younger. I'm better." Rivers followed him into the forest.

Nick saw something glint beside a fallen tree.

He bellowed, drowning out all other sounds in the forest as he ran another hundred meters before stopping and facing Rivers. "Yes, but I have one thing you'll never have."

Rivers' attention slipped briefly. "What? What could you have that

I don't have?"

"Friends." Nick dove to the ground.

Rivers leapt up, grabbed a tree branch, and said, "You can't kill me, Trailer - "

Nick closed his eyes and screamed, "Now!"

The trees swayed far behind Rivers.

"But I can."

Rivers spun as he let go of the branch. "Major?"

Two armor-piercing shells punched through Rivers' right and left pectorals. Rivers started shrieking. Nick saw Donaldson's HULC vibrating.

Donaldson swung the M16 up and fired.

Nick heard the distinctive whoosh of CrowdPleasers.

Donaldson unloaded all ninety-nine rounds into Rivers chest and abdomen. "That ought to soften you up, you bastard."

Rivers lurched towards him.

Donaldson didn't have time to load another magazine onto the M16 and dropped it.

The Benelli fell into his hand. The six remaining shells fired in less than a second, sending an expanding cloud of angry 12 gauge hornets in Rivers' direction.

Rivers screamed but didn't fall.

Donaldson let go the Benelli and lifted the Ruger, its clip bearing mixed full metal and explosive tips.

Rivers dodged the first four rounds.

The fifth round blew his left arm off.

The sixth round ripped through his shoulder, erupting out his back with blood and bone fragments.

Donaldson didn't have a chance to fire a seventh round.

Rivers grabbed the rifle barrel.

"I told you not to play with these." Rivers bent the barrel against the HULC.

Nick plowed into them, turning them so that Jim landed on top.

Rivers got up faster than either Jim or Nick and slammed his foot down as Nick rolled out of the way.

"Old man! Old Man! Old Man!" Rivers smashed his feet into the earth, a bizarre clog dancer attempting to crush Nick underfoot. Nick rolled and dodged his stomps.

The Mk-79 swung over Jim's shoulder. He ran up behind Rivers and buried the muzzle in Rivers' back.

Rivers crushed the Mk-79 into the HULC and then into Donaldson's shoulder.

Rivers backed away and asked, "What do you think now, Major? I'm the best, right?"

Jim looked at him and, as calmly as he could, said, "No, you're not the best. You're too stupid to be the best. I don't know why I bother with you. You don't know what you're talking about. You're too stupid to know anything."

Rivers eyes went wide with horror. Jim continued, "You were a mistake. A bad, bad mistake. I should have shot the nurse and flushed you down the toilet when she brought you out to me."

Rivers reached for him and missed, sobbing. He stood, stretching his spine and reaching again, his sobs turned to shrieks of rage.

Donaldson activated the HULC's lifters until he stood taller than the stretched Rivers. He stared down at him and spoke calmly, "You stupid, stupid boy."

Donaldson backhanded Rivers as hard as he could, using the full weight of the HULC to deliver the blow. "You foolish, ignorant piece of shit kid. God damn but I should have ended you when that bitch that spawned you brought you home."

Rivers reached again and let loose an ear-shattering ululation.

All of Rivers' attention focused on Donaldson. Donaldson screamed and backhanded him again, "I hate you, you little bastard." Donaldson slapped Rivers' face, forehand and backhand, with each pass of the words, "I hate you.

"Hate you.

"*Hate you.*"

Rivers slowed. He grabbed the HULC with his remaining arm, lost his grip, fumbled recovering, finally got it back and lifted.

He pulled his head back and opened his mouth wide, spit and blood dripping from his teeth, his nictating membranes pulled up.

His shrieking stopped as he snapped Donaldson towards his mouth.

Nick kicked Donaldson out of Rivers' grip.

Donaldson fell back and landed hard, blood flowing from ruptured eardrums.

Nick screamed every childhood curse he could think of, all he could remember, screaming them in a little child's voice, "I don't want to be around you anymore, Tommy. You're stupid, you're ugly, and your mother dresses you funny. You don't know how to play any good games; nobody likes you and I don't, either. Go home!"

Rivers stood over Jim, his eyes going from one to the other.

Nick hollered, "Go away, Tommy. You're no fun anymore."

"You're a very bad boy, Thomas, a mistake of the worst kind," Donaldson spoke as evenly as he could, declaring a fact, not an opinion. He remembered a line from Rivers' 201, something his father often threatened him with, "Do you know there are starving kids in South America who would love to come live here with me? I think I should get rid of you and get one of them."

Rivers kept looking from one to the other. "But, but, but - "

"There you go again, son," Donaldson said. "What're you doing? Counting assholes?"

Donaldson stood up. The 45-70 came into his hand.

He buried the muzzle under Rivers' jaw. "You dumb prick."

He closed his eyes and pulled once.

Rivers went stiff as the 400 grain, uranium cased slug rampaged up, through, and out his skull.

Donaldson angled the muzzle lower and pulled again.

Rivers' body began to relax.

Donaldson kept his eyes closed as Rivers' brains, mucous, blood, throat, and tongue painted his face, pushed out of Rivers' eyes, nose and mouth by the pressure of the small missile burrowing through him.

Donaldson lowered the muzzle and pulled again, lowered and pulled, lowered and pulled.

The hammer hit empty chambers. He let the weapon fall.

Rivers' beautiful Aryan body lay before him, motionless.

There was nothing left to the back of Rivers' head. The beautiful smile remained.

Nick limped over to him. "What kept you?"

Donaldson started to take off the HULC. "I wanted to catch him with his pants down."

"Can he come back from that?"

"I'd doubt it, why?"

Nick held out his hand. "Give me the comm. I want to be the hero in this one."

Five minutes later they held onto each other, hobbling down the logging road, Donaldson out of the HULC, ordnance, body armor, and BDU. Overhead and back at the logging camp, Minich's lone WarCloud's FFARs and Mistrals disintegrated Rivers' remains.

The WarCloud gathered them a few minutes later and left.

Donaldson tapped Minich on the shoulder. "Karen?"

Minich looked from one man to the other. He shook his head, no.

They passed over where they'd left the Grande. Nick focused on the ground where he last held her. He started shaking, his eyes, tear-filled, pleading with Donaldson. "Help me," he whispered.

Donaldson grabbed Minich. "Put us down."

"What?"

"Put us down, now!"

Trailer jumped out before the WarCloud landed. He knelt where he'd last held Karen and raised his fist, bringing it down slowly to the ground, then faster and harder, banging a hole into the earth. He spoke quietly at first. His voice grew louder and louder until it matched his victory yell at its greatest, "I held you, Karen. I held you just like you wanted. I held you."

The hole became a puddle filled with Nick's tears as Donaldson watched.

Nick whispered, "You were the only person to ever love me." His eyes fixed on the puddle.

A few sobs later Donaldson joined him.

Did you enjoy **The Augmented Man***?*

Please write a review on Amazon http://nlb. pub/Augmented and Goodreads http://nlb.pub/ GAugmented (and our thanks!)

Become a member of Joseph's blog and read excerpts of **The Augmented Man's** *sequel*

I'll Raise a Cup to You, My Darling

http://nlb.pub/JoinJoseph

Follow Joseph on
BookBub http://nlb.pub/BookBub
Goodreads http://nlb.pub/Goodreads
Facebook http://nlb.pub/Facebook
Twitter http://nlb.pub/Twitter
Instagram http://nlb.pub/Instagram
Pinterest http://nlb.pub/Pinterest
LinkedIn http://nlb.pub/LinkedIn

Avoiding Self-Destructive Behaviors

The first thing you need to know is that the best way to avoid self-destructive behaviors — those things you do which you don't mean to do that sabotage your work, your partnerships, your life. That's why such behaviors are also often called self-sabotaging and self-defeating behaviors — is to not have them.

That's kind of like "Just say 'No' to drugs," isn't it? Don't want to sabotage yourself? Then don't.

The good news is that just about everybody on the planet has some self-defeating behaviors. Self-defeating behaviors — in their more useful form — are known as our *protective instincts*. Protective instincts are those things that stop us from walking off cliffs, intentionally touching live high tension power lines, things like that. Protective instincts stop us from doing things that might hurt us.

Very useful, don't you think?

Then how did something so very useful become something so … unuseful? Basically self -destructive, -defeating and -sabotaging be- haviors are given to us (that's right. They're given to us) in childhood.

We hear our mothers say things to our fathers, our fathers to our mothers, a much older and probably care-giving sibling to someone else. We see something done that should not have been done or seen. We believe we did a good thing, something to be proud of, and are punished for it.

Any and all of these things (and many others) occur repeatedly and when we're too young to understand them, to separate the people from the acts or the words, we get wounded in ways too penetrating and permanent to recognize.

The wounding is psycho-emotional, the most difficult to heal. The body, luckily, doesn't remember pain. When the body is wounded it sends a message to the brain, "That hurt! Don't do it again", but it doesn't remember the pain itself. That's the brain's job, to remember to help us avoid.

Which is what happens when we're older, supposedly wiser, going after a job, a promotion, a client, a lover, a friend

Then, suddenly poof, for reasons hidden away, not recognized because we as adults can't access the childhood memories that caused these kinds of trauma (without help and training, anyway), the memories and pains associated with them reveal themselves in behaviors that cause us to put on the brakes, to stop the win, to avoid doing whatever it is we're doing, to defeat, sabotage, and destroy our best efforts by turning them into worst efforts.

Triggering Events

Any behavior is a response to an internal or external event. More accurately, all behaviors are external manifestations of internal responses to internal or external events (what are called BMIRs - Behavioral Manifestation of Internal Response). We drive our cars, cook our dinners, hug others, and push still others away because our lifelong memories dictate how we respond to events happening around us now.

The same is true for self -defeating, destructive, etc., behaviors. We respond in the moment with a life time of experience. What we need to do is recognize what events trigger which behaviors.

An Example

A small company CEO always seemed to take vacations whenever a client was ready to sign, a product was about to be released, a milestone was about to be achieved, … , whenever anything critical to company progress was going to happen, the CEO … well … vanished. Couldn't be reached by phone, by email, knocks on the door or requests to family and friends.

Company success was unobtainable because the individual leading the company psycho-emotionally refused to lead when the need for leadership was at its peak.

And it was all traceable to a mother who never honored a father's best efforts, demonstrated that lack of honoring in front of her children, and, as this individual grew, refused to honor this individual's best efforts as well.

When the repeated message is that no best effort is worthy, the desire to put forth a best effort fades — after all, it won't be honored — so while the conscious mind wants us to achieve, the lifetime of experience instructs us to avoid.

Changing Responses

Knowing your personal history of self -destructive, -defeating, -sabotaging, … behaviors is part of the solution and is best done with professional help. After that knowledge comes learning to recognize what events trigger those behaviors. This takes a willingness to become self-aware that in itself can be a difficult and painful journey (although an incredibly worthwhile one (in my opinion) for those so willing).

It is while on this last journey that we learn to control our behaviors, to respond to events as we wish to rather than how we used to, to change what we were to what we can be.

It is up to us as individuals to decide.

Addendum

The person who taught me these things has long passed and I'm writing this post to pass on that learning to a friend, the CEO mentioned above, and including another lesson from this same master: My journey is my goal, my path is my prize.

Knowing, learning and changing is what life is all about. No matter where your path takes you, rejoice in it. No matter what your journey entails, relish it.

Fear of Rejection

I was contacted by someone whose personal life is interfering with their public life.

First, in a Facebook, LinkedIn, YouTube, Twitter world, I detect some kind of oxymoron in the thought that public and private lives are still separate.

Second, throughout all history it has been impossible for most people — barring sociopaths — to keep their private life and public life separate. I've known some people who are remarkably adept at compartmentalizing things and this doesn't mean they're keeping things separate, only that they're letting specific things through.

The reason it's impossible to keep different aspects of our lives separate is because all aspects of our lives are "powered" by our core psychologies and beliefs. Someone who's a joy on the job and a terror at home is simply bringing their work frustrations home and letting them out there. The reason people act out at home (private life) more than at work (public life) is because the relative safety of the home allows for more of the core to manifest itself.

Usually.

But this chapter is about *Fear of Rejection*, so let's get to it … This individual's family-of-origin (the core family group that raised you) didn't support open emotionality (Note to parents: unless children learn how to express their emotions openly they'll never learn when it's not safe to do so). This lack of support planted a seed of emotional confusion and frustration.

Such seeds usually sprout polarity type demonstrations. The individual either grows cold (never having learned how to demonstrate emotions healthily the safest thing for them to do is shut theirs down when presented with yours) or demonstrates their emotions too easily and often (never having learned how to demonstrate emotions healthily they've never learned boundaries and limits to their own emotional displays). At the best of times there's a median ground where the individual doesn't grow completely cold with certain individuals or learns with whom it is safe to be emotional.

In this case, that seed was watered when a poor partner choice paired them with someone who could not honor commitments and philandered. Often.

And what sprouted is a fear of rejection.

As noted above, this fear wasn't compartmentalized to one aspect of life. What happened in their private life manifested in their public life. Seeking a new job, they decided the potential employer was not interested (and worse, if you know how these phobias make themselves known).

So they contacted me for some advice, and I share that advice with all those possibly facing similar fears.

Advice to the fearful

Your partner (I assume now an ex-partner)'s philandering was an indication of their psyche, not yours. You've decided their actions were due to some lack or inability on your part hence you've "developed a fear of rejection".

"Fear of rejection" isn't something that happens overnight. Nobody wakes up one morning, stretches, throws back the covers, looks smilingly into the sun and declares, "Yes, from this day forward I shall fear rejection!" This response - because that's what it is, it's a response to your environment - was something taught to you and learned over time. Because it was taught and learned, because it's not part of how you're designed to work, it can be unlearned, untaught, and more useful responses can take its place.

By the way, you were designed to be wonderful. Just like everybody else. If you're not wonderful right now, it's someone else's responsibility. Your parents, your partners, your co-workers, your supervisors, your friends, ...

But (*BUT!!!*) if you're reading this right now, you are being invited to take responsibility *from them* - they're obviously not good stewards of you - and put it where it belongs, *in you.*

Scary, I know, that "taking responsibility for yourself" part. We are what we've put our greatest efforts into creating and it took us our whole lives to become the way we are. It's tough to re-do a work of art so far along in its creation and that's okay, we're designed to be able to do it. It's part of that evolutionary process that's in our DNA.

I would offer that you've created a tool for dealing with certain types of information. Now you must decide if the tool you've developed — a fear of rejection — is the best tool for dealing with the "no information coming in" type of information, the "negative" information, and other certain types of information. Dealing with negative information - the type of information we'd rather not have - is pretty easy. First determine if it's valid information. It is? Then change the reason for the negative information (maybe it's time to change a job because of a harsh boss, change a partner because they don't care about you, change your brand of soap or laundry detergent, ...). It isn't valid? Ignore it and its source.

Right. Now let's deal with the "no information coming in" type of information. Often when people are waiting for a response from someone or something and they get no response whatsoever, they imagine the worst. In relationships (professional and personal) this becomes fear of rejection.

So first recognize you're using the fear of rejection tool to deal with "no information coming in".

Next, recognize that information is coming in, simply not information you have a good tool for. The information is "no information" because (without boring you with jargon) an information "vacuum" can not exist. The vacuum is being filled with information from your past experiences, and specifically your "fear of rejection" experiences.

As with your partner, so with this potential employer: whatever their response, they're making a statement about themselves, not about you. Your life-partner's philandering was a statement of their limits, their lack, and how they sought to fill them. It was a demonstration of their lack of tools and had nothing to do with you.

Really, truly, it is so. Believe it.

There's a tool I use, not specific to "fear of rejection" although I'm betting it would work quite well because it is a "fill the vacuum with correct information" tool. I contact people and ask them, "Have you made a decision yet?"

I know, you're shocked that I would be direct and to the point, yes?

This tool is built on another tool, an Eliadean tool, known as "choice is better than no choice". I believe knowing is better than not knowing, hence my desire to know as a fact that I'm "rejected" is stronger than my desire to remain ignorant of such a fact because knowing facts allows me choices. Not knowing limits my choices.

Knowing something is a fact allows me to make decisions and choices based on that piece of information. Not knowing makes me a victim of my ignorance, traps me in a well of uncertainty, and forces me to stop functioning until I learn what fact applies.

More to the case here, it causes me to live a life of fear rather than a life of joy, bliss, happiness, love, … And I do know that how I choose to live my life directly affects all those around me. Living a life of fear will cause me to demonstrate fear-based behaviors to everyone I'm in contact with, especially those I love. If I interact daily with children? They will learn the "fear of rejection" lesson and the more I interact with them the better they will learn it.

So for me I'll chose a life of bliss, joy, happiness and love because I'd rather people drink those things from my cup than any others.

Rewarding Your Critical Actors

Do you have a little voice inside your head that warns you about things you're about to do? Maybe it goes beyond warning you, perhaps it out and out chides you or even yells so loudly it stops you dead in your tracks?

Congratulations, you've been in touch with what people studying learning models call your *critic* (not a surprising name considering what it does, is it?).

Do you have a little voice inside your head that makes suggestions on how to get the most out of whatever you're about to do? Maybe it goes beyond suggestions, maybe it reminds you of what worked and what didn't in the past? Maybe it demands this path be followed over that path?

Congratulations again, now you're talking with your *actor*.

Want to learn how to confuse them or even shut them up completely? It's probably obvious (once you think about it) that our mind's actor and critic come from different parts of the brain. The critic comes from the front part of the brain where reasoning occurs, the actor from the rear of the brain where we process vision and memory (generally speaking).

Both are necessary. They're part of what's called *instrumental conditioning* and constitute the most basic form of *adaptive behavior.* Adaptive behavior and instrumental conditioning are very important to our survival as individuals and as a species. We adapt how we behave in order to maximize rewards and minimize punishments, and that process of adapting is done in (hopefully) small steps by conditioning ourselves to our environment.

The actor reminds us what happened before in similar environments and helps us predict what to do in the present environment. The critic predicts future gains and losses by evaluating present conditions and information out of our direct experience. We need both of them. They work in tandem for most of us and people lacking one or the other tend to take unnecessary risks or avoid new situations altogether.

But what if your critic-actor is too critical or too … umm … actorial?

Both critic and actor cause the brain to send hormonal signals through the body. Most often these signals are survival oriented — great for the jungle and possibly night walks in a city, not quite the same as deciding what you should purchase or whether or not to get on that really big roller coaster.

So here's how to deal with both and let you — your hopefully rational, thinking, intelligent self — make the decisions.

First, Agree

People think this is an odd suggestion and it comes from lots of studies. When your critic is saying "No, don't! Danger, Will Robinson! Danger!" respond with "Thanks. That's good advice. I appreciate your letting me know that" or something similar. Strangely enough, all the critic really wants to know is that you're paying attention to warning signs in the environment. Letting your critic know you're doing so is often enough to either shut it up or quiet it down, at least for a while. Similarly, agree with your actor. Same rules apply.

Second, Take a Deep Breath

Remember those hormonal signals I mentioned? Those signals are survival based, as in fight or flight. Taking a deep breath, centering yourself, maybe even closing your eyes for a second, all send counter-signals telling your brain and body "It's okay. You can relax now. I'm here." Think of something funny, a joke or some such. Put a smile on your face. A real smile, not just a polite one. You'll find you can think clearer when you do.

Third, Act Intentionally

Your critic and actor are exerting all sorts of energy to tell you what might, possibly could, or should happen. The truth is neither they nor you know what will happen. What you do know is what's happening right "now" in the moment of the decision. This is where you take control of your adaptive learning and instrumental conditioning to your own best benefit. Decide what option looks best "as far as the eye can see" so to speak and make a deal with your actor and critic. Ask them to cover your back and let you know if something needs your attention. Nothing quiets these primitive parts of the mind more than asking them to help. Seriously.

Lastly, Take Small Steps

You've chosen a path, now move in that direction. Just a little, not a lot. Are you still okay? Everything still good? Great. Lather, Rinse, Repeat. The moment you can't see what's going on or things stop being okay, back up to your last safe spot and decide if you want to continue or not.

Summary

Your actor and critic are there for a reason. The goal is to use them rather than letting them abuse you.

Enjoy.

Curious about more of Joseph's fiction?

http://nlb.pub/TalesV1

Here are excerpts from three *Tales Told Round Celestial Campfires* stories. Enjoy!

Cymodoce

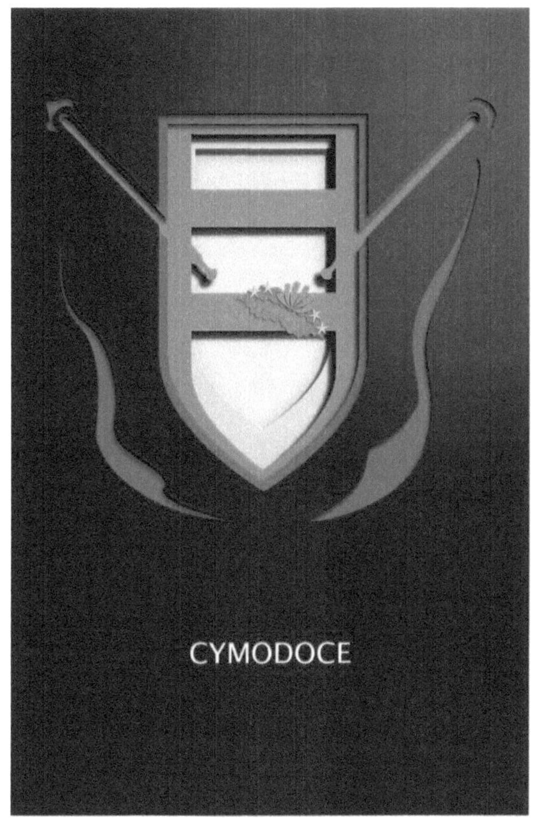

"How happy could I be with either
Were t'other dear charmer away!
But while ye thus tease me together,
To neither a word will I say."

Synopsis

Jenny Packwood, a single mother of three-year-old twins Davy and Cymmi and ASL interpreter/teacher in New York City, returns to her family's Maine Coast cabin for a summer away. There she remembers the near-dead man she found on the beach whom she nursed back to health.

Her kindness and his tenderness resulted in a night's quiet passion. He was gone when she woke, taking nothing nor using her skiff to get to shore.

He never returned.

Now back on the island with the children from their one encounter, Jenny finds seashell necklaces and deep-water pearls - gifts similar to her lover's previous visit - on her dock, in her boat, and on the path up to her cabin.

One night he returns. He knows the children are his.

And he wants one to come with him.

Excerpt

Jenny silently guided the rowboat to the dock, all the while keeping one eye on her three-year-old twins, Davy and Cymmi, sitting in front of her. When the boat was next to the mooring Jenny grabbed a line, pulled the boat to the dock and tied it. It was the first time she'd been to the island since the twins were born. Her parents, who died within a week of each other the previous fall, left her the dock, the boat, the cabin, the two acres of land, and only property taxes and upkeep to concern her.

Davy fidgeted. "Mommy, I'm hungry. Can we eat now?" She put a finger to her lips and Davy pouted. Cymmi was leaning over the side of the boat, splashing her hands in the water. She paused, looked out over the waves, then splashed harder.

Jenny moored the boat, lifted a lunch basket and helped the children onto the dock. "Mom," Davy whined, "I'm hungry."

"We'll go up to the cabin and eat. Okay, Davy?" They started up the narrow path.

"Mom, Cymmi's still by the water."

Jenny looked up. Cymmi was in up to her ankles. Jenny dropped the lunch basket, ran back and lifted Cymmi from the water. Her feet glistened. Cymmi kept looking at the waves as Jenny sat her by the lunch basket, took out a container of fresh water and poured it over Cymmi's feet. The tiny, silvery marks began to fade and Jenny signed /COME /EAT /NOW /PLAY /LATER /OKAY/?// She took Cymmi's hand and gently pulled her along.

Much later, when Jenny had put the children to bed, she walked down the path and sat on the dock. She took off her sandals and swished her feet in the ocean. Across the Sound she could see the lights of the Maine coast. The island had always been a quiet place. Even in the heat of the tourist season, when Route 1, heard if not seen across the Sound, was a tangle of campers, buses, and hitchhikers, the island was left to the three New York families who owned it and had cabins there.

The sounds of summer came across the water. She tried to match the sounds with the lights. Fuzzy rock music came from Beniroo's, an old icehouse turned bar and nightclub. When Beniroo's music paused she could hear a calliope and, intermittently, people giddily screaming. That would be Funland. She could see the Ferris wheel spinning and the roller coaster trestle climbing into the sky. Search lights swept back and forth, sweeping the ocean mists inland and then back out to sea. To the north she could pick out the tinny guitar and muffled bass of The Word's tent meeting, preaching God's message to the summer sinners.

Something tickled her foot and she jerked it from the water. Soon the tide would turn and go out. Fundy had powerful tides, aided this night by the moon overhead. There was a splash out by the rocks. Something bobbed briefly about forty feet from her. She heard another splash, saw a rippling approach her through the waves. / HELLO/?//

"Mommy?" Davy's voice pulled her back to dry land.

There was a slight almost soundless splash in the water.

Jenny's heart pounded. She fumbled getting up. "Yes, Davy?"

He walked over to her. "Who're you talking to?"

She smiled and ruffled his hair. "Just the fishes. I told them we came back this summer. Now, what are you doing out of bed?"

"I couldn't sleep."

She lifted him up so he could ride her hip as she walked. He wrapped his arms around her neck and cradled his head in her shoulder. "Come on, little man, you can sleep with me tonight." Davy's arms hung limp by his sides before they got back to the cabin.

She put Davy in her own bed and checked Cymmi before returning to the kitchen. There she made herself a cup of coffee and, from a window, watched the coast lights go out, one by one.

"If you live knowing only a process, you can never have all your options. If you live knowing there are options, one of them can be to partake in the process, they tell me."

Synopsis

Leaving behind his estranged wife and son, xenopologist Gordon Banks sets out with an advance team on a mission to explore the distant planet Aguirra. There, the team discovers the Goatmen: wise aboriginals with a rich telekinetic history preserved through entheogenic ritual. Nicknamed "Journeyer" by the Goatmen, Gordon Banks is invited to their village to live amongst them and participate in their customs. He soon realizes that the Goatmen are not the only intelligent life form on Aguirra and - in the process - embarks on a path of self-discovery. Set against the backdrop of interstellar colonialism, The Goatmen of Aguirra proposes that one's destiny can be achieved on a path taken to avoid it.

Excerpt

705015:216 - We've landed in a grotto, near the center of Hochebene's Altiplano, but closer to the Towers of God than not. On one side of the grotto is the only run of clear water for some thirty kilometers, and I've noted with Sanders that this could be a problem as all native fauna encountered thus far follow the same biologies as we. Immediately upon landing, Sanders ordered Tellweiller, Nash, and Galen to construct a blind. We are now a boulder, one among several, that slid into the grotto when we lowered a rumbler to cover our landing.

Nash estimates two standard hours before sunrise.

Early estimates indicated Aguirra was three and a half to four billion years old. Now, with readings coming in about the deep core and mantle, we place it closer to five. Gravity is one-point-one standard and the atmosphere is quite like Earth's only sweeter due to a higher $O3$ content. There is also a free floating enzyme, essentially carbolic anhydrase, which explains some of the evolutionary adaptations on the planet. Everything we've observed is based on the nitrocarbon cycle – everything we've recorded from space and robotics shows up as a variation on some earth fauna – and the carbolic anhydrase probably helps redaction and reduction in the $O3$ rich atmosphere when a stressing agent is introduced.

Due to the atmosphere there is a perpetual slight pink tint in the sky, much like before an intense electrical storm back home. This area, Hochebene's Altiplano to the Towers of God, is a paragneiss formed we're not sure how long ago by glaciation. It is difficult to estimate because the atmosphere mediates the planetary temperature such that weathering is neither gradual nor minimal – Hopkin's Bioclimatic Law doesn't seem to apply. There are seasons in the temperate zones but without the fluctuations of four true seasons. Summer temperature extremes range from -19°C to 33°C. Winter temperatures also vary by about twenty degrees, from -25°C to 5°C. These temperatures are for our current location, 43°N, 8000m altitude, and, as I've mentioned earlier, shrouded to the west by the Towers of God.

To our immediate east is the rock wall we worked hard to resemble, the rise of the grotto, then the expanse of the high plain for several kilometers. Although comprised principally of paragneiss and granite with only slight eruptions of soil, a hardy tundral grass grows in clumps all around. Our guess is the grass serves to anchor what little soil there is in place. There are wind storms – one is due in another hour – when Astarte 217 rises over the altiplano and begins churning this high, thin air with the thicker, deep valley air far below.

These grasses are richly verdant, their tops a slight yellow as if gently burned. Galen collected some samples when the blind was completed and says the yellowing is a pollen. Thus we learn immediately that these verdant clusters aren't true grasses and that there is some pollenizing agent, perhaps only the wind, which is at work. If the robotics sent into these highlands hadn't met such abrupt and catastrophic ends, we might know more about Aguirra's highland life, at least in this area.

There is still a carpet of snow, albeit thin and frayed in some areas, stretching a kilometer from the entrance to the altiplano to the Towers of God even though this continent is now in high summer. The snow, Nash says, is due to the altitude and rarified atmosphere. Even with the carpet of white, this is a desert, with cold, dry steppes leading to the Towers.

In contrast to earth flora, there appears to be no treeline. While there are no trees on the altiplano, there are five here in the grotto ranging from two to two-fifty meters in height. They appear something like succulent scotch pines, kind of chubby Christmas trees. They have no root systems and, according to Galen, all five trees are extensions of the same growth and are more like vines than trees, growing like Sequoias in the northern California forests. If they are vines, it explains their limbs being naked on one side and holding fast against the grotto's walls. They're being succulents so close to a clear water supply indicates that the water might be seasonal.

There are several similar although much smaller trees, these resembling elms and birch although Galen's report might show different, growing to our west and in the runoff fissures of the Towers. From there these trees grow up to the crowns of the Towers, becoming deeper and denser with altitude, giving the appearance of twin green-haired giants out in the distance. Based on this and other evidence Galen claims these are not true "trees". If Galen's contention about the succulents is accurate, there are but one or two of these "trees" sending their shoots, binding and girding like some giant's phylacteries, up the Towers.

The most noticeable feature of the landscape, the one we all knew would be most breath-

taking, are the Towers themselves. We are eight kilometers above sea level and the Towers rise another eight above us. They are the largest vertical features on all of Aguirra, even and symmetrical in every geologic detail, with their expansive flat plained plateau heads, each five-point-five kilometers in diameter, separated by zero-point-five kilometers horizontal and a four kilometer drop. There are a few passes down the Towers, more like torrents than actual passes in their slope and grain, and various hanging, piedmont, and steppe glaciers coming down the Towers' sides. The best climb, if one were necessary, seems to be along a bergschrund on the immediate faces of each.

Tellweiller has no explanation for the Towers' formation, although it is obvious from their age they were formed in the prebiologic days of the planet.

Although I am not a religious man, standing at their feet and hearing the winds, it is not difficult to imagine the whispers the ancient Greeks heard about Mt. Olympus. I can understand why these features were named the Towers of God.

Mani He

MANI HE

"The more you accept your fear, the greater your courage will become."
"Some places, they'll be like nightmares. Other places, they'll be like your sweetest dreams. Go towards your sweetest dreams, Mani He."

Synopsis

Anthony Morelli is on the fast track becoming Boston's next high-finance wunderkind. But his ascendency has an unforeseen cost; a soon-to-retire workmate is fired to make room for him. His organization's CEO only wants a "man's man" in the role and tells Anthony to prove himself via a solo trip to the organization's northern New Hampshire hunting cabin for a weekend.

Just be sure to bring home a trophy to hang in his office.

But Anthony was raised to respect The Wild. His Native American grandfather told him stories about the animal spirits, told Tony The Old Ones were his friends. Now Tony's childhood beliefs want his ascending star to travel another sky.

Anthony agrees to the trip and what Tony learns changes him forever.

Excerpt

Anthony Morelli saw the badger across the street as he came out of South Station, where the MBTA's southern terminus washed people towards One Financial Place. Anthony wore his St. James suit – bright grays with a black pinstripe – with cream oxford shirt and red and gold pumped satin tie, diamond studs, stockings which blended with his trousers, and black wingtips. It was an early Boston Fall and Channel-4 forecasted light drizzle. Morelli's raincoat was draped over his left arm and his accountant's case pulled down his right like a ship's keel in a storm. Today he made the presentation showing the errors in Thompson's plan.

The badger sat on a pretzel wagon. People were buying soft pretzels with mustard, soft pretzels with cheese, soft pretzels with extra salt. The badger was passing small talk and change and nobody else seemed to notice.

Morelli stopped and stared. The smell of coal-cooked chestnuts, peanuts and pretzels came over the diesel and street-level smog of Boston. His mouth watered and he remembered his father teaching him how to flip peanuts and catch them in his mouth.

The badger looked at Tony and hollered, "REDhots! PRETzels! GETcha-GETcha REDhots! PRETzels!"

If Anthony wore his glasses, he'd've adjusted them. Today he wore his contacts but his hands went to his face anyway. The badger waved at him and laughed, mimicking Tony's hand movements. The badger started pedaling his pretzel wagon and rolled away, calling out "REDhots! GETcha REDhots!"

Tony went into One Financial Place, made his presentation, shook hands, got his back patted, and was thanked personally by the Old Man. Brumhall, the Old Man, looked fifty and was well past seventy-five. His eyes were clear and sharp and his mind had never dulled. Haggedorn, Brumhall's number two, stopped Tony outside Thompson's door. "Anthony, excellent! You planned this? Excellent. Impressed me, right here," Haggedorn tapped his heart. "The Old Man and I gotta talk. It'll be excellent. Thompson. Have to let him go. Too bad. It'll be excellent."

Just then Thompson opened his door, stared at the two men, excused himself, and walked towards the restroom.

Tony looked at Thompson, the way the man's shoulders sagged, the way his chin quivered. Tony swallowed and felt a lump like a badger claw etch its way down his throat, crashing into his stomach like a bus into a pushcart. He wanted to say releasing Thompson wasn't part of his plan. Instead he dug into his pocket for the roll of TUMS his wife, Grace, gave him when he left the house, popped one in his mouth, and made a note to pick up a fresh roll when he went for lunch.

The Old Man came up to them a few moments after Thompson returned to his office. "Mr. Morelli, take the afternoon off. You come in tomorrow, you stop here." Brumhall pointed at Thompson's door and nodded to his number two, acting as if Tony no longer existed. "Mr. Haggedorn." The Old Man opened Thompson's door without knocking.

Haggedorn nodded. Before entering Thompson's office and while the door was opened, he said, "The American Express office. Third

Floor. Our branch, right there. Excellent. Stop in there. Big surprise. It'll be excellent."

Tony said, "I need to get my things."

Haggedorn said, "Already taken care of. Third Floor. American Express. Excellent," and closed Thompson's door.

Tony, still stunned and feeling hollow, took the stairs.

There was a Platinum Plus card with the company name on it waiting for him on the third floor. He smiled, lifted the card to his nose and inhaled like it was a roll of bills and he was an old-time gambler. Another whiff and the smell of platinum plastic rubbed the sting of Thompson's misfortune away. "Excellent." He sniffed the card again.

He took a cab home. From the Financial District to dying but ethnic Revere, even though his mail went thirty miles away to a PO box in affluent and upscale Newton. As the cab went through the Callahan Tunnel the lights went out. The cab starting bucking and kicking, as if the gas and brake had suddenly become alien to the burnt-ash-black West Somalian cab driver. The cab started to weave and horns blared in front, in back, and to the sides of them. Tony leaned forward and tapped on the glass. The burnt-ash-black man looked over his shoulder and Tony slumped back into his seat.

The West Somalian driver was a moose, the driver's dreadlocks weaving through the moose's antlers. He bellowed apologetically in the driver's pidgin English, "Sorry. In my country, we have nothing like this."

Outside his home, Tony gave the West Somalian moose a fifty dollar tip. The moose lifted the bill to his nose much as Tony had done with the Platinum card, inhaled, kissed the bill, then inhaled again. He smiled at Tony and Tony thought he said "Ganja." Tony couldn't be sure because there were grasses and weeds dripping from the driver's mouth. He pulled a U-ey, waved at Tony and left.

Tony waved until Grace called him inside. "Why're you home? Are you okay? You didn't get fired, did you?"

He explained. They celebrated. Later, they went to a quiet little bistro back in the North End, a place they knew from childhood, a place where they were part of the family. They spent the day sipping espressos and talking their first generation Italian-American English with Danté, the owner and the man who introduced them. Tony jumped up from his chair and hurried Grace into her coat when Danté brought some antipasto and linguine pesto.

"Anthony, what's wrong?" asked Grace.

"Nothing. I … I don't feel good. Too much strain. I have to go home."

A long, thin, pink tongue snapped out of a lizard's face atop Danté's body. "Antonio, stai male?" The lizard said.

Tony's face blanched and he wouldn't look the lizard in the eye. The lizard grabbed the water pitcher and a bowl from an empty table. He put the bowl down in front of Tony and poured some water in it, then sprinkled some olive oil on top of the water and placed the salt shaker beside the bowl. He made the sign of the evil eye and motioned Tony to pick up the salt. "Malocchio." The lizard stared fixedly at the bowl of water and oil, waiting for Tony to finish the evil eye ceremony.

At hearing the intervention against misfortune, Tony looked up again. Danté was once again old Danté, the man they'd both known since childhood. The scaly lizard's face and great round eyes, seen for a moment, were gone. His tongue was hidden in his mouth and not whipping about casting for flies as it had been a moment before.

Not believing in the old ways but honoring his friend, Tony sprinkled some salt in his hand, pressed it to his forehead, made the sign of the Cross with his thumb against his forehead and dipped the thumb into the oily water. The oil separated, fleeing from the salt as it lowered the specific gravity of the water. Tony knew the science but couldn't bring himself to shatter the old man's faith. "Si, amico mio. Si."

Late that night, Tony and Grace lay in bed. "It sounds like you've been working too hard, Tony. I don't mind being rich, but I don't want to be rich alone." She rolled on top of him and straddled him. "You die, Mister, and I'll have somebody else in this bed before your breath is cold."

It was an old joke. They both laughed. Up against the wall on the other side of the room and in a line of sight behind Grace's head, a spider built a web above Tony's closet. Tony's eyes focused and zoomed on the spider as if they were camera lenses. Grace was still laughing and rocking on his hips. He saw the spider look up from her web building, hold a pedipalp in front of her eyes and shake it like a finger, shaking her head, "no", as if in warning.

Then the spider was just a simple spider, building a web. Tony's last thought as he went to sleep was, "How did I know it was a 'she'?"

He woke up before the alarm went off. It was daylight and he saw by the clock he had about ten minutes of sleep left. He rolled over, towards his dresser and away from his wife. The badger was picking through the things on his dresser.

It looked up at him and said, "You got any juju-bees?"

Tony shook his head, no.

"How about toys, you got any toys? Coyote likes toys. That dumb shit's always playing with toys."

Another voice called from the hallway. The voice echoed and Tony knew it was coming from the pulldown stairs that led to the attic. "Found 'em." He heard something bumping up in the rafters then the same voice squealed, "Hey, look at this! Tonkas! The kid's got Tonkas!"

The alarm brizzed over Tony's head and Badger said, "See you later, kid. Gotta go."

Grace swacked the alarm silent and said, "Wake up, hon. Time to make me a millionaire."

Tony opened his eyes and reached on his dresser for his glasses. They weren't were he left them the night before. They were shifted a few inches to the right. A coldness shivered him despite the warmth of the bed. On his way to the bathroom he saw the attic stairs bolted and secured in the ceiling and laughed at himself. "Probably got up last night and moved my glasses myself," he mumbled.

In the bathroom he started the shower, turned to the toilet and fell backwards into the tub when he lifted the seat.

Grace called from the bedroom, "You okay, hon?"

"Yeah. Yeah, sure. Just slipped." He turned the shower to cold and held his head under the blast of frigid water. "Okay. I'm awake," he whispered. Drops of cold water trickled down his face, chest and shoulders as he looked back in the toilet. A child's bow and arrow were wedged in the seat.

His old bow and arrow. The bow and arrow which he'd packed under the Tonkas in his toy chest in the attic. The old bow and arrow his grandfather had given him. Holding them he remembered his grandfather's smell, a laborer's smell, his grandfather strong like a farmer. "My people use to be warriors," he once told Tony. "That was long before I met your grandmother." He remembered going to meet other old men with his grandfather, other old men who wore the strange turquoise and silver, bone and bead jewelry his grandfather wore. Then, too soon it seemed, Grandfather John died and the bow and arrow, the old men with the funny jewelry, were no more.

The arrow was rubber tipped and the rubber suction cup was old and cracked. The plastic feathers were stripped in places. The bow was also plastic, with a string made of heavy thread. Feathers and thunderbirds and Indians on horses were painted on the bow. He picked them up and memories of playing Indian as a child came back, as if the memories were waiting like mountain lions in the bow and arrow, waiting to pounce as soon as he touched it.

He lifted the bow and arrow to his shoulder and took aim, hearing himself and others chanting childhood rhymes and verse, mixes of broken English and Hollywood Indians, as he swept the bow and arrow around the bathroom, his arms somehow tiny once again so the toys became big and real and he wasn't Tony Morelli anymore but Little Chief White Feather once again.

He stopped smiling when he took aim at himself in the bathroom mirror. Behind his reflection, a mountain lion pulled back the shower curtain, held out a paw and pointed at the sink. "You wanna hand me the soap there, buddy?"

Tony skipped breakfast and went to work. Haggedorn met him as he got off the elevator at the eighteenth floor. "Anthony. Excellent. New office. Right here. It's yours. It's excellent." It was Thompson's office. A corner office. Two walls of floor-to-ceiling tinted windows with blinds tied to the environmental system. All Anthony had to do was set the amount of light and heat he wanted and the blinds would open and close to accommodate. When necessary, lights and ventilators took up the slack. The name plate on the door – his door, his name. Excellent! – was gold, as was the one on his desk, which was huge. The desk was as big as his bed and the office – his office. Excellent! – was the size of his living room. Along one wall was a multiplexing entertainment system and, at the press of a button, a bar which could rotate from fully alcoholic to totally dry, depending on who you were trying to impress. The other wall had a full length black brocade leather couch. The walls were dark oak, matching the desk. The upholstery of both Tony's chair and the two opposite his desk matched the couch's black. The rug, an inch-thick plush, was gray. He had two computers on his desk and a twenty-channel phone system. The phone's listings were all the ones he'd had in his old office. His accountant's case was there. Along the walls were plants and floral arrangements from various people in the firm and clients he didn't know he had.

As Haggedorn left, the office procession began. Several people came through, all shaking his hand and congratulating him. He looked into their faces as they came and left; this one was too hungry, this one would wait. This one would ally with whoever offered the most, this one would remain loyal.

He stayed late, enjoying the feel of a vibrating, reclining, twelve axes of movement, heated chair and kicked his legs up onto an oak desk so thick it would take six strong men to lift. Somebody knocked on his door. "Yes?"

"Cleaning crew, Mr. Morelli."

Tony checked his watch, a gift from Grace from their dating days when wishes were horses and the two of them rode. "Come on in.

You guys don't waste any time, do you? Office has only been closed about an hour."

The door opened and a hawk pushed a cleaning cart into the room. A hummingbird followed in behind the hawk. Both were dressed in clean and neatly pressed "Ace Cleaning Services" uniforms. The hawk's uniform had a white name tag over the right breast pocket which held an Ace Cleaning Services pocket-protector filled with pencils. Stitched in red was "Sparky". The hummingbird was obviously new because he had no pencils and his name was a red-on-white iron-on tag and not stitched in, therefore showing no permanence. He was "Bob". The hummingbird wore earbuds and hummed a tune Tony couldn't place.

"We try not to waste any time, Mr. Morelli," said Sparky the Hawk. "Sometimes, though, people keep us waiting their whole life."

Hummingbird Bob nodded, "Yeah."

They took out spray bottles and stain removers and went to work.

Haggedorn came in with the Old Man. He looked around the office, told Sparky the Hawk and Hummingbird Bob they were doing a good job and he appreciated their consistency as if there was nothing strange about them, then faced Tony. "You like it here, Mr. Morelli?" asked Brumhall. "This office satisfy you?"

"Yes, sir, thank you. And please call me 'Tony'."

Brumhall nodded slowly, measuring Tony with some internal gauge. "May I see your watch then, Tony?"

"Beg pardon, sir?"

"Your watch."

Tony peeled it from his wrist. Brumhall inspected it. "This watch have any significance to you?"

Tony, his eyes on the watch, swallowed. "No."

"Good." Brumhall tossed the watch into the trash basket on Sparky the Hawk's cart and turned back to Tony. "Mr. Haggedorn."

Tony watched Haggedorn open a black case. Out of the corner of his eye he watched Sparky the Hawk grab Hummingbird Bob's hands as the latter dove for Tony's old watch. Brumhall said nothing until Haggedorn gave Tony the black case.

A new watch. Rivier platinum, with more dials and gauges than Tony imagined he'd find in a fighter cockpit. The back had his name, the date, and "Welcome to The Club."

"You play tennis, Tony?" Brumhall asked.

"No, sir."

Brumhall brow creased. "No? What about Racquetball?"

"No, sir, not that either."

Brumhall turned briefly to Haggedorn then back to Tony. "Golf?"

Tony was about to answer in the negative when Haggedorn interrupted, his voice slightly higher and his face a little whiter than usual, "Outdoorsman. And excellent, Mr. Brumhall. Our Tony. Gun in hand. Right, Tony?"

Before Tony could answer, Haggedorn continued. "Hiking. Camping. Being alone. One man against nature. The outdoor thing. And excellent."

Brumhall considered this for a moment. "You like to hunt?"

Behind Brumhall, Haggedorn stared into Tony's eyes and nodded vigorously. Tony answered, "Yeah."

Hummingbird Bob dropped his spray bottle into the bar's sink. "Sorry."

Brumhall stared at Bob for a second then said, "The company's got a cabin up in New Hampshire." His looked back at Tony, "Did you know that?"

"No sir."

"Is it hunting season, Haggedorn? Is there something he can go up there and kill?"

"Yes, Mr. Brumhall. Something. Something excellent."

"Good. Give him the keys, Haggedorn. Call ahead and make sure he's got provisions for three days. I'll see you on Monday, Mr. Morelli. I'd like to see something strapped to the hood of your car when you come back. Am I understood?" The Old Man's eyes were clear crystals bearing into Tony's face.

"Yes, sir. I think so."

"Good."

Coming Soon From Northern Lights Publishing

Stay up on early reads, special offers, and gift opportunities! Join our mailing list at http://nlb.pub/nlbmailings

June 2023: The Inheritors

Tommy was told he was different by his family, his friends, and his teachers. He was special. Then one day he disappeared, prompting a mystery that would span millennia and bring together individuals from all walks of life from the distant past to the near future. Reaching out across all the world's civilizations through all time, The Inheritors tells the story of the hidden costs of immortality, the innocent lives exploited in its pursuit, and the unlikely heroes who make the ultimate sacrifice to exact justice.

September 2023: The Shaman

Gio Fortuna, a boy spurned by his parents for being "slow," is raised by his grandfather in the ways of the Practice, a rich esoteric discipline drawing upon mystic traditions passed down over thousands of years from a multitude of cultures. Written in five parts chronicling Gio's life, The Shaman sees Fortuna embark on a journey from initiate to adept, young boy to old man, as he navigates a network of teachers, each with their own unique lessons and challenges. Steeped in wisdom applicable to all, The Shaman is an inspiring story that proposes a unique path to self-discovery and growth unlike anything written before.

December 2023: Search

Two young boys and their guardian go missing in the Maine woods. No one has a clue, no one comes forward offering information, and the police are powerless to provide the boys' family with any answers. The boys' older sister learns about Gio Fortuna through a friend and asks him to help. Search chronicles one life-changing event in The Shaman's life, an event causing Gio to realize the use of his grandfather's teachings and their purpose in both his life and the lives of others.

THREE QUESTIONS FOR YOU

1. *Did you know most readers rely on other readers' reviews and comments to make their book buying decisions? Ongoing research begun in mid-2022 indicates reviews and comments are better decision drivers than video teasers, author interviews, author blogs, and everything else combined.*
2. *Did you know most on- and off-line bookstores - from the smallest indie to the largest megastore - rely on reader reviews and comments to decide which books to put on their shelves?*
3. *Did you enjoy* The Augmented Man?

Help Northern Lights as a publisher and Joseph Carrabis as an author by reviewing The Augmented Man *on Amazon http://nlb.pub/Augmented Goodreads http://nlb.pub/GAugmented, Barnes&Noble, BookBub, NetGalley, your favorite reader Facebook and LinkedIn groups, TikTok, Instagram, anywhere and everywhere.*

Let's Kick It Up A Notch!

Send a link to your online review of a Northern Lights Publishing book to Reviews@NorthernLightsPublishing.com and we'll give you a 35% discount on your next Northern Lights Publishing ePub or Print book.

Not Enough? Let's Kick It Up Another Notch!

You can share that 35% discount with up to ten friends, family, neighbors, we won't mind, and you'll have our thanks.

Join Northern Lights Publishing's Journey
http://nlb.pub/JoinNorthernLights

About Northern Lights Publishing

Northern Lights Publishing/Press is an association of five professionals (one graphic artist, one marketer, one editor/book designer, one copyeditor, one editor/educator/author) and a rotating group of ten published authors and poets all of whom are passionate readers. Financial backing is provided by a small group of investors led by Susan and Joseph Carrabis through the NextStage Evolution Corporation. Everyone receives remuneration and owns an equal share of the company with the exception of Susan and Joseph Carrabis.

We're developing our publishing/marketing model so we're not accepting submissions at present.

We'll open our doors to submissions (and announce it through various social networks) once we're sure we can break even and preferably turn a profit. Until then, wish us well.

It's an exciting journey and one we'd love to share, but only after we're sure we can successfully navigate the publishing seas.

Also by Joseph Carrabis

Non-Fiction

That Th!nk You Do - http://nlb.pub/TTYDv1

That Th!nk You Do is based on a series of blog posts Joseph wrote between 2008 and 2016. They dealt with ways his research in fields as diverse as neuroscience, linguistics, psychology, sociology, anthropology and other disciplines could be put to practical use to help people better their lives.

If you ever wonder about how to think like an expert, the difference between your inner critic and the actor within, your ability to be heard, the value of being a musician, how to protect yourself from liars or how to overcome fears, you will find answers in this book..

Reading Virtual Minds Volume I: Science and History - http://nlb.pub/Minds1

The science and history behind NextStage Evolution's Evolution Technology

Reading Virtual Minds Volume II: Experience and Expectation - http://nlb.pub/Minds2

Learnings and Take-Aways from NextStage Evolution's research and studies

Reading Virtual Minds Volume III: Fair-Exchange and Social Networks - http://nlb.pub/Minds3

Learnings and Take-Aways from NextStage Evolution's research and studies applied specifically on on- and off-line social interactions

Fiction: Novels

Empty Sky - http://nlb.pub/EmptySky

What if you're a young boy, Jamie McPherson, whose mother has been missing for over a year and whose father starts falling in and out of coma? What if you hold onto your aging dog, Shem, who's always been with you and always protected you, because the world isn't safe anymore?

And what if in the midst all that's happening, The Moon asks you to help her save the world's dreams?

Earl Pangiosi's greatest desire, since childhood, has been to control and manipulate people. Working for the NSA, Earl learns that people's dreams - their nonconscious minds - guide their conscious decisions. Control their dreams - weaponize them - and you control people at an unprecedented level.

Jamie will not face Pangiosi alone. The Moon sends her Guardians, winged, shapeshifting wolves; and her children, The Oneiroi, little black silhouettes, shadows in the darkness of night, whose multi-colored, multifaceted, crystalline eyes serve as kaleidoscopic Gates — little rainbow bridges allowing humans passage from one dream reality to the next, to help Jamie.

Pangiosi sends the Native American giant, Nighthorse, to stop Jamie. But Nighthorse's grandfather introduced him to Wovoka, the DreamWorld, as a child. Going after Jamie, Nighthorse finds one of the Oneiroi's Eye-Gates and realizes his grandfather may not have been such a fool after all.

Meanwhile the Moon brings together a team of "Dreamers" to help Jamie. One such Dreamer is ANN, a supercomputer who can blend dream and waking realities via Penrose Consciousnesses, quantum superpositions.

If they fail, Pangiosi and the NSA will control the world.

The Augmented Man - http://nlb.pub/Augmented

What do you do with a deadly weapon when it's no longer needed?

Nicholas Trailer is the last of The Augmented Men, beings created first by society and completed by a political group the public can't even imagine exists. Captain James Donaldson takes severely abused and traumatized children and modifies them into monsters capable of the most horrifying deeds without feeling any remorse or regret.

But the horrors of war never stay on the battlefield. They always come home.

Battling what society and science has made him, Nick Trailer discovers he is loved. From the horrors of childhood to the horrors of a war, what does it take for someone to find true love and peace? Especially when everyone has their own agenda, from the senators who sanctioned his making to the Governor of Maine who wants to use Nick's struggle to propel himself to the White House.

The Augmented Men were good at war, perhaps a little too good. Now they have to come home … or do they? What do you do with man-made monsters?

Nick must decide if his friends are his friends and if his enemies are his enemies, all while protecting the woman he loves.

And are you truly the last of your kind?

What if you must remain a monster to defeat a monster? Will you sacrifice love to protect what you love?

Fiction: Anthologies

Tales Told 'Round Celestial Campfires - http://nlb.pub/TalesV1
Includes:

Binky (available separately at http://nlb.pub/Binky)

What if you run an inner-city health clinic and are tired of fighting budget cuts, politics, protestors, police, … ? And what if you question your purpose because caring is no longer cost-effective? And what if you meet a bright, beautiful child who leads you to a child who died sixty years ago? And what if that child asks you to save its life?

The Boy Who Loved Horses (available separately at http://nlb.pub/Horses)

What if you're born and raised Hill but got City educated and now you drivin a big state issue Buick back into Hill 'cause you gonna show them you something else? And what if one town you drive through's got secrets it don't want nobody to know? And what if you plan to tell City those secrets and those secrets got they own idea who you gonna tell?

Canis Major (available separately at http://nlb.pub/CanisMajor)

What if you're a WereMan, human when the moon is full, a beast when not, and your father died before explaining your gift to you? And what if your fully human mother did the best she could but couldn't really understand your needs? And what if you're tired of being alone and afraid and once, just once, you want to hold someone and not be afraid of their fear?

Cold War (available separately at http://nlb.pub/ColdWar)

What if your last deployment left you so damaged driving a school bus tops your employable skills? And what if the kids laugh at you because you can't talk right and twitch at nothing? And what if the military calls you back, says they can make you a man again. Or get close. And what if you're so lonely, angry and tired you say sure without realizing they plan to leave you out in the cold, forever?

Cymodoce (available separately at http://nlb.pub/Cymodoce)

What if the only man you've ever given yourself to isn't a man at all? And what if you gave birth to twins, the son wholly yours, the daughter wholly his? And what if your daughter needs to return to her father in order to survive? And what if her survival means never seeing her again, and her brother losing his sister forever?

Dancers in the Eye of Chronos (available separately at http://nlb.pub/Dancers)

What if your love so delights the Gods they grant you immortality. But you learn love is meant to age, to mature, to grow and change in ways the Gods can't imagine. After millennia, they strip their gift from you. But that's what you wanted; to hold your lover's face one last time before darkness falls. Or is your love so strong it outlives the Gods themselves?

The Goatmen of Aguirra (available separately at http://nlb.pub/Goatmen)

What if you've signed onto a deep space mission and left behind a wife and young son? And what if your mission takes to you a supposedly uninhabited planet that harbors intelligent life that values family above all else? And what if they take you into their family to heal you? And what if, finally healed, your shipmates abandon you when the mission is called home?

Mani He (available separately at http://nlb.pub/ManiHe)

What if you've acquired your dream job but destroyed another man's life and career to get it? And what if the president of your company hands you a rifle and the keys to his mountain cabin with the instructions "Bring me back something to make me proud"? And what if the spirits in the mountains have their own ideas of what it means to be proud?

Power Unlimited (available separately at http://nlb.pub/PowerUnlimited)

What if Eddie's kid brother Tommy idolizes you guys at the gym and wants to be like you but you know he's not really built for it. And what if he sends away for some "GET BIG FAST" Muscle Pill exercise programs? And what if he starts looking like The Hulk and King Kong had a baby? And what if the people who make those Pills want them back?

Sema (available separately at http://nlb.pub/Sema)
What if a beautiful woman discovers you and your friends are beings living side-by-side with humans since the beginning of time? And what if she discovers you have abilities beyond imagination and she, too, has gifts no mortal should possess? And what if, having no knowledge of your kind, has trained with a Darkness humans can't imagine, never suspecting a Light beyond mortals' dreams?

The Settlement (available separately at http://nlb.pub/Settlement)
What if you're a young, hotshot, wildly successful asteroid miner who hasn't seen your parents since you joined the corp underage? And what if your parents are getting divorced and each is laying claim to guardianship of your fortune? And what if your parents never knew why you joined the corp or what you had to give up to get a ship of your own?

Them Doore Girls (available separately at http://nlb.pub/Doore)
What if the woman you love is the mistress of something else, something so monstrous, so hideous its summoning her creates ocean storms? And what if she knows this entity will destroy her, you, your village and all those you know if she denies it? And what if you know she goes to it willingly because it threatened to kill you, her one love, if she doesn't yield to its wishes?

Those Wings Which Tire, They Have Upheld Me (available separately at http://nlb.pub/Wings)
What if you're a little boy with brain cancer whose doctors say they can cure you by replacing your eyes with an experimental device? And

what if that experimental device lets you see your guardian angel? And what if seeing your guardian angel makes you best friends with the class trouble-maker? And what if the class bully finds out you talk to angels?

The Weight (available separately at http://nlb.pub/Weight)
What if you've been a success at everything you've done in your life and decide to retrace a hike you took when wishes were horses and beggars could ride? And what if you met one of your heroes on that long ago hike and - miracle of miracles - you meet him again? And what if your hero isn't your hero and says you took something from it way back when and now it wants it back?

Winter Winds (available separately at http://nlb.pub/Winds)
What if you're sitting in your favorite chair, your son on your lap, helping him with his homework when you see something in the fields outside your house? And what if you turn on the floodlights and see unimaginable creatures battling in your fields? And what if your son and wife tell you you're the strange one because those fantastical creatures battling in your field are as natural as natural can be?

Follow Joseph's work in magazines and other anthologies at https://josephcarrabis.com/tag/im-published-here/

You can find most of Joseph's work at http://nlb.pub/amazon

About The Author

Joseph Carrabis told stories to anyone who would listen starting in childhood, wrote his first stories in gradeschool, and started getting paid for his writing in 1978. His work history includes periods as a long-haul trucker, apprentice butcher, apprentice coffee buyer/broker, lumberjack, Cold Regions researcher, mathematician, semanticist, semioticist, physicist, educator, Chief Data Scientist, Chief Research Scientist, and Chief Research Officer. He was an original member of the NYAS/UN's Scientists Without Borders program and held patents covering mathematics, anthropology, neuroscience, and linguistics. After patenting a technology he created in his basement and creating an international company, he retired from corporate life. Now he spends his time writing fiction based on his experiences. His work appears regularly in anthologies and his own novels. You can often find him playing with his dog, Boo, and snuggling with his wife, Susan. Learn more about him at https://josephcarrabis.com and his work at http://nlb.pub/amazon.